FULL
FADOM
FIVE

FULL
FADOM
FIVE

DAVID C.C. BOURGEOIS

Baraka
Books

Montréal

ISBN 978-1-77186-312-4 pbk; 978-1-77186-320-9 epub; 978-1-77186-321-6 pdf

Cover by Maison 1608
Book Design by Folio infographie
Editing and proofreading: Blossom Thom, Elise Moser, Anne Marie Marko, Daniel J. Rowe

Legal Deposit, 2nd quarter 2023
Bibliothèque et Archives nationales du Québec
Library and Archives Canada

Published by Baraka Books of Montreal

Printed and bound in Quebec

Trade Distribution & Returns
Canada – UTP Distribution: UTPdistribution.com

United States
Independent Publishers Group: IPGbook.com

We acknowledge the support from the Société de développement des entreprises culturelles (SODEC) and the Government of Quebec tax credit for book publishing administered by SODEC.

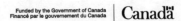

For Megan

In my heart's core, ay, in my heart of heart

Full fadom fiue thy Father lies,
Of his bones are Corrall made:
Those are pearles that were his eies,
Nothing of him that doth fade,
But doth suffer a Sea-change
Into something rich, & strange:

–The Tempest

PART ONE

The Isle Is Full of Noises

I

With the sloping shoulders of the island above, and the wide sea below, a runner was tracing the worn, rising line of the highway's winding, his breathing even and deep, his lungs full of salty air and the taste of a morning thundershower. He leaned into the inclination, pacing himself as the burn began to kindle in his legs above the knees. The sun, small and red and oozing like a cracked egg across the horizon, cast on the road before him his lanky shadow, whose every easy stride he envied. Sleep the night before had been a long time coming, and now he felt like an idiotic salmon: slim and spent, and yet still kicking his way upstream. Twice he had run the Cape and twice the punishing North Mountain legs of the relay, but it was years since he had raced, or with any frequency attempted anything harder than a slow six-miler on even ground. Now when he returned home he found the climbs debilitating. He had to suffer to rebuild his fitness. Two weeks prior, on his first attempt, he had found himself afflicted with a strange panic, a bodily fear, as though he were braced with iron ribs that could not accommodate his heart's need nor his lungs'. And what would that be like, to suffocate with air in endless supply around him? Would he arrive on the hilltop triumphant and, like the first marathoner, cry victory and instantly drop dead? Under the rubric of a sunrise climb, the island seemed designed to teach humility.

His chest felt like a door his heart was trying to break down, but he tried to ignore it. Nothing kills the heart so much as thought. Time was, his grandfather was wont to lope along the coast and his father too. Likewise the laurel-chasing Olympians across the sea, and day-running couriers of the islandy, peninsular ancient world, and

3

persistence hunters everywhere, from the Indigenous peoples of Australia and northern Mexico to the dogged foragers of the Kalahari, who in remotest prehistory learned to patiently run springboks and hartebeests to exhaustion. Since *Homo* first became *erectus* were a million years and more of adaptation striding endlessly forward, one blind hand-off at a time. Or maybe more. He had read somewhere that humans ran before they thought—though that knowledge profited him little now. His breath was growing laboured and, from the stinging in his heel, his gait uneven as he made the unforgiving ascent.

He knew that should he have to slacken his pace, or should he cramp and half fold over, still he could will himself to pick 'em up and put 'em down. And that, even should he arrive at the summit with his body miserable and hardly moving, nevertheless his organs would be intact and working fine. The body lives by processes of work and rest. The muscle fibres ratchet on and off. The effort produces lactate, which the body then removes. Or if instead the muscles, under too much strain, become a lactic acid oasis that the body's conduits cannot carry rapidly enough away, then the muscles suffer from fatigue and burn, grow penitent, and sometimes knuckle under. But then the body rests. It siphons off the liquid fire, adapts, and in these successions grows fitter, stronger.

The hill was steep and stretched out before him. The waves and his pounding feet beat down their ragged rhythms. His thighs were burning and his knees appealed for mercy. Numbness spread into his hips and groin. His heart and lungs, he knew, were on the threshold. Bodily imperatives filled his mind, and wordless expletives. No shame in resting.

But the body is not the mind.

A river ran through him, and a turning wheel.

He upped his pace.

Thoughts about his ailing grandparents in their cottage, and his son half a continent away, and the smell of stale breath on the pillow beside him, pulled at his attention, but he let them slip away. There was only the road beneath him, and the sky above, and the cool, wet breeze on his face. He felt his trunk draw in, his torso lengthen, his hips unwind and slightly roll. He shortened his stride and the cramping in his legs began to ebb, his ribs expand more freely. To be like a cord: not so tight it snaps, nor so loose it goes slack. To abide in tension. To hum with use. A thrill of adrenaline burst through him and, as if suspended by a string atop his skull, he felt taller, lighter, and drawn up. If a passing driver, gearing down, should happen to inspect him, he would wonder how a man so flushed and straining could have a smile inscribed across his face. Then up and over he went at last, slowing down and walking only once the summit lay beneath him, after which his breathing grew easier and his smile too. For the moment, his feelings uncomplicated themselves into something next of kin to happiness. He left the road behind, stepping with one weak leg over the guardrail, and then the limping other, into the open field that led to the graveyard.

The grounds there were untended. Species of weeds and grasses competed for success among the stones and deadwood. Not far distant, perhaps a quarter mile, the clifftop narrowed into a rocky point, like a ship's prow jutting out into the sea. Unlike so many cemeteries along the coast, this one had been devised by some Cartesian gravedigger. No haphazard plotting of stones here, but the rigorous coordination of remains. As he traversed the graveyard, he imagined he could see the x's and y's of grid-lines strung out over the terrain. A square stone marked the resting place of Great-Grandfather Lamarck, his wife's stone by its side. A large white crucifix stood mast-like in the centre, to mark the grave of the Unknown Sailor. Simple, granite stones, round and white like bleached skulls, marked the graves of all who had washed ashore and could not be accounted for. Of the others, many were very old and many of their inscriptions were worn. As he walked towards the point he noted those he knew from his grandfather's stories.

For instance, Ang and Asa Stuart, sealers who were lost on the ice floes one April when a sou'wester came hauling-in and pushed the brash ice out to sea; they were buried side by side, exactly as they were discovered when the wind veered and pushed their frozen bodies back to shore. Or Murdo Donovan: a shipwright—out of Lunenburg, if he remembered right—who built the *Kittiwake*, which was later lost in a fall storm. She was captained by Murdo's son, Johnny, the last sight of whom was had by a friend, captain of the *Sea Lion's Mane*, who saw her rolling over and tried to reach her, and even got so near that he could see poor Johnny lashed to the wheel before a high swell divided them and she disappeared. The story went that Old Murdo was inconsolable and Johnny's mother, if you ever asked about her boy, would just reply, maybe from her seat on the porch where she would do her knitting, "Well, he's not back yet." Nearby was Bobby Morris, who even before the Depression hadn't two dimes to rub together. In the summer of the rum, when a vessel bound for Chéticamp went down and spilled its cargo on the sea, he went overboard of his boat trying to gaff a crate of the loot and wouldn't let it go, even when it flipped him underneath and nearly choked him out, and the boys were forced to fetch it aboard before him because, he said, he'd rather drown than go another week without a nip. He lived to a hundred and six.

Then there was Donald Hill, lying not far off, who stood up to the monopolists and helped to organize the Co-op. A brave man, people always said. He married twice. His first wife was an uncompromising miser that wouldn't give you the smell of a greased rag; his second was such a spendthrift he had to have her advertised. And there was also Hill's oft-wed sister, Flory, who married and buried the Gilles brothers—not two, mind you, which would have been improbable enough, but three, one after the other, the last when she was forty—and each one dead of a heart attack before his son saw his second birthday. The town moralists were scandalized—some even insinuated that she herself had done them in—so too were the local historians, who never did forgive her for being an aunt to her own children, who were themselves all cousins to their brothers.

Some of the miners were buried near each other. Under a simple cross lay Charlie-Dan Aucoin from Margaree, who was still known by some in town as the Frenchman who in his youth performed exorcisms on possessed milk cows. And another Frenchman lay nearby: Adrien Melanson, who married a Scotchman's daughter and paid for it the rest of his life. She was a terrible scold and Melanson, a timid man by nature, was forced to weather her tempers. She used to beat him with a wooden spoon too big for cooking, and once, when he brought home a pal from work for a cup of tea without asking, she chased him underneath the bed, where she swung it at him and threatened to do worse if he didn't come out that instant, to which he replied from between the bedposts, "Like hell! Your threats don't scare me!" A Bible verse was written across his stone: *I sought the LORD, and He heard me; and delivered me from all my fears.* His wife picked it out herself.

Then there was Bill McPherson, who ran the hoist, and his wife Ket, who in a nasty winter in the 1940s birthed her twins all by herself before Bill could make it back with the midwife; and Simon Pettipas, whose daughter ran off with the Mi'kmaq fiddler; and Father Leon, a lazy sponge who best served his parish by leaving it and was later returned for burying because no other would have him; and Henry Arsenault, a bootlegger (and a good one), who made a nice little dime justifying the preachers' complaints that the parishioners abandoned themselves to the excesses of drink. His cortege was an unsteady mile long.

His mother's grave lay farther out towards the point among the newer stones. From the edge of a large, rocky knob he plucked a lonely harebell, likely the last he'd see for the season, with three dropping blue-white bells, and placed it at the foot of the stone:

Léa Lamarck née Doucet

1948-1970

He had a rubbing of it at home, and a rubbing also of the stone shield that lay flat in the grass to the left of his mother's, which marked no body but pointed out towards the sea that was his father's tomb. He hovered over it before walking out along the grassy promontory.

The entire network was there: the invisible rigging of a few dozen families that, still living in his grandfather's stories, seemed to fill the island with voices. Standing at the cliff's edge, with the sun and wide sky perched on his shoulders, he looked back across the cove. At one end of town stood the Protestant Church and at the other the Roman, like two old coots who've talked all day, so many days, that now their patter, like the rout of the waves or the cries of the gulls that ride them, seldom registers. He sat down in the grass, looking east, and drew in his knees. Whales could be seen sometimes, and seals roughhousing in the surf, and seabirds plunging from great heights—but not today. The wind was up and everywhere the waves were washing hard along the coast. It was as though the island were a ship with her sails full, and she conveying her passengers all, alive or otherwise, across uncharted waters to lands beyond the horizon.

ᚢ

Swifter and more pleasant was the run back: the air was cool, the road silent, the trees just barely hinted at the red-gold turning of their leaves. His heel ached and his knees jarred somewhat from the downhill, but his body otherwise was sound. Before long he neared St. George's United, which marked the edge of town. Beyond it he could see the shop windows on Main Street winking at each other in the sunlight, and beyond that, far out to sea, the sky was overcast with a belly of cloud, brushed pink and pale blue as in a Renaissance painting.

Though it was early, all the lights were on in Don's convenience and, despite the Closed sign that hung from it, the door was cracked open. He stopped and looked in. Don stood with his back to the entrance, interrupted in the act of restocking the periodicals. From the door it was impossible to tell which one Don was holding, but it was clear that he held it sideways and was examining its folded-out length. As he opened the door, its brass bell rang and Don tried to cram his reading into the rack.

"Sign says we're closed, don't it?"

"No exceptions?"

Don, recognizing the voice, looked over his shoulder. "Noah. You're up early."

"You know. The early bird."

The flesh above Don's beard grew pink. "If I'd known it was you I wouldn't have startled and ruined that poor girl's figure." He turned to the rack and removed the damaged magazine. He held it out to Noah, who declined, then he shrugged and tossed it into a small bin beside the cash.

"So what brings you?"

"I know it's outside hours, but since you're here I thought I'd get the mail, if there's any."

Don nodded and went to the back of the store. There was a small counter and a door with a Canada Post sign. "Got a couple of things yesterday."

As the door was narrow and Don was not, he had to squeeze his stoutness through. "So's the wind sharp?" he asked. He began to rummage through the piles of boxes and letters.

"Enough to shave your face," Noah answered.

"I'll have to keep my cheeks out of it. The wife's forbid me shaving. Claims it's 'cause she fell in love with my beard, but I think it's jealousy. She wants to keep me ugly so the women don't swoon for me."

Don returned with two envelopes. Noah glanced down as he received them. Government of Canada. The one addressed to Peter Lamarck, 10 Shore Lane, Mission Point, NS. The other to Modeste Lamarck. The pension cheques.

"Thanks, Don. My grandmother will be glad to have these."

Don leaned back against the counter and slipped his hands into his pockets. "You know, I thought you were in Toronto."

"I was, but after last winter the gutters needed fixing. And they'd almost run out of firewood. I meant to come in the spring only I couldn't get the time."

"They must be happy to have you. Your gran especially. How long you staying?"

"I fly out tomorrow."

"That's too bad. How's Felix?"

"Going on ten."

"Jesus. Already?"

"In the blink of an eye."

"Jesus. And your grandfather? I haven't seen him since Easter, but I thought he looked pretty good. Had a bit more face to wash, but so do I."

"If it were only his hair receding ..."

Don frowned and nodded his head. "Your grandmother hasn't been by in almost as long. Some of the old girls take turns getting the mail for her. The ones that aren't in the Home."

"When she leaves the house the old man runs off. If he gets much worse she'll have to put him on a leash."

"Oh, don't say that." Don frowned. "He's a great man. You know he taught me art and science at St. Mike's back when it was still a high school."

"Can't say I'm surprised. As I understand it, if you grew up Catholic anywhere in the township he taught you."

"He must have broken up a fight every other day at least," Don said. "And those days by rights he could've used the stick on you, but instead he had you into the gym and made you take up boxing, which he said was more civilized. Lord knows we were little savages, the lot of us. There wasn't hardly a lad didn't get a lesson or two. There was this time my brother got a year's probation and a seven pm curfew for vandalizing the church door. Dad was working nights and my sisters were too young for Mom to leave at home or haul around, so your grandfather spoke to the judge and for the next year he drove my brother to hockey twice a week himself. I bet you didn't know about that."

"No, I didn't," Noah said.

"I didn't think you would. Even then he didn't talk about it. He didn't want to shame my brother or my folks by making a show. He did it all secret." Don hesitated. "I can't think of a nicer thing anyone ever did for us."

Noah smiled, but sadly. "I doubt he even remembers."

"Well, we never forgot it. You know, my brother's a crown attorney in Ottawa now. So, if your gran's having a hard time ..."

Noah's heart, like a fighter, lurched defensively, bobbing on the inside. "Thanks, Don, but you know how she is."

"Proud as an ill-struck nail is how she is. There's hands all over that would pitch in if only she'd ask. You tell her I said so." Don shoved his hands in his pocket. Then he frowned like an uneasy schoolboy. "Only mind you don't tell her how I said it."

Unwinding a little, Noah laughed. "All right. You realize, though, that he wouldn't even know who you are."

"Maybe, but I still know who he is."

A burst of air shoved against the door. It squealed through the crack and rang the bell faintly. Don and Noah turned to look at it. The stop sign on the corner shivered in the wind, rolling with the punches.

"Might be in for a rough" Don said.

"Feels like it."

"Good thing you got out early, then. Say, did you hear about the drowning? Down at the Horton's yesterday it was all anyone was talking about. That fellow up from New England who went overboard a few weeks ago. I guess he washed up day before yesterday a bit dismembered. They were saying how they carted him off to the hospital and they're trying to put him back together before they ship him home."

Noah grew numb. He really didn't want to think about what he was thinking about, and he was trying not to. Don just leaned into the scuttlebutt.

"Old Mal Burns had it from his daughter—she's a nurse over at the General—he says they're still missing a few bits."

Noah's gaze slipped towards the door. Don noticed and fell silent too.

"I should probably get back," Noah said.

"Sure. I should finish up with the magazines."

"I bet you should."

The two men eyed each other and shared a momentary look of mischief.

"Stop by next time you're in town," Don said.

"I will."

"And you tell your gran."

"Count on it."

ㄱ

With the mail in hand Noah picked up his run, his body buffeting for home against the wind's hard jabs. At the corner stood St. Joseph's. Beyond was the small creek that mostly ran beneath the streets in culverts until it emptied at the wharf, where the priest used to hold a dockside blessing for the fleet in spring, and beyond that was the old lobster plant, which the co-op built around the same time as the study clubs, though those disappeared after the war, long before the plant closed down. Past the plant, his grandparents' cottage was just half a mile out and half a mile again down a long lane that finished on a stretch of open field beside the sea. As the yards passed beneath Noah's feet, he began to really want a shower and he expected to be warming under it within minutes, but as he neared the house he spotted a tall man with wild, white hair climbing down a rocky ledge exposed by the tide. "Shit," he said.

Noah hurried to prevent him, but his grandfather was lithe and nimble. Fifty years since and he could still fit into his service uniform. *If the brain be not sound then all the members will be amiss.* Saint Jerome was full of shit. Noah jogged past the firepit and over the lawn, but by the time he scrambled down the ledge, the old man was already on the pebbled beach, sitting there, patient as a sea stack, facing into the east wind, which beat the water along the shore and likewise the thinning waves of his hair. Noah joined him and gazed with him out over the water. "You shouldn't be out here," he said.

The old man's face cinched up and his wrinkles deepened. "Don't tell me. You're mine, you know." His eyes narrowed and he pointed an accusing finger at the waves. "Sounds like … sounds … you know, the quiet talk."

"Whispering."

"That's it. Telling secrets … like I don't know—but I know." He lifted his nose and closed his eyes. "Wind's up, too," he said.

Noah tried to be encouraging. "I don't think we need to worry about it. Whatever they're saying, they're keeping it to themselves."

"Don't tell me. I kept your son, Laz, so don't tell me."

"No, Gramps, you've forgotten. I'm Noah. Laz died a long time ago."

The old man looked into his grandson's eyes, which were like his grandson's father's eyes, and like his own eyes too, which began to fill with tears. "Don't talk about that other guy," he said.

"Do you remember—"

"No, no, no, no, no. A fool plows it." The old man's eyes flooded now in earnest. "Plows where it doesn't grow."

"I'm sorry," Noah said. He reached up and with his sleeve tried to dry his grandfather's tears, but the old man turned away proudly. Several bursts of wind assailed them. Noah felt his own eyes grow wet from the blows, and from his grandfather's failure to remember. "The wind's up all right. It's making mine water too." He wiped his own eyes, then he tried again to dry his grandfather's. This time the old man let him. "My sweat's getting cold. How about we go in. See if Gran's got breakfast on."

Though it was hardly necessary, Noah helped his grandfather back to the house. Inside, the kitchen lights were on and the kettle was hot. A wet tea bag slumped on a saucer next to the stove, but his grandmother was nowhere to be seen. Noah tossed the mail on the counter and took down a cup for his grandfather. He dropped in a new bag and filled it with water, then he coaxed the old man to sit at the table. "Gran's likely making the bed. She'll be out soon." The old man smiled and patted him on the hand.

Noah left the kitchen and climbed the narrow stairs to his bedroom, which was squeezed into the attic. From beneath the blankets a nest of blonde hair peeked, and then the head it was attached to. Noah turned away and began to strip down. His clothes were soaked and clinging to him.

"Christ, you're up early," the head said. Maggy's head, and her beery breath.

Noah worked away at a double-knot in his shoelace. "There's nothing like exercise for a hangover."

"That so? You know, I'm a bit hung over myself. How about you slide back in here." Maggy patted the bed.

"Not now."

"I think you owe me. You fucked like you were late for an appointment." Maggy undulated beneath the blankets, but Noah was not looking. "Come on. It's cold and I'm still naked under here. I was led to believe you were an early riser."

"You missed it. I was up an hour ago and you slept through it," Noah said. The hard nubs in his laces at last co-operated and he removed his shoes. Then he began to slide his sweats down.

"Look at that arse," Maggy said. "Rosy red like the morning sun. How can you say I missed you rising when I'm up at the crack of dawn?"

"It may look like the sun, but trust me, it's a moon."

Noah rummaged through his suitcase for something to cover himself. He pulled out a cleanish pair of pants and, gitchless, pulled them on. "I need to see to my grandparents," he said.

Maggy rose up on one elbow, revealing her bare shoulders. "Your grandmother already saw to me. She was sweet. She came up with some tea while you were out."

Noah's stomach turned a little and stirred the dregs of his hangover. He had hoped to sneak Maggy out and avoid the conversation he now would have to have with his grandmother. He picked a shirt up off the floor and pressed it to his face. It smelled not too foul and he pulled it on. Behind him, Maggy was sliding out of bed and beginning to dress. Noah turned his head just enough to peep.

"She asked if I'd be staying for breakfast. I said I didn't know."

Her unspoken question begged an answer he didn't know how to put. He needed a moment to think, but the room was small enough that it was hard to avoid facing her, and awkward to keep trying, so he turned and answered, wretchedly, that he would rather she didn't. "Sorry. It's hard with my grandfather the way he is. Strange faces confuse him."

"I understand," Maggy replied quickly.

Noah gave her a thankful smile, but it was short-lived. On the bedside table, beneath an empty teacup, he saw his papers were disordered and some of them lightly stained with rings of orange pekoe. She had gone through them.

"I hope you don't mind," Maggy said. "I got bored. Are you writing some kind of book?"

"No."

She pulled up her underwear and then, hopping, her jeans. Distracted, Noah was too slow to stop her snatching up the pages. Determined not to let her get a rise, he hardly fought when she spun her body around to keep them out of reach. He was too bushed anyway to put up a fight. Standing at the window with her back to him, she began to read aloud:

When my father was about ten or twelve, he and your great-granddad went down the road to a nearby farm and picked up two chicks that he named Cain and Abel (even though they turned out to be hens). They used to race them up and down the hall, which your great-gran put up with, but not always happily because of the mess they left. And because of the scratches they put into her floor when they got older. And because of all the cheering. She killed and butchered her own chickens back then. She would take one out to the wood pile and all at once slap it down on a stump and chop its head off. Sometimes it would slip from her hand, and then it would run headless around the yard and my father would laugh and laugh. When my father was still too young to use the hatchet, she showed him how to break their necks with a sharp twist and pull. But he wasn't strong enough, and chicken necks are rubbery. Mostly he succeeded only in irritating his chicken, which seemed to squawk "stop it" each time he torqued its head. He had a tender streak, too, and as Cain and Abel got big he didn't like the thought of eating them, especially if he had to choose which one to sacrifice first, and which one second, and might have to do the killing himself. So one day, when Great-gran was out shopping, he and your great-granddad each tucked one under his arm, and walked them down the road to the farm where they were hatched, and tossed them in with the rest of the chickens. Cain and Abel might get eaten anyway, but likely not for a while and not by them. Meat wasn't cheap in those days, and when your great-gran found out she got so riled that for a week she fed them nothing but weasel stew. She told them: If you want chicken so bad, you know where to get it.

When Maggy finished, she let the pages sag in her hands. "Sounds like a book to me."

Noah picked up a folder and opened it for Maggy. She inserted the pages and he shoved it into a bag beside the bed. "It's not. It's just stories my grandfather used to tell me. I'm writing them out for Felix. I want him to know his great-grandfather."

"Oh," she said. Then she looked her eyes into him. "Why don't you bring Felix down when you come?"

Noah didn't have an answer, and he was relieved that Maggy didn't wait for one. She slipped her bra over her shoulders and, reaching back with both hands, fastened it. Noah wondered if, when she was young, the boys at school had asked her could she touch her elbows behind her back, and had she been fooled, or had she not, and (if she had not) had she tried to do it anyway.

"How much have you got?" she asked. "Is that all of it?"

"No, I'm still missing a lot."

"I mean, do you have more than just those?"

"Oh. Yes. Back in Toronto."

She pulled her hair back and fastened it with an elastic from her pocket. Then she put on her shirt and sat down on the bed to button it. She still wasn't leaving. Noah gave in and sat down beside her. "When do you go back?" she asked.

"Tomorrow."

"Be careful with all your flying in and flying out. You're getting awful from-away on us." Maggy laughed, though not unkindly. "I suppose you've got to get back to Felix. Is he splitting time between you?"

"Not exactly," Noah answered. "I can visit anytime, but he stays with Cate."

Maggy took his hand and leaned against him. She dropped her head on his shoulder. "How long has that been going on?"

"A couple of years, I guess."

"And you're still trying to work it out," she said, pushing.

Noah didn't want to answer, but she waited. "Not really," he said.

She reached out and ran her finger along the curve of his wedding band. "Then why don't you take the ring off?" Maggy waited once again, but this time Noah couldn't answer. "Look at you," she said, "just like in high school, still mooning over her. With your big, beautiful calf eyes." Maggy turned her cheek and pressed it more firmly into his shoulder. Then she shifted her hand to his thigh. "Can't you stay a little longer?"

Noah took her hand in his, and let his silence stand in for an apology. Maggy sat back up.

"Do you have time for breakfast tomorrow?" she asked. "Or is this goodbye?"

"I'm meeting Ray for breakfast. Then I'm taking the bus to the airport."

"I wonder how he's doing this morning." She tugged at her ponytail. "He was bad when we left, and looked set to get worse."

"He's doing better than his brother, I bet. Joe was well-nigh unconscious."

"That's 'cause he knocked up his girl."

"He didn't," Noah said, surprised. No one had said anything about it.

"That's what I hear. I guess she got tired of being taken for granted and stopped taking her pill without telling him."

Noah felt a sudden, belly-stabbing fear, and his face slacked enough for Maggy to notice. She laughed brightly.

"Don't worry. I don't want you that bad," she said. "But don't start thinking I'm money in the bank. You do, and next time you're in town you'll find you're overdrawn." Maggy reached down and pulled on her socks. "Maybe I'll go down to Chance's. There's lots of guys there that don't need waiting for."

"Isn't that a cougar bar now?" Noah said. He said it without thinking and quickly regretted it. Maggy was only fooling.

"Listen, love: I don't mind being your regular vacation thing, but I don't want people getting the wrong idea about me. Next time you're in town, take the ring off." She stood up and posed. "Besides, I'm not so far gone am I?" Her tone was flippant and she showed no outward sign of injury. She shot him a wink.

"Sorry, Maggy," he said.

She leaned over him and ran her fingers through his damp hair. "Don't sweat it." Then she kissed him on the forehead and quietly hurried out and down the stairs.

As the lungs following a long exhalation, or in the heart's interim when it lurches, the room felt emptier than it would have had she never been there at all, and Noah, slouched on the edge of his bed, contemplated in silence the dull, scarred contour of his wedding ring. He took it between his thumb and forefinger like the dial of a padlock and spun it. He could still hear the priest's instructions. *In its circularity, the ring is a symbol of wholeness, and of the unending commitment of man and wife, sanctified by the undying love of their Creator, and, for those that undertake the sacrament of marriage, of the blessing conferred upon them by the holy rites.* Removing it, Noah wrenched open a door to the dark galleries of his memory where, like relics of the dead, his thoughts and feelings lay sometimes secretly buried. From these, if he scrutinized them—as he scrutinized the distorted reflections, tilting to and fro on the ring's golden inner surface, of the strata of his face—he could interpolate a picture of himself, almost.

Ninth grade, the gauntlet of windows down the road to McKinnon's kitchen party, Cate in trousers, like her girlfriends when they collected her, all of them with skirts underneath. The first disobediences. Not yet fourteen, but treason in the blood already. For the first time really dancing. The sharp inward breath and the lightning flash. Why she had been suddenly forbidden to play in her room with him, or go walking in his company alone past dark. Her father's unreason, and his distrust: a debt like a circle no steps could square. "Time After Time" on the radio and peppermint on her breath. The initial confusion of her curved hips and his hands fast upon them, and how it blew his mind. The electric fear. Her moist lips and his, a closed ring. Like the sea before a storm, a tempest beneath his calm.

The bedroom window in their first apartment, poorly sealed and loose in the jamb. The bedroom colder than her father, which was saying something. The winter air breathed right in. Soft rime grew in swirls and feathers, exquisite and diaphanous, creeping across the panes. The pale moonlight refracted through the delicate paisleys of ice and frost. The room illuminated. The sharp silhouettes of the lamp, the clothes rack, the brick and board bookshelves. One night the heat had gone out. So cold they tripled their blankets. Two young people huddled for warmth. He watched her ghostly heat rising as she slept.

Early morning. A hard-on urgent enough to pry his eyes open. The moon's pale aperture long vanished. The room dark as a tomb. The warmth of Cate's body, and the small concavity of her waist, her rear's roundness. The room cold, but he hotter than the hinges of hell. Her silence, her stillness, hardly moving. Their bodies entwined, chiasmatic, crossed where her flesh encircled his, one flesh. Not only his heart pulsing. Lightheaded, holding his breath. A shiver, not from the cold. Then the ill-divining: her stillness and her silence appalling. She had hardly waked, much less spoken, and he had hardly waited. The whole thing so like in a dream. The wildness of his need, and the small, forgotten square of the condom wrapper unopened on the bedside table. A nocturnal omission. In his secret heart his error written.

And the way the window, which he never did fix, thawed and froze, keeping time with the pulse of winter's days and nights, until the threads of ice, the veins and slivers, bloated. The intricate lines of hoarfrost swollen. Hard ropes too thick to clear. The moonlight that slipped through the ice, blunted and diffuse. Laundry on the floor in heaps, and extinguished tea lights on the dresser. Her body tucked away, opposite his. Beneath her chin the heavy blankets trammelled and her hair. Her cheek pale and cold. He, trying not to think, but thinking. The bed springs silent. The come and go of winters passing.

How he wanted more and more to encircle her in his arms and kiss it all into oblivion, and how he tried. But she could not compartmentalize her hurts, nor could he her unending catalogue of injuries. Each advance he made was fraught with anticipated disappointment, freighted with their failures, and failed. The wound you let go septic because it stings too much to disinfect. His hand a stranger to her, trespassing on her hip, driven off. The desolate exhalations. Their love grown strange. And then: the rupture. The unmendable regret. He and Catherine Bass, in a contumulate bed. A forgotten, crinkled square of paper bearing a number and a name. A suspicion confirmed, a confession without redress. The account without reckoning. A long time coming. And after: nothing can be safely trusted.

The soft wings of morning had alighted on the bed. In the silence of the room, Noah became aware of how his heart was tolling like a bell. Around his naked finger, the impression of his ring persisted in clearly cut lines, almost like a brand. The flesh there was polished with spinning. He thought: two people, one of them him and the other someone who loved him, had made a marriage with mutual feelings and promises they never lived up to, and when it died they lingered awhile beside the corpse, like speechless and uncertain children at a wake for someone they hardly knew, until at last they buried it. It was strange to think that a piece of metal, squeezed between his finger and thumb, was all that remained. It was just an artifact now, and he felt like a tomb raider, only without the thrill of discovery. He sighed a hard, disburdening exhalation. His legs and hips were starting to lock up. He set the ring down on the bedside table, atop the folder and its pages. *When the world falls into sin.* Saint Jerome again. He needed that shower.

ʊ

Towel in hand, Noah came down the stairs and looked into the kitchen. It smelled of buttered toast. His grandmother was at the stove with her back to him, but he saw how her elbow circled and could hear her rattle and scrape in the porridge pot. He approached and gave her a kiss. Her stiff silver curls tickled his cheek. "Where's Gramps?" he asked.

"In the toilet. When I came down I found him pacing with his tea and talking not a lot of sense. Care to explain?"

Noah reached around her to open the oven and she shifted to one side. He took a piece of toast from inside and then sat at the table. "I might have asked him about Dad."

In reflex, his grandmother's free hand went to her hair; her fingers slid into the curls and curled around them. "Noah, would you please stop doing that? You know it winds him up."

"He was down at the water again."

His grandmother put down the spoon and turned to him. "Again? Jesus, when I went to start the wash he was still in bed. I swear I'm gonna have to put a bell on him—"

"If you need help watching him, we can get the nurse to come more often—"

"—or maybe a leash."

"—or maybe get someone to come full time."

Persevering little pockets of air began to pop up and whistle through the oatmeal. She turned and resumed her stirring. "That's far too expensive. We can manage."

"What about the money I sent you?" Noah asked.

"You're always trying to spare yourself short," she answered. "I've got it in an account for Felix."

Noah bit into his toast, chewing harder than he needed. "Gran, that money was for you. I can take care of Felix—"

"And we can take care of ourselves."

Noah draped his towel over a chair and sat down at the table. The kitchen was warm from the oven and the stove and the steaming kettle. Cramming the rest of his toast, he chewed deliberately for a long while. At last he swallowed. "What was the last offer?"

"They wanted to tear the house down, so I told them to forget it," his grandmother said. "Anyway, where would we go?" She did not turn to answer. She was watching the porridge thicken.

Each trip home was like watching time lapse photography of his grandfather's illness. It always seemed to be advancing more quickly than it was, and Noah had to fight against a sense of urgency that caused him to consider, like a ruminant chewing over and over again his indigestible forage, the growing need to move his grandparents into a home. While safely in Toronto, he could easily imagine the conversation in which he laid out for his grandmother the various reasons why, but once he got down home again he blocked right up.

Up against the south side of the house behind the lilacs, there was a little nook where he used to play when he was young, and a tire swing on the sugar maple, which he still would use sometimes, especially when the wind was up and the folding of the surf became so hypnotic that seconds stretched to minutes and a short swing could fill a half hour before you knew it. Neither kitchen nor bathroom, though both were well cared for, had been renovated in Noah's lifetime, which made the house feel suspended in some decade before he was born, when cheap wood paneling, and hideously coloured carpet, and vile orange melamine counter-tops were thought attractive. In the parlour, which was of a more ancient, Green Gables appearance, the walls were plaster and prone to cracking, framed by simple, century-old crown moulding, and the carpets were elegantly patterned and tightly woven, worn around the doorways and charred in little pocks around the fireplace, which sometimes spat out embers. There was also a small upright piano that his grandfather still could play and did from time to time. On the walls hung his grandfather's charcoal sketches, as well as faded prints of Renaissance paintings, the two largest being the *Primavera* and *Nascita di Venere* by Botticelli. In one corner was their small television and facing it the rocking chair that Noah's grandfather used to sit in and watch the game on Saturdays. A mirror hung over the hearth, with sconces shaped like candles on either side. On the mantelpiece numerous pictures were displayed: one of Noah's grandfather kitted out before the war; one of his grandmother, with her mischievous young eyes a-twinkle, and her girls, all short-haired and fancied up in their courting dresses, huddled close around her; a few of Noah when he was a child; one of his parents on their wedding day, and one of him and Cate on theirs; and one of Felix from the last time he visited. It was like a side-chapel, and Noah's grandmother devoted a little time to it each day to preserve it from any accumulation of dust.

These items, and so many others, not to mention all the sounds and smells and daily routines, all reminded Noah that this was their home, and his home, and his dead father's too, so that even now, when presented with an opportunity to say what was becoming so obvious— that his grandmother was no longer able to care for her husband and herself and the house too, all on her own—Noah wavered. He could not imagine his grandmother without her kitchen, or either of them without the ocean in their backyard. He balked at the likelihood, his grandmother requiring so little care and his grandfather so much, that they would be housed separately. When she was a small, pretty girl, Noah's grandmother had come into the Co-op. His grandfather had just enlisted with the Highlanders and was lending a hand before shipping out. He took one look and knew she was the one. After she left, he said, "Dad, I'm going to marry that girl." And his father said, "Well aren't you a big feelin' lad. Don't she get a say?"

After the war she had her say, and said it. He was hired on at the high school. They bought the house that first year and had lived here since. But while his grandfather still took to his chair in the evenings, he was increasingly silent, and his grandmother now went weeks without seeing her girls, skipping even their monthly bridge nights. It was time he nudged them along, but Noah knew that after fifty years together it would break their hearts to be parted. When he tried to speak, he felt his voice penned in. He felt like a cosset, eager to cut loose, but fearful of nipping at the hand that strokes it. He watched his grandmother stir the pot and the time for speaking passed. She turned her head slightly to look at him.

"Noah, promise me you'll stop asking him about your father. There's no use plowing a barren field."

Noah smiled. "That's what he said."

She looked at her grandson in surprise. "Really?"

"Sort of."

"Exactly. Sort of." She frowned. "I think you've got about as much out of him as you're like to."

"Some days he's better," said Noah.

"Some days he hasn't sense enough to make a nickel."

The kettle started to squeal and Noah's grandmother turned to lift it off the burner. "Do you want some tea?" Noah felt a little pain in his chest as he watched her use the slumped, sodden bag from the saucer. She turned and saw him watching. "Waste not, want not," she said. Then she placed the cup and saucer before him on the table. "How was your run?"

"Fine." He swirled and muddled the tea bag with his spoon. "I stopped for the mail. The cheques came. I left them on the counter."

"Oh, good."

"And Don sends his best. He wanted me to tell you that if you need anything you only have to ask."

"That's sweet of him. Don always was a good lad, when he wasn't being foolish."

Down the hall the toilet flushed and the bathroom door opened. The old man then appeared in the doorway and entered the kitchen with his shirt tucked so well into his pants that it poked out through his open zipper.

"Oh, Peter," his wife said, "your fly's down." She moved towards her husband, but Noah reached him first.

"No worries," Noah said. "If it can't get up it can't get out, right Gramps?"

Noah's grandmother placed two bowls of porridge on the table. "Lord knows that's the truth. And to think he used to wake up with his eyes wide open."

The old man cackled as Noah tucked the shirttail in and zipped. "Come on, Gramps." Noah sat his grandfather down and, remembering how the old man's arthritis sometimes acted up in the morning, took a tube of Bengay from an upper cupboard. He squeezed a little into his palm, placed the tube on the table, and began to rub the cream vigorously into his grandfather's hands. The smell of menthol and camphor filled their noses.

"Ho ho!" the old man said, and whistled in appreciation. Then loudly he said, "Toast!"

"Yes, yes, dear, it's coming."

His wife set a plate of buttered toast on the table and then turned back to the stove.

"Avy, Avy," the old man said. "Come here." He reached up and took her cheeks in his hands and pulled her lips to his. Receiving his kiss, she placed her hands on his cheeks too and held them there a moment before pulling away.

"I love you too. Now let me get the dishes started." She turned and started running water in the sink.

"Now …" the old man said. He clapped his hands upright together twice. "Now the … you know …" He clapped them again.

"I'll do it," Noah said, sitting. They held their hands together solemnly and bowed their heads, then Noah intoned, "In the name of the Father and of the Son and of the Holy Ghost, whoever eats the fastest gets the most."

"Noah!" his grandmother said, turning her disapproving face on him.

The old man opened his eyes and, smiling, slapped his hands on the table. "Good, lad. Good." Then he took his spoon and began to eat.

"Noah, you shouldn't make fun."

"Who do you think taught me?"

"Do you see what a terrible influence you were, Peter?"

Noah's grandfather still smiled. His grandmother, mildly rueful, shook her head. Then, remembering suddenly, she said to Noah, "I forgot about your friend. Shall I make another cup for her?"

"No, she couldn't stay."

"No? Came in the fog and left in the morning, did she?"

Noah stiffened. His grandmother put some detergent in the water and started piling in the few dishes that lay on the counter. She began to scrub the porridge pot.

"When I was growing up we had a name for girls like that, and it wasn't *friend*. Nothing so dressed-up."

"Gran—"

"I knew this one girl ... the poor dear was so walleyed she could lie on her back and look down a well. Thought she had to go grassin' up on skin hill with all the boys to get any attention. Caused her poor mother no end of grief, God rest her. It was a relief to everyone when she married a nice boy from somewhere away. Of course, that just made her mean and jealous. She dogged him something awful just in case he got up to something. Had eyes in the back of her head almost." She turned off the water. "Do you know what the problem is? You're all too casual."

"Gran, I know—"

"Don't give me your I-knows. You ought to know." She bore down equally on Noah and the porridge pot, her elbow and tongue both wagging. "You remember what happened to Johnny McKenzie and Maddy Donovan when they got themselves pregnant? When he told his parents, they kicked him out and told him to get a job. She didn't even tell her parents. She was what, seventeen? Just going up fool's hill. And her parents had warned her, if she got herself knocked up they weren't taking care of her mistake. When they finally found out, her mother swore to me it was just an idle threat, just to keep her in line, and that she never thought she'd get herself an abortion. You remember what happened to them? They dropped out of school and shacked up, but they couldn't get enough to make ends meet so both of them had to go back to their parents with their tails between their legs. And now where are they?"

"I don't know."

She put down the pot and turned to face him. "Now you're talking sensible. You don't know. And I don't neither, but I bet they wish they could have done things different." Noah wanted to interject, but by now his grandmother was off and steaming like the kettle. "And if you don't get yourself pregnant you get your diseases. You won't believe what I heard the other day when I stopped for a tea at the Hortons. There were these two girls talking, and do you know what they're teaching them at school? They're teaching that, when you sleep with a boy, you sleep with everyone he's ever slept with. Sounds like they've got signs in the corridors and everything down at the high school. And, Lord help me, if the one girl didn't say to the other that she kind of liked the thought of that. Said she always had a thing for the girl her boyfriend used to go with, only she was too shy to tell her." Noah watched his grandmother's fair face redden. "Honest to frig," she said, "the things you hear at the Hortons."

"Gran ..." Noah pleaded.

She dunked her hands in the water and started washing a teacup. "It's no wonder you kids can't stay married these days."

"You're one to talk, Gran," Noah said, fed up at last. "The way Gramps told it, when you two were still courting he had you over the snowbank behind the curling rink."

His grandmother dropped the cup clanking into the sink and spun around. "Noah! You mind your tongue. It was different with us. He was my only one and we both told each other so and meant it." She tried to pick up the glass, but it slipped again from her shaking hands. "Damn it, Noah, you've got me all bothered now."

She took a deep breath and steadied her hands, then she picked up the glass again. After several moments of silence, she asked, "So, did he tell you anything else?"

"Not that bears repeating."

Noah was about to return to his breakfast, but noticed that the tube of Bengay had moved and the cap was off. Glancing up, he saw his grandfather sliding his spoon from between his lips.

"Gramps, you didn't ..."

It was immediately apparent that he had. The old man started coughing and mucus began to pour out from his nose and down over his lips. Noah quickly snatched a long strip of paper towels, and his grandmother caught her husband under the arms and hurried him to the sink, where he hacked and snorted as his body tried to flush his whole head clean. It took several minutes and dozens of spasms before the old man's body relaxed and the phlegm stopped flowing. Noah's grandmother removed a handkerchief from her husband's pocket and dried his eyes and cheeks and mouth.

"Wow," the old man said, eyes wide. He smiled, amazed.

Gently, she forced her husband back to the table and patted him on the shoulder. Then she turned on her grandson. "Jesus, Noah. You can't leave that stuff lying around."

26

She quickly wetted a new cloth and wiped the table, but that was only the beginning. Realizing that the floor needed cleaning too, she just sighed and sank back against the counter. In the excitement, her curls had become wet and a little wispy. She looked older.

Noah slumped into his chair. He no longer had any appetite for the globs of porridge in his bowl. "I'm leaving tomorrow," he said, pushing it away.

"That's good," his grandmother replied, adding hurriedly, "Felix will be missing you."

Noah agreed.

"When you go, there's an envelope on the table by the front door. It's some stuff of your grandfather's that I found a while back when I was vacuuming behind the filing cabinet."

"Oh?"

"There's some papers, a few letters he wrote from the war, some newspaper clippings. It's not much."

"It's not nothing," Noah said. "You know, at the convenience this morning, Don told me how Gramps drove his brother to hockey for a year when he was on probation."

Noah's grandmother opened her mouth in surprise. "I'd forgotten all about that." She smiled at her husband, then frowned, then shook her head. He was finished eating and was now licking the empty bowl clean. "Why don't you take him somewhere. I've got to get this floor cleaned, and I don't even want to think about the sink."

Noah took his grandfather by the hand and led him into the parlour. He sat the old man down on the piano bench, and took the rocking chair for himself. He wondered how they would manage, and when he would be able to return, and what was in the envelope by the door. In the kitchen, his grandmother was talking to herself: "I swear to God, when I said *till death* I didn't think he'd live this long." In the parlour, the piano sang with the perfectly remembered notes of "Ma Virginie."

2

"So where did you get to last night?" Raymond Cormier asked.

Though it smelled less of the sea air its name promised, and more of burnt coffee and infrequently changed fryer oil, the Seaside Diner was full of customers. Most were locals, but one or two had suitcases and, like Noah, were waiting for the airport bus. Noah sat with his friend in a corner at a window table so he could watch for it. He looked hard for it.

"If you don't fess up, I'll have to catechize you."

The look on Noah's face was confession enough for Ray.

"You went home with Maggy didn't you."

"No," Noah said, defensively. He sipped his coffee. "She went home with me."

"Jesus, Plugger. You know better."

"If you let it drop, I'll get the tab."

"Sold," Ray said, slapping his palm on the table, "to the guilty-looking gentleman in the corner."

Noah had rather look guilty than as badly hung over and haggard as Ray, with his anemic complexion and puffy eyes, and he said as much.

"It's a miracle I don't look worse. Shit, I'm still half in the bag."

"What happened after I left?"

"Well, first we closed the Ceilidh House. Then we wanted to keep drinking, but Walt forgot to stop for liquor, so we had to make do with the Schooners in the back of his truck. They'd been there most of the summer, but what are you gonna do?"

"You drank that?"

"It was that or switch to water. We were too hammered to notice anyway. We dropped Joe off sometime after four, and then Walt and

I drove back to his place to crash. I doubt Joe even made it inside. He probably passed out in the yard again."

"He was blind drunk even before I left," Noah said, amazed.

"He didn't want to see the morning."

"Yeah, Maggy told me. Did his girl really skip her pill?"

"He's not saying, but it sounds like dirty pool to me. You know, I read somewhere that women skipping their pills is the number one cause of pregnancy."

"Really?" Noah said. "I thought it was sperm."

He smiled, and Ray smiled too and nodded his approval. The two men, amid the ambient clatter of the café, grew momentarily silent. Noah had been poking away at his fried egg with a fork whose tines were bent askew. He was about to break open and spill the yolk, but instead he tried to straighten his utensil.

A young man exited the café, followed by his wife with a stroller. As he held the door, a pigeon scurried in and began hopping down the aisle. Noah's curious expression as he watched it scavenge near the table drew his friend's attention. Ray kicked at it and it scurried away. "Filthy things." Undeterred, it returned, risking a blow to nab the crumbs around their feet. "Among the island's first immigrants," Ray said, in the style of a *Hinterland Who's Who*, "the common pigeon was first introduced to North America at Port Royal, Nova Scotia, in sixteen-ought-six. At the time domesticated, the resilient species quickly adapted to the local climate and became feral, spreading widely across the continent." Ray swung his leg once more at the creature, but it hopped laterally and carried on with beady-eyed indifference. Ray frowned, but let it be.

"You can't fault their persistence," Noah said.

"This is true. They were fruitful and multiplied. Now they're a nuisance, as the good Lord no doubt intended."

A loud, catastrophic-sounding crash cut them off, and the café fell momentarily silent. There followed an unpleasant string of curses from the kitchen. Some people returned to their conversations, some craned to better hear the aftermath. Noah wondered about Joe. "Is he going to marry her?"

"Oh, probably," Ray answered, once his curiosity about the kitchen petered out. "They've been steady off and on for a couple of years now.

He probably would have married her anyway, if she'd asked. I just don't think he had much of a notion for wanting kids just yet."

"Will he be able to stay in school?"

"I doubt it. Almost everyone I know who went to school doesn't have kids, and everyone who had kids didn't go to school. Things being as they are you might as well sign right up for welfare. I don't know how you and Cate did it."

"We didn't, quite."

Ray nodded. Noah watched as his friend's thoughts withdrew to some distant part of his brain. He was choosing his words. "Are you going to be OK?"

Noah set his head confidently nodding. "I've been out of work before. It'll work out."

"What are you going to do after you get back?"

"Cate said I could stay with them while I'm looking."

"It's the least she can do," Ray said, punctuating in the air with his fork. A large drop of syrup arced across the table. "How is she, anyway?"

"The same," Noah said. "Only more so."

Ray nodded. Then he dug his fork into a pancake. "How are your prospects?"

Noah hesitated. "Poor," he said, finally. "If things don't improve, I may have to try my hand at something else."

"If it makes you feel better, it's no different at Fisheries."

"That's supposed to make me feel better?"

"They keep telling me I have to pay my dues." Ray stabbed at his breakfast. "Well it's been five years and all I can get are these one year contracts. Condescending shits. Their parents set them up with everything—social security, health care—they'll devour it all if we let them."

Noah nodded. "I can't even get a doctor in Toronto. My guess is, by the time we start going in for colonoscopies there'll be no money left for lube."

"Fuck it," Ray said. "Lube's for pussies anyway."

The young couple at the table behind them fell silent. Across the aisle, two sixty-something men were glancing with conspicuous irritation. Noah alerted Ray to their discomfort. Ray, as conspicuously, looked them over. "God forbid we offend the ancientry," he said pointedly. "Every time the market so much as hiccups their sphincters pucker up a little tighter. *Cut taxes. No more corporate liability, or environmental oversight, or financial regulation.* I say it's economic cannibalism. They're underwriters profiting from their own ruin. It's like robbing Peter to pay Paul, you see? Like ... the leachate from the tar ponds. That shit gets in everywhere and it poisons everything. Who's going to pay to clean that up?"

Noah glanced around. The diners beside them and behind were once again in conversation.

"You watch," Ray continued. "When the market really bucks it'll get bad. And then it'll get worse. More of us will get laid off, and pretty soon people at your kitchen parties will be eyeing their beer with suspicion. That's what happens in a recession. And how many of them had to put themselves through school with full-time jobs for minimum wage? Or were tens of thousands in debt when they finished? Or couldn't find jobs while their parents were finding ways not to retire?"

"I don't think I'll ever be able to retire," Noah said.

"You and me both, Plugger. Was there ever a generation that took more and left less?" Ray shook his head in disgust. "I mean, my parents have three cars between them. Three!"

"How are your folks?"

"They're all right, I guess. They want me to move out."

Ray sipped his coffee. Noah looked out the window. Across the street an old woman was sitting by the bus stop. Her hands were folded one over the other and a small suitcase rested by her feet. Behind her was a red-brick house, a gallery with hooked rugs, too reverent paintings and other homespuns. There was a tiny mining museum too, filled with letters, photographs and drawings, and various lanterns, picks and shovels donated by families who treasured them so little, or in some cases so much, that they didn't want to keep them. The town's hopeful testament to the island's faded golden age, its donation box was often empty. Beside the gallery and museum was the Medical Associates, which seemed a grand name for just two doctors and a half-blind dentist.

"So, how's your grandfather," Ray asked.

"Sometimes better, sometimes worse," Noah said. "Yesterday he ate some Bengay at breakfast."

"Oh no, really?"

"Yeah. You'd never imagine an old man's head could have so much phlegm in it."

Ray shuddered and shook his head. Then he smiled. "You know who's ben-gay?"

Ray indicated the young couple at the table behind him. Facing Noah was a young woman, attractive, not more than twenty-three or twenty-four. Her eyes were fixed on her companion, whose small frame sat erect and forward-leaning. His back being to Noah, his face was hidden, but his choirboy voice was animated and his body too.

"I tried a couple of times with girls after you and I broke up, but it was nothing like this. The sensations … I mean, I never suspected. I thought I was going to fly to pieces. He was the one that taught me how to really give head." The young man leaned in further, conspiratorially, but raised his voice a little. "The secret is sibilance. The slightly hollow shape in the tongue, and where to place it. And the articulation, all around the corona, especially near the glans. And then it's all about the friction. Stiff and slow and smooth. Once I started to get it down, I felt like a debutante at her coming-out party. I swear, moving to Montreal was the best decision I ever made. I don't think I'd ever have come out otherwise." He scratched his neck and adjusted his shirt. The young woman's eyes were wide. "I think my parents are worried about my sisters, though. Now that the city's sullied one of their children, they're afraid it'll happen to the girls too."

"He's gotten worse," Ray said. "I used to think it was just his braces, but now it sounds like his tongue's too big for his mouth."

"Who is it?"

"Paul Renn."

"Should I remember him?"

"He was a few years behind us. Joe knew him. He used to play the Virgin Mary for the Nativity at Christmas."

Noah nodded, remembering.

"Joe said he used to try to make him play tea party with his mother's good china," Ray said. "It's hard to believe there was ever a closet big enough for him to hide in. I hope he's careful not to get all fancy-pants about it when he's around here, though. He'll get worse than the dirty looks those old fellers shot us."

Noah thought of lisps and looks and secret handshakes and other shibboleths. The young woman was smiling at Renn, but the smile was tight. It was sympathetic and confidential, but there was something hollow and costly in it, something pyrrhic. "It's sad," Noah said.

"That he'll get a beating if he's not careful? Yeah, I'd say that's sad."

"No ... I mean, yes that too, but ... she's in love with him and he doesn't even see it."

Ray half swung around to look, then stopped and straightened himself. "You think so?" he asked.

"She's thinking how she's always loved him. She's thinking how he'd squire her up and down and treat her better than any of the others. She'd marry him if she could."

"It would take some serious alchemy to get what she's after. She'd have to transmute him first." Then Ray chuckled. "You know, marriage is a lot like alchemy."

"Because it turns lead into gold?" Noah suggested.

"No. Because it doesn't work." Then, almost by the way, Ray added, "You know, I've seen Maggy give you a look like that on occasion."

Noah didn't answer. From his plate he took a piece of buttered toast and used it to break open his remaining egg. The golden yolk spilled everywhere and Noah dabbed hurriedly to sop it up.

ᠸ

A few hours later, Noah was trying to get comfortable in his window seat. Peering down, he saw the landscape far below slowly drifting rearward in the changing afternoon light, like in a schoolboy's diorama. Below lay Annapolis Royal, which had been Port Royal before it was usurped, and had also been, before that, the green Annapolis fundament, whose shores the Mi'kmaq alone used to fish. From Digby in the southeast, counterclockwise, lay the Annapolis, Cornwallis, Avon, Shubenacadie, Salmon, Farrells, Tantramar, Memramcook, Petitcodiac, Shepody, Upper Salmon, Quiddy, Little Salmon, Big

Salmon, Saint John, Magaguadavic and Saint Croix rivers, all partici-
pants in the great, peristaltic inpouring and venting where the sea and
river waters came into the Fundy Basin. Salmon farms, Noah knew,
lined the outer bay on both sides, but he could not see them.

There had been a party the night that Noah's father died. Three
friends separately remembered that his parents had argued violently.
These recollections were largely synoptic, but there were divergences.
Also, the years had edited and excised so much, and in all likelihood
added too, that the versions could be neither corroborated nor confirmed. They might all be true, or part of each. Noah kept copies of
their statements folded in his notebook, but he had more or less committed them to memory.

Version 1: "I remember Laz and Léa yellin' at each other in the
bedroom—you could hear it down the hall—and then Laz came out
and Léa following and still giving it to him—they carried right on
through the kitchen and out the door, right into the rain. I don't have
the slightest idea what the matter was. When was that, April? And you
would have been not much more than two, I think." [John Poirier,
realtor. Friend of Laz Lamarck and Léa, née Doucet. 19 August 1991
at his Halifax office]

Version 2: "The two of them were pretty hot, but I don't remember what for or what they said, although I do remember feelin' right
unsettled when they come through the kitchen 'cause Léa was beside
herself with cryin' and Laz weren't havin' any of it and just left without
so much as a word to any of us. And her with no ride home. And then
the next day I heard how Laz had gone and drowned in that storm."
[Sarah Nicols, née Ross, nurse. Childhood friend of Léa Lamarck, née
Doucet. 9 August 1993, at Dartmouth General Hospital]

Version 3: "The booze that night was plentiful, mind you, and
they'd been drinkin', but then we'd all been, and at some point they
went into the bedroom down the hall of that little bungalow—I can't
say why, though I wondered at the time, 'cause I weren't goin' in to
find out—didn't want an eyeful o'nethers, see?—and then things got
loud in there, and at first I thought they were just havin' a bit of a roll,
but it didn't take no time to hear that it were more of a tussle. Well,
I was noodlin' at the piano and tryin' to drown them out with a reel,

see? Then in comes Janet Deveau who starts to give it to me about the sweat ring my beer is leavin' on the piano, and I says what right has she got to give me hell for nothin', and she says she's got the right 'cause it's her house and her piano, and I figure she's got me on that one, so I down the beer and go to the kitchen to get another. Now, while my head's in the fridge lookin', I hear Laz and Léa come out of the bedroom and down the hall towards the kitchen and I realize that I don't know where I put my opener, the one with the O'Keefe on it, which I always liked 'cause it was my father's so I don't want to lose it. So as my head's in there your folks come into the kitchen, though I don't hear what they're saying 'cause of the racket from the fridge my head's in, but when I stand up they're out on the porch and Zeph MacDermid is gettin' in between 'em, and I think that maybe Laz knows where I put my opener or maybe has his own that I can borrow till I find mine. So I go out to ask and I see Laz punch Zeph right in the snoot and bloody him all up, which surprises me seein' they were always pals and such, and Laz goes off and gets in his car and I go up to Zeph to ask if he's OK and has he seen my opener, but he just goes walkin' off with his hand over his nose, and your mother's in tears but tells me it's on my key ring, which I had clipped to my pants so as I wouldn't lose 'em, which I was always doin' at parties, and sure enough there it is right on my keys like she says. So then I crack my beer and tell your mother that I'll get her home if she wants, 'cause to tell you true—and I loved your father, don't get me wrong, and wouldn't have wished him no harm—but I always had a sweetness for your mother and thought we could have been sweet on each other maybe if things had turned out other than they did. 'Course, as I said there were plentiful booze that night, so I can't say as I don't have some of the details amiss, but then with Laz dyin' that same night some of it got burned in, see?" [Alexander Beaton, former captain of the hockey team, current regular at Hill's Bar, occasional guest of the North Sydney drunk tank. Friend of Laz Lamarck and Léa, née Doucet. 14 August 1993, half-drunk at Tim Horton's at time of interview]

Being the most colourful and complete, it was Beaton's narrative that Noah found the most compelling, but coming from a man drunk both when the events occurred and when retelling them it was hardly reliable. It also, like the others, didn't tell him what he really wanted to know. What mattered most remained a blank.

The cause seemed not to have been his father's job, nor money. Laz worked in the cannery, which as occupations go was neither noble nor very profitable, but the pay was steady and, though a clever man and capable of better employment, he had a wife and child to care for and, as Noah's grandmother had explained, those days the job you had was always better than the job you wished for. It wasn't like he spent his days breathing coal dust one mile down and three miles out in the soot and darkness beneath the ocean floor.

What little money he did earn appeared, judging by the twenty or so account statements Noah discovered loose in a box, to be deposited every two weeks without exception. Had his father been a drinker or a gambler, the money would have been spent before it was ever earned, but they seemed to have lived carefully from month to month, with-drawing regular, small amounts, enough for rent and food and maybe a little extra for the three of them. When they died, the estate left neither obligations nor bequests besides himself.

Which caused Noah to sometimes wonder if maybe that was what it amounted to: the third person. It was not uncommon. When Felix was born, he and Cate had not been prepared for the reality of dividing their affections. It was like when small waves strike a floating dock and get it rocking, but at a different pace than they strike it, and there's a struggle in the rhythm and it's hard to follow. Or like when he ran with music and sometimes found it difficult to keep his cadence when his three steps had to fit into the music's two, or vice-versa. Or like years ago that duet his grandfather tried to teach him, where the left hand played the melody in double time while the right hand played in triple, and they found it impossible to stay together and snarled it every time and the whole thing fell to pieces, which with his marriage was more or less exactly how it all went down.

But Noah had to be careful, and when he indulged in such analo-gies reminded himself to take care, to avoid reading his father's story through the lens of his own. There was no reason to implicate himself, apart from his own insinuative conscience, which too readily knitted itself to his father's circumstances at the one end and to his son's at the other. Concentrating only on the facts, however—all that his grandparents had been able and willing to say; and what little he had discovered from his mother's parents, now dead, and her siblings, older almost by a generation and having migrated and become estranged after she married an Anglo; and whatever his parents' friends could remember, which in the end wasn't much—it left Noah feeling like all the king's men. Like the lines of the rivers below, the details paid out into the rift his imagination opened up, where they slacked and tangled until, at last, they unspooled entirely, leaving him bereft and empty.

The scraps contained in his grandmother's envelope, which he withdrew from the bag at his feet, were likewise tantalizing letdowns: letters from London, where his grandfather had been stationed, addressed to Modeste Avy and cross-written to save on paper and skirt the censors; clippings of fading newsprint, mostly of book reviews from the *Chronicle Herald*, but also some local reports on Laz's hockey team from when he was quite young; and, most torturous, a page sparsely covered in his grandfather's hurried handwriting. It was dated 12 April 1969, which Noah recognized as the date of his father's funeral. His grandfather had underlined this so many times that the pen had nearly torn through. The ideas were full of randomness. Orphaned words and abortive phrases bore witness to his grandfather's distraction. Nothing was worked out. Strange uncertainty in the hand so confident and controlled in letters to his girl back home. It bore evidence of crumpling. Hardly hoping that somewhere on the page was something he had overlooked, Noah read it again.

<u>*12 April 1969*</u>

a eulogy is supposed to be a ~~*recitation of a commemoration of a remembering*~~

<u>*Things I remember:*</u>
teaching him to tie his skates—he kept crossing the laces into the wrong holes
reading him books and then watching him go to the shelves on his own
raking the leaves and shovelling the snow
the night he cooked his first fricot

his books go unread ~~*and his shoes unscuffed*~~
~~*when a child dies his bed stays forever made, his toys say put away*~~
~~*his shirts stay folded with no shoulders to fill them*~~
his things fall into <u>disuse</u>

~~*why did he make the deci*~~
~~*idiotic decision to go out in that storm*~~
idiotic

When children leave you always think that if they need you they'll call and you can go get them

Children are the   ~~*anchor line?*~~
            ~~*the anchor?*~~
            ~~*the boat*~~

There are things ~~*we should have talked about*~~ ~~*I should have said to him*~~ *things we should have said*

Consolations: *graduation*
               marriage
               ~~*he is beyond poverty and labour and whatever pain he suffered*~~
               others have suffered worse than we common woe
               a grandchild
               continuance
               after the flood a little branch
               the family tree

crooked roots and branches that couldn't be made straight
man and wife and child   *a threefold cord*
~~*there was a man somewhere that he would have become and now I shall not know him*~~
why didn't he talk to us?
For a teacher loses all his influence whose words are rendered null by his deeds.

                                       fish food

Clipped to the back of the page on a small piece of paper was a note: *These were Gramps' notes for your father's eulogy. He didn't end up using them. He only said he guessed they hadn't really known each other and he wished they had.* Noah reclined in his seat and closed his eyes.

A storm on a savage sea, gnashing in the deep cleft of the Atlantic basin. Such hiss and steam are breathed into the air and the air so thick and dark—like something out of the first act of the history of the world. A vessel, small and trim, breasting the molten waters, its make-or-break engine banging out a clamour like a fist on a kitchen table. The wind spits salt rain and sleet. On the shore, beneath the hunched shoulders of the rocky island, the scrub spruce cower in the snarling face of a living gale. Up-along, the sea heaves in every inlet, pummelling away all this side of the island. In the harbour the boats pitch and tug against their moorings. The traps and tackle sit tight if fastened to the dock or, if not, they're thrown about the wharf. Shutters everywhere are all clamped down and the doors bolted, or they're rattling off their hinges. A blow to strip the paint clean off. All the streets of town are empty.

But now behold: a thunder crack and follows a silence in the heavens. The sea stills. The wind and waters take a breather. The village steeple, tall in the scant light and draughty, whispers an intermittent, timid ring of bell–song. The boat now heaves a little less, but, even so, faint's the hope that she'll escape a wracking. Why take a boat out in these waters? No dry foot neither. An able pilot gone so far strange that he would make for out and throw himself into the open chops of the sea.

Now comes a big wave and the winds hauling in, and he brings her about and puts her nose right into it. His shimmy's soaked and sticking to him, and his hair's blown back, and his eyes are only knife-cuts of white in the lightning flash. Up and up he goes, climbing the swell, its fingers curling over and coming down to get him. They rend the hull and pluck him from his seat: a man in such need of a pool of still water that he had to go five fathom deep and more to find it. And he does. The cold, dark wet plunges in around him. His lungs are flooded, his limbs go lank, what light is in his eyes goes dark, and he's chewed open by the sea and sinking slowly into the ooze. With no other vessels to devour, the storm goes vainly at the shore, screaming and clawing all it can. The land's old shoulders suffer the blows, and the sky, unrelenting, empties right out.

Before long Noah fell asleep. In the afternoon sun, his flight was only a distant flash of silver and the crisp line of its contrail, into the vague blue of the sky, fading.

PART TWO

By Accident Most Strange

3

Perched in Rosedale atop one of the Don Valley's small ravines, the three-storey Georgian home of Owen Trover glowed in fledgling rays of sun that glided silently across the city sprawl. Trover himself—already showered, shaven, and half-dressed—was settled into the leather cushions of his window chair and casting a crisp shadow across the soft wool rug. In one hand, quarter-folded, he held the financial pages of the daily paper, and at his elbow, on a side table, lay a silver tray with what was left of his breakfast: a few lonesome clusters of granola, crumbs of wholegrain toast, and a dozen or so cherry pits exposed at the silver's edge. Clutching a dessert spoon like a curette, he toyed distractedly with the remains. Leaning back into the chair, he lifted his legs onto the ottoman and his robe fell open slightly at the chest and thighs, exposing his smooth trunk and trousers. A warm breeze was prowling through the salon.

Discreetly, Trover's personal assistant entered from the hallway carrying a tea service in both hands and a substantial memorandum book under his arm. Trover dropped his spoon and paper on the breakfast tray, and lowered his legs to make room for the tea. The tray held a pot, two inverted cups, a serviette, and a small cake, rectangular like a gold brick. He poured the tea. "I assume Ms. Jensen made it home without incident," Trover said. "She had an early appointment."

"Yes. The car returned while you were in the pool."

Trover curled his hands around the cup and tasted. "Mmm. Excellent. Thank you, Clement."

"Rooibos orange ginger," Clement said, answering before Trover could ask.

"It's good. Make sure we keep some of that around."

Clement jotted down the instruction. "You enjoyed your breakfast."

"A question?"

"An observation. You savaged your tray."

"It's true. But, in my defence, I was famished. I think it's the new regimen. I'm starting to feel like the thirty-year-old me. Or how I imagine him anyway." With both hands he patted his lean torso. "When I came in from my swim this morning I caught myself in the mirror and couldn't believe how good I looked. I even turned myself on a little."

"That's ridiculous."

"I agree, it is ridiculous ... how good I look. I don't know how you can stand it."

"Let's go with professionalism."

"How unflappable of you." Trover sipped the steaming bush tea. "This really is fine. Sit your professionalism down and have some." His assistant poured himself a cup and sat stiffly on the adjacent chesterfield. Across his lap his notebook was waiting and, in his hand, a stylus poised. "The guest list," Trover said.

"We can expect 115, if no one cancels."

"The premier and his wife?"

"Otherwise engaged."

"Our dear director of advancement will be disappointed. I tried to tell her. What was the last book he read? *Mr. Silly*, I think. I suppose it's just as well, though. He sees more civic value in a parking lot. He would have soured the milk."

"Without question."

"You remember the book I had you send to persuade him."

"Atwood, wasn't it?"

Trover closed his eyes. "*The Circle Game*. First edition. Red cloth. Just the slightest toning of the pages." He sighed. "It was a fine copy. Not as fine as mine, but still. Not easy to come by. I bet he uses it as a coaster."

"Perhaps he finds the jacket design confusing."

Trover smiled. "Well. You've reminded Frau Direktor to be more selective in her choice of staff?"

"I have."

Gleeful, Trover reminisced, "Last time, one of those nitwits went after the Missus Doctor Stanley Hill. She was in a wheelchair, recovering from cancer surgery, and when he made *the ask* he suggested she make a bequest—"

"If not for her sutures, she might have made him take his own advice."

"I've told you before?" Trover asked.

"I was there."

"Odd that I don't remember."

"You remember just fine. You're just disappointed I didn't pretend not to."

Trover's esteem appeared in his renewed smile. "Remind me not to trust you too far. You're too clever by half." Rising from his chair, Trover put down his tea and directed himself towards the walk-in that divided the salon from the bedroom. He removed his robe and stood sleek and shirtless before the vanity. "Go on," he called into the salon. With a small pair of scissors, he began to nip a small cluster of enterprising ear hairs that had earlier escaped his attention.

"The musicians are booked," Clement said loudly. "A trio for the afternoon, a DJ for the evening."

"And he understands he's to avoid anything too current or too well known? I want the music energetic but unassuming; I want toe tapping, but not dancing; and certainly not singing."

"Is that likely?"

"It's an open bar, and some of the guests are students or graduates. It's not impossible. Help him with the program if you think he needs it. You're still on the happy side of youth."

"I'll speak with him."

Satisfied, Trover turned from the mirror and engaged his sartorial faculties. He examined his collection of shirts and pulled a pale blue of soft broadcloth to go with the chestnut wool of his trousers. He donned the shirt and lifted his braces into place.

"I've also spoken with the caterers," Clement continued. "They've provided a bar list and their suggested comestibles."

"Good. Arrange for a tasting before the end of the week. And arrange it here. I want them familiar with the kitchen." Trover selected

47

a tie—red, with silver-blue pin dots—and slung it over his shoulder. He returned to the salon. "Transportation?"

"Several cars are booked to collect the guests you indicated, and they'll be on call to take them home."

"When that's done, make sure some of the others of less substance are offered rides as well. It sends the right message. They'll go home feeling that they've arrived."

"Of course." Clement's pen darted across the page. "The patio lighting has also been arranged. And floating candle barges."

"Fish?" Trover asked.

"They won't survive in the pool."

"Pity."

"Propane heaters have been reserved in case it's cold. And the cleaning has been scheduled, before and after."

"The acrobats?"

"Twins from Montreal. Their fee was paltry, so I booked them at the Royal York. They're young enough to find that exciting. They've sent their technical needs. I would suggest the centre of the entry hall. There's room enough. It will make an impression as the guests arrive."

"Make sure their costumes are understated—shape yes, skin no. The energy can be erotic, but not indecent. And nothing too frenetic. Think: moving sculptures. I want diversion, not distraction." Trover approached the tea service and reached for the little cake, a small concession in his usual dietary reserve. He held it to his nose. It smelled of almonds.

"A financier," Clement said.

Trover devoured it and cleaned his fingers on the serviette. He then approached a mirror on the wall by the salon door, intended for last-minute adjustments and for guests. "I will also need a date."

Clement studied his employer. "Am I to infer that I should find you one?"

"I have no doubt you could, Clement, but that would be coarse."

"Perhaps Ms. Jensen."

Trover adjusted the loose lengths of his tie and began the habitual dance of right-over-left, then up-through-and-left, then back-around-front, and through, and right, then all-the-way-round, and up-behind, and down-and-through. "Ms. Jensen is lovely, and a suitable companion in her own way, but a date is like a tie—even the flattering are not for all occasions. I need a date for this party." Trover snugged the knot and stood preening before his own reflection.

"The tie is exquisite," Clement said.

"Yes. The Windsor knot should be worn more often. It's elegant, more difficult to tie than the Half Windsor, and broad enough to be almost, but not quite, ostentatious."

4

"But think about the opening scene: 'Which of you shall we say doth love us most?'"

Cecelia Lines scanned for sympathetic listeners, but the seminar room was full of skeptics. At the distant end sat two young men wearing ironic T-shirts. Greg's read, Stop Plate Tectonics and Anthony's, too small, exclaimed Your Boyfriend Thinks I'm Hot! Under the fluorescent lights, their glassy eyes suggested they had consumed a mainly liquid lunch again. To her immediate right was a young woman, Marion, whose traffic-sign doodles commonly communicated her indifference to everyone in the room, including Professor Handly, who sometimes allowed himself overtly disdainful glances at her pages. Across the table sat Approaches to Shakespeare's other students: Kelly, a sharp-nosed woman with a bolt through the cartilage of her right ear and a short, off-centre Mohawk that resembled a cockscomb; to her right, round-faced Jesper, always with a stupid grin and nodding, especially when Professor Handly was speaking, as if his head were being patted by the unseen hand of scholarly approbation; and finally, directly opposite Cecelia, an angular, young woman, barely twenty years old, she guessed, censorious and fond of interruption: Jessica Cleary. Cecelia felt them readying their objections. She steadied her nerves with a sustained breath that surely only she could hear. A fasten-safety-belts sign appeared in Marion's notebook and Jessica wore her habitual, withering expression. Handly's curious stare, forbearing and indulgent, was a distraction.

"Lear forces his daughters to compete for their marriage portions in a kind of love auction. Can you imagine anything more self-serving and manipulative? And, worse, his daughters' natural rivalries are exposed not only to each other, but also to the court, their husbands, and Cordelia's suitors." She envisioned them, the serpentine sisters gnawing, in their relentless reckoning, on each other's tails. "Think about the way he presides over the scene: the old king, the beloved father, basking in the glow of his daughters' and his subjects' love … until Cordelia speaks. From there the scene degenerates into a mess of petulant curses and banishments."

"Which is only what she deserves," said Greg. A shot across her bow. "This is a political scene, not a private one. Lear isn't asking for the real thing, only lip service. It's just the formality of state business. Goneril and Regan get it, but Cordelia doesn't. Her disobedience undermines her king. If you ask me, there's a whiff of treason in her backtalk."

"But isn't the scene as much about family as politics?" Cecelia was accommodating, but firm. "Sure, the political is front and centre, but don't we need to acknowledge the degree to which the daughters' reactions are governed by their familial relationships? Otherwise we risk misunderstanding what happens as badly as Lear does."

With beery eyes Greg looked at Cecelia, unconvinced. "For a royal family, a public appearance is state business."

"No, for every family a public appearance is state business."

Her rebuttal gave him pause. She hurried to hammer it home. "Who trusts the ministry of a preacher whose own children misbehave? What parent doesn't feel a little embarrassed when her child makes a boneheaded play and blows the game? What child isn't … isn't haunted by a parent whose disappointed face says, as clearly as words could ever do, you have failed, and in failing you have shamed both yourself and me? I'm betting everyone in this room has experienced that at one time or another. Even the loving mother who kisses her son in the schoolyard is trespassing. The other boys don't let him forget it." Cecelia thought she sensed a kind of suspension in her audience. "The important question is: why does Cordelia refuse to play along? The secret lies in the play's seldom discussed opening lines, where another child is embarrassed by an inconsiderate father. Gloucester introduces Edmund for the first time to his friend, Kent, and the son is forced to listen as his father not only acknowledges his illegitimacy, but also as he boasts to his friend that his mother was a good lay. 'There was good sport at his making,' Gloucester says. Imagine it. Edmund puts up with it in that scene, but later he goes on at length about his bastardy, and afterwards he takes vengeance on both his father and his brother for it. Shakespeare places this scene right before Lear opens the bidding because he wants it to inform our understanding of the love auction: Lear exposes his relationships with his daughters by wrenching the private world of the family into the public world of the court."

Cecelia could sense that Greg wanted to intervene again, so she hurried ahead. It was her seminar, after all. "A few years ago my parents renewed their wedding vows. Thirty years of intermittent marital bliss. They booked the church they were married in, and sent invitations to their friends and relatives. They sat together in front of the altar, and I remember vividly how uncomfortable I felt as they not only reminisced about their courtship and their marriage, but in fact reenacted some of it. My father even serenaded my mother with his guitar like when they were teenagers. And not only was I forced to witness the intimate and earnest devotedness of my parents—not to mention the strangely obliging spectatorship of their friends—but I was forced to participate, along with my sister. She performed on the church piano, something by Cole Porter, I think, and I was asked to read a poem. I found the idea excruciating. I couldn't tell them why because I hardly understood it myself at the time, so I stalled: I said I didn't know what to read. I said hardly any decent love poems are happy at all, much less unequivocally happy, as the occasion demanded. They then told me they would be happiest if I wrote them a poem, after all I went to school for poetry." The remark drew smiles from a few of the students, and Handly too.

"So my sister sat at the piano and played, and I stood by the pulpit and read 'Let me not to the marriage of true minds,' and my parents sat centre stage where they could proudly watch, and be watched proudly watching, as if to say to all their friends, "See this? See what we made?" Then they renewed their vows, and I watched from a pew where everyone could see me watching." Cecelia remembered her discomfort, the ceremony a kind of surgical procedure, her ribs cracked open on an anatomizing table, and the congregation gazing with fascination from the gallery as her insides were presented for examination. Fleetingly she wondered would it help to say so. "There's something inherently damaging about baring our souls to audiences. That's why Lear's demand that his daughters bargain with their love is so obscene."

Jesper coughed affectedly. "I'd like to propose an intervention. Are we even talking about the same kind of thing when we say love?" His eyes looked not at Cecelia but at Professor Handly. "In a play written four hundred years ago the concept of familial love is bound to differ from ours. With infant mortality generally much higher in early modern England, especially in London, and with the constant threat of plague … I mean, aren't we assuming parents loved their children the way we do?"

Cecelia frowned, annoyed. "I wasn't aware you had any children."

Professor Handly, apparently thinking the question was neither meant for Cecelia, as perhaps it wasn't, nor even particularly stupid, interceded: "Actually there is considerable documentary evidence in the form of letters and journals, mostly by men but also by some women, that show parents' affection for the children was no less strong than today. David Cressy collects and categorizes much of this." Jesper's head kept nodding happily as he listened to Handly dismiss his conjecture. "There's one belonging to an Exeter man who lost six consecutive children in infancy. He writes of his and his wife's struggle to cope with their losses, mostly through a combination of Christian patience and prayer. It's really very moving." Handly proffered Cecelia a reassuring smile, and made a show of it. He was being solicitous—and presumptuous. She was able to fend for herself, and eager.

"We don't even need the documentary evidence," she said, fixing first on Handly, then on Jesper. "Think of Capulet's despair when Juliet is found dead the morning of her wedding—he and his entire family are incoherent in their grief. Or think of the way Constance is inconsolable after the loss of her son, Arthur. Or Macduff's wordless horror when he learns of the massacre of 'all his pretty chickens.' Shakespeare's plays are haunted by the deaths of children. But it's not a question of whether parents and children love each other in Shakespeare, or whether they love each other differently. It's that what Lear is asking for is more than love. It is something unnatural. That's why Cordelia says, 'Sure I shall never marry like my sisters, to love my father all'—the real question is, what do we owe our parents? What exactly is Cordelia indebted to her father for, and what is it fair for him to expect in return?"

Jessica Cleary flung herself back into her chair and raised her hand severely. "I'm sorry, but aren't you being melodramatic? For one thing, baring your soul right now, in front of this audience, doesn't seem to be doing you much damage. In fact, you're counting on it to arouse sympathy for your argument. Don't you think this whole line of reasoning smacks of eisegesis?" Jessica glanced, as Jesper had, to Professor Handly, then back at Cecelia. Her flat stare underlined her contempt. "It's what's commonly called reading into the text. What if I have a great relationship with my parents?"

"Then your reasoning is at least as eisegetical as mine." It was sometimes difficult to know when Jessica was irritated, her smile so nearly resembled her frown, but not this time. Cecelia had nipped her good.

"But what's your critical framework?" Jessica barked. "New Historicism? Feminism? New Criticism, maybe?"

"How about opportunism? Is that a framework?" Cecelia asked with deliberate nerve.

"But you can't take a little history, some pop psychology, and your autobiography, roll it together willy-nilly and call it criticism."

Jessica's objection came out whining, like an animal who thinks she's scavenging a carcass and gets a fight instead. Cecelia noted it with pleasure. She allowed herself to pause and examine the room. The flow of interventions seemed stoppered for the moment, though Jessica's gaze remained unyielding. "These are the fundamental and generic conditions of family life. Debts unpaid and unpayable, the need to be a part of and yet still separate from one's relations, the demanding renegotiations that take place as sons and daughters become husbands and wives, and then fathers and mothers. Ideally, in that order. What Shakespeare is dramatizing is the family's constant threat to our identities. These are high stakes, so the contention is vicious and vindictive. That's why the family tends towards self-destruction. Lear himself says it. 'Filial ingratitude. Is it not as this mouth should tear this hand for lifting food to it?'"

"I think you're right to blame Lear as a father, but I agree with Greg," Kelly said. She had been silent for most of the seminar. "You have to concede that it's his tremendous political error that dooms him. As anyone in his audience would have known, dividing a kingdom only leads to instability and civil war."

"I can concede that," Cecelia replied—fairly, she hoped—"but I don't think that blame is the most useful way of understanding the scene."

Greg leaped right in. "And, as I said before, Cordelia is at least as much to blame for not playing her part in the politics of the scene."

Cecelia tried to only nudge him: "Yes, but my point is that family strife is intractable and inescapable. Blame just isn't a useful way of evaluating behaviour in families because everybody is always to blame for something."

"That's true," Kelly said. "It's hard to blame the victim of an oppressive system for trying to resist its imperatives."

Cecelia's eyes narrowed and she frowned. "That's really not what I said. I mean that there's a natural—"

Jessica, ever-ready, pounced: "You keep using that word. Too often the word *natural* is just a cover for unquestioned assumptions. The play has to be examined through the culturally coded practices of its time. Cordelia's refusal to obey her father threatens the cosmic order, the "Great Chain of Being," where man is set above woman and father above daughter."

Kelly sensed a swerve and piled on: "Then maybe Cordelia is better understood as a contradiction in the early modern coding of gender. She is a disobedient but loving daughter. In a time and place where women were either submissive or shrewish, she doesn't fit into any of the culturally intelligible frameworks."

"Exactly," Jessica said. The merest baring of her teeth showed through her thin lips. "The whole problem with gender is that it's performed—a repetition of stylized acts in time. There is no essential self. No self-determined identity, independent of time and place and circumstances. Identity is just what you do, when and where you do it."

"So if my boyfriend and I do it in Lake Simcoe," Cecelia asked, "does that make me a fish?" The various looks of surprise and annoyance around the table told her that she had blundered. It was a joke her father would have made. Beside her, Marion was sketching a yield sign. Jessica continued, ignoring Cecelia entirely.

"Cordelia's refusal to flatter her father calls into question the ontological premises of an androcentric world. She's playing a role that her family and friends and country can't interpret. She has no place there."

"But the way he calls Cordelia his 'sometime daughter'"—Cecelia hurried to say—"I mean, there are some titles you can't abdicate—"

JESSICA. The whole play demonstrates women's lack of self-determination. Scene after scene dramatizes the male's attempt to assign and enforce his gender norms while violently suppressing female agency: Cordelia is disowned, and when they stop serving their father's purposes Goneril and Regan are rejected. A woman standing up for herself socially, politically, or even sexually is seen as monstrous in the play.

HANDLY. Lear does despise his own emotions because they make him womanish: *Hysterica Passio*, he calls it—the passion of the womb—"how this mother swells up towards my heart," he says.

JESPER. And notice that there are no mothers in the play. What do we make of that?

HANDLY. And don't forget that it's not just early modern men who expressed these views. Some of the most scathing attacks on women were written by members of their own sex. The few extant pamphlets and tracts we have by women testify—

JESSICA. Yes, their collaboration with the patriarchal hegemony evidences even more clearly the anxieties circulating in the cultural marketplace of early modern England.

KELLY. Just look at Goneril and Regan. The way they betray their sister and then each other is a dramatization of that very thing. Are they or are they not the archetypal wicked step-sisters?

Yes, the wickedness of sorority and its savage instincts. Jessica was showing off. Kelly trying to keep up. At dinner, Cecelia's sister, who was into her second trimester, would make a big deal again. The light would reflect brightly off the mirror and the picture frames and the polished table, and Rose would be lit up like a collectible doll. A fat one. The entire evening would orbit around her. Which was only natural. Around the conference table the chatter continued, but Cecelia's attention was half-hearted. At her elbow, another road sign—octagonal and heavily drawn—now adorned the page of Marion's notebook. Fair enough. She wondered would Noah remember her seminar. And would he come to dinner if she asked him. It might give them something else to talk about. Sliding lower in her chair, she looked up and let her gaze be drawn into the dull whiteness of the ceiling. None of them understood what she was trying to say, and she never seemed able to make them. Listening to the arguments cross and begin to tangle, she decided she had been doomed from the beginning and that nothing could have prevented it. Nothing, she thought, will come of nothing. Now there was nothing left but to drift mutely along, amid the hurly-burly of a helmless ship of fools. Suck it Lear. You earned that paycheck.

Hurrying, Cecelia descended the fan-shaped east stair into the cool shadow of Old Vic. In the quad the leaves of the maples shimmered in the sun, and the many-fingered vines, still summer-green, hung from the old grey stones of Burwash Hall. The office windows contained avian silhouettes, black like pupils, to warn errant songbirds who otherwise would not see till it was too late what was coming. She had once rescued a sparrow after it plunged full steam into her bedroom window. Stunned and barely moving except for the rapid pulsing of its breast—she had never touched a bird before. It was even softer than she imagined, its feet tiny and hot. She asked her father could she keep it, but it grew more and more anxious as it recovered. Just ten years old and careless, she was not yet capable of moderation. Her affections, like the quivering orb of feathers in her hand, flouted every effort to restrain them. When the sparrow flitted away she stood scanning the trees a long time after it had disappeared.

Seated sidesaddle on one of the benches, a pair of students were going at it like spring stoats, the sun filtering through the leaves, ermining their shoulders in shifts of light and shade. They went on necking so excitedly that Cecelia half expected them to tip over. When at last their mouths uncoupled, they pressed close like mourning doves. Beaks nudging. Only Cecelia and the gargoyles watching.

Then Cecelia saw Anthony coming out of Pratt, moving in her direction. After the seminar, as they were all dispersing, he had approached and quietly said how much he liked her talk. Frustrated, she had blown him off with a curt thank you and a quick departure. She had felt the sharp line of her lips curve into a smiling knife—her mother's lips, her sister's—and had noted the discomfort it caused him. She hadn't meant to be rude, but he wouldn't know that. She could feel her temper, and she had no desire to test it. As he was crossing the path she turned away, before he noticed her she hoped, and started walking. She felt Old Vic's eyes looking down on her. She could have spat for irritation.

She fled along the narrow path between the dining hall and the open pit where the tennis courts used to be, then turned onto Charles Street and saw, framed on either side by trees, the McLaughlin Planetarium's domed roof across the avenue, stained like a used diaphragm. Stopping at the corner by the Museum Station entrance, she waited for a break in the traffic. Noah was waiting for her in Diabolos, a coffee shop named for a mason who made a ghost of his partner in order to devil away with his savings and his woman. She checked her watch. Despite Professor Handly having kept her longer than she wanted, happily she would not be late. She would not have time, though, to stop at Massey to change and drop off her bag.

At University Avenue she felt the dull rumble of the northbound subway underfoot, and the vrrroush of cars. It was faster to cross above ground and not too perilous. The motorists, with so much open road ahead, would not mind giving way to let her safely pass. Had it been later she would have gone underground and not have tried the drivers' patience. At rush hour it was worth your life to steal a foot or two to weave through. A gap opened behind a short convoy of vans and she jogged over the six lanes, her long hair tailing out behind her in the gentle slipstream.

Continuing west, she slipped into the alley and rounded Falconer Hall. The shade was cool but humid. It had rained hard all night. Up the south stairway and behind EJB she climbed. In the patch of lawn they called the G-spot, a handful of students were noodling with their instruments on the spongy turf. The space was exposed to the sun, the heat verging on disagreeable. In the distance she could see the Trinity towers, and beyond them the trim concrete bulwark of Robarts Library breasting the green treetops of Philosopher's Walk. Checking the time again, she hurried across to the farther stairs and there descended to the path below, which followed the dried up and all-but-forgotten run of Taddle Creek. Two men from the physical plant were groundskeeping: one guided a droning mower over the long knoll by the iron fence, the other was edging the footpath, holding off the green's unwanted advances. The men stopped to look her over. She was starting to sweat.

Trying to ignore it, she fell in behind a pair of undergraduates. Owners of four long legs, showing up almost to the cheeks. Above their miniskirts, they wore tanks—one floral, one pink—equally gaudy.

"But she's such a slut."

"You're one to talk. How many guys are you sleeping with right now?"

"Only two. The guys you sleep with you don't even call back."

"That's not slutty, is it?"

Their conversation, for wit, was like their skirts for fabric: wanting, and about as modest. It occurred to Cecelia that a university was like a great garden where students—annual or perennial, hardy or delicate—endeavoured to grow, but like the vines at Burwash found themselves at intervals cut back. Her mother insisted that her gardens thrived because of her sagacious and unsentimental training, but how many maple seedlings, she wondered, green-winged and hopeful, had fallen to her keen shears. Stumping lamely home to her apartment, how often had she herself, after class or dinner with her parents, like those same vines and sprouts, felt altogether shorn. Her seminar hadn't gone the way she'd hoped. And not just the seminar.

Where the footpath rose to the street, the view opened up towards Queen's Park and the well-groomed demesnes of Trinity College. The 94 bus curled loudly onto Hoskin and interrupted Cecelia's overhearing. The girls then crossed towards Wycliffe. They seemed, like her, headed towards UC. Her father's college. None of his professors still taught there. Many were likely dead. He had dropped out after a year. Even so, he had been disappointed when she chose Vic. He still had some of the friends he made there. The girls turned again towards the clock tower. Cecelia got the uncomfortable feeling they might suspect her of following. She should not have been so short with Anthony.

The wide lawn of Back Campus was a brownish green, roughed up from heavy use, though it was not at that moment crowded. Frisbees flew, hanging long enough in the air that even she might have caught one. The sun, the transparent blue of the sky, and all of the play beneath, punctuated by shouts and laughter, made her wish she were more inclined to recreation. She had spent two hours indoors enduring homilies—not only theirs but also her own—then suffered through a soliloquy (with asides) in Handly's office that she was trying to forget, which was no easy proposition. She wished that she were one of those unwinding on the green.

Two young men were near the fence, shirtless and tossing a football. Farther off, two smiling young women alternated between shouting at them and talking to each other in a show of covertness. Cecelia smiled a little too, enjoying the athletic flexion of their arms and torsos, the faint glistening of their perspiration. The beguiling persuasion of the male body in motion. The girls were watching the boys, and being watched watching. They were sunning their legs and leaning back on their arms, which made their shoulders appear rolled back and their breasts more prominent. The taller boy was showing off and the one girl, brunette with long, lean legs, was making sure he knew that she knew it. Beside her, the other girl, blonde, was doing likewise, but she was also being careful to direct her eyes more often—though with less intensity—at the other boy, shorter and more muscular certainly, but more plodding too and maybe not so deft or good-looking as his friend. Though she was careful to hide it, he was her consolation, as she was his, judging by his attentions which, like his better-looking friend's, were clearly intended for her rival. Cecelia felt a quaver of emotion shake her. Though short-lived and fugitive, nonetheless it left her guarded.

Westerly rose the squat nubbin of the Fisher Library holding Robarts by the hand like its short, sulky daughter. The muscled boy threw the football long and out of reach, and the brunette hurried with her long legs to get it. The blonde drew up her knees as though she would follow, but instead let her legs fall open slightly. The way the tall boy stopped and looked at her, he probably could see right up her skirt. Cecelia sure could.

One of the ditzy, mini-skirted girls on the path before her raised her arm in a wide, sweeping professorial gesture, baldly parodic even viewed from behind. "Sleeping with your TA is just a sound investment. Think of them as dividend-bearing stocks. In fact, I think I'll write my senior paper on it. *Grading in the Sexual Marketplace.* Of course, it'll take time to draw up the questionnaire and interview a statistically meaningful sample of female respondents, but I'm confident that by mid-term I can produce a yield index. Variables to include: frequency of coitus, intensity, position, and program of study."

"Don't forget a subjective measure of TA hotness, as a control," her friend said.

"Desirability, independent of anticipated gains. Check."

"And what about male respondents?"

The undergrads stumbled into each other, overcome with cackling. Cecelia didn't know what to think—*How many guys, statistically meaningful, yield index*—they were and were not what they seemed.

In her distraction, she nearly tripped over the football, which wobbled unexpectedly into the road a few inches from her feet. She picked it up and turned. The jouncing muscles of the tall boy were jogging towards her. With a nervous step and a lurching, flipper-like motion she tossed it. The boy's large hands secured the ball, and he smiled in thanks, throwing in a wink at Cecelia's embarrassment. He then fired the ball to his friend. Adept at making a pass, he made a fine one. Handily.

Up the worn stairs of Old Vic she had gone to Professor Handly's office. The door when she arrived stood open and he stood at the window with arms folded, peering into the quad. Before she could knock he turned, smiling, and invited her to sit down. Built-in shelves covered one entire wall and, except for a small electric kettle, were more or less stuffed with books. Sets of Oxfords and Ardens took up whole rows. Professional quarterlies, also some of Handly's own monographs, several copies of each, took up others. She sensed that he was observing her interest. Her curiosity had a habit of running off if she gave it too much lead, so she reined it in and took a seat at the desk. He sat opposite her and lifted a white teacup to his smiling mouth; his eyes examined her over the half-moon of the porcelain lip.

He asked her, was this her first time? Cecelia hesitated, unsure of his intention. Was this her first graduate seminar? He asked because a graduate seminar was different from an undergraduate presentation. And doing it with students more experienced could feel intimidating sometimes. It could leave one feeling a bit vulnerable. A bit like somebody's tagalong kid sister. Not that he meant she should feel that way, not at all. He only meant that if she did, it was only natural. No doubt she was still adjusting to the demands of coursework? Cecelia nodded. Not to worry, he said. He understood entirely, and wanted to start by telling her how very pleased he was with her seminar. Was she surprised? She oughtn't to be. Her reading of the play was sensitive, he said, and frank. He had never really considered Edmund's humiliation as a foreshadowing of the love test, but really it prepares so economically for everything that follows. It seemed obvious now. That was one of the greatest pleasures of his profession. The *infinite variety*, he said, quoting. However much he gave to his students, they often gave him so much more in return. Though some credit had to be given to the material too. He chuckled and Cecelia smiled. The great books, he said, have a way of surprising you, catching you off your guard and unawares.

He had sometimes sat in his office all day reading or writing, and for long stretches been so entirely unsuspecting of the passage of time that hours later, when he looked up from his desk, he was surprised to find the light had dwindled without his realizing, and that the sunlight through the window, and the first glow of the lamps in the quad, had uncovered something starkly unfamiliar in the shelves and chairs and other furnishings. Like he was in someone else's room, and had been all along, only he hadn't known it. Except that he wasn't and hadn't been. It was both his own and not his own. Reading could be like that. You could go back to the same book five or ten years later, find the shadows on the page had shifted, and wonder how you could have missed so much the times before. He was—he was not about to say how old he was, but certainly he was no longer a young man—and even so he found himself every few years full of wonder at how much more there was. Great books don't give it up all at once, he said. That was part of the attraction. The way they every time catch your breath. It was a kind of fecundity. Perhaps the one fundamental and essential attribute of literary beauty. That was why he always wrote in his books, and had done since he was in high school. Did she annotate her books? he asked. Cecelia said she did. He thought she did. He had stolen a glance or two. Though many and maybe even most of his old copies were in storage, he kept a few on hand. Those pencilled marginalia were a record of all the things his favourite books had meant to him, and he went back to them from time to time to commune with the parts of himself that had passed out of the world.

He grew quiet then. He seemed sad and glanced up at his shelves. Did he write in all the books he read, Cecelia asked. Yes, he whispered. He asked her would she like to see something. He rose and adroitly retrieved a small book, hardbound and beaten up, the cloth scratched and stained and the boards a little warped. He placed it in front of her. He and his father never got on very well, he said, vouchsafing a confidence. He died when he was young, just out of high school. Going through his father's things he had found this copy of *Cymbeline*, a copy from when his father was at school and not much younger than himself, and as he held it his heart had pumped harder, as though his blood were grown clotten. Cecelia lifted the book and, as he seemed to want her to, she began to leaf through. He stood over her and cocked his head, watching. It was a chance, he said, to speak to who his father was when they were of an age and, as she could see, the pages were untouched. His mother said he likely never got around to reading it. In that moment he had felt his father's death more strongly than when he stopped breathing in his hospital bed at St. Mike's. We don't really live in the present, he said. Our thoughts are just the vehicles for our desires, vectors reaching out or in, ahead or behind, but always aimed at something somewhere else beyond our reach. He hoped she would forgive his waxing metaphorical.

With sageness she nodded, acknowledging his disclosure. It was very sad that he had missed that chance. Smiling sadly too, she returned his *Cymbeline*. He replaced it and sat down again. Existence in time, he said. *Nostos algos*. She was still too young to know, but that was the real tragedy. Like Edmund's bastardy: an injury beyond repair or redress. He was glad she had alerted him to that aspect of the play. Hers was a fine example of the merits of close reading, attentiveness to detail, sensitivity to language. He also liked the way she refused to hide behind the jargon of this or that theory, refused to mindlessly band with the dogmatists in the class. Starting from her own experience. A little New Criticism, a little Reader-Response, and a lot gutsy. However, gutsy could only take her so far, he said, and he and she both knew it. Her interpretation lacked grounding and context. It was something he might set as a topic for an undergraduate paper.

Cecelia confessed that midway through she realized it wasn't going well, but by then she didn't see what she could do. Leaning forward, he hurried to explain that she shouldn't take his criticisms too hard, nor personally. He was just doing his job. It was up to him to flush out assumptions, fallacies, tautologies, needless flourishes of rhetoric. But he liked to think he did so always with understanding and indulgence. He liked to think of himself as part hunter, part retriever. A sharp eye and a soft mouth. To a student who was bright enough, and worth the trouble, he could be gentle once he'd shot her down. Her problem was self-consciousness. She needed more of it. She needed to attempt a more theoretical approach, even if she deliberately ran against it. Had she read Bloom's book, *The Western Canon*? She had not, she said. There was a chapter, "A Shakespearean Reading of Freud." He argues that Freud was so intimidated by Shakespeare that he simultaneously appropriated his representations of human psychology, and repudiated them for being inferior to his own. From a strictly professional perspective, it was perhaps more hocus pocus than scholarship, and he wasn't sure how much scrutiny it could bear from either camp, but it was clever enough. It deserved attention. Alternatively, she might use Bradley as a model, though he was now out of fashion. Or perhaps Greenblatt. Part historicist, part formalist, and a steady hand at the helm. Or if she didn't like theory, she could do history. Only she must place her work on a firm foundation. There was no such thing, he said, as criticism *ex nihilo*.

He paused to study her and sip his tea. Did she want an academic cáreer? Or was she a hobbyist, content with an acronym to append to correspondences? Not that he thought her unserious—she mustn't misunderstand—but that he knew how quickly even flaming passions could fizzle. Sometimes a promising undergraduate would ask him if there were consequences to delaying her graduate studies. Taking a year to travel, or paying off her debts, or seeing where a relationship was headed. Students like that he unfortunately had to write off. Once out of school, most would never return, no matter their intentions at the outset. How readily an aberrance, even a small one, passed into abeyance. In a blinking, he assured her. She must decide for herself how serious she was. However, she needn't worry about the seminar for now. He liked to observe his students awhile before finally assigning a grade, in case anything came up later to make him reconsider. He didn't assume they were born knowing. His course was meant to help initiate them into the professional study of literature, which was to say that he was there to help her, if she were willing and open.

Whether she wanted to admit it or not, he said, Jessica Cleary had it down cold. She was, he conceded, perhaps fiercer than was, strictly speaking, collegial. And she could be contemptuous at times, which was unwise. Contempt could blunt both intellect and imagination. Jessica should beware of that, he said, and Cecelia too. If she didn't believe him, she should believe the masonry: ABEUNT STUDIA IN MORES. Studies pass into character. For all that, though, Jessica was sharp. She knew how to tango. She would make it. Which was not to say that Cecelia should allow herself to be baited. It was important, even should they bury their points hilt-deep, that they still be able to go for drinks after. Civilized relations between colleagues were the foundation of academic life. She knew, didn't she, that universities everywhere were turning to sessionals, precarious part-time appointments? Competition for tenured posts was becoming fierce. All things being equal, a committee would go with the candidate they thought they could best stand to work with. Collegiality was the tiebreaker. It could give her a leg over. It was, after all, the most noble and venerable aim of higher education: the establishment and nurturing of a fellowship, a congregation of lives devoted to learning and teaching, a community dedicated to the flourishing of its members and their common interests. He liked that word—*flourishing*—the Aristotelian ethos. Human flourishing as the end of all ethical thought and action. She had read her Aristotle, hadn't she? Yes, she said. Some of it, at least. He was so glad, he said.

It was one of the greatest pleasures—the breath of life, if she would forgive his poeticization—to find oneself in a position to share experiences with like-minded young men and women, some of whom would go on to academic careers themselves. Some of whom might become colleagues, or even friends. He himself was very fortunate that many of his former students were still a part of his life, some of them at this very university. Those friendships were precious to him. Intellectually, certainly, but in other ways too. It was a former student who got him out of the house again after his divorce. She introduced him to Latin dancing, of all things.

Leaning forward, he asked did she like to dance. He had, in the last few years, taken up athletics again after years of largely sedentary existence, but he found running and going to the gym so solitary and impersonal that he could never stick to it. He had often wanted to be more active, he confessed, but the pressure to fulfill his obligations to the university and to publish, even for a tenured professor, were considerable, and he had learned long ago that one could develop either the mind or the body, unless one were content to sacrifice the excellence of both. He had always tried to maintain a nominal corporeal fitness, but he noted, summoning a look of sheepishness, that he had been forced to give ground on that front. Time is limited and unrelenting, he said. You really can't give your best hours to more than one thing, and he had decided long ago to dedicate himself to the life of the mind. But as it happened, he actually liked to dance, only he had never known because he had been too single- and too closed-minded to allow himself the chance to learn. Now he went dancing several nights a week—could she believe it?—and he could fit into his Armani jackets again. He still believed, he said, that the most noble human aspirations were to empathy in matters of feeling and, in matters of judgment, wisdom; but one could not be blind to fitness and beauty in matters of the body.

Didn't she find that one's attraction to another's thoughts and feelings left their mark more deeply when intensified by an accompanying physical attraction? He was sure she understood him, being herself, in every aforementioned way, an undeniably attractive young woman.

ठ

The Back Campus lawn, where it was not roughed-up and sullied, was vibrant green and inviting. And yet, all she could think about was Handly's pass. His attentions unwanted, aberrant *in mores*, unrespecting of professional boundaries. It left her stomach tightly coiled, like the spinning of the boys' pigskin.

Cecelia turned into the quad, where a handful of people haunted the veranda, smoking mostly cigarettes and drinking coffee in paper cups. She skirted brusquely past them and into the college. As it was still lunchtime, the Junior Common Room was bustling. There was a line at the Diabolos counter and the sofas were full, as were most of the tables, but she quickly spotted Noah waiting by the hearth with a chair, kitty-corner to his, reserved for her. With a wave and a still-distracted smile she caught his eye as she approached. He had before him a small pile of books and two coffees which she hoped had not gotten cold. As she approached, she saw the cups were still steaming, and she knew that he could see that she was too. He rose to greet her and asked cautiously how she was doing.

As she sat beside him she felt the background noise of the room draw in around them with a comforting sense of enclosure. And though she had meant not to—in fact she had wanted to bind it up again so tightly that she herself could once again become unconscious of it—nonetheless, she found herself launching into the story as though knuckling down to an assigned but disagreeable book: break the spine and get down to business.

When she had done, Noah shook his head. "Aristotelian ethics as a pick up line ... A-*ri*-sto-*tee*-lian."

"I know," Cecelia said. "It sounds like some kind of reptile."

"So does he. As far as come-ons go, I suppose it does have the virtue of being novel. 'Human flourishing, says Aristotle, is to be found in the golden mean. Please, dear, spread those vices a little more so we can find your virtue.' Fear it, Cecelia. Beware the ivory tower."

"Don't. I feel sick enough about it already." Cecelia frowned. "Should I have seen it coming?"

"Umm ..."

"Please don't."

"You said it."

"No, you thought it."

"I couldn't not think it. I read somewhere it's genetics. Coded onto the chromosomal locus linked to male sexual determination."

"Sexual determination in males. Who knew?" Attempting to make light, Cecelia's face nonetheless registered her dismay. "Are you ever not thinking about it?"

"Maybe sometimes. Not often. I think a lot of men just get good at compartmentalizing."

"What I want to know," she said, "is whether he'll try it again."

"Sounds like he doesn't want you to give it up all at once. Remember: he likes *fecundity*."

"Oh god, he's a predator. Isn't he."

"It's possible. I doubt this was his first time."

"It just all came out so artlessly. It was like he was dropping his guard. I actually felt sorry for him when he was talking about his father. I suppose he had it all planned out, though. Or he's done it so many times it's just instinctive. Is that a distinction without a difference?"

"I think he sounds lonely."

Cecelia's eyes widened. "So that's what you think, is it?"

"It's still wrong," Noah hurried to say. "But it's kind of sad too, from a certain point of view."

Cecelia frowned again. Noah's response was irritatingly even-handed. He was always so nice, which she liked; but she would have liked it more to have him take her side.

"Short answer? Yes, I think he'll try it again," Noah said. "He sounds kind of old hand."

"Then how can I trust him to tell me if I'm any good?"

"You shouldn't anyway. Better the hammer than the nail. If you don't know, no one can tell you."

It was a careless remark meant kindly. She wondered why were men always remarking on things. And did he know he had hit the nail on the head? Dead nuts. To judge from his steady smile, he seemed instead to think it should be reassuring, which it wasn't, though his smile was, and the unwavering gaze of his kind eyes. They had met for coffee a number of times, and twice for drinks, but this was the first time she felt that he had really asked her out. She got the feeling he could be interested. She thought she could be too. They got on well enough, they bantered. She could imagine her father liking him. As she had before, she wondered would he come to dinner. Later she would ask him.

Cecelia glanced at the small stack of books by Noah's arm. She noted the university labels. "Those must be overdue," she said.

"Just picked them up," Noah replied. "My borrowing privileges haven't been revoked yet. They're slow to catch that sometimes. Also, I have ex-colleagues who aren't likely to get around to it immediately."

She turned the spines to better appraise the titles. One she thought she recognized. *Tales from Shakespeare.* She took the book, leafed through its prefacing pages to the opening chapter, and read aloud. "There was a certain island in the sea, the only inhabitants of which were an old man, and his young daughter Miranda, a very beautiful young lady. She came to this island so young, that she had no memory of having seen any other human face than her father's."

"It's for Felix. You made me think of it."

"That's sweet. Maybe," she added hesitantly, "I could meet him sometime." Noah took the book back, smiling, but there was something cautious in his expression.

"I'd like that. Only Cate's shifts are all over the place right now, so I'll have to ask her first."

Something happens to the eyes, Cecelia thought, when we have said something too much, or too sensitive, or too touching: it's like the effect you get at an aquarium when you see an animal suddenly charge towards the glass and you recoil, even though you know it can't get at you; or it's the opposite, the way an animal, not realizing that we can't get at it, retreats when we get too close or tap inquisitively on the glass; or it's both. "It's nice she's letting you stay with her."

"Yes, it is."

"That must be hard. For both of you."

His fingers traced the letters embossed on the cover, and he looked at his watch. "We've done harder. This isn't so bad, at least for now. We're pretty good at giving each other space."

Cecelia wondered what he meant when he said *harder* and *pretty good* and also *space*.

"I'm trying not to wear out my welcome," he added.

Indeed. Men were a lot like metaphors: even when they said exactly what you wanted, somehow they didn't. She leaned back in her chair and grew more conscious of the bustle around them. They had talked of nothing but her creepy professor, and Noah's estranged wife. Not a hopeful beginning.

"Tell you what," Noah said, pushing back his chair and standing. "You've had a hard day. Come with me."

She asked him where, but Noah only smiled and told her once again to come. He led her out of the college and back into the bright light of Back Campus. In a few minutes they had crossed St. George and Harbord, and entered at the second floor of the Fisher Library. Cecelia had never been inside. Thousands of volumes, shelved in towering stacks, lined the building's tiered circumference. She expected to see readers everywhere on the walkways, browsing, but apart from the young man at the desk, who smiled and greeted them as Noah ushered her inside, it seemed to be empty. Down on the ground floor, however, there were signs of life. Noah took her around several disorienting turns to a cluttered room in a seemingly lost corner of the tower. Its many shelves and cases stood full of books and long, brass binding tools and screw-top bottles. On a low table near the door sat a heavy paper press, its wheel and screw and steel plate compressing she didn't know what between a pair of plywood boards. In the centre of the room, lit by overhead fluorescent lights and three tall, thin windows like arrow slits on the far wall, was a large workstation, its surface a cluttered, ugly, light-green melamine. A tall, greying woman was stooped over it like a question mark. Her hands were occupied with placing a thin strip of wooden moulding around a small glass case. She tried to blow an uncooperative strand of hair from her face, but it was partly wrapped around the arm of her glasses and resisted.

"Steady there, you bastard," the woman said.

Cecelia stopped, nervously. The woman secured the trim with an elastic band. She then stood up straight and removed her glasses, pulling out several long hairs as she did.

"Not me, I hope," Noah said.

She smiled at Noah and, looking up at a clock on the wall, she said, "You come most carefully upon your hour. Is this her? Can she keep her mouth shut?" Then she questioned Cecelia directly: "Can you keep your mouth shut?"

Cecelia hesitated and Noah interposed himself. "Of course she can, but I haven't told her anything at all yet. Dora, this is Cecelia Lines. She's a friend of mine. Cecelia, this is Dora Curtis, the Fisher's conservator. Conservatrice. Conservatrix? Are those words?"

"They are now," Dora said. She took Cecelia's hand. "So, you can keep your mouth shut, right?"

The conservationist's delicate-seeming fingers were hard-squeezing, like her screw press. Cecelia said she could, and was a little relieved to have the use of her hand once more.

"You're sure this is no trouble, Dora?" Noah asked.

"Of course not, as long as you trust her. Seems a little late to be asking, though."

The various uncertainties made Cecelia uncomfortable, but the woman seemed jovial enough. The antagonism seemed more in friendly banter than in earnest, and directed more at Noah than herself, but there was an edge to it she wanted not to test.

"Only a few of us know about this, and we've been sworn to secrecy, so if it gets out, it won't be hard to figure who let it out," Dora said.

She went to a nearby table and retrieved a small, thin archival box. As she returned she was smiling mischievously, with her eyes narrowed and one corner of her mouth upturned. She placed the box before them on the workstation and invited Cecelia to open it. As Cecelia breathed in the air of conspiracy, her interest grew into an indistinct, ungrounded excitement. Lifting the hinged lid, she revealed what appeared to be a folded piece of thick paper. It was somewhat stained, seemingly dirty, and stiff to the touch.

"Be careful," Noah said quickly and reached to stay her hand. "Let me help you."

"Relax. She won't hurt it," Dora said. "That vellum will outlive us all by a thousand years. I could wet it down, press it flat and twenty minutes later it would fold itself right up again no worse for wear."

Cecelia withdrew the calfskin and began carefully to unfold it. Sensible to its shyness, she coaxed it gently to open and looked, first at the cleaner, whiter inner surface of the vellum, and then at the dark and slightly browned words inscribed illegibly across it. Cecelia was scarcely aware that Dora, ignoring Noah entirely, had shouldered up and was talking quickly in her ear.

"It was discovered a couple of months ago in Halifax. There's an old company there—bankers at one time but now an investment firm or something—they had no idea how complete their archives were or how far back they went because they were rescued from a ruined building after the Great Explosion, so they recently implemented an archival program. They turned up a bunch of ledgers, letters, stationery in general, some of it from an importing company that must have used the same building sometime before they moved in. It's written in secretary hand. That's why it's so hard to read."

Not just hard, but for Cecelia impossible. She could make out hardly any of the strangely ornamented script. She simply stared at the words, helpless of their meaning. Dora's description continued uninterrupted.

"This is a goldsmith acting as a receiver of deposits, something not common until almost the eighteenth century. This is fifty years before the earliest records of it. And it's not a penal bond, which suggests that he must have known the man and trusted this goldsmith to deposit so large a sum. She's a rare bird. There are hardly any ledgers extant from this period, so hundreds of scholars of early modern England will be interested, and scholars of banking history too. The most curious thing is that it exists at all. Sometimes these promissory notes were nullified by a formal acquittance, but more often they were just slashed or destroyed. It's possible that an acquittance was issued and lost, but it's also possible that the note was never presented to the receiver."

Noah was now plotted at Cecelia's other shoulder. He reached in to help her press the indenture flat against the tabletop. She looked at the bottom of the page. One signature she could not make out at all, but the other caused her stomach to spin.

"It's been authenticated. The terms aren't in his handwriting, but the signature is consistent with the others. There's the spurred *a*, for example." Dora indicated, as she described it to Cecelia, the small but striking alpha hanging from the *h* like a pitcher plant. "And the spelling is the same as on the Blackfriars mortgage."

She continued to explain the definitive features, but Cecelia was no longer with Dora Curtis and Noah in the conservation room of the first floor of the Fisher Library. Instead, she had crossed four hundred years and thousands of miles to the dark, lamplit shop of a London goldsmith where stood, she imagined, a man with a fine jerkin, and well-cut breeches, and a thoughtful eye, and a balding head, and a serious countenance. A man worthy of a frontispiece, leaning over the indentured copies, signing at the bottom of each, with pen and ink, *Wm Shakspere.*

Suddenly aware how scant of breath she had become, Cecelia turned wide-eyed to Noah. As far as first dates went, she thought, if this was their first date, it was equivalent to hauling in a Hail Mary.

5

"I'm telling you, everybody will make money on this. Management, shareholders, the captive firms. Everybody. The transaction fees, restructuring and redundancy costs, the potential loan losses: those will all get capitalized as assets. Write up a goodwill and intangible asset account, and presto: earnings accretive. Everyone will get a raise. Some of it won't need to be written off at all. CEOs have wet dreams about this kind of legacy transaction. For the people that make this happen, there'll be an empty chair in any room they want."

The telephone was on speaker and Owen Trover had his back to it, reclining cross-legged in his chair and surveying the expanse of the city, which stretched north and west beneath his office high atop BCE Place. The neighbouring office towers glowed orange in the reflected light of the setting sun, and the CN Tower was a burnished bone, its antenna shooting forth from the knob head of the Skypod high above the cityscape. A boyish smile lingered on Trover's otherwise languid face. He interrupted the caller's disembodied dullness.

"Dick, listen. It's a valid business strategy. A merger would increase their market share at home, and position them to compete internationally. They need less government interference on this, not more. The province gets it. They're getting out of the business of being in business. You watch. In a year or two they'll sell off Hydro and the 407, balance the budget, cut taxes again—they'll make the feds look like communists."

The voice tried to muster an objection, but Trover forestalled it before it was fully formed.

"No, I don't think it's a matter of perspective. Ask anyone on the board of one of these banks. It's a small country. The only way to keep growing is to start making bigger bets in the global markets. They need Ottawa to clear the way. They need an irreversible policy decision that will unfetter them for good. Dick, you're on the Treasury Board. It's not like you're short on opportunity. Tell him as often as it takes. Tell him so often he starts to have dreams about it."

Ignoring the discontent at the other end, Trover said a peremptory goodbye. Unhurriedly, he swiveled in his chair away from the view to face his desk and the telephone, whose line he disconnected with the push of a button. He then buzzed his assistant, Ms. Li, who entered immediately and began setting the conference table for a light dinner.

"I think a large bouquet of mixed flowers sent to the Honourable Member's wife would not be a wasted gesture. She's a lovely and sensible woman. He trusts her more than he trusts himself. She likes gladioluses, I think. The sword lily. What's that for, remembrance? Strength of character?"

"For a dozen things or more no doubt," Ms. Li said. "Flowers aren't choosy."

"Indeed. Sword lily, then. She'll know what it means. What did you end up ordering?"

"Three small ceviches: salmon, tuna, lobster and shrimp—"

"That's four ceviches."

"It's three, actually. Also, a mango salad."

"It's not much," Trover said.

"You have a late dinner appointment with Mr. Reinholt of the Deutsche Bank."

Trover remembered.

"They said delivery in thirty minutes," Ms. Li said. "It's not too late to order for Mr. Potts, if you wish. He's waiting outside."

"No, that's all right. He won't be staying long."

"Very well. There's sparkling water in the cooler and Don Julio 1942 in the cabinet."

"Ms. Li, you are superb."

Ms. Li, well-aware, nodded her head and turned towards the door, exiting with such command that Mr. Potts, who waited at the threshold, had to quickly step aside. It was with a kind of reflexive timidity, then, that he entered and closed the door behind him.

Trover rose from his chair to greet his guest. "Nice to see you, Eric. You're well, I hope."

"Yes, Owen, thank you."

Trover approached the cabinet where he kept his spirits. He retrieved the tequila, poured himself a small glass, and offered some to Potts.

"No, thank you," Potts said. However, under Trover's deliberate scrutiny he waffled. "All right, maybe just a little. Is it strong?"

"It'll do." Into another glass Trover poured as much as he himself had taken and more. He placed it in Potts's hand, which dipped from the unanticipated weight of the crystal. "How are things, Eric? How is your wife?"

Potts raised the glass to his nose too quickly and caught the unpleasant rush of evaporating alcohol, which also caused his eyes to water slightly.

"My partner is fine. Thank you for asking."

"Oh yes, partner. Of course. Good for you." Trover sat himself down on a lounge chair and invited Mr. Potts to do the same. "So tell me, Eric, how's my baby doing?"

"The stand and mount are finished. We're just waiting on the museum glass for the display case. If you don't mind me asking, Owen, how long do you plan on keeping it in your private collection?"

"I was thinking forever." Trover drank a half-mouthful and, as he savoured, studied his guest's discomfort.

"Oh." Struggling with how to proceed, Potts took a sip of his drink and winced slightly. Once he had recovered, he said carefully, "It's just that with all of your other gifts ... well, when you brought us the indenture I understood that you would be donating it."

"I can see how you might have thought that, but I don't recall ever saying it."

"The vice-president of advancement has asked me to draft a press release."

"I'm sorry you misunderstood. That will be a difficult conversation."

A long silence grew between them, uncomfortably for Mr. Potts, who was noticeably disoriented. From his jacket pocket there came the electronic pulse of a cellular phone. With a sigh half-way between annoyance and relief, accompanied by a rehearsed *excuse-me* look, he retrieved and answered it. Instantly a shrill and incoherent barking, also audible to Trover, assaulted his ear. Trover went to the liquor cabinet, more out of a sense of propriety than to freshen his drink, although he took the opportunity. He returned to his seat only after Potts pocketed his phone.

"What can I say?" Potts said with an apologetic shrug.

"I would say that you either hired the wrong people or didn't train them well enough to get along without you for an hour and a half. Either that or you make them call you for every little decision because you're under the misapprehension that a ringing cell phone announces your importance."

"It was our new CAO," Potts said, explaining.

"The one you poached from Melbourne?"

"Yes, her. She has an appealing way of cutting through red tape, but her induction has been a bit more chaotic than expected. It seems several grievances are being filed every week against her." Potts frowned and glanced at his glass, but he declined to drink from it.

"Buck up, Eric. You can't let a dingo loose in a library and then be surprised when some babies get eaten."

Potts nodded in agreement. "You know, Owen, I've been wondering. Why Shakespeare? I understand you have a good little collection."

"Nostalgia, I suppose," Trover answered. "The complete works was the first book I ever bought myself. I bought it with money from a prize I won in grade school."

"I see. Is it rare too?"

"In my innocence I did think when I bought it that maybe I had stumbled onto something special. Alas, no. Just an old second-hand copy. An utterly pedestrian, workaday Oxford edition. Thousands of them were printed."

"Still, it must have sentimental value. Even in a collection like yours."

"It would have, but I lost it years ago."

"Oh, that's too bad," Potts said. Then he added, "But if there were thousands of copies …"

Trover looked him over, but instead of picking up the thread he changed the subject.

"So, my indenture: it will be ready when? End of the week?"

"I think so, yes. The museum glass will protect it from light damage when you want to view it, but you'll want to leave the cover on otherwise. And you'll want to keep the humidity as close to fifty percent as you can."

"Yes, I know all about that, Eric."

"Of course. I can arrange to have it dropped off at your home when it's ready."

"No, I'll have my assistant retrieve it Friday afternoon."

"Sure. Simply have him contact my office with a time."

"This is very good news, Eric. Thank you," Trover said, smiling. "I half expected there would be some hiccup."

Potts looked away momentarily, and Trover detected his apprehension.

"Eric, kindly describe the exact nature of your cock-up."

"It's just that your request for discretion wasn't so strictly followed as it should have been. I suppose I didn't impress upon them quite strongly enough that discretion in this case meant complete secrecy."

Trover sighed and set aside his drink. "How many?" He folded his hands neatly on his lap and waited.

On his fingers, Potts began to enumerate. "Well, there's you and me, our conservationist, the vice-president, the authenticators and your man in Halifax—"

"Eric."

"There are two."

"And how did they find out?"

"Well, one is a former employee, Noah Lamarck."

"Former?"

"He had a temporary contract with the library, but it wasn't renewed."

"The dingo?" Trover asked.

"Uh, yes. We're reducing staff through attrition. The other is a graduate student in the Department of English. I don't know much about her. Nothing, actually."

Trover raised his glass but did not drink from it. Instead he swirled it under his nose, breathing calmly and not looking at the university man. "So two people with no investment in my interests, one of whom no longer has ties with the university at all, are free to tell anyone they wish about my indenture."

"No, Owen. Dora has assured me—"

"And wasn't she sworn to secrecy too? And you? And yet now an ex-employee, and a young woman with no reason to keep quiet about it, both know. How did this happen?"

"Apparently they stumbled on our conservator while she was working on it."

"What's the girl's name?"

"Cecelia something, I think."

"Cecelia Something of the Department of English, you think."

"I'll find out."

"And then you'll call my P.A., Clement Rowse, whose card you can ask for as you pass by Ms. Li's desk. In the meantime, I would like you to arrange a special appointment or bursary for one student to inventory and describe the remaining papers. That student will be your Cecelia Something."

"I'll have to see if we have the funding."

"Eric, you're the chief librarian." Trover paused, his eyes communicating irritation, but also interest. "You know, Eric, so many people have this unaccountable expectation that they will receive something for nothing. For instance, I have always been a proud benefactor of the library's special collections, and a great champion of yours, especially to the Vice-Chair of the Governing Council, who has taken a fascinating dislike to you and your tenure."

"We'll find the funds," Potts said quickly.

"Thank you."

"And what about Lamarck?"

"Send his contact information. I'll speak with him. And now, if you don't mind ..."

"Of course, Owen."

"Just see Ms. Li on your way out. I'll expect the indenture on Friday."

"Yes, of course."

Potts turned towards the door.

"And Eric, see if you can't prevent anyone else from discovering my indenture, at least until I decide to unveil it."

"I'll take care of it," Potts said eagerly over his shoulder as he exited the office.

Trover called after him: "And give my regards to your partner …"

"Roger." Potts barely turned around to reply.

"Yes, my regards to Roger."

Trover tried vainly to resist an unattractive furrowing of his brow. Then he lifted the telephone receiver and, pressing a button, connected immediately with his assistant.

"Clement, Eric Potts will be calling you. After he does, find out what you can about a librarian recently laid off at the Fisher: Noah Lamarck."

PART THREE

That Hath Such People in It

6

So slowly that even with the windows open they were wilting, the taxi by tangled lefts and rights approached its destination in Rosedale. The afternoon sun was unrelenting, mood-altering. It was no cooler in the shade. Twice, Cecelia's friend accused the driver of taking them for a ride. When the city got like this the sidewalks and asphalt strips, whether wide or narrow, tree-lined or flanked by storefronts, swallowed up the heat by day and, by night, disgorged it in all directions. Every block was a radiator. The breeze, when there was one, was a whispered suggestion, an insufferable tease that stoked a longing for relief that never came. Your body could sometimes ache from the heat, and what it tried to expel got squeezed back in. It was worse in summer—in the summer you steamed like a vegetable. But even falls had been unseasonable in recent years, much hotter and more humid than Cecelia remembered them being when she was a child. Although perhaps she was just less sensible to it then, or less averse to sweating. This week had been especially bad. Rain enough to saturate the air, but neither breeze enough to blow nor sun enough to burn it away. The city was a sauna. There was even a smog advisory, and it was the first week of October.

Cecelia raised her eyes towards the sky, hoping that she might see clouds and that they might be moving. Instead she saw only the suffocating haze and a handful of birds circling. She thought at first they might be hawks. Sometimes hawks could be spotted gliding, especially over the parks, or scouting the river valley for songbirds and other prey. Last year in winter she had stumbled on a peregrine falcon, white and stunning, settled on a low-slung tree limb in Philosopher's Walk behind the Conservatory. With the snow heaped on either side of the path, she had gone in over her knees to get a look. She was then surprised to discover that in its talons it held a pigeon, pale grey and brown and lifeless, and she watched in fascination as it ransacked the plumage. The birds circling were not hawks, though. Hawks kept to themselves. Their numbers and black bellies marked these birds as turkey vultures, scanning the streets and sidewalks for carrion.

Groundhogs across the city lived hard by the tracks, and she had sometimes seen foxes sniffing them out. Squirrels, late in the year, would eat the last of the elderberries, which by then had started to ferment, and the hitherto faultless aerialists, *Rodentia trapezius*, would become intoxicated and fall from the trees—the only circumstance in which she had ever seen that happen. Along the bluffs there were coyotes picking off dogs and cats, and sizing up unattended children, and she had once seen a raccoon big enough to stare down a German shepherd, at a cross-walk, waiting on its haunches for the light to change. The city was full of wild animals, like the people who lived there, adapting.

The taxi slowed to make a turn. At the corner a scruffy vagrant was giving a trashcan a good rummage. He was old, but how old was hard to say, his filth was so extraordinary. He wore a cap and a ratty T-shirt and trousers torn off unevenly below the knees. He had matted hair and a fierce sweat on, and surely not enough to eat. He glanced at them, but kept an eye on his shopping cart, crammed to overflowing with castoffs. Living off the land, as derelicts in urban environments do: his whole life was in there. From the cart's wire frame hung a collection of discarded bottles and cans in plastic bags, all that he had scavenged and sorted since dawn on his expedition to the antipodean reaches of the Rosedale Valley. The empties he was adding to his store had no doubt been discarded overnight by roaming packs of high-schoolers. One contained a swampy mouthful, which he downed. He checked that his bags were intact and secure. In his volatile micro-economy a crash could massively deflate his currency. Then, more attentive to the neighbourhood's cleanliness than to his own, he pulled out a whisk and dustpan and tidied up.

If it were winter he wouldn't feel so light-headed. If it were winter and cold enough, he could have sheltered at St. Simon's. He paused, stooping, to catch his breath. Maybe make his way to the Good Shepherd. It would take some doing in this heat. But a bit of luck and he might be in time to get a bed—and afterwards a shower. If not, then sleep in Regent Park with the sparrows. As he stood up, panting, the taxi passed. With his arm he dried his brow. His face, what showed of it above his beard, was streaked with grime.

"I swear I'll lose my mind if I don't get some air," Janet said. "This heat is killing me."

"Please relax," Cecelia whispered.

"Thirty seconds. Thirty. Then I start screaming."

"Please don't," the driver said.

"Drive your car," Janet ordered. "It should be illegal to drive a taxi without air conditioning."

On either side of the street, trees and fantastically expensive houses loomed. Cecelia had been summoned. She must have caught someone's eye. Not Handly, she hoped. Perhaps the chair, but nobody said. Like stagecraft to a spectator, it was a mystery to her how these things worked. She got on well with the graduate secretary. Unlike some, Cecelia didn't make her problems his. He said the library's director of advancement wanted the department to send a couple of students. The host an important benefactor. She was too young to remember *Lifestyles of the Rich and Famous*, he said, but she would see affluence and privilege like she wouldn't believe. She only had to go, and take a friend if she wanted, and have a good time. It occurred to her that, while she had been through the neighbourhood a few times, she had never really been in it. She imagined that behind the suburban backdrop were bankers and athletes, politicians and celebrities, sunning themselves in their designer yards, or wading in their custom pools, or doing yoga with personal trainers, while their children played and their nannies minded, and their little dogs panted on their patios. She envisioned afternoon cocktails and expensive bottles of chilled wine whose necks beaded like hers, only refreshingly.

Janet turned sharply, presenting Cecelia with a view of her back.

"Do I look OK? I'd rather go home than walk in there with sweat stains."

"You could get out here," the driver offered.

A small procession of cars appeared before them. People were being dropped off near a large Georgian home. A low, iron fence spanned the narrow frontage, and a handful of guests were filing through the gate. Beyond that a flower garden and dwarf shrubs lined the stone path, in obedience to a rigid geometry. Cecelia and Janet disembarked and followed the others to the door, through which they could hear music. The change in temperature as Cecelia entered was so sudden she began to erupt in goosebumps.

A moment later they found themselves in an astonishing two-storey entry hall. Its high ceilings were trimmed with lavish cornice mouldings. At one end of the hall rose a staircase of rich, dark wood, with wide steps and ornately turned spindles; in a nearby corner, in huddled detachment, a trio was playing inconspicuous jazz; and suspended above her head was a broad chandelier whose crystals reflected and glowed star-like on the cloudy Carrara floor. Cecelia halted at the foot of the stair, taking it in. It was not just a question of style, though this was rich and elegant, nor even of materials, though they were of surpassing quality. No, it was simply that where the edges of the plaster moulding, the wooden risers, and the marble tiles abutted, the joints were even and precise and true. Nothing so announces quality as the care with which a thing is put together. Her father had taught her that, she realized. Not that he would have liked the hall. He would have called it excessive and pretentious, but he would have expounded on the excellence of the joints, excellence that required more skill and time and care, and cost more money, than any prefab, slap-dash, middle-class renovator could conceive of spending.

All around her, people were performing greetings: handshakes and embraces abounded, and airy kisses were evidently *de rigueur*. The Gallic demonstrations of pleasure seemed genuine and unaffected, for some. Cecelia shifted on her feet and turned appraisingly about, waiting to see what she should do next. Guests were continuing to arrive and although some, like her, lingered in the hall to look around, most moved ahead into the adjoining rooms with little hesitation. Two young men, both tall and broad-shouldered, moved handsomely among them. Janet examined them closely.

"Doctors," she conjectured.

Cecelia watched them stroll comfortably away. They were laughing. At one crowded threshold the shorter one raised his hand and pressed his friend to enter first. His shoulder moved beautifully in the jacket.

"Lawyers," Cecelia countered. "Those are really good suits."

Janet began to follow. "Let's find out."

"Not just yet. OK?" Cecelia whispered.

Janet stared at her. "I don't understand. Are we supposed to just stand here?"

On the landing above, a man appeared. Lean and alert, he approached the balustrade. He rested his hands there on the railing and scrutinized the animated milling in the hall. A tall, beautiful woman, with all her dark and silky Middle-Eastern hair dangling over one shoulder like a tassel, swept with gentle condescension forward to his arm.

"No, of course not," Cecelia said. "But could we pace ourselves?"

Janet laughed softly and looped her arm through her friend's. "If you like, but when I track them down later you'll have to settle for leftovers."

As they moved with the other invitees, Cecelia looked up and saw the man smiling. His gaze settled momentarily on her and Janet, she thought, but then it glided by. Taking in the crowd at the door and the visitors milling in the hall, he looked on with approbation. He seemed accustomed to it. An inveterate approbator. He placed his hands behind his back and drew himself erect, approbating over the ongoing arrival of his guests.

The dining room had been converted to a bar for the occasion. A long table was pushed towards one wall, and behind it were two attractive young men in white, with the old-timey sleeve garters and braces of a Prohibition speakeasy. One was mixing spirits and the other dispensing wine from ice-filled buckets. Below another opulent chandelier, where the table would normally have stood, a line of guests had formed, some thirsty from the heat, some from the anticipation, and some from the impatience that heat and anticipation often breed. Many were less

demure than they pretended. Even as they engaged in friendly conversation their eyes skipped towards the drink service in case there
emerged more auspicious pathways to the booze.

"Get in there," Janet said. "You know you need it."

She thrust Cecelia ahead and right through to the bar. Little cards
stood here and there, and listed the alternatives, but the words signi-
fied nothing to Cecelia. She only knew she wanted a white. When the
bartender asked, she said she would have a glass of the Chardonnay.

"We have a few. Do you have a preference?"

Tongue-tied and arrested by this unforeseen complication, Cecelia
helplessly returned the young man's engaging smile.

"If you want something refreshing and easy, we have a classic gunflint
Chablis. Or if you're in the mood for something rounder, a bit buttery,
we have a nice Mâcon." Cecelia pondered. She wanted something
refreshing, but questioned which would be the more discerning choice.
In the shuffling and shouldering around her, she could feel people growing irritated. Their drinks were not getting poured. The kind-smiling
bartender persisted. "Or maybe ... would you like something special?"

"She sure would," Janet said. She manoeuvred herself alongside.

"Mostly people are drinking the French whites, but I have a really
great Napa Chardonnay here. And not one of your cloying, overblown
jugs of oak-driven swill. It's lively. Pear and melon, citrus and mineral.
There's smoky vanilla, but it's so restrained the subtle fruit layers express
themselves effortlessly. This is the wine that won the Judgment of Paris."

"I thought the Judgment of Paris was won by the Greeks," Cecelia
said. Janet poked her so hard she flinched.

"No, Chateau Montelena," the bartender corrected. There was a
moment's hesitation, in which an apprehension of misunderstanding
slightly blistered his professional veneer. "It's twice the wine the other
two are," he said, encouraging her. "I'd love to open a bottle."

"Then I'd love to try it." Cecelia smiled and tried to iron out any
lingering irreverence. It was a relief to see him skip away. She hoped
she had not made him feel ridiculous.

"Don't get clever, Lines," Janet whispered. "We're here to have fun,
not throw around apples of discord."

"Now who's being clever?"

The bartender returned and poured the wine. It glistened yellow-gold against the white of the table linen. She lifted the glass by the stem, as she had been taught, and tried to thank the young man, but already he was on to Janet.

"For you too?" he asked.

"I don't know," Janet simpered. "I hardly know anything about wine. What do you think would pair best with my mood? I'm feeling effervescent."

"Champagne, then."

"That does sound tempting. But do you think it's very good?" she asked. "Seduce me. Make me want it."

Cecelia, about to taste her wine, stopped and marvelled at Janet's boldness. How easily she could do this: check her brains at the door, pretend her mother had not, like so many other waspish, Toronto ladies of privilege, taught her to uphold the old etiquettes. How effortlessly she could play. In a curious moment of disembodiment, Cecelia watched herself as her head shook and her lips pursed. It was not deliberate, but it was not unconscious either, and while she did not endorse it—her own prudish disapproval—neither could she entirely disown it. It came from a part of her that mostly she kept closeted away, like an unfashionable dress handed down to her as an heirloom that she would never wear, but could not bring herself to discard. It was an unattractive habit, this readiness to censure. She was only glad Janet and the bartender were too absorbed in one another to note it. Cecelia watched as he slid closer and lovingly presented a dripping bottle from a nearby bucket.

"This comes from a small producer in the Marne Valley, where the south-facing slopes produce ripe wines with lots of aroma. It's mostly Pinot Meunier and it's left on its lees six years. The nose has dried fruits with a suggestive spiciness, and in the mouth ..." He delayed, mid-expression, and leaned in. His eyes became more penetrating and Janet cocked her head with interest, inviting him to continue. "It's like a ripe pear and a sticky bun making love on your tongue. And the finish is long. It seems to go on forever."

Cecelia thought she saw Janet's composure waver, and her knees a little too.

"Give me the bubbly sex wine."

The bartender smiled and filled a fluted glass. As he handed it to her, she looked at him lingeringly, her eyes like the champagne, limpid and sparkling.

"Thanks," she said, regaining her cool. "When I come back later, I want you to give it to me again."

As they moved away through the crowd, Cecelia tasted her flat California Chardonnay. She thought she could detect the melon, but she wasn't sure. It being twice the wine, she tried to like it twice as much, but Janet's left her wondering.

ᚢ

The living room was so large that, without crowding, it accommodated two dozen or more, and it was teeming with exchanges—the varied, vehement confabulation of opinionated men and women, some well-established and some as yet pretending—and these exchanges were accompanied by the inevitable social outgassing and competition you would expect as secondary effects of all that mingling. The walls featured paintings of varying style and scale, and throughout the room stood plinths and pedestals for sculptures; the seats and sofas were oriented to promote their contemplation, though few noticed. Inconvenienced by a temporary absence of servers, one philistine had even rested his empty glass on a plinth next to one of Fafard's recumbent bovines.

In one corner Rick Stafford, the young radio personality, was in conversation with literary it girl Anna Bronn-Carlson, who having written two little-noticed books—*The Wheat Goes on Forever*, and *How to Escape from a Tightly Locked Cabinet*—was suddenly all the rage for her breakout novel, *In the Streetcar Suburbs Things Will Only Get Worse*. Since launching his popular arts program three years ago, Stafford was explaining, he had notched his belt many times over with hard-to-land actors, musicians, and other personalities, and now his star was on the rise. He was poised to be an arbiter of cool from coast to coast; he was about to score a deal for American syndication; and he was pitching a battle of the books concept. She knew—didn't she?—that with the right press she could get herself listed for one of the big prizes. He would check with his producers. Maybe he could make something happen. Maybe she would like to discuss it over drinks sometime. She tried to explain how it really didn't work that way.

Within earshot of their conversation were Matthew Carver, who had only recently arrived in the city to take the helm as CAO of the film festival, and Chris Marlowe (the auspiciously named), who cut quite a figure in the entertainment community, owing to his seats on the advisory boards of several key arts institutions whose net economic impact annually surpassed one hundred million. Both men had listened to Stafford's show and disliked him intensely: in part for his fawning, imbecilic, softball interviews; and in part for his turns of phrase, like all the somethings that were the new something else; and in part for the fact that all the things for which they disliked him were precisely responsible for his success. How far national radio had fallen, they agreed, if stupid was the new sophistication, and the new Pied Piper of pop culture was using his fifteen minutes to have a go at a literary debutante.

By the fireplace, over drinks, Melissa Kohler was making her case to columnist Reg Butler, whose steadfast conviction was that her book on the widening income gap and the disappearing middle class, while intelligent and important, might as well be a voice in the wilderness. If she hoped to parlay it into a run at political office, it was ill-timed and only good for being forgotten. Aspirations to a federal or provincial nomination were wildly unrealistic. Municipally she might be able to do something, but it was better not to get involved in that meat-grinder. Better to wait for public opinion to swing around. It always did. Kohler frowned a little, though not from Butler's assessment, with which she secretly agreed. No, her Sauvignon blanc had turned disappointingly warm in her hand. Caroline Underhill from City Hall, herself a crusader for low-income housing and public libraries, interjected and told her not to listen. Butler knew nothing about local politics, she said. He insisted he knew plenty, only he didn't give a shit.

Elsewhere in the room stood the highly connected litigator, and Vice-Chair of the Ontario Securities Commission, Alan Jacobs, advocating for reform to securities regulations, which to journalist and occasional television pundit Jeremy Reynolds he described as "reach-arounds-for-grifters." And standing not far off was Richard Kavanagh, the shit-disturbing city planner who counted among his friends Bob

Rae, and even admitted to it; who, even with the writing on the wall, refused to glad-hand with the schoolboy Conservatives, preferring to give them and their hall monitor politics the finger. And there was also Friend of the Library Jack Whiting, a thirty-year veteran of various bank and insurance boards, going on about how Sydney Fisher gave his First Folio to McGill and later stole it back—walked right in and took it, and then gave it to U of T along with a rare book library to house it—and how that guy had stones. And Whiting's friend and tennis partner, Victor Barker, president and CEO of Tudor Securities, chair of the Board of Trustees for SickKids: around town he was known as the banker with a heart—not because other bankers didn't have hearts, but because his still beat from time to time.

And among these and the many other middle-aged and conspicuous men and women at the apexes of their professional and social domains, hovered cautiously the young and eager: students and junior professionals, like tick birds, bright-eyed and gregarious, hopeful of lighting on the rump of an interesting or advantageous conversation. On the whole it was a curious menagerie, eclectic as any natural ecosystem, and in its differences as yielding to taxonomy. Cecelia, however, was like a solitary western scientist, plunked down in some remote jungle. She had no idea who any of these people were and, lacking a frame of reference, had no idea where to begin. Janet had gone off to explore, so Cecelia was on her own. She looked for something familiar to which she could gravitate.

One end of the room was anchored by an enormous canvas—a chaotic, motley patchwork of coloured oils flung against and forced upon the canvas with frenetic, unpainterly gestures. It stretched almost from floor to ceiling and ran several wingspans wide. It had attracted the attention of a small congress of enthusiasts, two of whom were in such vehement disagreement it was evident to all that something was at stake. No doubt they were dating.

"No. Listen. Riopelle is Lyrical Abstraction," the young man said categorically.

"Don't be stupid. This is no different from Abstract Expressionism," replied his ostensible girlfriend. "It's like a Rothko, after Pollock got his grubby hands on it."

"Oh, did they teach you that in medicine? Of the two of us, which one is actually taking art history?"

"Go ahead, take a course in it. Learn how to do it yourself, for all I care." She stamped her foot in irritation and he threw his arm up in appeal, but the canvas wasn't taking sides.

A woman of thirty or thirty-five was watching them, and nearby a brace of middle-aged men were themselves hungrily eyeing her. This woman's dress was modest in front, with a high neckline and three-quarter sleeves. Lace-fringed and elegant, but in an old-world, Victorian sort of way: it was neither fashionable, nor even classic, really. It was also not quite fitting: her curves were so generous they taxed the resilience of the skirt. "I wouldn't discount it just because it has affinities," the woman said. "Art doesn't get made in a vacuum."

"That's just an academic perspective," the girlfriend said knowingly.

"No, look closely. The impasto—the oil so thick it's almost tumid—pressed on with knives and trowels. And the use of white. Riopelle doesn't just drip it on the floor like Pollock. He throws it at the canvas in long, glossy ropes. His technique is so vigorous, his expression virile." She paused, adoring, and gazed up at the canvas. "Riopelle's influence and fame aren't so great as Rothko and Pollock's. But in four hundred years, who knows?"

Cecelia watched the couple, but it seemed they were less invested in the painting now than in each other's resentment. After a moment they moved off, to be replaced by the two gentlemen observers.

Stepping forward, one said to the woman, "You seem to know a lot about art."

"I hope so. I'm at the AGO."

He introduced himself as Rohan Batra, a fund manager with Furness Financial, and she herself as Monica Delorme, curatorial assistant at the Art Gallery of Ontario. She offered her hand, and he clasped it.

"Doctor Charles Abrams," said the other man, joining in. "I think I saw you here last year. How do you know Owen?"

"We met ... well it's almost ten years now. I was doing a senior paper on Wolfe's copy of Gray's *Elegy*, which the Fisher owns. He came across me in the library and asked me what I was doing. When I told him, he quoted from the margins: 'How ineffectual are often our own unaided exertions, especially in early life. How many shining lights owe to patronage and affluence what their talents would never procure them.' He's been so generous to me. He helped me get my first job, and I helped him get this painting."

She turned about, her eyes searching the room, but their host was not there. After that the conversation quickly petered out and the gentlemen excused themselves to a wide ottoman an elderly couple had just vacated.

"I swear, sometimes I think Owen is compensating for something," Batra said, observing the extravagance of the surroundings. "He's got this place done up like a museum. At least half of these are new."

"I like museums," Abrams said, looking in the direction of Monica Delorme. "You can stand behind the ladies, looking at their asses for long stretches, and they don't get uncomfortable."

"I bet they do, Doctor Abrams."

Abrams shrugged indifferently. The two gentlemen chuckled. They didn't seem to realize that Cecelia was still near enough to overhear. She hoped they didn't realize. Then Batra's face drew tight.

"What is it?" his friend asked.

"Moffat is here. Over in the corner. That's a conversation I'd like to avoid. He'll come looking for me the second his wife is buzzed enough that he can slip away."

"So you've got about fifteen minutes."

Batra frowned and shook his head.

"What's the big deal?" Abrams asked.

"Bre-X. He got in late and didn't get out at all. I keep telling him. I can do risk management. What I can't do is risk elimination. How was I supposed to know they were salting the samples?"

"He's still mad?"

"Still. Again. Take your pick. He's hounding me like it's personal. I told him, everybody got shafted on that one. Now he wants to chuck his tech portfolio too. He's killing me."

They peered off into the corner. A tall, grey-headed man in a double-breasted suit stood talking with several other guests. His gaze drifted towards them and they turned to avoid it.

"Goddamn tight-ass," Batra said, worrying at his cuff. "He'll lose his fortune. He's a patient of yours, isn't he? So you know."

Cradling the glass bulb of his tumbler, Doctor Abrams' fingers, by means of gentle palpitations, turned it slowly in his palm. Rather than answer, he looked back at Monica Delorme. "You know, museums should serve booze. That would shake things up."

"True. But it's probably safer the way it is."

"For the art?"

"For the women," Batra corrected. He leaned back on his hands and looked once more at the painting. "A Riopelle. What did she say it was? Abstract Expressionism?"

"Something like that."

"The way she talked about it made it sound so dirty."

Abrams frowned. "I'm a doctor. Trust me. Expression can be a dirty word."

Monica Delorme, now alone, was still standing by the painting. She seemed to be stationed there, protective of her proximity, as though she were relying on it somehow. Cecelia no longer felt the need to linger.

As she made her way through the crowd towards the back of the house, Cecelia passed young James Milburn of the Advancement Office. He was pressing Dr. Henry Greene.

"You understand, the roof leaks and there's water infiltration down the walls. During last year's thaw there was a river running just inches from some of the manuscripts. We were hoping you would consider a gift, perhaps a hundred thousand, to help us preserve the collections."

Greene said nothing. Instead, he removed a handkerchief from his pocket and lightly dabbed his brow; then he scrutinized the moist cotton and began to square it with calculated precision, unhurriedly aligning one pressed edge at a time.

"You do understand," Milburn continued, "the books inside the Fisher are worth more than all the buildings on St. George combined. Come by sometime and I'll show you what your support would mean. We would love to put your name on something, or your father's name, if you prefer."

"So, you envision what? A plaque in appreciation of the Henry Greene butyl liner?"

Cecelia tried to slip through the living room doors, only to be hindered by George Bleury and Robert Heiden, venture partners at First-In Capital. They were in determined-but-lopsided disagreement, and Bleury was using his friend as an excuse to hold forth and disgorge motes of experience to the clutch of hungry aspirants who were coveyed around them, ignorant of their obstruction.

"So I'm in the middle of my due diligence and I find out this guy has a string of backers but no business plan. I couldn't fucking believe it. Pardon my French, but come on."

"Why don't you just walk out on it?" Heiden asked.

"Well it's not like I don't want to, but you've got to be careful which bridges you burn," he said. Casting around his little circle of influence, he expanded: "Listen, any time you think about screwing someone on a deal, think twice. And then think again. If it's the last thing you'll ever need from him, then fine. If not, take the long view. Think win-win. Otherwise he'll get you back. Besides, he's married to my sister. Oh, and when I asked to see the books guess who he calls."

Heiden felt disinclined to play the feed for his preening friend.

"I'll tell you who," Bleury said. "Darnel Jackson. Their operation's so Mickey Mouse that accounting's just one guy, and it's Darnel fucking Jackson."

"You're shitting me," Heiden said.

"I know, right? He's such a self-righteous tit."

"To be fair. His wife died not long ago."

"To be fair, he probably killed her. I spent three weeks working with him in '92 and it nearly killed me." Bleury drank heavily from his rocks glass and with an emphatic flourish prepared his brood for a dose of philosophy. "Ninety percent of the job is people. You want a real business curriculum? Have the HR courses taught by accountants and the management courses taught by psychologists. The rest you can get from a book."

"I don't understand," a young woman said. "How did he get a backer without a business plan?"

"The same way anyone gets anything. He knew somebody. This guy," he motioned to Heiden, "he never applied for a job in his life. How long have you been in this game?"

"Long enough. I started—"

"They don't need the whole story, Robert," Bleury said. Then he said, to all in general, "All you need to know is that he knew somebody. And now you know somebody. We won't be with First-In forever. In three to five we'll be out on our own and you'll want to give us a call."

He savoured the last drops of his whisky, and the soundness of his own advice. Then he rattled the ice in his empty glass. "First things first, though. I need another drink."

ਤ

On the expansive upper patio at the rear of the house, the air was still humid. Owing to the trees and thick undergrowth that rose up from the ravine and surrounded the property, the temperature was a little less than streetside, but not enough. It felt like an incubator. The guests were roosting mildly here and there in dopey little hatches: some hanging out near the doorways, others by the railings, a few tucked around by the side of the house. Relatively few of these were men, it seemed. Or, at any rate, their turnover was high. In the brief time Cecelia spent looking for somewhere to situate herself, several came out, spoke a few words to this person or that or to each other, and hastily excused themselves back into the comfort of the air conditioning. Even the lightest suits were suffocating: the best silks worsted by the heat. Janet, presumably, was still in search of her lawyers, so Cecelia sat down on an empty bench seat beside a party of garrulous women.

Rebecca Mason, Ellen Harrison, and Julia Jones had been friends since high school, and Louisa Peck, a PR maven whose firm ran damage control for many of the city's cultural illuminati—and occasionally for a few of the guests at this very party—had known them since university. Their manner and appearance were deceptively youthful. They were remarkably well preserved—or else enhanced, or expertly camouflaged, or perhaps all three. They lounged comfortably on a set of patio furniture, their dresses like their opinions, breezy and conducive to ventilation.

"Owen throws such good parties," said Julia, a long and elegantly proportioned woman with a waist like a hinge. "If only he did more often."

"Yeah, I don't know anyone who tries this hard," Rebecca said.

"That's one good thing about new money, at least," Louisa said. "Ooh, and did you notice the bartenders?"

Rebecca nodded and said, "What a relief they actually knew something about wine. Last week Bill and I ate at Auteur and they tried to make us drink a flawed wine. It wasn't even a matter of opinion. It had these little hard bits on the cork and the waiter actually tried to tell us it was nothing to worry about. Called them wine diamonds. Can you believe that? So, Bill told the manager that if he wasn't going to have an actual sommelier on staff he should go open an Olive Garden." The women nodded their endorsement as Rebecca coquetted prettily in her seat. "After that the server spent the rest of the meal overcompensating. You should have seen him flirting with me."

Ellen Harrison, the shyer, more silent of the foursome, was short and slightly round, albeit only compared to her lithesome friends. She was very attractive, not that there was even the slenderest consolation in that. She fidgeted, eager to include herself, her smile meek and searching. "Did Bill tell the manager that too?" she asked.

"No. But only 'cause he didn't notice," Rebecca said.

A few steps from this gaggling, at the centre of another group, stood the man from the balustrade, his dark-haired companion absent and his arm temporarily unadorned. Uniquely among the men, he seemed at ease with the heat. Cecelia guessed that he must be the host, Mr. Owen Trover. The way others fawned unabashedly, like earnest spaniels, suggested it. He was not wholly attentive to them, though. Wandering, his interest seemed, like Cecelia's, drawn to the chatterboxy socialites beside her. His lips tucked into a slight smile. He seemed to find them amusing.

"Speaking of flirting, Julia ..." Ellen said. She trailed off and, with an upturning of her nose, she indicated a mismatched couple standing in proximity, not only to the French doors, but also to each other. The gentleman, older and greying, was leaning over a university girl. His stance aspired to rakishness, though he was much too stiff and agitated to make it, possibly because of the way the young lady's fingers were gently to-and-fro-ing across his forearm.

"Oh, I see," said Julia. Her lips see-sawed into an indulgent smile.

"Look at her," said Louisa with unmuffled disdain. "If that skirt was any shorter it would be a belt. Flat as a board too. What do they see in these schoolgirl skinny Minnies?"

"I bet she can eat anything she wants and not get fat," said Rebecca.

"Maybe. Or maybe she's one of those girls that can eat croissants for breakfast every day until it's too late, and then she gains twenty pounds all at once and can never get them off again." Louisa studied the woman ravenishly. "I really hope so."

"I don't know," Ellen said. "I heard that croissants are actually one of the lowest calorie breakfast foods. If you make them small enough." Her friends, their attention still diverted, did not hear her.

"She can't be older than nineteen or twenty. What can they possibly have to talk about?" Rebecca said, frowning.

"Daddy issues," Louisa theorized. "A touch of grey, a bit of fatherly approval, and she gets all moist."

"Oh Daddy, but I try so hard to be a good little girl," Rebecca cooed, suddenly delighted.

"I bet she bends over for a wink and a pat on the head," said Louisa.

"You're one to talk," said Julia. "You used to give it away like a food bank."

"Bite your tongue, bitch!"

Rebecca interrupted: "So, what, you're saying it doesn't bother you to see some pubescent floozy with petticoat-perfect legs jobbing your husband's arm?"

Julia shrugged. "That's why I do Pilates."

"What's Pilates?" Ellen asked.

"It's how you keep your husband interested in you after forty."

"You should try it, Ellen," Louisa crowed. "Even with three kids, you're not the unhopefullest forty-seven-year-old I know."

Ellen could not help but sulk a little. "'Cause it's working so well for Julia."

Stretching back in her chair—her skirt uprising and her breasts outstanding against the bodice of her dress—Julia shot a piercing whistle across the patio. Her husband jerked upright in embarrassment, and his mouth, aiming first at his wife and then at the university girl, spouted dry and ineffectual excuses. The women laughed, and the young woman skipped away while he all but folded over in defeat.

"Oh, poor thing," said Rebecca, sounding not very sympathetic.

Julia smiled. "He'll get over it."

From his nearby conversation, Trover glanced at Cecelia and smiled. Then he winked, as though cahootsing. She smiled too but with instinctive reserve, flustered by his unaccountable familiarity. Rising, she turned away and approached the nearby iron railing. Below, on the lower terrace, three women—young and mildly intoxicated—sat at the edge of the lap pool, dangling their bare feet in the water and occasionally kicking little splashes onto each other's exposed thighs, making a show of themselves and receiving stares of disapproval and desire that, in equal measure, they unrestrainedly enjoyed.

Peripherally, Cecelia thought she saw Janet, but when she looked for her she was gone. Trover, though, was looking at her again, or still. She felt uncomfortably self-aware, as though her insides were out. She made deliberate steps back to her seat, conscious that they should convey the appearance of purpose, so that he would not suspect she was alone for any reason other than her desire to be. She tried to own the comfort she counterfeited, but it was difficult with Trover's eyes, like two abacus beads, following her back and forth across the patio. Dropping onto the edge of the chair, she perched with one leg over the other, keeping her chest forward and shoulders back, not immodestly, but enough to keep her from sweating against the fabric of the chair. Looking up, she saw that Trover was once more with his dark-haired companion. Cecelia averted her gaze and tried not to check again.

Somewhere distant but approaching, a siren sounded; but shielded by the brick and mortar of the house on one side, and the vegetation of the ravine on the other, the guests were made to endure only its muffled whining, and not even that for long, as it cut out before its crescendo reached the point of ruffling their calm.

"God this heat is offensive. I was starting to hope that ambulance was for me," Louisa said.

"That's just the change whispering in your ear," Rebecca teased.

"Shut up."

"You shouldn't tease about that," Ellen said. "I spoke with Anne last week and she's having a terrible time with it, and now the cancer's back too."

"I thought the hysterectomy was supposed to take care of that," Louisa said, frowning.

"How's she holding up?" Julia asked.

"She sounds good on the whole. The chemo's not so bad. It's the hot flashes she says are killing her."

"She would say that," Julia said. She shook her head and smiled admiringly.

"What's the prognosis?" Louisa asked.

"She'll beat it," Julia insisted.

"They can cure almost anything these days," Rebecca said. "Remember the AIDS epidemic? Like, hardly at all, right? That's 'cause they've got it completely under control."

"Except for in Africa," Julia noted.

"OK, but that's not the same thing."

"And they have a whole team working on her," Ellen confirmed.

"And yet I can't even find a GP I like," Louisa said. "I've tried three in the past six months and I just don't like any of them."

"Is that so, Goldilocks?" Julia asked.

"Don't get superior, Missus-Doctor Chief of Surgery," Rebecca snapped.

"Oh, but Julia," Ellen interjected, "you remember that eighty-year-old I got sent to when my doctor was on mat leave."

Louisa laughed. "The one whose hands shook?"

"It's not funny. He shoved the speculum in cold and, when he realized he forgot the swab, just left it dangling there while he went to get it."

The lips of all four women screwed into tight frowns. Even the seemingly unflappable Julia quavered.

"It's 'cause of all the immigrants, you know," Rebecca pronounced. "Them and their anchor babies."

"Don't be stupid," Julia said.

"Or they let their foreign relatives borrow their health cards for surgical procedures. Some of these people are rich in their own countries, but here they can get it for nothing. Seriously. Bill wasn't born rich, you know. His parents owned an appliance store on Bloor West, and he had to build himself up from nothing. But these people, all they have to do is cook up a story about how bad it is in some backward, unpronounceable country and they get free dental, just like that. And they're not even real Canadians."

"Jesus, Becca. That's a terrible thing to say," Ellen said.

She looked to Julia to see if she would say something. Rebecca brandished her glass and downed a good long showy sip.

"Well, sometimes I do feel a little bad about it. But then the alcohol kicks in."

"Becks, if you ever read anything besides *Vogue* and *Cosmo* you couldn't be such an ignoramus," Julia said.

"Don't be tedious, Julia. If I wanted my head filled with all sorts of ideas, I'd go back and finish my dissertation."

"Sorry, did I say ignoramus?" Julia asked. "I meant to say vicious twat."

"Excuse me, Ms. Lines." At Cecelia's elbow a gentleman had appeared. "I'm Clement Rowse, Mr. Trover's assistant. If you're not otherwise engaged, Mr. Trover was wondering if you might find a moment to speak with him."

"Oh?"

"Perhaps now would be at your convenience?"

Cecelia didn't quite understand what was happening, but she knew she didn't like to be ordered about. His manner was so restrained and categorical, however, that it left the impression she ought not to dally. "Oh, of course. Only where should I ..." She cast her eyes over the patio.

"He said he would find you in the living room."

She tried to convey her irritation by drinking off the last of her glass at one go, but she had been nursing it and now it was so cloying that her mouth curled unpleasantly and ruined the effect. Rowse only nodded politely and returned to the house. There was no longer any sign of Trover on the terrace, and the lounging women continued to blather, their bloodless disregard a study in vapidity.

Ա

At a comfortable distance, Cecelia followed Rowse inside. The whisky-downing gentlemen and the small handful of young hopefuls who still hovered around them were obstructing doorways again, this time to the dining room and bar. They had been joined, in the interim, by another man whose disagreement with them was beginning to carry, and Rowse paused in apparent assessment.

"No, of course not. You always want to be one hundred percent invested. All I'm saying is there's a massive correction coming. So whatever you do, don't unhedge yourself for a quick gain. Start offloading liabilities instead, and start buying undervalued assets: like, drop Nortel and think about Apple."

"Ladies and gentlemen, Tony Nicols: the Pessimist of Bay Street," Bleury said.

"I'm just trying to remind them," Nicols objected, "it's in the swing that the real money gets made, but they need enough liquidity to make the most of it."

"The rumour is he's a closet pinko."

"That's horseshit," Nicols replied.

"Ask him why he objects to a thirty percent tax cut."

"Are you still on that? I told you, I'm not against cutting taxes, but Harris cut so much so fast the debt actually increased by twenty billion. That makes him either a liar or an idiot."

"Like I said: pinko."

Nicols threw up his hands. "This from a guy who thinks amalgamation is going to work out."

"It'll work for me."

"You watch," Nicols said. "Once that happens, every second mayor will be a buffoon and the outer neighbourhoods will start turning into slums. Jane and Finch is halfway there already. How good is that for business?"

"Jane and Finch? The name rings a bell."

Nicols excused himself with deliberate politeness. After he had gone, one of the young hangers-on ventured to ask if liquidity was really so important.

"Liquidity is of paramount importance," Bleury said, lifting his glass. "But that's what the open bar is for." He might have said more but Rowse, on his way by, clipped his shoulder, causing him to spill most of his drink on the floor.

"I'm so sorry," Rowse said. "I'll get someone to clean this up immediately."

Bleury and Heiden were forced to move towards the patio. A number of their followers took the opportunity to explore other options.

As Cecelia entered the living room, she found it empty. The crowd had shifted to the entry hall, so she positioned herself just inside the doorway, peeking between the huddled spectators. Its entire circumference was lined with people; some had even taken seats on the great staircase to get a better view of the acrobats. The chandelier had been dimmed. Its glow cast gentle shadows over the bodies of the performers. Two young women. Twins. Muscular, but supple enough to draw their legs into almost any position. Even all the way behind their backs so that their toes could touch their heads. They balanced on each other, moving around an invisible centre in dreamy equilibrium like mirror reflections. Propped as they were, each on the other, there was something disturbing about how far they could bend without falling. The jazz of mid-afternoon had given way to gently pulsating electronica. The guests stood motionless and entranced.

"Good lord, the excess!" said a whispered voice at her elbow. "Who hires acrobats for a garden party?"

Cecelia started and nearly dropped her glass. It was Trover. He smiled easily, and she might have responded, but his eyes remained fixed on the performance. The acrobats shifted fluidly with the elegance of apparent ease from each position to the next for several minutes. Then, in a final act of astounding strength and skill, the one flipped and the other hoisted her into a handstand so that her toes reached up almost to the chandelier and—end on end, their hands joining them—they gazed the length of their arms into each other's eyes. They remained there longer than Cecelia could believe. At last they nodded, and let each other go, and settled gracefully side by side to the floor.

The lights grew brighter and Cecelia found she was holding her breath. The performers, to the delight of the applauding guests, took turns bowing and doing flips and laybacks and other tricks.

"My goodness, those girls are bendy," Trover said. "But I should be careful not to praise them in terms that could be mistaken for prurience. I'm not running a gentlemen's club after all. Did you enjoy it?"

"I've never seen anything like it," Cecelia said.

"I'm Owen."

"Cecelia."

"Yes, I know. I understand you have an interest in the Swan of Avon. I may have something else you would enjoy seeing."

Finding his meaning enigmatical, Cecelia was unsure how to respond. He was nearly a head taller than she, and he could have loomed over her had he chosen to, but instead he had stooped forward, conspiratorially, and though he seemed self-satisfied, even a little smug, nonetheless his smile was boyish and inviting. She tried to feel at ease.

Trover pulled a key from his pocket and unlocked the door. Within, the room was barely illuminated, only by a faint diffusion of sunlight through a pair of thick window shades. He stepped aside to allow Cecelia to enter and, slipping in after, turned on the overhead lights. The walls were lined with bookshelves and framed drawings. To one side a modest writing desk and chair, and to the other a loveseat with coffee and end tables, were the only furnishings. On the desk sat a thin archival box, and on the coffee table a curious piece of gnarled wood. Closing the door, he asked Cecelia was she a book person. It sounded rhetorical. As she scanned the room, he relieved her of her glass and placed it on the end table. He invited her to poke around—she wouldn't hurt anything, he said.

She circled the room, eyeing the shelves one by one and scanning the spines. One whole wall seemed to be poetry, some soft-covered, some cloth-bound, most of those with jackets. First editions, Trover explained. Another contained books much older and more variable in size, but with bindings more uniform in that all were leather, many with their gilding more or less preserved. A few of the shelves displayed small objects and ephemera, and one held archival boxes, cartons of dull grey, and a glass display case. She hesitated to lay hands on anything, but Trover encouraged her.

She began with an unevenly shaped coin, a trade token from 1621. Yellow and grey with age, it was one of the oldest struck in Canada, used for barter in the Avalon Colony and bearing the initials of David Kirke, one-time governor of Newfoundland and a tavern-keeper who had a license to make his own money. Cecelia had never seen anything like it. She turned it over in her hand. He used to have another, he boasted, but this one was better.

"Used to have?"

"I couldn't look at it without seeing how much inferior it was to its sibling here, so I sold it."

He then pointed to the desiccated piece of wood on the coffee table. A miniature black spruce: krummholz from a conservation area inside the Arctic Circle. A thousand or more years old, with rings thin and wound tight like a tiny scroll, it was one of the rarest things he owned.

"I had to bribe some people to get this," he said, covertly, "and I'd have to bribe some more if I told the wrong person what it is."

From the shelf below she pulled a heavy, large format book and set it beside the dwarf tree to examine: a book of wildflowers of the Dominion of Canada, with hand-coloured sketches, almost as old as Confederation. Though beautiful it was not very rare, he explained, nor valuable in any marketable sense, but between every page was a specimen of each species, pressed and preserved, no doubt hunted unrelentingly over many years, perhaps a lifetime. Cecelia sat down and he, leaning over, helped her open it slowly. There was *Amelanchier humilis*, he said, called the low serviceberry—she turned some pages—and *Campanula rotundifolia*, the harebell, which was for remembrance.

"I guarantee you, nobody in the world has one like it. Just imagine the persistence."

When she had finished, Trover returned the book to its place. He then went to the shelf with the empty display case. It stood somewhat apart from the other shelves, and from it he pulled an archival box. It housed a thick leather-bound volume, which he handed to her, and which when she opened it caused her to shoot out a little "O!" The headline read, *MR. WILLIAM SHAKESPEARES COMEDIES, HISTORIES, & TRAGEDIES. Published according to the True Originall Copies.*

"Is this … is this really a First Folio?" She had never handled one before. After too long gaping in silence, she looked up and again took stock. "And in all the boxes?"

"A few sheets of an anonymous author plot, a few letters with reports of performances, a prompt book for an anonymous play, two early quartos, including *Much Ado*—documents from the Elizabethan stage, essentially." He also had various almanacs and dictionaries, he said, as well as pamphlets and tracts, treatises, some lovely Bibles. Some later stage history too: a couple of prompt books belonging to Garrick; one of Edmund Kean's from when he starred opposite his son Charles; some commemorative programs, as well as personal correspondence between actors; copies of plays annotated by John Gielgud, and a couple that once belonged to Gielgud's great-aunts, Dame Ellen Terry and her second-fiddle sister, Kate. Trover hesitated, thinking. Also some handwritten notes from Paul Robeson's 1930 London *Othello*, which had he attempted it in the United States could well have ended in more murders than in all of Shakespeare.

"It's so eclectic," Cecelia said. "Is there a system to it?"

"It's what I could get my hands on."

"That's a kind of system, I guess."

Trover laughed. "A costly one. I went about it exactly backwards. I started out buying mostly first editions by writers I knew, or knew of, when I was at the university. Nobody was collecting them, so it seemed like somewhere I could plant my flag. I should have listened to Miss Brown, who used to run the university's rare book room. Now here I am, thirty years later. Canadian titles are still dirt cheap, but if you're after Renaissance London, good luck. Institutions own most of it and the only way to liberate anything really interesting is to pay somebody off, or threaten them. When I was much younger, I was outbid twice at auction for a folio. This one I ransomed from a bankrupt lord who shied from the auction house cut. Which was just dandy with me. I much prefer the sanity of a private understanding to the hysteria of public auctions. All of that *which of you doth love us most.*"

"You know, I gave a seminar just a few weeks ago on *Lear*."

"You don't say."

Cecelia leafed unhurriedly through the folio, pausing here and there to read a passage of greyish text. "It's so beautiful," she said.

"Only if you haven't seen any others." Trover sighed. "The binding is tight and in good condition, but it's not original—it's not even the first rebinding, and the spine has been re-backed. It's also been trimmed pretty savagely, so it's a smallish copy. And, of course, it's incomplete. Some of the pages are substitutes from a Second Folio, and most of the preliminaries are facsimiles. Good ones, but still."

"I didn't realize a person could be disappointed in a First Folio." Cecelia laboured to see the deficiencies. "Is the Fisher's copy better?"

"Oh yes. Much finer, I'm afraid. The 'Rosebud' copy. Even its flaws are more beautiful. I've often been quite jealous of it, in fact." Trover took back the volume and returned it to its shelf. Then he directed her to the writing desk and indicated that she should sit. "But it does make me feel better to know that they have nothing quite like this."

He gestured at the grey box on the desktop. It was wide and thin but unremarkable, and Cecelia, having been drawn to the more overtly displayed of Trover's collectibles, had more or less overlooked it when she entered. He slid it in front of her.

At his invitation, she lifted the lid and found within a folded piece of vellum that, when she opened it, made her catch her breath. She knew she ought to play it cool. However, in the time it took to get her head around the situation, she had been just sitting there mutely. Now, no matter what she pretended, be it surprise or ignorance or even curiosity, she knew it would be unconvincing—and, anyway, she was too stunned for words.

"Gotcha," Trover whispered.

"It's yours," Cecelia said at last, stupidly. "You knew."

In answer Trover only smiled, the proud father of his dearest things, and Cecelia saw in his clear, proud smile with sudden clarity that this had not been a free invitation, nor of her own deserving. Her intuition had been truer than she realized, and it now began to eat at her like a subtle worm, hungry and seeking out her centre. She had not been invited here, to sit before the indenture, because she had attracted someone's attention. Instead it was a chance convergence of discrete trajectories. The document, her friendship with Noah, the disastrous interview with Handly that left her in need of a bolstering, which Noah had sensed and tried to supply—these had set in motion a series of off-stage events that had led her to the private library of Owen Trover, at a garden party. It was hard to ignore the extent of her own irrelevance to the outcome of these accidents. She felt like the victim of a peeping Tom. The lidless box might as well have been an open window and all her nakedness discovered.

"So this is why I was invited to your party. Because somebody couldn't keep their mouth shut."

"You're less surprised than I imagined," Trover answered. He seemed disappointed.

"I'm surprised you have it here. I thought it was the university's."

"Yes, they thought that too. But I don't need them to babysit it for me."

Trover reached for the box and Cecelia released the indenture, which folded back in on itself. He placed it atop the glass case.

"I might let them have it eventually, but not yet. Not until I've had a chance to enjoy it. And not until I've been completely thorough. You've seen it before. What's your take on it?"

Cecelia did not answer immediately.

"Don't play foolish," he said. "What did you do after Ms. Curtis showed it to you?"

She didn't like how he stood there expectantly, as though he enjoyed putting her on the spot. "I read Schoenbaum's *Documentary Life*," she said a last. "Then I read everything he referenced that I could get my hands on. Then a couple of biographies."

"And now you know exactly as much as anyone, which is next to nothing. So, like I said, what's your take?"

Irritated at his insistence, she quickly recapitulated the facts as she remembered them. How in 1603, or thereabouts, Shakespeare took a room with Christopher Mountjoy—a French Huguenot and a maker of tyres and wigs on Silver Street—and got caught up in a domestic drama. How Mountjoy's daughter and his apprentice, Stephen Belott, fell in love and Mrs. Mountjoy asked Shakespeare to encourage the match, shortly after which, they married and agreed to live with the Mountjoys and keep working for the family business. Later there was a falling out between Mountjoy and Belott over money, accommodations and, probably, the usual stress of children living with their parents after they're old enough not to. Maybe young Stephen forgot to replace the silver wire he used. Maybe Mountjoy got tired of hearing the newlyweds consummating their marriage at all hours of the night. Maybe the two men never liked each other, which might explain why Mrs. Mountjoy asked for Shakespeare's help in the first place. Then, after Mrs. Mountjoy died, the Belotts moved out, Mountjoy disowned his daughter and refused to pay them the dowry he promised, and in 1612 Belott sued him for it. Shakespeare was called to testify for the Belotts, but when he was asked how much money Mountjoy had promised, he claimed he couldn't remember and, as a result, the Belotts got next to nothing.

This was discovered at the start of the century by the Wallaces, an American scholar and his wife, among old court records. But this indenture made the whole, strange story even stranger. Why would Shakespeare leave so much money? It wasn't just a lot of money—it was roughly the difference between what Belott said he was promised and what he actually received. Did he feel guilty for forgetting the amount and letting down a young couple whose match he helped make? But then why not leave the money to Belott himself? Unless Belott had done something to alienate him. In one of the court documents, both Mountjoy and Belott are described as *débauchéz*. Maybe Shakespeare was on better terms with Missus Mountjoy than with Mister, and maybe it was the same with the Belotts. If she had to, Cecelia would guess that Shakespeare refused to take the side of either debauched Frenchman, and the only way to help the missus and not the mister was to leave money for their son, whom Shakespeare likely knew from when he lived with them in Silver Street. By the time Belott died in 1646 he was on his second wife. His will makes mention of several daughters but no son, which means either that the son was dead, or was thought dead, or that they were estranged.

"It's impossible to know if the sum was ever paid," Cecelia said, "but given the indenture wasn't destroyed and it wasn't accompanied by an acquittance, I'd put my money on the son dying before he could claim it. Maybe he caught the plague, or a drunkard's knife. It could also be a forgery, despite your authenticators. It's a large sum. It's hard to believe Shakespeare would pay it out of his own pocket. But then again, it seems like he and Mrs. Mountjoy were close, and it seems both had questionable notions of marital fidelity. She seems to have had an affair with the neighbourhood grocer, and Shakespeare could be tempted, if the sonnets are to be believed. But there's no way of knowing. That's my take."

Trover's eyes narrowed and with unsettling stillness examined her. Then he perched on the corner of the desk. "When the archivists were going through the mystery boxes, they found it slipped between the pages of a ledger. They couldn't read it, so they called an acquaintance of mine at King's College, who called me when he realized what it was. He owed me a favour. So I called up the company president, and told him I was a professor of history researching pre–World War II economics in Canada. I paid him about five times what the boxes were worth, which was a tiny fraction of what that indenture alone could fetch. He was just happy to be rid of it all."

Trover smiled the small, satisfied smile of a child who has outman- oeuvred his parents—who, harbouring a desire to stay indoors when they have told him to go play in the yard, commits a transgression just serious enough to secure his own grounding—a quiet smile of cunning superiority.

"So now I have an indenture with Shakespeare's name on it, and a collection of other documents that might shed some light on it, and the few people who know about it, including the authenticators, have agreed to keep quiet for the next twelve months."

"I don't understand," Cecelia said.

"Think of it, Ms. Lines: really new discoveries aren't just his- toric—they're historical, as in, they're history. This indenture isn't the best thing that's been found in eighty years. It's the only thing. It's absolutely singular. Now it's mine, and no one can take it away from me, but imagine if this little foundling here had a brother or a sister out there somewhere. If there's an even greater discovery just waiting, and this indenture or the boxes it came with can point the way … To be candid, Ms. Lines, I want it. But it will take some finesse. It would be best if any investigations were made secretly. That way, if anything is found maybe I can make a deal, ideally before the owner knows what he's got. It's the only way. If something turns up, if it's important in any way … if the people at Harvard or Yale find out, it will all be for nothing. Not even I have the resources to compete with them. Word will get out eventually. You found out, after all, despite my explicit instructions. No doubt the ship will spring other leaks. But if there's anything in those archives, well, twelve months will be enough of a head start. If there isn't, then twelve months might as well be twelve years. It's back to random chance at that point, and the authenticators, and anyone else who's interested, might as well have a go. What I need right now is someone to inventory it all and see if it leads anywhere. And to do it quietly. I've arranged a research assistantship, if you're interested."

Cecelia said nothing immediately, but that too said plenty.

"You seem unhappy," Trover observed.

"I let myself think I'd done something right to get invited to this party, but it turns out it was just dumb luck. It's a little embarrassing."

"You know, the Ancient Greeks believed luck was part of a person's character. It was luck I got the indenture. And even if luck got you in the door, you kept yourself from getting shown out."

Cecelia avoided his eyes. Instead, she gazed vaguely at the shelves. From the muffled light at the windows she sensed the sun was setting, and she began to be aware again, as she had not been since she entered the library, of the sounds of the party still going on beyond the door. The music and merriment had both grown louder and more agitated.

"Twelve months doesn't seem like much time," she said at last.

"Time enough to launch a career."

He said it pointedly, and Cecelia experienced a great lumping, involuntary spasm of excitement.

"In nine years," Trover said, "the Wallaces examined more than a million records in an unreadable script. I'm guessing a couple of months is enough time for you to get through a few thousand written mostly in clean cursive."

Cecelia opened her mouth to accept the offer, but stopped herself as she was taken by a sudden inspiration. She demurred instead. "It's a tempting offer, but I don't know anything about archives. I wouldn't even know how to begin."

Trover's eyes studied her. His gaze was forthright and piercing; it was a look of calculated penetration, and Cecelia was relieved that a disarming smile followed apace. "Perhaps you're thinking of the young man who let you in on my little secret? Yes, I think that would be a sensible arrangement. You're friends. He knows how to work with archives. And he's recently been laid off, I understand."

"He does need a job." She blushed to hear the indelicacy of her own explanation, which Trover's shrewdness had rushed her into.

"It's not in my power to get him his job back, if that's what you're hoping. And he's not a student, so I can't drum up an RAship for him too. But suppose I contact Mr. Lamarck myself and offer him a stipend to assist you. I imagine that would satisfy everyone's concerns."

Cecelia felt herself give in. Unwinding, she experienced a surprising little burst of confidence. It shot up through her, blossoming like an adrenaline flower.

ᴜ

In the entry hall James Milburn and another junior staffer, Cory Hayes, had scuttled into the vicinity of David Fredericks. He was talking with Louisa Peck.

"It's just that books aren't people," Louisa said.

"You're not wrong," Fredericks agreed. "Everyone gives in their own way. Your firm has opened up all sorts of new directions for our capital campaigns. After everything you've done, you know I would never twist your arm."

"I know you wouldn't, but I was wondering. Do you have anything in advanced cancer research that I could support? Not something generic. Something really promising."

"That would be wonderful. Can I give you a call at the office next week? I'll have to ask one of my colleagues for details, but I know there are people at the Faculty of Medicine your support could really do something for."

Milburn and Hayes drew back from the conversation.

"How does he do that?" Hayes asked, glancing back.

"I know," Milburn said. "I beetle around this party for nearly three hours and can't get anyone to give a shit. He has a few drinks and a good time and they're throwing it at him."

"It comes out so naturally," Hayes said, still watching. "How do you even learn to fake sincerity like that?"

Milburn sneered like he'd eaten a small turd. "Forget it. Let's just try to enjoy the rest of the party. Maybe we'll fall into something. People are sure to be looser about it now that the ambulance is gone."

"What was that about, anyway?"

"Heart attack, I heard somebody say. Not anyone here, though. On the street, I think."

Hayes contemplated the consequences. "God, can you imagine having to segue from that?"

"If there's a way," Milburn said, "I bet Fredericks knows it."

ច

Back at the bar Robert Heiden checked his watch. George Bleury was still going strong.

"Every time she stays home for her sick kid, every time she talks about getting flex time, she tries to make it my problem. And now she's bitching me out about her equity settlement. Well, fuck her. I called payroll. I told them not to hurry. She'll get it when she gets it."

"George, can we please get back to the pitch? We can't just hire a headhunter and wait. We need to have a package ready, with incentives. Maybe if we consolidate our synergies we can leverage some of our resources ..."

"You know, ninety percent of this job is people," Bleury said, oblivious. "Take the Jews, for instance. I've got a friend in textiles and he can't grow his business 'cause they run the market like a cabal. It's this far and no farther, he says."

Heiden stood there stunned. "You didn't just say that."

"Don't get me wrong. I'm the first person to be understanding and all that, but they're ruthless. And organized. It's some kind of cultural trait. That's why so many end up being doctors or lawyers."

"Six million in death camps and you're saying the Jews are ruthless."

"You know, the Holocaust is one of the great lies of Western history. Don't misunderstand me, I'm not saying it didn't happen. But do you know who funded it? The wealthy Jewish families that owned the banks. They funded the Nazi party and the Bolsheviks. They did it to destabilize Europe and grow their Zionism. That's what the Holocaust was. Rich Jews killing poor ones to establish the State of Israel."

"That's the most willfully hateful and stupid thing I've ever heard you say. And that's a competitive category."

"No, there's this book about it. What's it called? I forget who wrote it, but it's amazing the way he lays it all out."

"You know I'm Jewish, right?"

"I'm saying this all wrong. Let me leverage some more whisky for you, just a little. To sharpen the saw? I mean, it's crap whisky—you need to go to Scotland and pay three hundred dollars and then you'll see what shit whisky you've been drinking all your life—"

"Maybe you've leveraged enough whisky, you anti-Semite."

"Maybe you can leverage my cock—sorry, Bob. Sorry. I didn't mean that. But it's not racist. They just happen to be Jews. I mean, I'd never say this to just anyone, but I know you'll hear me out."

After the dimness of the library, the full glare of the entry hall made Cecelia feel as though she were spotlighted—that and the attention Trover was encouraging from a pair of gentlemen, a father and son, to whom she had just been introduced. The three of them were fanned out before her like a proscenium. She found herself invigorated by thoughts of the indenture and, when Trover described her as one of the university's bright young things, she felt reflected in her complexion the glow of his praise.

"I've only just discovered her tonight," Trover said.

The elder gentleman shook hands with Cecelia. Trover had introduced him as Richard Paris, founder and CEO of Mickle Food Mart Companies Limited.

"One of the university's young scholars. Shakespeare, isn't it? She's just starting graduate work, but I expect it won't be long until she hits her mark."

"You'll kill me with much cherishing," Cecelia said.

A pause in the air, a little awkwardness. The younger Paris, Jason Paris, giving her a good looking over. He was rather good-looking himself, though a little too aware of it. Swept back hair, sleek narrow shoes, the trim cut of his suit, even the oblique knotting of his tie: his entire look conveyed an urbane and dashing disposition suggestive of speed. It was as though he consulted *louche* in a thesaurus before getting out of bed in the morning. Still, he was very good looking.

"Shakespeare. Pfft!" he said, with the reserve of a whispered fart. "He was an imposter, you know. Just a front for the Duke of Something-or-other. I bet they don't teach you that in school."

Cecelia had not considered before how much like refinement boredom and condescension could appear, but she considered it now. "Based on the historical record," she said to young Paris, "I think most scholars would agree that there's every reason to believe Shakespeare wrote the plays."

"No peasant could write about what he wrote about."

"His father was a glover, an alderman, and even a bailiff. That's hardly the same thing as a peasant."

"Fine, but he didn't even go to university. Seems obvious to me."

"He went to the Stratford grammar school," Cecelia said, "which was more demanding than some undergraduate degrees. What's your degree in?"

"Now listen—"

"Honestly, I could do a whole soliloquy on the subject, but I'll save you the trouble of listening to it. The conspiracy theories begin and end with snobbery. There it is."

Another pause in the air, also awkward, but of a different sort.

"Well then," Paris said, breezily. "I think I'll cast off. I heard a rumour there's a really good bottle of Scotch at the bar, if you know to ask for it." With a vaguely aimed bowing of his head, he backed away and departed.

"His degree was in outdoor recreation," Richard Paris said. "He likes to ski."

His eyebrows rose, just a little, and no doubt unconsciously, but from this Cecelia inferred that he was experiencing again a mild and chronic disappointment. Nonetheless his demeanour towards her remained gentle and kind, and she felt the need to apologize.

"Sorry. I have a sharp tongue," she said. "Sometimes I forget to mind it."

Mr. Paris smiled in momentary contemplation. "I think Shakespeare likely had a good ear, discipline, and humaneness. In my experience that combination is more uncommon than good fortune in one's choice of parents." He paused, and his eyes followed his son, who was negotiating his way towards the bar. "Well, perhaps I'll join him for that Scotch and then we'll get going. Cecelia, it was very nice meeting you. Good night, Owen."

Cecelia was fearful she had embarrassed her host. Once Mr. Paris was far enough removed, she apologized again. "I'm sorry. I should have softened it. It would have been more polite to say it's hard to see past our prejudices." Then, correcting herself further, she added, "I mean, for any of us."

"The theory is nonsense. I would have said so myself, but I thought it would be more fun to let you do it."

"I embarrassed his father too," she said, determined.

"I doubt it. Richard was a Rhodes Scholar. If he was embarrassed, it wasn't you that did it."

From where they stood in the hall, Cecelia, now at liberty to gaze, could see through the wide doorway and across the living room. At the far end she saw Janet in conversation with the imposing beauty she had first seen gliding to Trover's side on the balustrade. The conversation appeared more than casual, and their postures less than dispassionate. For two people who had only just met, they were being surprisingly familiar. Janet gazed fixedly, however to Cecelia it seemed that the woman, without ever quite ignoring Janet, was also keeping her dark falcon eyes a little on the bias. Without other company, Cecelia and Trover were now exposed and the woman quickly spotted them. Assured that they were watching, she then leaned towards Janet and said something with an air of covertness, while also feathering her fingers through Janet's hair.

"Isn't that your date?" Cecelia asked.

"Indeed," Trover said. "Isn't that yours?"

"Not exactly."

The woman's eyes cut swiftly across the room. Laughing, she placed her hand on Janet's arm. Trover, unruffled, stood watching. "I get the impression she's staging a spectacle for me. But it's no worse than I deserve. I have been rather inconstant in my affections."

"Herodotus had a saying: 'Never trust a woman who wiggles her bottom; she's after your barn.' There's some more Greek philosophy for you."

"That's some good counsel. However, now that I've seen her flirting with your friend, it would be rude of me not to be a little jealous. Cecelia, I'll have my assistant get in touch soon. He'll set up access to the collection and answer any questions you have. After that, you'll have complete freedom to work. I'll be entirely hands off. And, of course, you'll keep this quiet …"

"Locked in the closet," Cecelia said, tap-tapping her forehead.

"Then enjoy the rest of the party. It's been a pleasure."

With a mock flourish and a nod of lordly deference, Trover concluded. Then he crossed the room to insert himself between their flirting companions. Cecelia watched him make a show of it, as though he had been summoned to do so. A few moments later, Janet was on her own and, to judge by her slight unsteadiness, a little buzzed from the alcohol, or perhaps the sexual energy. Likely both. Now alone, she began to search the room dazedly with her eyes, but Cecelia quickly scooted back into the bar for another drink. She wasn't ready for that just yet.

With the heat of the afternoon now mostly dissipated, the distribution of the sexes had reversed itself: to escape the growing chill the women were indoors mainly, and the men, at last able to display their suits comfortably, mainly on the patios. Here and there they were gathered into little assemblies, parliaments and prides one might say, flocks and trains, droves and dissimulations, schools and murders, rookeries and ostentations, lamentations, shrewdnesses, knots and knobs and other assembled veneries.

In the living room alone were several. Students admiring from afar a granddame of national literature: *That book changed my life. Which book? I like her newest even better. Oh, The Gleeful Cruellist?* And by the windows some professors gossiping like schoolgirls: *But he's your student. No, he was my student, now he just lives with me. God, what's this music now, is this hip hop? It's the Chemical Brothers. How do you—He's not the only one learning a thing or two from our arrangement.* Over by the Riopelle, two men just past mid-life, talking: *You mean Melinda, I took her out a few times. What was she like? I got so excited the first time I just exploded all over the place; it was like, what's that stuff you spray on ceilings? Spackle? Spackle, exactly; she was covered in it. Wow. I know. Would your wife ever let you? God, no. No, mine neither.* And eavesdropping nearby, two women acquainted with one of the wives in question: *She's not all that frigid, is she? I don't know, but would you blame her?* All of these and other snatches of conversation, Cecelia could hardly believe she was overhearing.

The patio was likewise populated. A woman angling away from the radio star: *But I don't want to date you; I want to work for you.* And that pair of students from before: *Well, I think Deconstruction is stupid! That's because you're too stupid to understand it. Then maybe we should just break up!* And the flat-chested young woman, she of the perfect legs, with a couple of her friends: *He thought he was the one who initiated it? That's so cute. But the way he looked when his wife whistled at him; my dog had that look right before we had him fixed. Still, he's pretty handsome; how much money do you think he makes?*

And yet: notwithstanding all of the vinolent confabulation, there was at least a show of civility in most quarters. A number of older men and women were making subdued but earnest farewells to acquaintances and friends; several groups of pleasantly reserved guests, relieved by the slow unravelling of the afternoon's humidity, were hanging around for a final drink or two; a number of gentlemen were smoking, and a few women too, and also the pair of well-tailored young lawyers, who with fat cigars between their fingers and showy gestures, were sewing sweet smelling filaments of tobacco smoke into the air. Despite the endless parade of overt luxury, you could almost get used to it over the course of a couple of hours, Cecelia thought, and no longer be so awed—by the bespoke suits, and fine silk ties, and couture dresses, and the expensive necklets, watches, and wine—except for how the many fragments of conversations, meaningless to the uninitiated, from time to time would remind you where you were, and that you didn't really belong.

It was just shy of seven and the night was coming on now; there remained only a smudge of sunset across the soft blue of the sky. The patio was lit mainly by hurricane lamps and the glow of the windows. Increasingly the scene was ornamented with little reflected flashes in people's wine and whisky glasses, and by their clinking, and more and more by the sounds of amiable, pizzicato chitchat. It had been amazing, a garner of influence and opportunity from which Trover had offered her a grain. She could not have scripted it more wondrously.

An old man lowered himself into a nearby chair. He seemed familiar and Cecelia thought maybe she had been vaguely aware of him for some time; perhaps he had been there off and on in that same chair all afternoon. He wore a suit that, though well cared for, was old and very rumpled, and a knitted necktie that, however neatly done, was monstrously unfashionable. He was also quiet and unassuming, both in speech and manner, and not exactly another of the assembled faux gentry. Cecelia might have recognized this had she not been so bewitched by all that she had seen and heard and, therefore, with casual disinterest, disregarded him. In other circumstances, with less on her mind, she might not have heard him as just another voice in the chorus of the privileged.

"It was touch and go there for a while with all that heat, but it's turned into a lovely evening," he said. When Cecelia didn't answer, he continued, "I see the women have moved indoors. People keep telling me I shouldn't make generalizations about the sexes, but I've never known a woman who didn't get cold in the evening. I hope you're not cold yourself."

"No, this is much better than the heat."

"I agree. I don't believe I've seen you here before."

"I've never been here before."

"It's marvellous, isn't it? I've lived in this neighbourhood my whole life, since before the boarding school relocated, so I'm a bit of a fixture, you see. Owen's such a nice young man. Not like a lot of these upstarts. A lot of spoiled children, I think. No interest in anybody but themselves, except to have an audience and put on a show. But Owen is a gentleman. He makes everyone feel that they're the centre of attention. Even an old man like myself is made to feel necessary. He was the first person to greet me when I arrived, you know. And he does it without pandering or condescending. He has the real thing: authority. He knows who he is. It wouldn't surprise me if he's still entirely sober. And I can't say the same for anyone else. Not even me. Of course, nobody notices an old man's inebriation, so long as he restrains himself. A gentleman's manners should be moderate in proportion to his intoxication. I myself have become increasingly unremarkable this evening."

Cecelia saw that he had a small measure of whisky in his glass.

"You seem to be one of the students," the old man continued. "Is that why you were invited?"

"I was invited because luck is part of a person's character."

"What a coincidence. So was I. What luck, you might wonder? Well, my family had a lot of money and, now that I'm the only one left, I have a lot of money." He leaned a little towards her. "Between you and me, they're hoping I'll leave it to the university. I think that's why they made me an emeritus professor too. It's supposed to be a fine honour, but all you really get is they let you keep your office. Or an office. And now that everyone I knew there is retired or dead, I don't have much use for it. I think that secretly they would like me to give it back, one way or another, if you understand me. You know, you remind me of someone from a long time ago. I've had thousands of students over the years and sadly I've forgotten most of them, but there's something about your eyes. Perhaps your mother?"

Just then, Janet emerged from the French doors and, seeing Cecelia, hurried towards her.

"No, my mother never went to school," Cecelia said.

"Where have you been?" Janet asked. "You disappeared for ages."

"I was with our host, watching him be jealous of you and his arm candy. The way she was looking at you made me think of a bird of prey." Cecelia made the remark casually. She did not see that when her friend turned away that it was not to survey the patio scene but to conceal that she was blushing.

"That's Professor Aliya Saqr. She teaches history of science. So, not really arm candy. She's out at Vic. I'm surprised you don't recognize her."

"Did you ever track down your lawyers?" Cecelia asked, changing the subject.

"That information is privileged."

With a nod Cecelia drew her friend's attention to where they were standing, smoking. The pair of them were taking draws so long and deep and (for cigar-smoking) awkwardly inexpert that you could be forgiven for finding it—as Cecelia and Janet did—more than a little suggestive.

"I tried to get their attention a few times, but they seemed more interested in each other than in striking up a conversation—I guess that explains it." Janet studied their extended lip action. "Wow. Even if they're not gay, I'm not going out with a guy who does that to his cigar."

On the lower patio something was happening, some commotion, that interrupted their conversation. A young woman was fishing for her bottle in the water—she even grazed its swaying neck with her fingers briefly—but then it veered suddenly and cruelly away, and thence she fell: first into a reach, then into a lunge, then into a panic, then into the pool. Fits of laughter erupted among the spectators below, mesmerized by the hilarity of their friend, now soaked and paddling like a mink with the bottle bobbing wildly at her side. It was time for Cecelia and Janet to be going.

They left the patio. The electronic music was not only louder inside, but louder than at any other point since they'd arrived. It gave Cecelia's steps a little lift. Janet asked who the old man was she'd been talking to, but Cecelia did not hear, nor was she especially listening. In the entry hall the acrobats were readying themselves, but to judge from the few guests gathering to watch, and those few remaining in the other rooms, this would be their last performance. Cecelia considered staying, but she was too overloaded to be very tempted, and a glance at Janet confirmed that she too was ready to make her exit.

Leaving behind the dwindling festivities, they hurried to the street where several black cars were queued and waiting. At the head of the line, beside a streetlight and an orphaned, junked out shopping cart, a driver signalled with an open door for them to come. They slipped right in and gave Janet's East Danforth address. As the air was cool now, and the humidity so much abated, they left the windows down to feel the breeze; and as Cecelia slumped back, she felt the expansiveness of her prospects with growing anticipation, as though an invisible hand had released her from its grasp, like the unlacing of a corset or the removal of a brace, the knots and folds of tension in her body unfurling and, for now, undone. The sunroof was open too, and in her state of giddy relief she felt like bursting through the hatch and disclosing her good fortune to the sky, the moon, to baffled pedestrians, to one and all, but the hypnotic passing of streetlights overhead lulled her into well-heeled contentment. She wondered how long it would last.

7

The glass and whitewashed lengths of steel of the galleria were supposed to be reminiscent of a forest canopy, but sitting inside on the steps of the Bay-Wellington Tower and gazing around him at the bustling, frenzied severity of men and women in their business attire, Noah thought the long white parabolic struts reminded him more of ribs than trees, and he imagined he and everyone within the atrium had been swallowed into the belly of a whale. He felt a childish desire to pull a fire alarm and watch the leviathan vomit onto Bay Street some of the teeming avarice that wriggled around inside. Alternatively, he could wait half an hour. The business day was nearly spent and the towers would soon empty. The occupants would head into rush hour with tens of thousands of the city's other career commuters.

Noah's day was just getting started. A man named Rowse had called the day before about a job that, mysteriously, was at the Fisher but not for the Fisher. He had said little more, only asking Noah to meet him at the foot of the tower at four thirty. However, Noah suspected it had something to do with the indenture, which had been the subject, albeit within a tiny circle, of several gossipy conversations on St. George Street. More than that he couldn't guess. Nonetheless, he felt the pleasurable anxiety of opportunity upon him. He had not worried very much at first when his contract had not been renewed, especially as it afforded him more time for Felix, but he was well aware the pogey wouldn't last forever.

Noah distinguished from the ambient noise of the atrium the crisp approach of shoes behind him. Turning his head, he saw a trim man with a black notebook in one hand. Noah stood and turned to greet him. "Mr. Rowse?"

"Mr. Lamarck," said Mr. Rowse. They shook hands. "I hope I haven't kept you waiting. If you'll come up to the office, Mr. Trover will be able to see you shortly."

Noah followed Trover's assistant to the bank of elevators behind the information desk. The silence in which they waited Noah at first construed as negligence, but then he changed his mind and decided it was correctness, studied and perfected. Rowse must have felt it was not only appropriate, but also needful that they discuss nothing in the public spaces of the building. This was confirmed when, once they were alone in the elevator, Rowse explained that Cecelia, whom he believed Noah knew from the university, had been given a research assistantship to inventory and describe all the contents of the collection in which the indenture—of which Mr. Trover knew Noah was aware—was discovered. It was not an extensive collection, he said, but large enough to challenge someone unfamiliar with the technical aspects of archival practices, however intelligent she might otherwise be. Mr. Trover felt that Noah's experience would be useful to her. Trover also hoped that, as Noah was no longer employed by the Fisher, he would be less inclined to throw any more grist to the rumour mill. He and Cecelia were to use the most scrupulous discretion. In the event the collection pointed the way to anything interesting, any publicity might cost Mr. Trover a considerable fortune. Their secrets were, therefore, to be jealously guarded. They would have to sign NDAs, Rowse said, but Mr. Trover was offering to pay him for his services as a consulting scholar for the duration of the project. There was never any question of Noah's answer.

When the elevator doors opened, Rowse steered Noah down a long hall and into a waiting room. A pair of double doors at one end opened and a woman exited. Through them Noah saw the rich interior of Trover's office, the large, expensive-looking desk, and behind it the man himself talking loudly on the phone. The woman turned to close the doors, but stopped, instructed by Trover's distant, waving arm to leave it be. Rowse introduced Noah to Ms. Li, who acknowledged him with a professionalism that was at once respectful and distant. After returning to her desk she made a point of ignoring him. Rowse then invited Noah to sit by the open doors. Inside, Trover was agitated.

"Don't say we're subtracting a third of the system. Say that we're adding two heavy hitters. Tell him we need to pool our resources so we get too big to fail—I'm not disagreeing, but capital markets are in disarray and there are deep concerns about the economy and systematic risk. There's a crisis coming and now's the time to strike. If we don't, the big boys in the foreign markets are going to overrun us and it will cost us even more, I can promise you. I'm talking branch cuts and closures, layoffs—Don't talk to me about conflicts of interest. Anyone with an investment account or shares with the banks is in a conflict of interest. And do you know how many pensions are publicly traded? Tony, what do you think will happen when people see the value of their nest eggs shrinking like your scrotum in a cold shower?—Exactly, so get it done."

After Trover hung up the phone, Rowse directed Noah to enter. The entire office was windows, and beyond them many of the city's towers swung like trees in the wind. Noah had never seen them from this vantage. Trover was at the bar pouring a drink into a low glass.

"You must be Noah," he said.

They shook hands and Trover offered Noah a drink, but he declined. Trover said he hoped Noah would not mind if he partook; after the day he had had, he felt the need for an indulgence. Then the two men sat in armchairs facing each other across what Noah would have called a living room or lounge, had he not been in an office building.

Swirling his drink gently, Trover said, "I assume Clement explained to you the contours of the offer. Do you have any questions?"

"No, I think I got it all. I'm happy to start as soon as you like."

"Before discussing your compensation?" Trover leaned back, affecting an air of magnanimous beneficence towards Noah. "If you don't mind, Noah, I'll give you this advice. Never agree to anything without first negotiating all of the terms. You should always walk into an interview knowing what you're worth and knowing what you're willing to settle for. Then you're in a position to judge the offer, which you should ask for before you give too much away. By already agreeing to do the job, you've put yourself in my hands. You've lost your leverage."

"Except you got my name from someone at the library, right? That means you knew my situation before you called. Which means I didn't have much leverage to begin with."

Trover acknowledged this with a small nod. His eyes narrowed, and he smiled faintly. Noah understood: he was being studied. "How long will the work last?"

"At least four months, I imagine. Twelve at the absolute most," Trover said. "But the sooner you finish the better, so long as you're thorough. It's exacting work. It has to be letter perfect."

"Salaried or hourly?"

"There will be no formal contract, if that's what you mean, but it won't be hourly. I'll give you a flat stipend, deposited biweekly."

"If there's no formal contract, then I assume this is all off the books? You won't be reporting it?"

Trover cocked his head and his smile grew. "Now that's an astute question."

Beneath Trover's continued appraisal was something—not exactly respect, yet indicative of re-estimation. "If it's off the books," Noah said, "then I would prefer cash payments that I could pick up at the library."

"Then cash it is," Trover said. Then he added, "And you can continue to collect your unemployment, for as long as it lasts."

It was something more than an observation. Instead of responding right away, Noah found himself wondering about Trover's age. His lean, athletic frame made him seem no more than forty, but the lines of his face, especially around the eyes, suggested he was older, and the eyes themselves especially were misleading. They were bright and energetic, certainly, but they were calculating and rapacious too, hungry. Noah would have to be calculating too. There was a pen and notepad on the table between them.

"I don't know much about business, but I think this is a case of fast, good, and cheap: pick any two." Noah leaned forward. He wrote a number on the pad and handed it over. "That's enough to cover rent and living expenses, and a little to set aside. If you think it's unreasonable, you could try to find someone else, but that will take time. Also, I realize my expertise is limited, and you could find others more qualified. But you say you're looking to keep this quiet. I already know about it, I know Cecelia, I can do the work, and I can start right away. Under other circumstances, you could easily do better, but right here and now, I'm the right choice. All I want is a fair wage, and a guaranteed minimum of six months, however long it takes."

"Be careful, Noah, I'm beginning to like you," Trover said. He swirled his drink and made a show of consideration. "I think we can agree on these terms, but I'll also be insisting that you keep me up to date periodically."

"Of course."

"What I mean is, Cecelia will be writing up reports on your progress, but I want you to quietly look them over and then, without telling her, let me know if there's anything she's forgotten, or perhaps left out."

There was something in his tone, in the way he said *left out*. Noah was not sure that he understood entirely, nor entirely sure that what he did understand he liked.

"As incredible as it may seem, this is the kind of thing people will sell out their friends and family for. Some people would even kill for it—mad people, certainly, obsessives and delusionals—but people nonetheless who, if push came to shove, would brain you with a shovel and not think twice. There are whole books about the mad and devious and criminal things people have done searching for Shakespeare's remains."

"I'm sure she wouldn't—"

"I agree, but I have to insist."

Noah hesitated. As he did, Trover sat up straight and with a sharp jerk adjusted his suit. He studied Noah momentarily.

"You strike me as a man of conscience," Trover said, his eyes unwavering. "Cecelia's your friend and you don't want to hide anything from her. I can respect that. And she strikes me as someone sensitive about manipulation, however benign or well-intentioned, so I understand if you feel uncomfortable hiding this from her. But I'll tell you bluntly: I don't trust in people. I trust in self-interest. If you want something, get it yourself and then hang on to it. That's what everyone else is doing. And if you need someone to do something for you, make it worth their while. Give them a reason to. I want you to corroborate her work for me. It's non-negotiable. But you know this is a good deal for you, so if your conscience stings, just remember: it's only a lie of omission, if you could even call it that, nothing your nose would stretch over. As long as you fill me in periodically, everyone will get what they want."

Money under the table was one thing; satisfying Trover's stipulation was quite another. Noah turned his gaze towards the windows, beyond which the towers of glass and steel stood swaying. Later, he would not be able to remember how long he resisted. Much longer than he imagined, but less long than he wished. Weighed down by his financial and other obligations, at last he accepted; and though by his course and freight he now risked running himself aground on more than shallow veniality, he tried to believe instead that he could navigate safely. The impressure of Trover's hand was firm and sure. It said don't worry, this will be a cinch.

8

The syncopation of their footsteps, the dull rubber one-two of his long strides and the more rapid click-cl-clack of Cecelia's heeled boots, kept uneven time in Noah's mind as they walked south from Bloor Street, along a stretch of sidewalk that skirted the length of a large park. Women in fall jackets were pushing strollers. Through the trees he thought he heard the shouts of youthful conflict and the clatter of hockey sticks. In the slight hollow of a baseball field several children were chasing a soccer ball, and a small dog was chasing them. Their schoolbags lay in a nearby heap, next to which a young girl in a heavy sweater sat reading. Cecelia had grown quiet as they neared her parents' home. Noah had never visited this part of the city.

"You grew up here," he said. He pointed at the children. "Were you the one with the ball or the book?"

"Sometimes one, sometimes the other."

At the next corner they turned away from the park and down a side street. On the north side, the houses stood on a small embankment, their large windows looking down on the houses adjacent. In the sky overhead hung a pearl-white moon, and only a nervy blush of sun remained. Cecelia turned up a steep driveway of interlocking brick and Noah followed a few steps behind. The lawn, though steeply pitched, was nonetheless well and evenly cut. In raised garden beds, plants had been cleared or cut back, and a few well-shaped rose bushes were staked and freshly mulched, burlap-ready for when the frost came. There was something just-so about this garden, so much unlike his grandmother's. Even the assiduous Virginia creeper was confined to small, allowed excesses here and there over the railway-tie planter boxes. Noah stopped and squatted to inspect it from the gardener's perspective. It was fine and orderly, if severe.

"You should see it in the summer," Cecelia said. "She's already dug up the less hardy plants. They're in the grow-op." Noah's raised brows conveyed his surprise and curiosity. "Don't get excited. It's not that kind. My dad set it up in the basement." Cecelia went ahead. She opened the screen door and knocked.

Noah stood from the planters and hurried to join her. "Do they keep it locked?" The neighbourhood seemed safe. The children in the park were more or less unsupervised.

Cecelia looked back over her shoulder, her expression wry or perhaps ironical. "I guess I don't have to knock." She reached for the handle, but it slipped her grasp. The door opened, swinging back to reveal a pair of large forearms and, appended to them, a tall, burly man in a T-shirt. "C!" With his large arms he dragged her over the threshold and into a bear hug; as he did, Noah saw how Cecelia's head drew back away from his shoulder. Her own arms, next to his so small and thin, unfolded only just enough to place her hands gently on his sides and no more. He released her and with some show examined her.

"You look great," he said. Then he wrenched his calloused hand around Noah's and introduced himself as Oliver.

Noah turned to Cecelia. "You didn't say you had a brother."

"Brother-in-law," Oliver said. Glancing at Cecelia, he burst into laughter. "Jesus. Good thing too!"

With a nod and a welcoming smile he invited them to follow into the front room, which lay to the right and through a double-wide doorway. Cecelia removed her jacket and Noah watched as she watched Oliver disappear. Then she bent over and started to unzip her boot. Noah began to remove his shoes. "He's nice." Cecelia only nodded. "Everything OK?"

"Yeah, fine," she said.

She smiled, but not without effort, and Noah smiled too, but not without curiosity.

"That almost sounded genuine," he said.

"He was supposed to be in Newfoundland until next week."

"What did he mean? 'Good thing too?'"

She didn't answer immediately. Half-bent and gull-like she stood one-footed, struggling with the zipper. Her soft dark hair trailed softly against Noah's hand. At last she heaved off her boot. "We used to date, that's all."

"Oh!" said Noah. "Sorry."

"No, it's fine," Cecelia said. Then she laughed. "Come on."

She led him into the front room, where Oliver and another man were in animated conversation over the sounds of a hockey game on the television. The elder, Cecelia's father, was on the couch, waving one hand violently and in the other steadying a beer bottle. The first words Noah heard clearly were, "Did you see that? Why doesn't somebody do something about that prick?"

"They did," Oliver said from a nearby chair. "Don't you remember?"

"That hardly counts. He should be skating around with his head in a sling."

"In a sling?" Oliver raised his beer to drink. His amused smile showed on either side of the bottle.

"Don't start with me," Cecelia's father replied. "In a sling, in a box, in a goddamn handbag: I don't care. As long as it's off his shoulders. That McCarty's a good one, but he didn't finish the job." He turned his head from the television to look directly at his son-in-law, a twist of derision on his lips. "You know, back in the day—"

"Back in the day?" Cecelia interrupted, walking up behind her father. "What does that even mean? What day?"

Cecelia's father looked back at his daughter. "What's wrong with that? I heard some of the kids at the shop saying it." Cecelia opened her mouth to respond, but he interrupted. "No you don't. You know the rule. You don't get to correct your father till you give him a hug."

"Alright," she said. She stooped over the back of the couch and put her arms around him.

When she released he turned more fully in his seat and looked her over. "Don't you look all prettied up." Then, turning to look at Noah, asked, "Who's your friend?"

"This is Noah."

"Call me Gary," he said and reached out his hand.

Like Oliver's, it was a calloused hand, but with sharp burrs of skin where the flesh had been carved and, in the saddle between forefinger and thumb, seemingly threaded. Like Oliver's it was strong. It felt like if he wanted he could screw it shut like a vise-grip. Gary let go and addressed his daughter.

"Go say hello to your mother. She and Rose are in the kitchen."

Cecelia looked at him a moment, and then at Noah. Squeezing Noah's arm gently, she turned and exited the living room. Gary turned his attention back to the television. Noah, unsure if he should sit or remain standing or maybe join Cecelia, placed his hands in his pockets and shifted his feet. On the television screen the play resumed, as did Gary.

"Back in the day ..." he said loudly.

He paused, listening. Noah looked to where Cecelia had gone, but there was no sign that she had heard. Gary shrugged and winked at him.

"You know anything about hockey?"

"Enough," Noah said.

Oliver caught Noah up: Claude Lemieux had followed one of the Leafs into the corner and taken out his strong leg, sending him sliding dangerously, feet first, into the boards. Both Oliver and Gary were understandably disgusted.

"Could have torn up his knee, easy. Or his ankle. Or dislocated his hip," Gary said. "Howe would have finished a guy like that. One-two-and-you're-through. Like he did Lou Fontinato. You guys are too young to know that fight."

"My father told me about it," Oliver said.

Gary didn't even look at him. He just shook his head. "Doesn't count. Hearing's not the same as seeing. I saw it." Eyes still on the game, Gary excitedly recounted how after a whistle Fontinato had tried to jump Howe behind the net, but it was Howe, always alert, who got the jump instead. "Remodelled his kitchen for him. Cheek, jaw, nose—smashed the plumbing right up. Lou was never the same after that. Two punches. That's all it took. Two and it was over. And Lou wasn't some nancy. He could throw 'em too. Back in the day, anyone who got into the league could fight and did his share."

"I call bullshit," Oliver said.

136

"What would you know? You weren't even alive when they still played real hockey. Gordie Howe hockey. Broad Street Bullies hockey."

"You mean like Bobby Clarke?" Noah asked, remembering his grandfather's deep and frequently expressed dislike for the Flyer captain.

"Yeah, didn't he mostly stand around yapping while Schultz and Mad Dog Kelly were laying out beatings?" Oliver said. He lifted his beer and drank.

"Yeah," Gary replied, "but he gave Kharlamov a limp in '72, so he gets a pass."

Oliver threw up his hands in frustration. "You're so full of shit sometimes, Gary. Anything I say, you just say I don't know what I'm talking about 'cause I wasn't around when the real stuff went down."

"And you act like the world's been around only since you set foot on it." Gary downed his beer, then added, "In fact, the next time you want to have an opinion about something, you should probably check with me first."

"So you're right 'cause you're an old fart."

"That's right."

Noah looked on in fascination at the remarkable double standards and arbitrary assertions of authority. A small part of him worried that the tension in the room, which had been until then light and amicable, was turning something close to hostile; nonetheless, he asked, "And when do we get to decide for ourselves?"

"When you talk to someone half your age, not double it," Gary said. His eyes were still on the television. "Or when you have kids of your own."

The image of his son flashed quickly in Noah's mind. He then saw Oliver open his mouth to speak, but quickly close it and instead stare at the television, or maybe not at the television but beyond it, maybe at the chair rail that encircled the room, or the ficus in the corner, or maybe only at the barren wall above the television screen.

"Sanctimonious ass," Oliver said finally.

Gary laughed and leaned towards Noah, as though to initiate a just-between-you-and-me, however one so loud that it was very much for Oliver's benefit and irritation. "If you want to know what someone's about, just rile him up a bit."

Then Oliver smiled, though grudgingly, and shook his head. Noah was uncertain how to respond. He felt himself broadcasting his uncertainty.

"Don't worry," Oliver said, "he hardly ever does it the first time he meets someone."

"I'm not against making an exception, though." Gary turned to Noah. "Go help yourself to a beer from the fridge and when you come back, if I don't like you any worse, maybe you'll get your turn."

As Noah set out to find the kitchen, behind him he heard Gary holler.

"Two by two, Noah. The more I drink, the more I like Oliver's company."

ਠ

The kitchen was at the rear of the house, through the dining room, from which it was separated by a swinging door. As he approached, Noah heard the muffled sounds of laughter. The door swung silently on its hinges when he opened it and inside he found the three women, their backs to him and unaware. Several dishes were keeping warm on the stove. A roast chicken was resting under foil on the counter and its aroma filled the room.

"I think it's great that he's on such good terms with her. I met Jenny Mills the other day coming out of a dollar store with three girls in tow. Not only is she not on good terms with her ex, he's not even making his support payments."

The young woman who was not Cecelia was speaking. She reached behind her neck with both hands and smoothed her reddish hair. She was taller than her sister by a hand or so and taller also, though by a smaller margin, than her redheaded mother. Noah wondered had they been talking about him long.

Standing at the farthest end of the counter from her mother and sister, Cecelia tiptoed to reach a pile of serving dishes in the upper cabinet. "I haven't seen her in ages. How did she look?"

"Like an old boot."

"Rose!" Cecelia said, surprised. She handed her sister a large bowl.

"Sorry, C. I know it's not nice, but it's true. She looked so worn out."

"Poor girl," their mother said, "she used to be gorgeous."

Swiping with her finger, Rose checked the bowl for dust. Then she plunged it into the sink and began to wash it. "They say a daughter steals her mother's beauty."

"I think you mean borrow," her mother said. "They borrow their mothers' beauty."

"That's what I said, didn't I? Borrowed?"

"Mmhmm," her mother said. "It's more likely that her husband wore it out."

"Well, she looked it." Rose lifted the bowl from the sink and handed it back to her sister. "I mean, it was sad how worn out she looked."

"I thought pregnant women were supposed to glow," Cecelia suggested.

"With boys they do," Rose said.

"I don't think my wife ever glowed when she was pregnant," Noah said. "She did sweat a lot, though."

At the sound of his voice, the three women looked back. Cecelia was darker of hair and complexion, and her mother touched somewhat by the effects of middle age, but to Noah it was apparent immediately that her mother's beauty had not been stolen, nor had it been borrowed or lent; rather it had been inherited, with the daughters' features evidently coalescent in their mother's. Moreover, as one would expect from three women of close relation, they shared elements not only of appearance but of expression too. Noah could hardly fail to notice this as all three gave him an identical regard of suspicion.

Cecelia then shifted on her feet, holding herself half-turned to him half-turned towards the counter. "This is Noah. He doesn't know how to make friends."

Cecelia's mother frowned playfully. "C. told me you were nice."

Rose was leaning back against the kitchen sink, examining him. She was otherwise so slender that, from behind, Noah had not realized how pregnant she was; her belly stood straight out like a bowsprit, or the nose of a blimp.

"I would have thought he was nice," Rose said, "if he hadn't opened his mouth."

"Are you nice, Noah?" Cecelia's mother asked.

The intensity of her green eyes bore down on him and Noah, a little unnerved, turned and smiled hopefully at Cecelia, but her expression was now merely amused. He was on his own.

At last, Cecelia's mother released him from her silent inspection. "I'm Susan. This is Rose." Her smile said she was letting him off the hook, and she turned back to the counter "You're as bad as my husband."

"That bad?" Noah asked.

Rose began to laugh. "Don't take it personally. He likes to tease. It's his version of being charming."

"He sent me for beer."

"Of course he did."

"I'll get them," Cecelia said, but Rose was already on the move. She brushed past Noah to the fridge, and a light perfume followed her.

"Beat you to it." Rose handed Noah three bottles, then she placed one hand on his shoulder, turning him towards the door. "Go enjoy your beer. Dinner's almost ready. You can tell the boys."

Noah looked over his shoulder at Cecelia. Her face was still smiling.

In the dining room, Oliver was near the buffet with his hands in his pockets and his eyes on the photographs. One was of the girls as infants, their bright blond hair shimmering in careful ringlets. Another showed them posing with hands crossed on their little skirts and smiles frozen on their little faces. There were family portraits too, and graduations, photos from Rose and Oliver's wedding, and also Gary and Susan's, the latter pair looking younger than their children were now. There was also a recent photograph of Cecelia's parents in semi-formal dress, flanked on one side by three men and on the other by three women. Noah offered Oliver one of the beers. He then started to ask about the photographs, but Gary appeared at his side and snatched a bottle from his hand.

"So, C. knows you from school? That's good," Gary said with playful conspiracy. "If things get heady, maybe you can translate."

Before Noah could respond, Cecelia and Rose bustled in from the kitchen. In turns they visited the china cabinet and began to set the table. Six dinner plates and six wine and water glasses, and silver from a large chest, and ringed napkins.

"Almost there, everyone," Susan called from the kitchen.

Rose eyed to Oliver, who followed her back to the kitchen. Cecelia sidled up to Noah.

"You have a photogenic family," Noah said. Cecelia smiled and made to answer, but her father got there first.

"I know," he said. "They're a good-lookin' bunch." He indicated one of the photos of the girls in ringlets. "Their mother spent hours getting those curls just right. It took so long we didn't even make it to the Sears that day and we had to go through the whole rigmarole again the day after. It was so bad I threatened to shave their heads to speed things up."

"He's making that up," Cecelia said.

"Are you sure?" Gary said.

Rose emerged again from the kitchen and Oliver after, she with a pitcher of ice water and he with a large carving knife and fork and several serving spoons. They placed them on the table, then Rose began searching the shelves behind her and Oliver returned to the kitchen. Gary put back nearly half his beer and exhaled deeply.

"This one here is a new one," he continued. "I mean, Sue just found it the other day. We lost a lot of our pictures years ago when our basement flooded and it's one of the few we've got of just the girls. She went right out and bought a frame for it."

He indicated a photograph with the two girls lying together on an oblong braided rug. Their faces were pressed hard together, and one appeared to be suffocating the other in a lethal hug. The strength of the squeeze was impressive. Even in still frame you could sense the desperate kicking of the victim's legs.

"They were great friends, you know. Almost Irish twins. When I was doing my apprenticeship and we were still dirt poor, they even shared a bed. They used to build up these nests with pillows and blankets they'd steal from the closet in the middle of the night, and then they'd take turns kicking each other out onto the floor. The giggling was enough to make you crazy. I don't know how many times we'd have to go in there to tell them to get to sleep. And every couple of nights someone would hit their head and they'd cry bloody murder and we'd have to let her sleep with us. And the next night they'd be at it again."

Gary laughed and a light blush had appeared on Cecelia's cheeks. Gary pinched one of them. "A couple of twin cherries, with their little cherry cheeks. So cute you could just eat them up. Do you have any brothers or sisters?"

Noah thought of Felix. He had several friends his age. He seemed happy enough. "No, it's just me," he said.

"Well, you might have dodged one there. I hate my brother and, believe me, the feeling's mutual. But my girls were such sweet things— they always got along well. Except for when they were teens. Then they fought over everything. There was this one time—I mean, they never would tell us what it was about exactly, but we sort of figured it out. C. and Oliver were dating at the time ..."

Gary hesitated. Cecelia's blush had disappeared and her face was strangely immobilized. Behind them, Rose had stopped moving. A frown flashed across her face, but she suppressed it so quickly that Noah could hardly interpret it. Her trivet-filled hands, however, went stiff.

"Did C. tell you about that?" Gary asked.

"She mentioned it," Noah said, growing uncomfortable.

Gary patted Noah on the back. "Oh good. I thought I might have gone too far there. Well, when we came downstairs they were screaming and clawing at each other like wild animals."

Noah kept his attention half on Cecelia's father, and half on Cecelia, and half on her sister—which he felt was too many halves by half. He wanted not to enjoy it, but Gary's enthusiasm was infectious and, despite himself, Noah found himself smiling a little and hoping it was not too much.

"We had a coon fight in the backyard here a few days ago, and it had nothing on these two," Gary continued. "They already had bruises coming and, when we pried them apart, C. tore out a fistful of Rose's hair. And I mean a fist full. Rose had to wear a hat for weeks. It looked so bad she even refused to go to the fall dance." He drank off the last of his beer. "Of course, girls get like that sometimes. But imagine, the two of them fighting over that boy. For a while there we weren't sure which way it was gonna go."

Oliver came through the kitchen door and stopped suddenly. He seemed to take in the discordant humour of the room. In his hands he held two uncorked bottles. "Anyone need wine?" Cecelia and Rose were already reaching for glasses.

Barging through the kitchen door, Susan noted the disarray and quickly set about repairing it. With a little bustling she got the knives properly to the right and forks to the left; and the napkins she positioned above the plates. She also reassigned the serving spoons. Familiar with the exercise, Gary slipped out. Shortly after, the opening bars of "Mrs. Robinson" infiltrated from the living room.

"Not too loud," Susan called, and the music quieted slightly.

Here and there in empty spaces she set candles and lit them. Then, with three orderly trips to the kitchen, Susan furnished the table while the others arranged themselves for dinner—Noah, by process of elimination, next to Rose and facing Cecelia. Finally, Susan backed one last time through the swinging door, her elbow raised to prevent it from jostling the platter she carried and the steaming bird upon it, to which she appointed her husband. Taking her seat opposite, she paused and subjected one and all to scrutiny and surveyance. "Arms off the table please, Oliver. Rose: napkin."

Susan removed her napkin from its ring and folded its white linen over her lap. Noah hurried to unroll his own and put it to its proper use.

"C.," Susan said.

It was said simply, but it caused Cecelia to sit up straight and stiff, albeit with a frown and evident irritation. She endured the correction with the obstinance of a leashed puppy.

"Rose, I hope that's not your wine," Susan said, doubling back.

"I'm allowed a small glass. Doctor's orders," Rose said, standing her ground against her mother's suspicion.

"And here we are again," Gary said. "All of us chickens in the same coop, and the old hen with such a variety of targets for a change. How nice."

"You take that back," Susan said.

"Nope." Gary laughed, then with marvellous exaggeration he rolled his sleeves, brandished the carving utensils, and set to work breaking down the chicken. He briskly reduced it to a carcass, disjointing and slicing with the deftness of a master butcher. Apparently everything about Gary required a certain amount of showmanship. While he carved, the others began to serve themselves. The dishes moved counterclockwise, in obedience to *Good Housekeeping* and the Emily Post school, and everyone helped themselves.

"Twice-baked potatoes with scallions and smoked paprika," Susan said, "and roasted red peppers with saffron, niçoise olives and mint. Sautéed chard and garlic. And roast chicken with chestnut stuffing."

Rose leaned in to smell the stuffing as it came to her. "Orange, coriander … thyme."

When finally a little of everything was on his plate, Gary temporized in admiration and addressed the company: "I would say grace, if only I knew who to address it to—the Lord, my wife, or Martha Stewart."

"That's a tough call," Cecelia said. "They're all jealous gods."

Susan pointed a finger at the pair of them, one after the other. "Keep talking, you two. See where it gets you."

"No, I mean it," Gary said with too much earnestness. "It's like something staged for a magazine. It's a good thing."

"I have no idea why I married you."

"Oh please. Noah, did you see our wedding photo? And the one from when we renewed our vows? Thirty years and I'm still dapper as the day we married. And if I'm so much trouble, why did she go and marry me all over again? Tell me that."

"I don't think I have an opinion," Noah said, practicing a cautious impartiality.

Gary cut a piece of meat from the bone and raised it to his mouth, but instead of eating it right away he held it aloft like a baton and, eyeing his wife with a twinkle of mischief, he began to enumerate.

"So, there's my good looks, for one. The camera doesn't lie. And then there's my charming personality, which you're all familiar with. But underneath it all, I think the real reason is I'm handy. You know, Noah, we lived here for years before we had the money to really renovate. And, of course, every hour I spend fixing my house is an hour I'm not getting paid to fix somebody else's, so I just kept putting it off. But as soon as the girls moved out, I said to myself, 'Get on it, Gary. Give your wife what she's been asking for all these years.' So I got on it, just for her. And I started with the plumbing."

"Dad," Cecelia said, uneasily.

"You know, I must have laid pipe in every room in the house," Gary continued.

"God, this is embarrassing," Rose said.

"What? Ask your mother. Sue, did I or did I not plumb everything I could get my hands on?"

"Cecelia told me you put a greenhouse in the basement," Noah said. It seemed like a safe interjection, and Rose touched an appreciative hand to his elbow.

"That's right. I set up a beautiful little hydroponic system for her down there. Come on, Sue. You're my high school sweetheart. Don't I take care of you?"

While her husband delighted himself in provocation, Susan had been eating small bites of her meal. Now she set down her fork and knife and addressed him. "You know, this house isn't the only fixer-upper I've had to live with. Just listen to yourself." Susan then looked around the table, gathering up her daughters' attention especially. "When a man's only been with one woman his whole life, he gets this idea of you in his head—in the biggest part of his brain, the part labelled woman—and then, because he doesn't have anything else to put in there, he fills it up with all sorts of absurd ideas. The more actual women he can fill it with, the fewer women he'll expect you to be." Then, to her husband, she said, "Darling, you're exhausting. And I swear, sometimes I wish a couple of other girls had broken you in a bit and saved me the trouble."

Noah buried his gaze in a potato. The others were sliding their utensils quietly across their plates or prodding at their food, except for Gary. Gary was gazing the length of the table at the woman who was, apparently, the only one he had ever loved. Then he started to laugh.

Had Noah been in Gary's place, he too might have laughed, but it would have been small and uncomfortable, or tightly apologetic, or maybe humble, slipping out like a confession. Gary's laughter, conversely, was resonant and unrestrained and, to judge by the roguish glint in his eye, unequivocally adoring. He placed his hands on his mouth and blew a vigorous kiss the length of the table. Susan shook her head, but smiled as she again took up her fork and knife. Oliver and the girls did likewise and before long they all were talking more freely and filling themselves with food and wine in the warmth of the candlelight and each other's company. Unexpectedly, and with some sentimentality, Noah considered that it was one of the most satisfying meals he could remember.

Not that he experienced no further moments of discomfort. Once the plates were cleared and a third bottle had been brought to the table, Noah was deprived of the excuse of a full mouth to limit his conversation, and though he was not averse to conversation in general, nevertheless as it was his first time meeting the Lineses, he knew there would be some attempts to draw him out, and he was not very much one for talk about himself, especially with strangers. And Cecelia's family were perhaps not strangers, but they were not exactly not strangers either. There was something both familiar and unfamiliar about them, which on the one hand was partly because Cecelia had prepared him, and partly because by now he knew Cecelia well enough to recognize in their demeanours something of her own, and partly because the boisterous relations of the household reminded him of some of his friends' rowdy family gatherings, such as Annie's or Adrien's, or even Ray's, despite the fact that his parents disliked each other and often disliked him too and he them; but on the other hand the seductive pleasures of the table were not a part of Noah's upbringing, most of his meals having been simple and inexpensive and taken at the small kitchen table, which his grandmother used to furnish with such parsimony. Moreover, the effortless rhythms of the Lines family banter made them seem welcoming and yet forbiddingly insular, as though their hospitality was both an invitation and a dare. The coincidence of these characteristics, the all-at-once-ness of them, at first filled Noah with the ambivalence of a landed alien in a foreign country, with anxieties and gentle yearnings in equal measure.

But there was something about the availability of their affections, even something about Gary's openly irascible sense of humour, that made Noah feel like he almost understood what it might have been like for him to have a family of his own like this, and at some point (somewhere between his fourth and fifth glasses of wine, he thought) he realized that his conflicting emotions were resolving themselves and he was having a straightforwardly good time.

He answered their questions easily. He had never really known his parents, and was generally estranged by circumstance and old grievances from what little extended family he had. His grandfather was suffering from dementia, which meant the last branch between him and that lineage was soon to be broken. The sadness of these reflections would normally have lingered, but the strength of the Lineses' interest, which they so readily and eagerly communicated, allowed Noah to speak his mind without hesitation or restraint: he cut right through his habitual resistance like a boat with her nose to the waves.

His son was nearly ten and old enough to understand what he was missing. He often asked about the old folks from the island who, because he had seen them so infrequently, existed more to him as an impression of benevolent spirits than actual, living people; and he had started asking questions about Noah's parents—like were they dead, and how, and why—most of which Noah had never been able to answer even for himself. It was an ongoing difficulty: what to do so Felix might feel a connection to people and a past he hardly knew, or had never known, of which he seemed nonetheless to feel the loss.

"Wait, you don't know how your parents died?" Rose asked.

"I know how, I just don't know why. Actually, I sort of know why my mother died. My grandmother says it was heartsickness. After my father died she took to wandering and one night she got out and died of exposure in the woods not far from home. I guess today we'd say she was clinically depressed, but heartsick is more to the point, I guess. My father's the bigger mystery. He just took a boat out into a storm and drowned."

"By himself?"

"All by himself. And my grandparents have no idea why."

The table became quiet and Cecelia looked at him with concern. "I had no idea," she said. "That must be so hard. Not knowing."

"I guess so, although they've always seemed pretty reconciled to it."

"No," Rose said, "she means for you."

Noah, wavering, pondered Rose's meaning and Cecelia's steady attentiveness. Dividing his attention between them, he raised his glass and drank off the remainder. "Yes, that too, I guess."

He would have ended there, but everyone was waiting. "At first I asked my parents' friends and family, but too much time had passed. The details had kind of unravelled. There are a lot of grievances too that are still pretty sharp. You know, after the Expulsion, French Protestants from the Jersey Islands brought Acadian refugees back to the island. The Jerseys owned the land and the only stores, and monopolized the shipping. It was outright exploitation for a long time. For people my age it's ancient history. None of it has anything to do with us. But my grandmother outraged her family by marrying a French Catholic, and my grandfather Doucet never forgave my mother for marrying my father, the Anglo son of a Frenchman who gave up his French. Her sisters were as bad. By the time she died they weren't speaking to her, so they couldn't tell me anything and didn't really want to anyway. So I'm just writing down everything I can get from my grandfather, and everything I can remember about his family."

He thought of Cate's father, with whom he had never been on good terms, and with whom he had taken issue even in the Sunday school. Noah didn't expect that to resolve itself until one or both of them gave up the ghost.

"We've been lucky, though. He can still mostly take care of himself. The other day I remembered something he said to me when I was just a kid. He said, 'I wiped your ass when you couldn't do it yourself. You get to do the same for me. That's the deal.'"

Gary laughed and said, "You hear that, girls? That's what kids are for. Don't forget it."

"Let's hope it doesn't come to that," Oliver said.

"I can't imagine," Rose said to Noah. "To have to watch that happen."

Noah had been carrying the conversation for some time, but he had not, he realized, quite been aware of the real weight of it. As if a spell had been broken, or a dream interrupted, Noah felt a momentary instability as he became aware of tensions in himself, and perhaps in the others, and felt himself pulled off his emotional axis. He poured himself another drink.

"Sorry," Rose said.

"No, it's alright," Noah reassured her. "For a while I thought it would help if I just kept talking to him, but he can't really keep it up anymore. His brain's full of slivers, and his mind's a tangle of tangles, and I can see he feels ashamed. It's a terrible, inchmeal kind of a disease. Like there are little holes in him everywhere, and a big one in the middle where maybe he used to know something useful about my father." He drank his wine. To his right Rose was frowning sadly, and Cecelia too from across the table and looking right at him. Noah hoped that someone would say something; he felt he had said quite enough.

"The world's a funny place," Gary said, obliging. "Something will turn up. Something always does."

Cecelia smiled at her father a little, and Noah nodded to communicate his appreciation.

"Like there was this article in the paper the other day," Gary continued. "This guy was writing that the molecules in the air have been around on earth for millions and millions of years—the exact same stuff floating around in the atmosphere all this time, never getting used up, just changing and turning up again somewhere else. So the oxygen molecules I'm breathing right now, they could be the same ones Einstein breathed a hundred years ago."

Susan hissed at Cecelia. "C., you stop that. You'll wear your eyes out rolling them." Her mouth was torqued into a disdainful knot that mirrored her daughter's.

Gary looked at the women in some confusion. "It's the same ones, you see? We're always breathing the same ones. So the air inside Einstein could be inside somebody else right now. Even one of us. You never know, right? What do you think of that?"

"That whatever it was that made Einstein special," Cecelia said, "it wasn't the air he breathed."

"I think your father meant it metaphorically," Oliver said.

"Don't put words in my mouth," Gary said. "What do you mean metaphorically? It's the same ones. Everybody breathes the same ones. If that doesn't matter, then why'd we send C. to London after high school? You said you just had to breathe the air."

Cecelia laughed suddenly in spite of herself, and Oliver too. Noah tried to restrain his amusement to avoid upsetting Gary, who had meant it to comfort him.

"I swear, Noah. I haven't understood a word she's said since she was sixteen. Has she dragged you through a conversation yet?"

Noah decided the question was rhetorical. "You know, Cecelia's working on a really interesting project right now at the rare book library. It's kind of like you said—"

Cecelia cut him off with a shake of her head and a whispered, "Noah."

He had meant it as a helpful intervention, as though chivalrously opening a door for her to walk through, but he could see that he had overstepped.

"What?" Gary asked. Cecelia hesitated. "What is it?"

"I've signed a nondisclosure agreement. Noah too."

"For the university? What is it, the Manhattan Project? Well, keep it to yourself if you want."

"It's not that." Cecelia wavered. "It's just, you can't tell this to anyone. Like, not anyone."

"Who am I gonna tell? The kids at the shop? The HVAC guy at my next job?"

"All right." Cecelia shifted in her seat. "I've been asked to investigate the origins of a four-hundred-year-old document. It was found in the archives of a defunct importing company in Halifax. It's an indentured promissory note between a London goldsmith, acting as a receiver of deposits …"

"Small words please," Rose said.

"… and William Shakespeare. The William Shakespeare. And I've been asked to study the entire set of papers it was found with, and to follow up any clues in case they lead anywhere. It's really exciting."

"So it's a piece of paper," Gary said. "A nondisclosure agreement over a piece of paper?"

"Well, vellum. But it's a record of deposit and Shakespeare's signature is on it."

Gary looked down the table at his daughter, then he reached behind him and pulled out his wallet. "Hold on. I think I've got an ATM receipt in here somewhere. You'd better hold on to it in case you want to write a book about me when I'm dead."

Cecelia fell back into her chair in disgust. "Jesus, Dad, this is a big deal!"

"Well, come on. A bank receipt? I was trying to say something significant, you know? About how nothing's ever lost and we're all connected. And then you come out with Shakespeare's banker."

Noah was regretting having extended the conversation, but tried nonetheless to defend Cecelia. "It's a fantastic opportunity. For now it's a bit of a secret, but once she's finished ..." Noah redirected to Cecelia. "You'll certainly get to publish something. And you'll have to give a talk on it at the university, right?"

"I suppose so," she said.

"You could come and hear it," Noah said to Gary.

"Shit, Noah, you mean you're one of them too? And I was starting to like you." Gary then saw Cecelia looking at him. "Darling, you know I wouldn't understand a word of it."

Rose was nodding. Noah, sitting beside her, was puzzled and again wanted to say something in Cecelia's defence, but he had interfered too much already. The buzz from the wine was fading.

Oliver put his arm around Cecelia's shoulder and squeezed. "I think it's exciting, C. If you give a talk on it, let me know and I'll see if I can book off. Assuming I'm not away on contract."

"Sorry, honey. We're very proud of you," Gary said, and laughed a little. "Sometimes, I even think you might actually be my daughter."

He gazed proudly at Cecelia, and explained to Noah, "We always said she could do anything she wanted as long as she worked hard enough. Even when she decided to do all this *art thou fart thou*. It was impossible to pry her away from her books. When she was a girl she used to get so mad sometimes that she couldn't even talk to us. Instead she used to write us letters with her big feelings spelled out in all these big words. By the time she was thirteen I had to go and buy a dictionary just to understand them. Can you believe that?"

"You know, I've still got one of those letters," Oliver said quickly, quietly, a small smile on his lips and in his eyes. "I found it a couple of years ago and I couldn't bring myself to get rid of it."

"I didn't know that," Rose said. She reached across the table and stole his big hand into hers. "That's kind of sweet, I think."

"Rose," Susan interrupted, "I think it might be time for your surprise. Why don't you get your father his present."

Susan began to clear the table and Cecelia lent a hand. Rose slipped into the living room. Gary watched with curiosity, but his youngest was already moving towards the vestibule. He turned to Oliver, but he only shrugged. When Rose returned, Susan and Cecelia were just getting back to their seats; she brought a paper gift bag with her and presented it to her father. Reaching in, he pulled out bunches of white tissue and then a tiny pink hockey jersey with a white maple leaf on the front, and on the back the number ninety-eight and the name Streit across the shoulders. He held it up for all to see. Oliver smiled proudly at his father-in-law.

"So it's a girl," Gary said. "Aren't you courageous."

Much hugging followed amongst the parents and children, and then chocolate torte for all to celebrate the news. Afterwards, the men indulged themselves in whisky and the late game on the television. Sitting next to him on the couch, Noah could see that Gary was all distracted grin and hardly paying attention to the skaters or the drone of the play-by-play.

Oliver noticed too. "Gary, tell me you're not getting sentimental. At least wait till we've got a baby to hand you."

"Go rot. I remember when Rose was just a wish I'd planted in her mother's womb."

"A wish?" Oliver replied. "If I'd known that, it wouldn't have taken us so long."

Behind them, the women were sitting around the table.

"I thought you didn't want to know," Cecelia said.

"I didn't at first, but the more I thought about having a tiny penis growing inside of me, the weirder I felt. I just had to know. Survey says: four chambers in the heart, a couple of kidneys, one stomach, one bladder, and no penises."

"When did you tell Mom?"

"She was there. Oliver couldn't get back for it."

"She's going to be big too, no surprise." Susan gestured at Oliver. "It's lucky your sister doesn't have an incompetent cervix. The doctor says hers is beautiful."

"I guess if there's one thing you want your cervix to be, it's competent," Cecelia said.

"That and screwed in straight," Rose said. "You don't want your baby having to work out any kinks in the hose. There was this woman in the waiting room even younger than me and already a mother, and when I asked her she said it sure rearranged a few things."

Cecelia winced. "I thought you were hoping for a boy."

"I was at first. We even tried. You can do that, you know. You have to have sex as close to ovulation as you can for a boy, and as far as possible for a girl. You have to really know your body. I got this book about it, it's called something like *Managing Your Fertility*. Do you know it? You have to read it. Every woman should read it."

"But it didn't work, did it."

"They conceived, didn't they?" Susan interjected. "That's all that matters."

"After the doctor put us on a schedule. We had to have sex every other day, and only every other day, to make sure Oliver built up enough sperm between attempts."

"I'm not sure I needed to know that," Cecelia said.

"But you know what he's like. He thought we should be trying more often. He figured if there was less sperm each time, at least it would be fresher."

Rose laughed loudly and looked to see if Oliver would react, but he and Gary were absorbed in their thoughts, or their drinks, or the game, or some combination of the three.

"Sounds romantic," Cecelia said.

"I told him the other day: the second best thing about being pregnant is that we can slow down a bit."

ᴒ

The visit carried on like this a little while, but it wasn't long before Noah sensed that it was winding down. Having insisted, he busied himself with washing the last few dishes. By then, Oliver was keeping Susan and Cecelia company at the table. Gary's cry—"Oliver, headman the puck!"—reminded Noah that the paterfamilias was still watching the game and still had his tumbler; the expression seemed to mean *pass the whisky*. There was something a little childlike about

Gary, a bit of innocence despite his mild indecencies. He took his licks as good as he gave, and he seemed to have about him the negligence of one who holds no grudges and so is surprised to find that others do. As Rose had said, he was a tease; but perhaps it was fairer to say his way was that of an old friend, whose take-you-for-granted familiarity makes delicacy not only superfluous but impolite. Oliver seemed to tolerate the verbal roughhousing with good humour, if not always affection. *When you have kids of your own.* By now Felix was in his pyjamas, brushing his teeth maybe, unless Cate had again not supervised and he had simply run the water until a convincing length of time had passed; in which case Felix might be crawling into bed to read, with the aftertaste of dinner in his mouth and the small triumph of a secret victory in his heart (an independence Noah admired in his son, though he would have foiled it and sent him back). Looking up from the sink, Noah saw a light on in the yard. By process of elimination, Noah surmised that Rose had gone outside for air. He drained the water and dried the glasses and, after folding the dishtowel over the handle of the oven door, he stepped outside. The cool night was invigorating after the meal and the drink and the steaming dishwater. He felt suddenly unencumbered.

Rose was at the far end of the yard, between a pair of fruit trees, facing away from him. The light from the porch lamp scarcely reached her, but enough for Noah to see a faint, tight coil of smoke rising over her shoulder. She corkscrewed herself around to see who it was had found her out; she seemed relieved that it was only Noah. She took a long, final drag and flicked the butt over the fence. She was barefoot, and wore a long, unbuttoned sweater, and she wrapped it around her and swayed as she walked. Noah's eyes followed her. He was tempted to approach and engage her in conversation, but there was something about the way she dug her toes in and the way she wasn't quite looking at him. Fearful he was intruding, Noah almost returned indoors, but there really was something—in the turn of her eyes and the patience of her gait, the way she stopped to run her fingers over a few of the sparsely clinging leaves, how she adjusted her weight from one hip to the other and how, when she turned just right, presenting herself in profile, with her arms uncrossed and her hands, with tender and hopeful caresses and defensive, going to the rounded shell of her abdomen—something that struck him with unrelenting vividness as reminiscent of Cate when she was pregnant. Of the way Cate adopted, bodily, a kind of anticipation—her flesh amassing, her hair thickening, her anatomy continent in everything except her unpredictable need to urinate—all of which amounted to a ripening and a fullness of her condition that Noah himself could hardly begin to understand. The tired arch in her back, her eyes downcast and studying the circling of her hands on her belly, wondering was she doing it right, and was he happy too, and did he still desire her, and all of the unreason and fear that he never entirely grasped. The way Cate would stand far away, right across the room as Rose across the yard now stood, and cast glances but not approach him, which (he did not immediately understand) she did to entice him to come to her without her asking (or almost) and put his arms around her and make her feel protected and safe and small, an uncharacteristic fragility in her. They had been so young, and all they could do was absorb and fret over all the dizzying dos and don'ts of doctors and midwives and parents and friends, and their endless inventory of instructions.

And it had been so troubling, especially for Cate, who was convinced that she was doing something dangerously wrong, when after Felix was born it had taken him a couple of weeks to get the hang of latching onto the breast. They had fed him, using a tiny tube connected to a bottle and running alongside a pinky finger that he took into his little mouth, with milk that Cate had pumped with an electric breast pump that pumped and pumped and kept on pumping until she felt like a dairy cow.

An identifiable but nameless feeling swelled in Noah's chest—the sensation astonishingly physical. It seemed to be an overlapping of sadness and regret and stoicism and longing and sweetness and grief, endlessly expanding yet fine and sharp as a pinprick. He had felt it before and sometimes wished there were a word to express all that it entailed. But there were other times when it was almost pleasant to dwell on the sensations, and how they were distinct, but not so much that he could quite demarcate where any one of them stopped being itself and became another. If his life were a thread extending from who he was to who he thought that he would be, then the separation from his wife was not simply a point along that line, but instead a place where that thread, pulled too tight, had snapped and recoiled, leaving him with two frayed ends and insufficient length to pull himself together again. Now here he was with an intense, instinctive desire to cross the lawn to Rose and to protect her in some indefinable way from some indefinable harm. It was a foolish feeling, originating with a woman he no longer had any claim to, and aroused by a woman he had only just met. It was as though he were following a template.

Noah saw that she was looking at him. She was standing at the end of the yard, silhouetted against the fence and flowers, and framed by the fruit trees and the nighttime glow of the city and the sky. Hoping to appear casual, he sat down on the step and waited as she approached.

"You're not cold?" he asked.

Rose patted her belly. "I've got the furnace on in the basement."

Then she sat down beside him and gazed in silence with him at the yard. The small evergreens were well and neatly shaped, and the other plants, as in front of the house, were mounded or staked or cut back and ready for wintering. The fallen leaves, all but a few, were in a pen for mulch or compost, and all but the highest hanging fruit had been harvested.

"You should see it in the summer," Rose said at last. "She winters the dahlias, and she forces columbine in the basement. Impatiens, cockscomb. Trillium in the spring, believe it or not. She even keeps the obedience at bay somehow. She's a bit of a genius, my mother."

Rose tried to raise her feet and wrap her arms around her knees, but her distension prevented it. Giving up, she sighed and dropped her feet back to the ground. She pulled her long hair back from her face. There were beads of sweat on her forehead.

"You know she bought us our first makeup kits when we were thirteen. She told us there was no such thing as an ugly girl, just a lazy one. Thirteen." She pursed her lips and, with the slightest of movements, shook her head. "I have to remind myself she was a young mother and probably didn't know any better."

"I knew less than nothing," Noah said.

Rose turned her face and looked directly at Noah and he felt his eyes, until now fixed on the blossoming fruit trees, drawn to hers.

"How long have you and C. been seeing each other?" she asked.

"You know, I'm not sure. It was a bit of a stutter start."

"She really likes you. Not that she would make a big deal, but I notice."

"Oh?"

"Like the way she always keeps left of you if she can help it, so you get her good side, and how she tries to give you a three-quarter profile. Haven't you noticed?"

Noah didn't think he had, not like Rose explained it, and he wondered if that meant something.

"She isn't very good at these things," Rose continued. "And she's so serious. I don't see why she can't be normal around us. She's always in her head." She paused and looked away, out into the yard. "You could be good for her, you know."

Noah let his gaze drift out and away too. "Should we go back inside?"

"In a minute." Rose pulled a box of mints from her pocket and popped a handful. Then she turned to Noah and said quietly, "You won't mention the cigarette, will you? I almost never smoke, and that's the first I've had since July, but Oliver would be furious. We've miscarried twice before, and I know I shouldn't, but family is always so stressful."

Noah nodded. They remained there, sitting next to one another on the step and looking out over the lawn and the garden in silence. But the silence did not last. The patio door swung open and Noah looked back to find Cecelia standing there, with the door pressed against her shoulder and the shadow and glow from the patio lights throwing her figure into relief. Noah was pleased to see her after the interval, and pleased to see a look of affection, warm and inviting, that was not confined to her eyes or lips or any other one of her features but floated over her entire face, notwithstanding that it followed a momentary, fettered hesitation, as though she feared she was interrupting. Then Oliver appeared over her shoulder. He poked Cecelia lightly in the side, a look of mischief on his face as her smile exploded into a shriek.

She cursed and swatted at him as he squeezed by and went to embrace his wife. Rose said she was tired, and Oliver confessed that he was still recovering from laying down twenty-five pounds of wire or more a day on the topsides for a couple of months. Welding at that pace, he was lucky he hadn't burned out entirely. It was time to go.

Susan embraced her children at the door, and Gary waved in inebriated recumbency from the couch. He proclaimed that he hoped to have the pleasure of meeting them all again soon, and they were welcome anytime. *Mi casa,* you *casa.* Rose and Oliver were parked a few streets over and offered Cecelia and Noah a lift to the subway, but they declined. The night sky was clear and the air crisp, exactly what Noah needed after a heavy meal and much drinking.

West and south they wandered, away from the avenue they had taken in the failing light of the afternoon. The neighbourhood trees seemed now more shadowy than substantial and they were creaking gently in the breeze. Noah imagined Cecelia as a child, seated in the park and studious, balancing a book on her crossed legs and brushing her dark hair out of her eyes. Rose, he guessed, would be near the same age, already perhaps a little taller, ebullient and social, curious of her sister's bookishness; and Oliver he imagined as one strong, roughhousing boy amongst many, lost in the single-mindedness of a game of soccer or road hockey. Felix was approaching the age when he too might find himself on his own in a city park on a fall afternoon, studying or playing, and soon Rose would have a little girl who would too someday. It made Noah happy to think about succession, even for people he had only just met. Rose and Oliver had struggled, but were happy now. Others had it worse. He thought about the kind of oversight and intervention some unfortunate people endured, often in vain; about thousands of dollars, about decades of medical expertise and advancement, cumulative and combined; about test tubes and hormones and the body's rhythms and imperatives; about reproductive isolation, having to go into a room, divorce love from procreation, pound one out in a dimly lit little room and, when the contractions come, ignore the pleasure and have the presence of mind to aim or you end up back in the waiting room explaining to the nurse (who might have been in your homeroom back in high school) why your little cup is empty.

Before long they won't need test tubes and catheters, he thought. It's surely just a matter of time before they invent a machine to take care of it all at once. A two seater, probably, with a vacuum pump at one end and a turkey baster at the other, and maybe a paint mixer in the middle, and you each sit down and your material is removed (pleasurably for the male, and for the female not so much), then into the mixer it goes before it's pumped back into the female and planted on the uterine wall. O ineffable Science! O modern day miracle! O emasculate contraption! Lamentations for the sterile, abandoned to the limits of medical science and their own flawed bodies. For all that he regretted the liberty he took that winter night all those years ago, and his carelessness, Noah counted his blessings for Cate's precipitous fertility and Felix's inadvertent conception. Far better to have had their boy and loved him and struggled for means than to struggle later—or maybe fail—to have him at all. Maybe Rose would have more children. Maybe her difficulties were behind her now. Maybe not. You could never tell. And what about Cecelia, whose life for years would be circumscribed and filled by her course of study and, after that, the scramble for employment? He wondered did Cecelia even want children.

They walked mutely together. Noah listened to the distant music of the city and the regular staccato, stride by slow stride, of their shoes on the cool concrete; he gazed at the bright singularity of the moon, at the distant luminescence of downtown office towers, and the evenly spaced street lamps. He caught himself studying her. Her hands were buried in her jacket pockets and her hair trembled in the breeze, rising and falling around her bent shoulders. Her eyes were on the sidewalk. She looked very beautiful, and it rattled Noah's heart a little, but her posture seemed so unhappy that a slimness of worry edged its way between his other feelings as he watched her. He wanted to step closer and maybe put his arm around her. "That was fun," he said. "I like your family."

"They liked you too," Cecelia replied.

"They seemed interested, anyway."

"They were very interested in you. Not so much in me."

"I don't know. Oliver seemed interested."

"He always is."

Their stroll had taken them along Bain Avenue to Broadview. Even at this hour there were more than a few vehicles passing north and south along the rim of Riverdale Park. Then Noah realized that Cecelia's cheeks were wet with tears. Only a few, but enough to glisten. She saw that he had noticed.

"Sorry, this is totally stupid," she said. "It's just that dinners with my family are so stressful. I'm glad you came."

Noah was tempted to reach over with his hand and dry her tears, which he thought perhaps she wanted—she had not dried them—and he thought he might kiss her too, lightly, in the crisp fall air under the soft glow of the streetlight. He laughed kindly and said that Rose had complained of the stress too. Then he lifted his hand to her cheek, but she turned away and cast her sad eyes away in the direction of the parklands.

"She's beautiful, isn't she," Cecelia said.

A feeling of confused alarm lit up Noah's conscience. "You have an attractive family," he said. Her eyes dropped and Noah, unsettled, wished he had said something else, or even nothing.

Cecelia stood there, unmoving, a champion of austerity. Then, without looking, she suddenly shot herself across the avenue. A horn exploded and tires screamed as she raced across the lanes. Noah was right behind her. When they reached the other side, Noah was frightened and angry, and Cecelia, shamefaced, was standing at the lip of the hollowed-out field, weeping.

"What the hell!" Noah said. "What is it?"

Cecelia dropped to the ground and put her head in her hands. Noah sat down, bewildered, at her side.

"Tell me," he said.

"It's idiotic." Sniffling, Cecelia dug her palms into her eyes and face. Then she looked at Noah and gave him a meek smile. "She turned out just like my mother."

She did not continue straightaway, but gathered herself, and Noah, afraid that speaking might precipitate another act of madness, waited quietly. When she did resume her explanation, her voice and breath were more controlled and she spoke with care.

"I was a late-bloomer in high school, and inexperienced. Boys noticed me, and I dated a little, but I never liked any of them enough to sleep with them. I held out so long I turned it into a bigger deal than it needed to be. It didn't help that Rose was sleeping with her boyfriends and giving me a hard time about it too, but I sure as hell wasn't going to do it just because they all said I was supposed to. I kind of internalized it, and it made me more reluctant with everyone I dated after that."

Cecelia's control faltered a little and her voice caught, but she continued.

"I knew Oliver in public school. Then I ran into him again the summer after high school and we started dating. He was lovely. He was patient and he didn't rush me. But when I brought him to meet my family, Rose sat beside him at the table. She ignored her own boyfriend and flirted with him all through dinner. After they left, she told me that Oliver was a keeper and that I'd better fuck him before he got bored with me like all the others. I was so angry I started that fight with her, but it wasn't enough."

She paused. She seemed tired.

"What happened?" Noah asked.

She spoke quietly. "I slept with her boyfriend instead. Just to show her. He came by to see her, but he was early and she wasn't home yet, and I was the only one there."

Noah could not conceal his confusion. He had no idea what to say.

"I know, it was horrid. I don't even know why I did it. I was like an insane person." She sighed. "His name was Jack."

She grew quiet again, and again she wept, though calmly, not uncontrollably as before. "Afterwards, I was so mortified that I couldn't let Oliver touch me, and I couldn't tell him why, and after a couple of weeks I broke it off. And Rose ... I could tell she knew, just by the way she looked at me ... She never said a word, though, and when I broke it off with Oliver she just stepped right in and took him."

"When did all this happen?"

"Years ago."

It was an old injury, and the tears she shed she had been shedding a long time, only on the inside; and now and then they filled her to overflowing and brimmed over in winding, wet, unpredictable paths down her cheeks. Noah wished that he could be a reservoir, a cup to

161

carry some of it for her, but of course that wasn't how it worked. "They seem like they're over it. Maybe you should let it go."

"I don't think she even told him." Cecelia dropped her head into her hands. "You know that chunk of hair my father mentioned? I've still got it, tucked away at the bottom of my jewellery box."

Noah smiled cautiously. "So I should keep on your good side."

Cecelia laughed and Noah relaxed a little. She wrapped her arms around her knees again and squeezed lightly. "I think at first she did it just to get me, but they're very happy now."

She had allowed him a glimpse of her broken heart. She had done as much at the front door when they had first arrived, and he had seen it himself in her timidity when Oliver put his arms around her, and in her voice when they spoke, but he had missed it somehow. Moments ago he had felt like kissing her. Now he felt ridiculous. She seemed small and sad, and censured by the memory of her indiscretions. His confidences with Rose on the patio and his own feelings took on troubling dimensions. He wondered had Cecelia misunderstood; and he wondered also was she contemplating that other life that veered away from hers, the one she might have led had things turned out differently, the marriage and child, and the home, and all of the things (many more than he could fathom) that to Cecelia were now a part of the afterlife of *if onlys*, where regrets never truly die, but loiter like ghosts around the heart. And he wondered about all of the fictions and frictions, and things said that can't be unsaid, and things done that can't be undone. He wondered too how people did it, how they negotiated the hopeless tangle of loyalties and rivalries that run over and around and through each other, cinched like a Gordian knot and choking each other off. And he imagined their lives, Cecelia's and Rose's, all of their confidences and Christmas mornings and picnics in the park and birthdays and afternoons in the garden and report cards and boys, frozen in time, like ropes of ice snarled this way and that, and incapable of loosening.

"I'm sorry. I shouldn't have dropped that on you," Cecelia said. "It's fine, really. Except for when it isn't." Her eyes drifted north towards the Danforth. "I don't know if I should have had less to drink or more."

Two streetcars clattered towards them, one either way. Noah watched as they passed each other smoothly, each enviably guided on its unwavering twin steel rails, discharging tiny sparks of light where their arms met with the crisscrossed wires overhead.

"Noah, do you love your family?"

Noah hesitated. It was not a question he had ever thought to ask himself. Asked by anyone else—even an old friend like Ray, or Cate, who had known him as long as he had known himself—he might have hedged. But sitting there he felt himself more disposed towards Cecelia in her penitent misery than he had felt towards anyone for a long time.

"I love my grandparents," he said finally. "As for my parents, I was about three when they died, so I'm not really sure I know what I feel about them. But I think about them a lot. And I hope that a part of them is somewhere and can feel that I'm thinking about them, and that it hurts a little. That's a kind of love, I guess."

His eyes had gone distant as he spoke and so it was not until he felt a faint, hesitant touch on his wrist that he realized Cecelia was reaching for his hand. He had wanted this, and more, but he felt a little empty, like he had bounced a cheque.

To the west, a little beyond where Danforth becomes Bloor Street, the towers of the downtown core glowed with innumerable points of light, incandescent blossoms emblazoning the steel and glass, like an electric garden. Cecelia leaned into Noah and her head dropped lightly on his shoulder, the scent of her hair and the warmth and weight of her body affecting him. With his own head leaning into hers, Noah's eyes scanned the length of road that ran downtown; they lingered especially on the viaduct, beneath which (though he could not see it) ran the Don River, cutting a dark wound through the valley; and he thought of all the ghosts of destitute and dejected people who, severing the ties that bound them to an indifferent world, had thrown themselves on the mercy of the earth's gravity and the river valley that came up to meet them.

PART FOUR

Advocate for an Imposter

9

With the long bell sounding, the elementary school on Orde Street announced the end of afternoon classes and unleashed a streaming riot of youth into the concrete yard. Released from the offices and strictures of schoolroom routine, the children burst through the doors as though a jailbreak were underway and once they cleared the outer fencing their getaways would be assured. The sky was hazy and there was no trace of snow, neither in the air nor on the ground. It was a grey look for Christmas vacation, and bleak. Nonetheless, even those not hostile to desks and chairs could be counted amongst the screaming, running, spitting, punching, laughing horde. Dressed in their oversized winter coats and hurtling this way and that, often uncontrollably, they descended upon waiting parents and unwary pedestrians with equal violence. Negotiating his way through this pinballing arcade of disorder was Felix Lamarck and, like most of the other children, he wore a grown-up's backpack, whose weight he was forced to lean into as he squeezed through the crowded gateway. From the sidewalk, he shouted his goodbyes and see-you-next-years, then stomped the short way home.

The house on McCaul Street was the worst house on a street of bad houses. Like many of them, a former massage parlour, it had become a moderately priced, poorly maintained rental property, the kind typically inhabited by students who for cheap lodging are happy to live eight to a four- or five-bedroom dwelling. The tiny front half was a century-old, red-bricked, two-storey structure, sturdy and true, but the rear was a 1960s addition with a poor foundation. It had settled over the years and it was now pulling away from the front so dramatically that the floor in the living room pitched a good ten degrees from level.

If intoxicated, or merely incautious, upon entering the rear of the house a person could stumble clean through the living room and into the kitchen. There wasn't a right angle in the place.

As soon as he came through the door, Felix dropped his bag and then his coat and raced to the couch, which, due to the angle of the floor, was effectively a recliner. He sprawled there—one foot on the armrest, the other dangling by the floor—and turned on the television. A hollow, metallic hammering was resonating up through the floor and there were voices behind him in the kitchen: Noah and Cecelia, engaged in vigorous debate.

After nearly three months of examination, which Cecelia had faithfully carved out of her weekly studies and schoolwork, she and Noah had inventoried and described the contents of the fifteen archival boxes that Trover had had delivered to the library for them, but these contained only the ledgers and letters and other stationery of a family enterprise, not the treasures they all (too expectantly, it seemed) had hoped for. Not that the contents were entirely barren of interest. They had traced the history of the indenture from its origins in seventeenth-century London to the Halifax basement where it was discovered.

The earliest ledger, into which the indenture had been folded, located a William Belott (presumably the son of Stephen and Mary Belott) in the American colony of Boston. It opened with lists of expenses and orders—the first for a sandy wig with silver brand and pearls—and also receipts of payment, all of it written in Belott's careful hand. This continued through six more ledgers before it was replaced in 1677 by the energetic and somewhat erratic scribbling of Samuel Belott, almost certainly a son taking up the business after the retirement, decline, or death of his father. There followed uninterrupted a string of Belotts, whose distinctive penmanships accounted for the history of the family business. Growing clientele and profits during the expansion of Boston and the fashion for wigs, followed by a century of consistent earnings overseen by Belotts John, William, Matthew, John and George (an astonishingly retentive crew in that the ledgers seemed an almost uninterrupted account of their dealings). Then came, as far as Cecelia and Noah could determine, a period of decline and worsening debts, as another John Belott was unable to adapt to the ever more wigless sovereign United States. First, he left Boston, then he left the colonies. Fleeing debts and jilting creditors, the Belotts—or this branch at any rate, perhaps joining the exodus of Loyalists—set themselves up in Halifax, where the ledgers showed them engaging in the importation of textiles and tailoring supplies. A few generations more did likewise until the last ledger, kept by yet another John Belott, ended abruptly in 1893. Letters from clients and bankers, and not much else, made up the remainder of the findings. As family records go it was a narrow one, but remarkably complete. And yet, for all that, it was little more than a money trail. If ever there was anything else of worth besides the indenture, it must have come unhitched and drifted off into the fog of history.

This much Noah and Cecelia agreed on, and also on what they might do next. In Boston and London there might be public and parish records, and therein the means of fanning out and perhaps following the faded trails of Belotts who had drifted away from the main line. Or, in Halifax, an old friend of Noah's, Andrew Coyle, could help them follow the remaining family footprints in the years after the ledgers ended, assuming there were any left to follow. Of these unpromising options, the latter was the less unpromising. Realistically, though, they were not likely to find anything more. Like so much scholarship, their work had turned secretarial.

What remained then to stimulate their disagreement was little, but it was enough: the indenture's strange origin. About this they had discovered exactly nothing, so their arguments amounted to baseless conjecture. Accordingly, their views grew only more fiercely entrenched. Now they were like two opossums staring each other down across the same carrion. Shakespeare's memory, Noah insisted, like the hand that signed his will, had been shaky. Unable to remember the agreed upon dowry, and apparently not fond of either Mountjoy or Belott, an aging Shakespeare made it up to young Mary by putting the money where neither could touch it, in the name of her son, whom Shakespeare must have known as a child on Silver Street and whom he surely pitied for having been born into such a den of covetousness.

Cecelia thought this theory mawkish. Mountjoy's wife, Marie, had been unfaithful with the local mercer. She obviously liked Shakespeare, since she asked him to arrange the marriage of her daughter. He obviously liked her because he acquiesced. They were the same age, as were their daughters, and both had lost children. Perhaps there were sympathies. Perhaps a romantic entanglement. If Mountjoy threatened him with publicizing the infidelity, it would have embarrassed Shakespeare, who was just barely gentrified and whose will, listing contingencies five generations long, suggested he cared as much or more for the standing of his ancestors and descendants than the posterity of his plays. Cecelia agreed that leaving the money to Marie's grandson could only mean he wanted it out of Belott's hands, but as Shakespeare was no stranger to liaisons … "Don't forget the dark mistress and the young man of the sonnets," she said, "and his estranged wife in Stratford."

"I don't see what that has to do with it," Noah said.

"He left her the second-best bed," Cecelia replied.

"It could have been the marriage bed," Noah insisted. "They made love in that bed."

"And it would have been less comfortable than whatever he bought for the New Place. He left his wife the less comfortable bed—the second-best bed."

"But an affair with Mountjoy's wife? Why multiply your assumptions when there are perfectly reasonable explanations?"

"That sounds like a sentimentalist's bastardization of Occam's razor," Cecelia said.

"Of me, you, and Brother Occam, which of us actually knows something about being married?" Noah countered. Too unkindly, he realized. Cecelia's eyes could not conceal that she was hurt. He pulled her into an embrace.

"You know, I'm supposed to be the expert here," she said. "I think you might respect my opinion a little more."

"I'm sorry. Of course I respect your opinion. I just think it's wrong."

In the basement, the hammering was growing in volume and vehemence, and it was now accompanied by Gary Lines' despairing entreaty, which the floor did little to muffle: "Why, why, why, why, why?"

"I should go down there," Noah said, releasing her. "Your father probably wants to hit me with a hammer, and I think I might have to let him." On his way through the living room, Noah evaded the ugly little Christmas tree and greeted his son by playfully swatting his foot from the arm of the couch. Then he took the door from the hallway, down the stairs in search of the wailing plumber.

The stone and concrete of the two foundations were badly stained with efflorescence and cut the basement into a tangle of short, narrow corridors, ill lit and damp, that so far as Noah could determine were largely unnecessary, as though at one time somebody must have had a plan, but could not be bothered following through. There were cracks, not only along the seams, but cutting through the concrete too, and extensive evidence of infiltration. The sharp clang of the hammer led Noah around a corner in time to see a large pipe swing free and drop to the floor, spilling water into an already wide pool at Gary's feet.

"It's like working in a bilge," Gary said over his shoulder.

Sweating heavily, he heaved the pipe to one side, then he knelt to catch his breath, and also Noah's eye. The question, unstated, was why they had let the drain become so badly clogged. The answer, essentially, was that they hadn't. The drains had been in bad shape before Cate and Felix moved in, and anyway it was the landlord's responsibility, only he refused to do anything about it because (he claimed) the drains had been clear when they moved in. He had made similar excuses for the house's other deficiencies, a list that included the water in the basement, the sinking foundation and the sloping floor, as well as cracks in the walls and under the baseboards where, in the fall, the mice began to nest and where, in the winter, cold air and frost crept in. During the coldest weeks, a thick layer of ice formed whose only virtue was that it blocked the wind, which otherwise they would have felt swirling around their feet. Then there were the windows, which all leaked, except in the bathrooms where they were painted shut, which led to mildew Cate could never entirely fight back. None of this, the landlord asserted, should hinder their enjoyment of the dwelling. However, if they felt strongly that it did they were welcome to argue before the rental board, should they opt for mediation.

A shorter answer, of course, was that Noah and Cate couldn't do it themselves and couldn't afford to pay someone. Gary was not happy. "I'm not gonna lie, Noah. It's a dog's breakfast down here." He stood up and slid a giant pipe cutter across the floor with his foot and began scraping out the open end of the stack connection. "At least you know where the shutoff is now. That's something. In a house like this, with no real insulation—what's in the walls anyway? probably newspaper, right? if that?—if your drain's not draining you get standing water, and then if the furnace goes even shutting off the water won't save you. The pipes will burst. Not a great big guy like this, maybe, but that just means something else will give out. Pipes will give out in places you don't even want to think about." Gary then turned to face him. "So listen, these pipes here are old and there's corrosion, but it's nothing I can't fix. But we've got to keep the drains clear. You get it?"

Noah surveyed the wreckage. It was considerable. "Fair enough," he said.

"No, pay attention. You see how the stack here is cast iron. So it won't just accept the new PVC. It needs a coupling. Now I can do that, but it won't make a difference if we don't keep things clear down here. You understand?"

"That sounds great, Gary."

"No it doesn't. You're not hearing me. There's the drains in here, and the sewers out there, and the two of them need to keep things clear between them. They need to communicate. They need to be free to express themselves. You understand what I'm talking about, right?"

It seemed Noah had not understood, but now he thought he was starting to. "We're talking about your daughter."

"No, we're talking about plumbing. Aren't you listening?" Gary said angrily. "We're two men and we can talk about plumbing because nobody said I couldn't talk to you about plumbing." He picked his hammer out of a puddle and dried it on his pants. "But I want to know the kind of guy my daughter's dating, especially because I'm fixing the drains in the house he's still sharing with his wife."

"Gary, I can't tell you how much this means," Noah said. "Money's tight and Cate doesn't get called in enough. We'd be in real trouble without you." Gary only grunted. "Look, I live mainly in the front two rooms and the kitchen. Cate and Felix have the second floor."

Finally, Gary nodded. "OK," he said, and patted Noah on the shoulder.

As Noah climbed the stairs, Gary shouted that he needed another hour to finish up, maybe a bit more. Upstairs, the women were talking in the kitchen. From the hallway he could hear the hesitation in Cate's voice, the kind common in people uncomfortable with charity. She was asking Cecelia again was she sure her father would take nothing for the work. As Noah entered, Cate was frowning and crunching between her teeth the cartilaginous ends of some leftover chicken bones, the rest of which were simmering in a small pot.

"Don't even ask him again," Cecelia reassured her. "At this point he would only be insulted. All Noah did was ask his advice. He's the one who offered."

Cate turned a bone over in her hand and cracked the tip open between her teeth and ground it down. Cecelia tried not to stare.

"We talked and it's fine," Noah said. "So stop worrying about it."

"And it's not too bad? He's not having to do too much?"

"It's nothing he can't handle. He needs another hour or so. I thought I could make a quick trip to the library."

"What for?" Cate asked.

"I left my address book. It's got Andrew's number in it."

"Don't forget I have to be at the hospital before five thirty."

Cecelia interrupted: "I can go."

"No, no," Noah said. "I'll take care of it."

"You're sure you won't be late?" Cate asked.

"Am I normally late?"

"Depends what do you mean. Late remembering a birthday? Or an anniversary? Late with a decision? With a compliment? An apology?"

"Come on."

"Trick question. It's all of the above."

"Maybe I should leave you two alone," Cecelia said.

"Oh sure, because this is what we used to call romantic," Cate said. "*I'll kick you in the shins* means *I love you.*"

"Don't threaten me with a good time," Noah said.

Cate removed some thin plastic containers from the cupboard and began ladling the broth into them.

"Listen, why don't you let me go for the book," Cecelia said. "Otherwise, I'll have nothing to do."

"You can handle your father, if it comes to that," Noah said.

"Oh, thanks."

"Just let me be gallant, and when I get back you'll have everything you need." Noah smiled. "Feel free to marvel."

"I'm marvelling," Cecelia said.

Noah kissed her quickly. "You're marvellous."

"Just don't be late," Cate repeated.

Noah grabbed his jacket and assured her that there was no need to worry. He knew exactly where to look.

ㅁ

He made his way up McCaul Street towards College and St. George. Loitering outside the Salvation Army building were several scruffy and impoverished men, mainly regulars. At times they could seem threatening, but they mostly went out of their way to seem otherwise. They ignored pedestrians in general, and children especially. Cate was less than happy with their proximity. Still, she rarely let her worry get the better of her. She had a gift for composure.

Like the first time he brought Cecelia home. Noah could read her discomfort, but to Cecelia she gave nothing away. When Felix lifted his hand into Cecelia's to shake and said he was delighted to meet her, Cate even allowed herself to be pleased. It was a charming scene. Before long, Felix's staid greetings became excited gallops to the door, and his well-mannered handshakes were abandoned for bearhugs. Very often these veered straight into a show and tell of some sort. Felix would hurriedly explain to Cecelia all the contents of this or that drawing he had made, or story he had read, or Lego structure he had built, with all of the signs of childhood infatuation. During one such visit, kneeling by the coffee table and describing an encounter with another child in the schoolyard, Felix became so excited that in a sudden spasm of energy he pitched forward and struck his face on the tabletop. He hit it hard enough that even Noah was concerned. Cecelia was terrified. When Felix came back up his eyes were wide, at first with surprise and then, as he pressed his fingers to his face, with fascination at the bleeding from his lower lip.

"Are you OK?" Cecelia asked.

"Oh yeah, I've been hurt worse than this," Felix answered.

"Are you sure?"

"I go to the playground all the time with Dad and you should see the blood!"

Doubtful, Noah called for Cate, who generally handled minor medical emergencies. One cold compress, five hours, and six stitches later, Felix was back from the hospital and his lip was once again intact. He played it like it was nothing.

In the weeks that followed they developed a routine. After spending the afternoon at the library, Cecelia and Noah would walk down to the house where Felix, not long arrived from school, would be waiting. When they entered, he would race to the door, ignore his father, and immediately take Cecelia by the hand and lead her up the stairs to his room. There he would clear his bed with a sweep of his arms and sit her down to tell her about his day: about how Sanjeev and Michael had punched each other over the new girl Kristy Chang; and how Nicole had gotten shy and forgotten how to long divide and cried when everyone laughed; and how Julia and Zoltan had decided not to be boyfriend and girlfriend anymore, which was probably good since they were too young to be getting serious, and they were telling different stories about who decided first to break up because neither one wanted to be the one who got dumped, but that probably they had decided together; and how in gym class he had almost won at dodgeball, and had lasted longer at arm burns than anybody except Harpreet, but that was OK because she was tougher than all the boys, and anyway he would be tougher than her in a few years. Some of this he described calmly, philosophically, as though a wise old man were stuffed inside his ten-year-old body, and some of it he acted out with an animal-like energy, sometimes lunging around the room like a monkey, and sometimes flopping fish-like on the mattress.

Sometimes, when he had finished, he would show off his reading for Cecelia. Instructing her not to move, he would race down the stairs to his bag, which he never carried to the second floor if he could help it, and return with his reader in hand. With the pride of acquired skill, he would read a new story for her, stopping frequently to explain the hard words to her so she would know he understood. Cate would occasionally check in on them, especially if Felix had homework, but otherwise she let them be. Cate was good that way. Only once did she express any concern.

One afternoon, from the next room where she was folding laundry and not trying very hard not to eavesdrop, she overheard them. Felix was explaining to Cecelia how he liked reading so much that he even read things his teachers didn't ask him to.

"So what do you like to read?" Cecelia asked.

"Oh, you know, whatever strikes me." Felix sometimes picked up such phrases and liked to audition them in this offhanded manner. "What do you like to read?" he asked her in return.

"Oh, you know, whatever strikes me."

"But what's your favourite?"

"My favourite? I guess that would be Shakespeare."

"I remember. My dad brought me his book."

"That wasn't the real Shakespeare, though."

"Oh? Who's the real Shakespeare?"

For a change, it was Cecelia who raced downstairs. She returned with a worn paperback and handed it to Felix. His eyes narrowed in concentration and he read slowly: *William Shakes-peare, the Twelfth Night.* He seemed to be guessing at *Shakespeare* and stumbled slightly over the title. Cecelia pointed out how he'd added the *the.* He tried again, successfully. Then she opened the book and asked him to try a bit. He stumbled sometimes, and sometimes leaned in close to follow his fingers across the page with his eyes, but plugged bravely away, with Cecelia helping as he went:

"O spirit of love. How quick and fresh art thoo—"

"It ends in *ow*, like when you skin your knee."

"Thou. That not-with-standing they—"

"Thy."

"Thy CA-pa-CI-ty—"

"Ca-PA-city."

"Thy ca-PA-city. Re-cei-veth—"

"Very good!"

"—as the sea. No—no—"

"Nought, like a knot in your shoelace, it means nothing."

"Nought enters there. Of what VA-li-DI-ty—"

"Va-LID-ity."

"Va-LID-ity and pitch so—soo—"

"Like *so air*. It's short for so ever."

"Soe'er. But falls into a-bat-ment—"

"A-bate-ment."

"A-bate-ment and low price. Even in a minute."

Felix let out a monstrous little sigh and put on a look of exhaustion. "That was really hard. I didn't hardly understand a single thing I said."

"Those are hard words," Cecelia agreed.

"Here, you read some."

He handed over the book and Cecelia turned to a dog-eared page, which Felix studied intently as she read aloud: "She never told her love, but let concealment, like a worm i' th' bud, feed on her damask cheek. She pined in thought, and with a green and yellow melancholy she sat like patience on a monument, smiling at grief. Was not this love indeed?"

She stopped and Felix looked up at her, impressed.

"What do you think?" she asked.

"I didn't know I could keep going at the end of the lines. It makes it sound like you know what it means." He took back the book and studied the words on the page. After a few moments he closed the pages with finality. "I'm too tired to try again right now, but do you think I could read Shakespeare like you one day?" He looked up at her hopefully.

"Of course."

"And you'll help me," Felix announced.

"Yes I will," she agreed.

Later, Cate admitted to Noah that she had sneaked around to the open doorway to observe them. She asked him was he sure it was a good idea for Felix to be reading something with so many hard words and which he was so unlikely to understand. She wondered would it hurt his confidence, or maybe turn reading into something laborious and even joyless. He told her that Cecelia had read *Macbeth* when she was his age. He didn't know how much she had understood, but it certainly hadn't hurt her. Cate had been unconvinced, and a little annoyed, but Noah only insisted Felix would be fine and they should let him read what he wanted. Felix was far too clever to get discouraged. Like many of the pleasures into which he would someday be initiated, like music or sports, or even sex, he didn't need to understand it all at once to like it. Noah got a good haranguing from Cate for that analogy.

But considering their unconventional domestic arrangement, with him and Cate romantically estranged but domestically conjoined, and Cecelia in the afternoons and evenings slowly insinuating herself, it was incredible to Noah that, in those initial weeks at least, their disagreement over Felix's reading was the only significant conflict. The one hiccup seemed to be Felix's infatuation with Cecelia which, however childlike at first, seemed to be growing into something more serious.

One afternoon, when Cate came through the door with the groceries, she found them playing cards on the living room floor. They were leaning in and slapping down cards with increasing urgency and, when Cate asked Felix to take a break to help her with the bags, he resisted—he was taking the opportunity to look down Cecelia's shirt. "Eyes up, mister," Cate said.

Caught in the act, Felix convulsed and fell forward across the playing cards and into Cecelia's arms. It was as though his feelings were trying to break down a door and barge out into the open. Curling up and turning away from his mother's gaze, he dropped his head into Cecelia's lap and lay there with his arms around her. Cate ignored his childish resistance and told him to get up. When he refused again, and Cecelia proved unable to pry him loose, Cate removed the bags to the kitchen herself, telling Felix, "That move won't work when you're twenty-five and it won't work now."

Noah waited for an evening when Cecelia was not around and Cate was working a shift at the hospital, then he went to Felix in his room and sat down amid the chaos of toys and clothes. When he asked if they could talk about boys and girls and how they feel about each other, Felix groaned and flopped sideways.

"Do we have to do all that again?"

"No, I guess we don't have to."

"Good. Last time Mom brought the diagrams from the hospital that showed just everything." His mouth twisted in discomfort.

"Fair enough. But you've been spending a lot of time with Cecelia, and your mom and I are wondering if maybe you're having some new feelings."

"It's all good. I just like her. She makes me happy and ..." Here his confidence wavered and he became suddenly shy. "And I want to hug her sometimes."

Noah smiled. "I feel the same way. You shouldn't look down her shirt, though. And you shouldn't throw yourself on her." Felix averted his eyes, and Noah took pity on him. "There's nothing wrong with giving her a hug when you feel like it, though." He stroked his son's head gently, and it nodded beneath his hand.

"OK," Felix said. Then he sat up straight and looked at Noah intently. "Dad, could I ask a question about babies, though?"

"But I thought you didn't want that talk." Forced to shake off his confusion, and in the anxious manner of so many fathers, bound in paternal obligation, fathering as their fathers fathered, back beyond the vanishing point of human history, Noah took a deep breath and began to explain how when a man and a woman love each other very much—

Felix rolled his eyes. "No no, you told me all that already. I want to know about gay babies." Noah had never heard of such a thing. "The ones with two dads or two moms. I see them sometimes in the park."

Noah pointed out that most of the pairs of men he saw with babies were not together like that, and that they were just friends, and both had wives somewhere.

"I know that. I mean the ones who hold hands and put their arms around each other. In school the teacher says gays and lesbians can't have their own babies, and that theirs are adopted." For some reason, the word *lesbian* sounded ridiculous and slightly unnerving spoken by his young son, and Noah only prayed the next word from his child's lips was not *surrogates*.

"But I don't understand why," Felix continued, "if they're in love, there isn't a way they can have their own babies."

"Well, you know how you have a curl in your hair, like your mother. And a split in your thumbnail."

"And your brown eyes."

"Exactly. Well, that's sort of the point. Some of it you get from her, and some from me. It's the differences that make a baby. You remember, it takes a sperm cell and an egg—"

"I know. But why is it that way?"

Noah frowned. "I don't know. I guess two men and two women aren't different enough." Of course, the argument was circular—even Felix could see that—so Noah retreated to tradition. "It's sort of like in the Bible story. When the animals were loaded two-by-two, male and female, into the ark to save them from the Flood. Or when the world was created by dividing it first into heaven and the earth, and light and dark, and land and sea. Things being different is how the world begins."

"Is that what made it good?" Felix asked.

"I don't know that either," Noah answered. "But differences are what make me me, and you you, and everybody themselves and not somebody else. I think that's good, at least."

"Then why do gay people go together?"

"Because they love each other, silly."

"So gay people love each other," Felix said carefully, "even though they can't make babies." He was thinking hard. "Does that mean that not-gay people can have babies even if they don't love each other?"

"Yes," Noah said cautiously. More and more, he dreaded the report he was going to have to make to Cate.

"So why do people love each other if they don't have to have babies?"

Question after question, it was nothing but curveballs and sliders. Noah considered his options. At last he put his arm around Felix. "You know, there's a very old story about that. Do you want to hear it?" Felix nodded. "So, the story goes that in the beginning people didn't look like they do now, but were round like balls with four arms and four legs, and one head with two faces looking opposite ways." To help explain, Noah took a pencil and paper from Felix's desk and began to sketch it out. "They also had four ears, and two sets of private parts, and there were three kinds of people: male people, female people, and male-female people. The males had two penises, and the females two vaginas—"

"And the male-females had one of each kind!" Felix's eyes grew wide as he anticipated the hermaphroditic genitals of the androgynous sex.

"Well, these people got too strong for their own good, and didn't want to do as they were told. So to make them easier to handle, the gods chopped them in half—head to toe—right down the middle. Then they twisted their heads around the other way so they could see where they'd been cut in half and have a think about what they'd done."

"Then their penises would look like tails," Felix said, suddenly laughing. Noah could not deny this. His drawing showed as much.

"Well, can you imagine what happened?" Noah asked. Felix shook his head in expectation. "They all missed their other halves and wanted to be whole again. So the pairs of males threw their arms around each other, and the females, and the single males and females that had been joined to each other. And they squeezed and cried, and kept trying until they forgot about anything else, and some of them even started to die of hunger. But when the gods saw how sad they were, they felt bad and decided to turn their privates—" Noah amended his drawing "— around to the front."

"So, no more tails," Felix observed wryly.

"That's right. And, if you believe that story, then each of us is just one half of what used to be a whole person. And love is each of us looking for our other half."

Felix said it sounded like a joke. Noah agreed. Then Felix asked, "But if there were males, and females, and male-females in the beginning, shouldn't there be twice as many gay people as not-gay people?"

It was surprisingly sound math from a ten-year-old. "It doesn't work that way in real life, though," Noah said. "Nature is biased the other way."

"OK," Felix said, ruminating, "but I know a boy who says he likes boys and girls. There aren't any people like that in the story."

Noah felt like he was falling behind.

"Will he fall in love with a boy and a girl at the same time?" Felix asked. He was no longer looking at Noah, and his voice had become quiet.

Noah answered slowly, "More likely he'll fall in love with a woman sometimes, and sometimes a man."

"But could he be with a girl and a boy at the same time? If he wanted to? Or a girl could be with a girl and a boy?"

Noah hesitated. "It's possible. I'm not sure it works out that way very often. Most people are looking for only one person at a time."

Felix hesitated too. "Dad," he asked finally, "do you think Mom or Cecelia is your other half?"

The question seemed very important to Felix, and Noah wished very badly to give a satisfactory answer. "I don't know, Felix."

"You always say I take after Mom. If you marry Cecelia, will I take after her?"

"It doesn't really work that way." Of course, Noah realized, this was not strictly true.

Felix nodded his head slowly, then he reached over and patted his father comfortingly on the knee. "OK," he said. "Good talk, Dad. Thanks."

Suddenly cheerful again, Felix had torn down the stairs and out to play in the yard, leaving Noah on the bed, alone and bewildered. Even now, weeks later, Noah could scarcely believe his son's adaptations, how amenable he was to sudden reconfigurations in his understanding of the world. It was almost miraculous. Upon receiving the report, Cate had asked him did he really think that Felix understood. Even now, Noah was forced to admit: of the two of them, it was Felix who seemed to have the better handle on it.

ᴝ

The clamour in the basement carried on after Noah left to fetch his book, as did the drone of the television in the living room. In the kitchen, Cate had finished with the stock, which was cooling on the countertop. Now she leaned by the window, drinking her tea in the last light of the shortened day. As always she left the bags in, which turned the water nearly black, strong enough to make your teeth cross. Cecelia took just enough milk in hers to turn it fawnish.

"We always did like to have a go," Cate said. "I hope you know it doesn't mean anything."

"Of course," Cecelia said.

"We don't do it on purpose. It's just a rut we fall into sometimes—one of the traps of marriage. Even when it's over, it isn't."

"I guess that's why they call it wedlock," Cecelia suggested.

"Exactly," Cate said, relieved. "There are just these things in a marriage ... sometimes it's hard to get free of them. It's a bit like when you wrap yourself too tight in a blanket, and when you wake up you can't move, and you start to panic." She was fidgeting with her cup. "Sorry. That sounds melodramatic doesn't it."

"Not as much as you think."

Cate smiled. "You know, I had these recurring dreams for a while. A faceless man pins me to the floor, and no matter how hard I scream I can't make a sound. They were so vivid, one time I had an anxiety attack when me and Felix were wrestling. He ended up kneeling on me with his hands on my shoulders and I panicked and jerked right up. Shot him right onto the floor."

"Really?"

"I know, right? And I can't even count the number of times I had to get out from under Noah in bed so that he wasn't on top of me." The television was still on and still loud, but Cate lowered her voice, shyly. "I never told anyone that. Not even Noah." She glanced over at the clock on the stove. "It probably has something to do with why I had the affair."

Cecelia's eyes widened briefly at Cate's unexpected candor.

"He didn't tell you, did he," Cate said.

"Not a word."

"That figures. He's good that way. I still felt terrible about it." Cate sat down and rested her elbows on the chipped melamine of the table. She looked right at Cecelia. "You know, I didn't think it would be, but it's been nice having you around."

Unsure how to respond, Cecelia tried to smile, but the trying was obvious.

"Oh, it's not weird, is it?" Cate asked.

"It is a little."

"OK, a little weird. But I've been here three years and I still hardly know anyone. And when you don't have anyone to talk to except a ten-year-old you go a little crazy, even if he is a sweetheart. I was uneasy when you started coming around, and I wasn't as welcoming as I could have been, but really it's turned out fine." Cate hesitated and her gaze drifted down towards her hands. "Actually, it's been nice to have a friend."

It seemed to Cecelia that there ought to be a limit to their confidence, but she could not decide where that limit lay. They had, indeed, begun a friendship. Or, at least, Cate had come to count on her. "Why did you come out here anyway?"

"Oh," Cate said slowly, "it's complicated. When we were still in Sydney, Noah would drive to his grandparents' house every day to help with the groceries, or rake the leaves, or get the mail. Anything that needed doing. He'd be there for hours on the weekends too. You wouldn't ever know there was anything wrong to look at him, but he would just sort of collapse when he got in. I think eventually he just had nothing left, but he didn't know it, and after I went back to school, we just tied ourselves up in knots trying to make it all work."

"Back?"

"Oh, I didn't go to university right away. And by the time Noah graduated we had loans to repay and a child to care for. It was only after Noah's job at the public library was solid enough that I decided to go back, except I just wanted to take the college program, and Noah wanted me to do the RN degree. Work was hard to come by, and some of our friends were already moving away. We got talking about leaving too, and he wanted me to have options."

"Makes sense," Cecelia said.

"If we were going to leave, sure," Cate countered, "but we weren't, you see? There wasn't much keeping me there—my family and I aren't close. But Noah, anytime he had a free afternoon or evening he was over helping his grandmother, or talking to his grandfather. Or he'd sit at the table writing all sorts of letters, looking for information on his parents. Even then you could see he wasn't going to find what he wanted, but there was no telling him. He either figures things out himself or he doesn't at all. He's like a dog on a bone sometimes. You may have noticed."

"I may have," Cecelia said. She laughed a little.

"To be fair, it's not so much that he never found out anything new. It's that nothing will tell him what he wants to know."

"Filling in the past isn't the same as fixing it," Cecelia suggested.

"Oh God, yes, exactly." Cate sighed, and her shoulders dropped in relief. "It's this hole inside him that he tries to fill with doing things for everybody else. When I went back to school, he started cooking the meals, and he did most of the cleaning and laundry, and all the shopping."

Cecelia laughed. "Cleaning, laundry, and shopping ... what a nightmare."

"I know, it sounds crazy to complain about it. And I didn't at first. At first it was an enormous help. Especially during midterms or finals. He had things so under control all I had to do was study and put Felix to bed with a story. But then something started to go wrong—" Cate unexpectedly broke off. She frowned and eyed her tea. "Have you ever had someone take care of everything for you?"

"Never," Cecelia answered quickly. Then she thought about it. "Except when I was a child, I guess."

Cate nodded. She turned her cup in her hands. "Before long I wasn't putting Felix to bed either—even when midterms were over. I just needed to do something that wasn't schoolwork, but every time I tried, Noah insisted on doing it for me. And the way he did it ... he was always encouraging and supportive ... but he started handling all of the finances too, which before we always did together. And it wasn't just that he managed them himself, but that he stopped taking me seriously when we argued about them. Like I'd given up my right to an opinion."

For Cecelia, it was an observation not without validity, but in Noah's absence she was not about to let it stand. "Maybe he needed someone to take care of him a little too."

"But he wouldn't let me," Cate insisted. "He thinks he can fix everything himself, and brushes off anybody that tries to help him. It wasn't just that he started taking things over. He started taking them away. And I never figured out how to take them back."

"That," Cecelia said carefully, "doesn't sound like him."

"No, of course not," Cate hurried to agree. "He never meant to. But it made me so unnecessary." She laughed suddenly, seemingly at herself and much to Cecelia's relief. "I should never have let him do it. I just felt guilty. I'm not like you—I hated school. I knew I'd never get through the degree program. And here he was, doing everything, and somehow always able to take on more, and because I couldn't … It was like a part of me disappeared, and the part that was left was a disappointment."

In the yard the bushes lurched and the windows rattled in a sudden gust. A cold draft swept along the floor.

"You know," Cate continued, "the way Noah was—I didn't have the words for it then, but I've thought a lot about it since. I think, for him every day was just a string of automatic reactions. They looked like decisions, but they weren't. The worse his grandfather's dementia got, and the more he took over for everyone, the more he was like a computer than a human being. When he looked like he was thinking, he was actually just following a program. Jesus, I even wrote it all out."

"You wrote it out?" Cecelia grinned in amusement. She didn't understand, but it sounded preposterous. "What, like … you wrote it down on paper?"

Cate nodded. "A few months ago, when I was deciding whether to let him move in. Hell, do you want to see it?"

Cecelia grew fearful and uncertain, but Cate had already risen and was retrieving her purse. She removed her wallet and, from deep inside one of the zippered pockets, she pulled out a tightly folded sheet of paper. She wavered briefly, and Cecelia almost hoped she would stop herself, but then she handed it over. Reluctantly, Cecelia opened its many folds, and before she let herself get caught up thinking too much about it, she pressed it flat on the table before her. It read:

Wake up at dawn *OR, IF NOT*, before; *IF* a weekday, run, *OR IF* a weekend, run more; *THEN* get Felix up; *THEN* make breakfast; *IF* I had morning class *AND IF* his grandparents were able *THEN* take Felix to them and go to work, *OR IF* I had morning class *AND IF* his grandparents were not able *THEN* stay home and watch Felix and make up the hours on a weekend, *OR IF* I had afternoon class *AND* his grandparents were able *THEN* go to work and pick Felix up at lunch and take him to them and go back to work, *OR IF* I had afternoon class *AND* his grandparents were not able *THEN* go to work and come home at lunch and watch Felix and make up the hours on a weekend, *OR IF* I had class all day *AND* his grandparents were able *THEN* take Felix to them and go to work, *OR IF* I had class all day *AND* his grandparents were not able *THEN* stay home and watch Felix and make up the hours on a weekend; *IF* Felix was with his grandparents *THEN* stop after work to pick him up and spend some time with them *OR IF* Felix was at home with me and not with his grandparents *THEN* stop after work to spend some time with them; *IF* a weeknight go shopping *OR* do laundry *OR* clean something, *OR IF* a weekend clean everything and dust and put away Felix's toys; *THEN* make dinner; *THEN* play with Felix; *THEN* put him to bed; *THEN* while I read to Felix, study the finances or his notebooks and enter new information, if any; *THEN* floss and clean his teeth; *THEN* attempt sexual intercourse; *IF* I was willing *THEN* succeed, *OR IF* I was too tired *AND* too tired to resist very strongly *THEN* succeed, *OR IF* I was too tired *AND* not too tired to resist *THEN* irritation; *THEN* sleep as many as five hours; *THEN* start over again.

Resisting the urge to read the absurdity a second time, Cecelia handed it back. "You know, it could almost be funny."

"I know, I know." Cate hurriedly refolded the evidence and tucked it back into her wallet. "But it doesn't mean anything."

"You colour coded it."

Cate slumped in her seat. "God, it is pretty childish, isn't it."

"Has he seen it?"

"Of course not!" Cate said. Then she frowned. "I'm sorry. I've put you in a terrible position."

Cecelia sipped her tea. She tried to imagine the kind of bewilderment or crisis that could make a person do something like that. She also considered what she might do in Cate's place. Not that, she assured herself. And yet. "Well, if he doesn't find out ..." Cate was sitting looking at her in anxious silence. "No harm done, right?"

"You know, you don't have to be so understanding."

"No, I guess I don't," Cecelia said. "I like to try, though."

Cate's lips curled into a tight, crooked smile. "I guess I just needed to remind myself what it was like, so I don't let it happen again."

Cecelia hesitated. "But didn't you ever talk about it?"

"I tried. I mean, I really did. But when I get emotional I can't explain anything. And he has this way of hearing and not hearing, you know? Like your words mean something different to him, or they turn into something else in his head. I sometimes wonder. If we'd just been better at talking, maybe I wouldn't have kicked him out."

"Wait," Cecelia said, "you kicked *him* out?" Without quite being conscious of it, she had been building a comfortable narrative, or if not comfortable, one that she could live with, and the admission of this new detail ill-fit the story she was telling herself.

"I sure did," Cate said.

"I just assumed—"

"Yeah. But no. No, after he found out about the affair he actually doubled down on our marriage. He was idiotic about it. He was ..." Cate searched for the word. It took her a while. "Merciless," she said at last. "He was mercilessly faithful to me."

She looked at Cecelia. She seemed to want to know if she understood her meaning. Cecelia was afraid she might.

"To be fair, it did work for a while. For a whole year we just white-knuckled it. We could go for weeks being civil to each other. But it always came up again. He said he wanted to let it go, but he said it so often I knew he couldn't. When I told him to leave, I closed the door behind him and my legs just gave out. I'd never broken up with anyone before."

Cecelia sat there, trying not to frown, but failing.

"And the worst part," Cate continued, "is that the other man—he was a classmate—he was just like Noah." She shook her head. "How stupid is that? If someone had told me we would end up living together again, I'd never have believed it."

For much of the conversation, a question had been lurking in Cecelia's mind, sidling up, slinking away, shifting to and fro like an anticipation, just out of reach of her awareness. "Cate," she asked, "how did you know when it was over?" The words were out of her mouth before she really appreciated the tug of war that had been going on inside her. Even as a part of her was trying to haul them back in. "Sorry. I'm sorry. You don't have to answer that."

Cate chuckled. "That's an easy one. The sex stopped working." She went to the counter and restarted the kettle. "Even thinking about sex made me feel sick. It was like my body knew the marriage was over before the rest of me. I could feel it in my guts."

"And you didn't tell him," Cecelia said.

Cate shook her head and leaned back against the counter. Perhaps a little wistfully.

"Our wills and fates do so contrary run," Cecelia observed, for want of other wisdom.

"I like that," Cate said. "It sounds almost like a poem."

Noah crossed Willcocks Street. Ahead, the library stood like a concrete redoubt, uncompromising and resolute, and when he arrived he hurried inside and right down to the ground floor, where the boxes were being stored. Walking the corridors, he experienced a sudden premonition of foolishness. Only the foolishness had already occurred. It was a post-monition. Realizing you've been stupid just in time to not be able to do anything about it—the way he and Cate had flirted before he left, and Cecelia had suggested she leave them alone. It was nothing. Just the radiation of an old fondness whose energy, fading since their lives had melted down, could be detected and even measured as a kind of marital half-life. Still, they had been incautious with Cecelia's feelings. He told himself he would be more careful, and he wondered was it possible that everything would work out all right.

The address book was not where Noah remembered it, but no harm done. It was a small room and after a few minutes, he found the brown pleather cover peeking out from behind one of the boxes. He snugged it into a pocket and turned to leave, but instead ran up against Owen Trover and his assistant, who were just entering the room. Noah and Trover stood there a moment, surprised and making polite apologies and pleasantries.

"This is an opportune coincidence. I was just saying to Clement— you remember Mr. Rowse?" Noah did remember, and acknowledged him. "I was saying that he should make a point of contacting you before the end of the week. But, in my experience, coincidences abound when you have an eye for opportunity. Suddenly here we are, you and me, brought together by … what? Shall we call it … serendipity?"

"If you want to," Noah said.

Trover laughed and slapped Noah on the shoulder. "I've just been with Mr. Potts. He was showing me some letters he's acquired for the Darwin collection—I expect you know all about that collection, with a name like yours—anyway I thought I might come down and see if anything was going on." He paused and smiled. Then he removed his coat and sat down at the small desk. The room really only held two people comfortably. Noah was more or less forced to pirouette to face him. "So what is going on?" Trover asked. "You were going to keep me informed."

"I thought I had."

"It's been weeks since I heard from either of you."

"I didn't think it was worth calling to tell you there was no news."

Trover was still smiling, but the smile was growing joyless. Vacant and ambiguous, it obscured whether he desired an apology or a reassurance or what.

"No news is also news," he said. "Listen, Noah, I promised Ms. Lines that I would be hands-off, and I'm trying to keep that promise. And, honestly, I can't say I'm surprised that she's been somewhat remiss. Classes. Papers. Her nose always in a book, I imagine. But I thought you, at least, might remember the importance of communicating with your patron." Noah's posture stiffened. He had been dressed down often enough to recognize the signs. "Noah, I didn't get to where I am by luck. I wasn't born into money or a good home. I grew up in the worst neighbourhoods and went to some very average schools, and there was no generous benefactor to give me a leg-up. It was just me, climbing one rung of the ladder at a time and not looking back."

"Sounds like most of us," Noah said.

"Perhaps." Trover scanned the room. Then he went to one of the boxes and opened the lid. He flipped idly through the contents, frowning the while. "You know, I'm not one to kid myself, so I've accepted that I'll never have the collection I want. For anything I want, for anything I have, there's almost always going to be another copy out there, and usually a better one, and usually unobtainable. I still remember the one that got away." He replaced the lid on the box. "First Folio, not in the Lee census. Owned by a succession of lords, fathers and sons, for two centuries until the last one sold off the family library to cover his debts. Bound in medium morocco, five bands on the spine, the second panel double-wide for the title and author, end-papers in good condition. It was the first I ever handled. I can still remember how soft and supple the pages were: imperfect ivory in colour, with age spots, but almost shimmering in gentle waves wherever you opened the book, the ink still dark and crisp. You would almost believe it had only just been printed. And it had notes scattered throughout, and in a few places the handwriting of a child practicing his letters. What kind of thrashing did he get for that, I wonder?"

"I can imagine," Noah said. He said it to humour him, but it had the side effect of redrawing Trover's attention.

"Now consider that the indenture, my indenture, isn't just a copy. It's the thing itself. And it's not like shares in a company, intellectual property, or even real estate. This is something you can hold in your hands. It exists outside the laws of economics. No one can diminish it or take it away. And what if there's more? Under the circumstances, I don't think it's unreasonable for me to expect that your updates, whatever they entail, be delivered in a regular and timely fashion." Trover spoke calmly, but there was no mistaking his intent. It was a straight-up reprimand. "Do you think that now might be a timely time?"

"I'm sorry. I didn't realize. Honestly, there's been nothing. If something had turned up, we would have told you immediately. We're just about to start writing up the description."

"And do you think there's anything more?"

"Beyond doubtful. It's hard to imagine there's still something to discover in the London records. I suppose it's possible there's something in the parish records in Boston, but since we've followed the Belotts as far as Halifax, we figured we should carry on from there. I have a friend who can help us, if there's anything left to trace in that direction. We were thinking of going in the new year, once the description is finished."

"Not before?"

"In case we missed something. It'll force us to go through it all again. Sometimes you notice things the second time around."

"See, Noah? You had lots of news." Trover sat down again. "I like your plan to follow the family. Family is important. It's important when you have it, and it's important when you don't. Did you know that I have no family at all? I find that bachelorhood suits me, so I suppose my books and paintings are the closest thing I'll ever have. But it's not the same as having a real family, is it? They don't feel hope or despair, they don't shiver when the heat goes out, or get hungry when the fridge is bare." While he was waxing philosophical, his gaze remained unfocused and upturned, taking in the cold fluorescent ceiling lights, but now they dropped and fixed on Noah. "Have you been careful with your money, Noah? I've wondered now and then what would happen if anyone found out you were receiving a salary from me while you continued to draw employment insurance?"

Noah's throat drew tight. His blood began to burn in his ears and pulse so strongly that he felt it in his eyes and lips and even his nose. Facing off with Trover, Noah refused to break his gaze, but as victories go it was worthless. He was fucked, and he knew it in his bones.

"I doubt any of it would trouble me," Trover continued, "but I imagine a fine and restitution would be a considerable burden for you. On top of that, you would then have to claim the income, wouldn't you? Have you been setting anything aside for tax season? Things could get precarious. It would be a shame if you had to leave that little house of yours, so conveniently located by your son's school. I wonder, where would you go?"

The question was rhetorical. There was nothing else to say. Noah understood perfectly and only wondered how he had not seen it before, that all along he'd been dancing at the end of Trover's line. He left without delay and headed for home. He didn't hear the rest of the conversation.

"It's like I said, Clement. The wife and child were the strings to pull. In fact, see what you can find about his grandparents. You said they raised him?"

"You won't actually follow through with it, though," Rowse said.

"I never threaten anything I wouldn't do. But it won't come to that. Anyway, he's really in no position to refuse, and has no reason to. I just wanted him to know." Trover rose from his chair and began to put on his coat. "I'm surprised. You're usually so steely about these things."

"But is it really necessary?" Rowse had not yet moved to follow.

"Remind me to show you the indenture sometime. 1612. So succinct they dispensed with guidelines. The labels and seals are missing, but the ink quality ... and you can even see the grain of the leather and a scar from the animal they skinned to get it."

The second floor had two small bathrooms, one at either end, and Cecelia had chosen the one in the front after deciding she didn't care to know how it felt to use a slanted toilet. Upstairs, the house seemed even smaller than below. As she stood washing her hands, Cecelia wondered at the absurdity of it all: Cate had stopped loving one man only to go chasing after his shadow in another. The sex had stopped working, she had said, and her hands had gestured vaguely at her whole anatomy. There was something to that. Looking up from the sink, Cecelia examined her reflection in the mirror and realized that she often thought about herself as though she were divided into a mind and a body, the way a house is divided into separate rooms. Down there was the stomach in the kitchen, and there, in the utility room, the liver and kidneys. The heart was working away in the pump room, the bowels and bladder in the toilet. She envisioned the compartments of her belly and her rib-studded torso, but it wasn't like that after all—no, it was open-concept. A sore wrist was sometimes caused by tension in her neck or shoulder. A pain in her right hip might be from something injured in her left. And she'd known people who, instead of saying they were tired, said they had a headache, or if they were stressed said their stomachs hurt. And they weren't just saying it. They felt it that way too, like their bodies did their thinking for them. So, there's the brain, maybe, working away in the den, but the door doesn't close all the way, nor the other doors neither, so all the noises from all the other organs doing their own things find their way in too.

As Cecelia returned to the main floor she noted for a second time how the stairs creaked under her weight, loudly and easily enough to betray her descent to Felix and Cate. Noah was a sound sleeper—Cate not, she imagined, though for no particular reason. In the night, surely they wakened Felix and one another alike with their footfalls. Certainly these stairs would give away a person's every step. Cecelia returned Felix's smile as she passed through the living room back into the kitchen. Cate was sipping her tea, but distractedly—her eyes were distant, as though in search of something. She gazed at Cecelia as she sat down, as though she might find it in her.

"You know," she said, "I think the truth is, I stopped really being a lover some time before Noah did. He kept trying a long time."

"He does like to try," Cecelia said quickly, surprising herself. She hesitated, her mouth slightly agape, her embarrassment catching her off guard. She wondered if she would get away with it, and whether she might find a way to retreat into some semblance of her habitual reticence. It was, however, not only impossible, but also unnecessary. Cate just put down her cup and laughed.

"No, no, it's fine," she said, sympathetically. "You're right. He's a generous lover. It's just that with me—well, we'd only been with each other, so we didn't know anything. I only found out later that he went and read all these manuals and articles. It made things … complicated."

"Doesn't sound like such a bad idea—"

"Sure, if all you want is to orgasm as efficiently and convincingly as possible. Don't get me wrong, at first he was really attentive—and it sure did the trick—but eventually it started to feel like he was just showing off. Sometimes it was even as if he was trying to keep me from pleasing him, like I must not be any good at it—which I am, by the way, very good, though it cost me my marriage to find that out."

Cecelia shifted in her seat, but Cate just leaned her head on her hand, and sighed. "It shouldn't be this hard. I mean, you should be able to fill out a form and get what you want."

Cecelia laughed too now. The idea was absurd, but she had a point. "Do you think that would make a difference?"

"Probably not," Cate admitted. "You know, I know how wrong it was having that affair, but it was just such a relief to discover that that part of me wasn't actually dead. That when a man kissed me I could still feel something."

Cate coughed and rubbed her nose with the back of her fingers. There was a box of tissues on the counter, and she hurried to get one. Cecelia sat patiently, trying not to study her too closely.

"You know, I thought I'd be able to breathe again if I could just start over. I was so sure it would be fine. But it's so expensive here. And the hospital misled me about how many hours I'd get. I mean, I could barely keep up with the bills ..."

Even as the tears broke through and ran freely down her cheeks and Cate's gaze dipped back into her memory, her mind apparently casting back to that time, Cecelia, by pure intuition, could see it plainly. Without thinking, she supplied what Cate was after: "And then Noah came."

Cate's eyes were growing red and she blew her nose. "I didn't even ask him. I tried not even to tell him how bad it was, but he called to talk to Felix one night and it all just came out. A week later he turned up at the house." She shook her head. "Even after what I did to him."

The television went silent briefly, for a commercial break, and in the silence they could hear the couch springs as Felix shifted in the next room. Cate balled up the tissue and spun it between her fingers. When the commercials began to run, she spoke again, but more quietly. "It probably wouldn't have made any difference if I had the degree, but it eats at me sometimes. Like maybe I could have saved more money, enough to get us through the fall until the colds and flus started to take out the regular staff." Over and over Cate worried at the tissue, spinning and gripping and pulling at it.

"I think you got it," Cecelia said, indicating with one raised eyebrow the devastated remains in Cate's hand.

Looking down, Cate saw and grinned a little, sheepishly, at what she had done. She rose, tossed it in the garbage and washed her hands. Then she dropped back onto her chair. "I just wish I could get over feeling like he had to rescue me."

"I don't know. You let him move in," Cecelia offered. "Maybe you rescued him."

Cate considered this. "You know, honestly, this is the best we've got along in a very long time. It's like we had to break up to remind ourselves why we were such good friends when we were kids."

Cecelia understood the intended meaning. Just the same, her face stiffened.

"But it can't really go on like this," Cate hurried to reassure her. "It isn't good for Felix to get the wrong idea, us living under the same roof again. Did Noah tell you about the fight we had a few months ago?".

"I think he prefers to keep that sort of thing just between you two—"

"We were like two cats in a bag. Felix saw some track and field thing on TV with Noah, and after decided he wanted to be a runner. He spent the summer begging Noah to take him training. Anyway, when Noah moved in they started going out a few times a week, and when he got good at that Felix got him to buy a stopwatch and take him to the track at Central Tech. He asked one day, after they'd come back, if we thought he could be a racer one day, and Noah told him he thought for sure, if he tried hard enough. I told him the most important thing was to have fun, and if he tried his hardest I'd be proud of him. Leave it to Felix to take it the wrong way. He said he sometimes thought he'd tried his best, but then he always remembered a moment when he let up a little, and if he hadn't then he'd have been even faster. He said he didn't know how to know. Maybe he'd never tried his best. I laughed it off at the time, but he was serious."

"That's intense."

"Right? And there was Noah, bragging about Felix's times every time they came back. The two of them, just winding each other up. Felix is relentless. If you tell him you're proud, he tries to impress you more. If you don't, he tries even harder to make up for the disappointment. He's just built that way. I mean, at a certain point, you just have to accept that they are who they are. Right out of the womb. But Noah should have known better and he just ignored me when I told him."

"So …"

"So Felix got sick. Very sick. He got a cough and then a fever, and he said he didn't feel good in his heart. And let me tell you, that's a scary-specific thing for your ten-year-old to tell you."

"Was he alright?" Cecelia asked. She thought about the little boy in the next room, and how he was clearly fine now, but also how glad she was that he was, and she even surprised herself by the strength of feeling.

"A slight pneumonia," Cate said, "and a transient cardiac arrhythmia. The doctor said not to worry, he was probably just overdoing it. And guess what the prescription was. Rest. And a break from the stopwatch."

"Which is basically what you said in the first place."

"It's exactly what I said."

Cecelia could see how even now, months later, Cate's feelings still hurt, and how on some level she still nursed them.

"God, I was furious. Those two ... and Noah ... It was one of those times when, you know, you're so angry you can't think of a single good thing about him, and yet you can recite a whole litany of every bad thing he's ever done." Cate was wagging her chin, and her mouth was twisted ruefully. "That's the problem with first loves."

Cecelia couldn't see the connection. "What is?"

"Well, most people break up and move on a few times, especially when they're young. So they can look back and say it didn't work out because he thought this, or she did that, or said whatever, and it's fine because then you get a fresh start and you can try not to make the same mistakes again. But when you don't break up with him, or if you get caught up with him again, it's not your last boyfriend who hurt you. It's him, you see? He's that guy. It can be hard not to feel like every new fight is the same as all the ones before."

"My parents were high school sweethearts," Cecelia said.

"Then they would know."

"But Felix seems OK," Cecelia redirected. She meant it as a statement, but it came out inflected as a question.

"He's fine." With a wave of her hand, Cate at last dismissed her remembered worry. "Kids are resilient. They mend quickly. But Noah ... him I could have killed."

For a while now, Cecelia realized, she had hardly moved. As for Cate, she seemed lost in thought, her lips pursed and angled to one side, as though she was chewing something over. Mulling, was the word that sprang to mind. In deep mull.

A sudden bang interrupted them, followed by commotion and cursing in the basement, loud enough that they could easily identify several profanities. The living room being nearer to the basement door, Felix must have heard them too. Cecelia rolled her eyes.

"Sorry. My dad gets like that when he's working. And sometimes when he's not."

"My dad's the same way," Cate said. Then she added, "You know, people always told me girls end up marrying their fathers, but I don't see it. Noah's nothing like mine. Actually, my father hates Noah. I bet he hasn't told you that either." It was hard for Cecelia to imagine Noah arousing an emotion as strong as hatred in anyone. "Too big for his britches, he used to say. He's one to talk. My father's the Great Explainer. He'll slowly explain you to death if you let him, or instantly shoot you dead at twenty paces or machine-gun you with his explanations. He can even do it without ever raising his voice. But Noah's been standing up to him since we were kids. He has a way of putting my father on his heels, and he's always hated that. He swore I'd regret marrying him. He told me with Noah right there in the room. Obviously we don't talk much anymore."

A part of Cecelia wanted to say how awful that sounded—Cate's break with her father, his unkindness—and how she was sorry for her. Another part, however, wanted something very different. She held herself in thought, uncertain.

"If you're wondering," Cate said, "no, I didn't. And I don't. Despite everything. No, my father probably feels pretty smug about it now, but he was wrong then and he still is. We were just too young. And a little careless."

Cate rose and looked into the living room. The television was still loud and she seemed reassured that Felix was still absorbed in his show. She returned to her seat and, lowering her voice a little, confessed that Felix had very much been inadvertently conceived. Cecelia's eyes opened briefly in surprise, but upon reflection it was not so surprising. These days, who in their right mind would choose to have a child so young, she wondered?

"Noah always wore a condom," Cate explained, "except for some reason one night he didn't. I let him think I was more asleep than I was, so we could just relax and enjoy it without overthinking ... but it turns out I'm breathtakingly fertile. I mean, I see women at the clinics who are desperate to conceive. For me, one slip-up is all it took. And the crazy things is, I was so innocent it didn't even faze me. I was totally casual about it. Like, of course I'll have a baby, and it will be wonderful, and I'll be so happy, and tra-la-la-la-la."

Cecelia burst out laughing and Cate too. It was so ridiculous, and the consequence was sitting in the next room lounging on the couch, oblivious to the cheerful naïveté that had followed his conception.

"How long did that last?" Cecelia asked.

"Oh, six or seven months, I think."

"Longer than I would have thought."

"Yeah, but I've noticed this about people. We don't realize things all at once. We kind of realize things over and over again in stages. It's like a defence mechanism, so after each shock you can get back on your feet before the next one turns your life upside down again. So first you realize you're having a baby, and after that you realize that you're actually having a person. Then you realize that you're not sure you're your own person yet, and this new person is going to be entirely dependent on you to help him turn into his own person too. And it keeps happening, right? Every five years or so you look back and realize everything you thought you knew was wrong, and you've been passing all of it on to your child the whole time. Somewhere after six months it was like flipping a switch. I guess there must have been a happy medium, somewhere between devil-may-care and panic attack, but I couldn't find it."

"And I'm guessing Noah just—"

"Noah just took it in stride, like everything. I think that's why he never takes my concerns seriously. I mean, like our first apartment—it was garbage, worse than this place—and the seal on our bedroom window was blown. I asked him to fix it, but he kept putting it off. He'd rather have a cold room and lots of blankets. And he liked the ice patterns that formed on the glass."

"The hoarfrost, you mean? To be fair, it is beautiful."

"I hated that window. I hated how cold the floor was every morning. And I worried Felix would catch a chill. He didn't, of course. Even then it was like they were siding against me." Cate leaned back and ran her hands through her hair. Several times she pulled it tight behind her head before finally letting it fall slack around her neck and shoulders. At last she said, "Noah used to lie awake at night, just staring at the moonlight through that window. Sometimes I lay there too, just wondering what he was thinking."

Cate had finished most of her second cup, and Cecelia wasn't going to finish hers, so Cate took them to the sink to rinse. She spoke over her shoulder. "But like I said, I still don't regret any of it. That was our first apartment. Felix was born there. We were happy there for a while. Our friends used to come. We had this huge surprise party for Noah's twenty-fifth birthday there and—"

"That's … almost five years right?" Cecelia asked suddenly. "Was that before or after you started with that other guy?"

Cate fell silent. When she turned, her eyes were seized with an uncomprehending wonder. "It feels like such a long time ago." She hesitated, visibly puzzling it over, then she shook her head and smiled. It was a sad smile, Cecelia saw at once—though Cate was trying not to let that show—as sad as she had seen from Cate perhaps in all the time that she had known her. And it seemed to grow sadder the longer she held it, her lips tensing, perhaps even twitching a little with the strain of holding it together. Then her shoulders fell, and she sighed deeply. "Jesus. What does it say about me that I can't remember if I was cheating on my husband when I planned his birthday party?"

The knocking in the basement started up again suddenly. It made them glance towards the kitchen door, and that was when they saw that Felix had been standing in the threshold. Cecelia quickly looked back at Cate, who stood arrested and wide-eyed, incapable as a statue. Her son's arrival shook her like a catastrophe.

"Don't worry, Mom," Felix said. "I already knew." He came in and took the empty chair next to Cecelia.

Cate's voice was weak and came slowly. "How?"

"I heard you on the phone one time. You were talking about his penis. I remember thinking that was only for Dad and me."

"How come you never said anything?"

"I don't know. I guess I didn't like to think about it."

Felix asked if he could have a cookie. Cate remained motionless at the counter, as though pinned back or otherwise affixed to it in some way, but Cecelia could see that she was trembling. The hammering in the basement grew louder. Then Cate glanced at the clock on the stove console. It was after five. "Shit! I'm going to be late. Where the hell is your father?"

At the front of the house, the door opened and banged shut. Cate stepped through the kitchen door, with Cecelia not far behind, as Noah stomped into the vestibule. "Sorry," he said in a single, half-swallowed syllable they could barely hear.

Cate opened her mouth to speak, but hesitated. Noah came down the hall, but he was avoiding looking at her. Felix slipped hastily back into the living room and dropped back onto the couch. He didn't bother about the cookie. Cate stepped aside for Noah to enter the kitchen, where he hastily filled a glass with water and gulped it down. Then, as Cate and Cecelia were eyeing the back of his head, a tremendous clang erupted from the basement. Something heavy and strong and hollow had dropped, and split, and the sound of it was ringing up through the floor.

"Does he have to make so much noise?" Cate snapped.

"If not for Gary you'd be paying for someone to make a racket," Noah said. He was still not looking at her.

"You mean we would be."

"Fine, we'd be paying for it."

Cate, undaunted, glared at Noah. "Oh, we're paying for it."

She turned and walked quickly down the hall and hurried up the stairs. From his back pocket, Noah removed a small book and tossed it on the table. Cecelia waited for him to say something, but he only leaned back against the counter. His gaze was blank, his thoughts somewhere else. She could hear Felix in the next room, flipping quickly from station to station on the television. He turned the volume up too.

Cecelia asked Noah if that was the address book. She asked him twice. Not really answering, he said she should finish the description. They needed to show Trover something. Cecelia asked him what was wrong. Nothing, he said. She looked at him, hard.

"You're lying," she said.

"No," he said.

"Yes," she said.

"Fine."

"That's no kind of answer."

"Fine," he said again.

Cecelia asked him why he wouldn't talk to her. Noah told her not to be ridiculous—he was talking to her. He stepped into the living room, with Cecelia following. He turned and looked at Felix. Their television only got twelve channels, but Felix was still changing them. Then Noah walked towards his room. Cate came rushing down the stairs. Pivoting sharply around the banister, she clipped Noah's shoulder trying to get by.

"You're in a fine mood," he said, rounding.

"You're late," she said.

"I can tell time."

"Sure. You just can't keep it. I get two shifts a week. I can't be late for one of them."

"That's my fault too, I guess."

"I didn't say that."

"That's what you mean," he said. "That's always what you mean."

"Fuck you, Noah!" Cate suddenly screamed. "You don't get to tell me what I mean!"

Cecelia wanted to escape, but there was nowhere to go, not even the basement, now suddenly quiet, and she was forced to watch the scene unspool. Cate struck him in the shoulder with her open hand. When that hardly moved him, she beat his chest twice with both hands. Noah only looked at her, then she began to cry. Without speaking, he turned and entered his room and left her weeping in the hall. Cecelia approached her carefully. She didn't know what else to do. When Noah stepped out of his room, he was on the telephone, but one look at Cecelia comforting his wife spun him right back in. She tried to explain to Cate that something was wrong that Noah wasn't saying, but she didn't want to listen. Noah, more quickly than seemed possible, emerged from his room with two bags packed.

They watched him retrieve his coat from beside the door. As he put it on he was explaining how he would call the neighbour's daughter to sit for Felix. Cecelia tried to say that she could stay. There was a chequebook on the desk, Noah said, with signed blanks for paying her, and Cate could use the others for whatever she needed. He had tried to fit everything into his bags, but he would have to leave some of it behind. He hoped that was OK. Cate wept silently as he itemized the circumstances of his departure.

Noah looked at her. "I have no idea what you want from me."

"An apology," Cate said, her voice small and shaken.

"I gave you one the second I got in."

"Noah, you can't," Cecelia said. She could not believe that Noah was really leaving. It was incomprehensible. "Noah, it's almost Christmas."

He stood in the doorway, impassive like a stone gargoyle, frowning as it all flowed through him. Then his face contorted. With one abrupt motion he caught up his bags and his arms, like pendulums, swung them back into his room. Then he walked out the door and dropped himself down on the stoop, exposing himself to the cold and the darkness. Cecelia followed after him, but stopped short of approaching. Cate looked at her watch. She would definitely be late now. She snatched up her jacket and slid out past them like a shadow. On her way she muttered an apology, but to which of them Cecelia could not say.

PART FIVE

Interval:

The Dark Backward and Abysm of Time

10

From the North Sea on the storm surge, the night white and cold in the splintered moonlight of a snowstorm. Coming southward, to where Cæsar's galleys first beheld the splayed seasides of Tamesis, her estuary bedded down in the shallow river valley. Inland, then, along her marsh-lined strands past Sheerness and Medway where, long before those Romans, the wide waters severed Briton chieftains and their rival blue-skinned brethren; and then upstream with the heavy churn, flanked by hills and floodplain, where the sea throbs and contracts in congress with the river, a spring tide teeming through the straight and unencumbered Gravesend Reach, into the belly of Anglia. From Gravesend onward, salt fading from the air, the brackish reach meandering through the shadows, the wind thrashing scrub trees up and down those shores where once King Ælfred stood, shores long before despoiled by Picts, and Scots, and Attacotti, shores which had and would again run red with blood of Saxons; and onward still, with the river as it cuts into high, dry land, hard around the Isle of Dogs, passing under Greenwich—the alluvium gathering, lining the river-bank—and Deptford's naval yard and store. Then suddenly west into the Pool, its edges knit with quays and quarters, the floodtide flowing past the white Caen stones—hunkered on a Roman ruin and gazing upstream over Lundenwic—of William the Bastard's Norman tower. To London Bridge now, with the river's speed, the shops and houses levered out above the waves, the waters rushing under, between the piers, and into the shielded tideway. Comes then the cluttered water-side—all brick and timber, stone and glass—which, like an apparition, looms but casts no reflection on the River Thames tonight. Darkly now her waters flow, ragged in the wind and falling snow. North she peers at hithes and havens, glances south to Bankside's stews and taverns, overtaking stairs, and wharves, and wherries by the dozen on her way. We land, at last, at Broken Wharf.

So called of being broken down and fallen into the river, the dilapidate quay shambles up from the riverside and ends in the flint and limestone of Thames Street. The riverside and all the ward is a motley of estates and parish churches, taverns and brothels. On the corner: Bygot House and the city's great water engine, whose wooden arms turn high above the gabled rooftops. And nearby: fishmongers and cheesemongers and merchants of divers trades, their signs battered and gently swinging from their storefronts. The Blacksmiths' Hall is not far off, and the Woodmongers' too. At Bennet's Hill stands St. Peter's Church, whose almshouses provide for many a hapless widow, and beyond that Addle Hill and Barkley's Inn. The length of Thames Street glimmers faintly all the way to Blackfriars, where the surrendered monastery stands.

From there begins Saint Andrew's Hill, at Puddle Wharf on Thames, and climbs beyond St. Andrew's Parish Church and the King's Wardrobe. Over Carter Lane and into Creed Lane it goes, and thence to Bowyer Row. At its westward end stands Ludgate and the crenellated stone of London Wall, and to the east the cathedral church, poor, spireless St. Paul's, and a clutter of bookstalls at its feet. Bibles and pamphlets, sermons and grammars, unbound playhouse quartos for six pence—morning come, the churchyard will bustle with pages bought and sold. Till then, the grounds are empty but for a watchman, ensconced and shivering in his stall.

Past Bowyer Row, the outstretched arms of Ave Mary Lane and Paternoster Row embrace the churchyard tenements. And from the corner where they meet, Warwick Lane strikes north, ending in the high street of Newgate Market, which is lined with stalls and shops for purveyance of all manner of victuals. At its eastern edge stands a great timber frame for weighing corn and meal, and in the west stands Newgate itself, with the parish of St. Sepulchre's beyond, and Giltspur Street running north to Pye Corner and St. Bartholomew's, where the sick and impotent are wont to lie in.

Beyond the hospital stairs the way opens into Smithfield. Here, upon a time, was a notable show of horses to be sold, and also swine, and sheep, and oxen, and all kinds of implements of husbandry. Here were tourneys held and feats of arms, and horses also run for wagers, but now the old uses are all given o'er, and now its once wide expanse is shrunken and compassed round with candlelight from inns and tenements and public houses, which line the half dozen lanes that run from Smithfield. Their upper stories o'erhang the streets, which are with narrow alleys notched throughout. In one a harlot stuffs her purse; in another a thief his long-knife draws; down a dark crevice a gentleman ingles his favour-ite boy. It is thus with strumpets, sneaks, and larcins that the quarter is peopled, for here in London's liberties the Watch would rather frolic within the alehouse walls than search for miscreants without. Tavern doors resound with the clamour of song and dance, and in the street pint-plenty husbands make their quick retires to wives they hope are long abed, not hiring beadles to cry them up and down for all to hear.

Candlelight glows throughout the ward, whence many's the mid-night fondling done, and many's the secret match that's made, and midwives sought for those in need. The cat toys with the mouse it hath catched, the dog nips fleas by's master's bed, the newborn stirs and cries out for the dug, and everywhere, as ever, in these small hours is the slow rhythm of night beat out.

For instance: at the head of Long Lane there stands a tyre maker's house, of timber and loam, a full three floors beneath two gables. Inside, the shop is dark, the countertops bare. Through the doorway, in the workshop, a wall of wire and thread, stacked high in heavy spools, is discernible with other commodities of the tyre maker's trade. The odour of glue and horsehair lingers, although 'tis hours since master and prentice put their needles and pliers away. In the scullery, a small, embarrassed clink of crockery betrays the presence of a young maiden, Jane. By a fire she stands, crushing herbs into a steaming cup. On the second floor there is shuffling in the parlour, the sound of hushed voices, and the tumble and flop of waste in the privy chute. Taking up the drink, she climbs the stairs and enters above.

The parlour is a modest chamber, well-lit with ill candles. At the table, half drunk and more than half asleep, sits a rumpled gentleman with hands scarred and blackened and an unkempt beard: her father, Stephen Belott. He leans against a barrel of wine that he hath placed upon the tabletop. In a corner, the gentleman's son, a young man of eighteen with dark eyes and a crooked nose, reads a large book by candlelight. With a bruised hand he sweeps away the foul-smelling tallow smoke. On one wall, a faded mural of the Deluge as drawn by some pious prior tenant. On another, a threadbare tapestry. Atop a short stool a young girl perches. With little fingers she darns a stocking, and with a little foot she rocks a cradle and the infant child within. A faint odour of old rushes from the greying floor mats. A smell of stale wine. The creak of the cradle and the young man's silence. The sound of the cup-bearer's footsteps, and something in the uppermost storey that she would rather not hear. Enter John, an apprentice, through the privy door.

BELOTT, *stirring, to John.* Villain, get the cards.

JANE. Good ev'n again, John. No winks for you, I see.

JOHN. 'Tis hard when we're two abed, Jane, and on his side your father's other prentice is tiring out the bailiff's daughter. (*Looks aloft. Muted sounds of grunts and giggles through the ceiling.*) He does love to ply his trade.

JANE. Father, we might open a house of resort for all the hobby-horses ridden here beneath your roofs.

JOHN. Poor Jane. Thou lackst a squire for thy saddle. An I were not indentured to thy father, I could take thee for a canter.

BELOTT, *fumbles for his cup.* Think twice before acting once, John.

JANE. Father, you must forbid these dalliances. We should lose our reputation, if we had any.

JOHN. Not so, Jane. Lose a good reputation, a bad takes its place. And, in truth, to many a young beau a bad reputation in woman is better than a good.

BELOTT. His time's his own. Let him spend it as he will.

SON, *looks up from his book.* To tally by his groans, his purse is already twice emptied. I marvel he hath any left to spend.

BELOTT. Peace, knave. No more from your corner. (*He drinks, slopping down his chin and onto his shirt, already soiled.*)

(*John retrieves a deck of cards and sits down at the table, but Belott once more has propped himself against the barrel.*)

JOHN. How is Madame Belott today, Jane?

JANE. More infirmer than before, but her wits are fine as five pence.

JOHN. And Doctor Ellyot? Hath he been round?

JANE. Aye, this evening.

BELOTT, *without rising*. And before that Mrs. Condell and her fine peacock of a husband too, preening about with that great doorstop of his. (*He indicates the book in his son's lap.*)

JOHN. A round of Primero, Master Belott? What say you?

(*Once again, Belott is nearly asleep. Enter another young maiden from an adjoining chamber. She carries a chamber pot and her linen is a little stained with blood. The little girl darns and rocks the cradle with more vigour. The faces of Jane and Belott's son are hard and intent upon their sister.*)

SON. What news, Ann?

ANN. Her coughing is more violent, but less frequent. She seems more settled and in better spirits than before. She asks for you, Will.

BELOTT, *grumbles, with eyes closed*. Again thy mother's minion, boy? By'r lady, she gave thee suck too long.

ANN, *to Jane*. Let him deliver the cup. I've to clean the pot and could use the company.

(*Jane studies the chamber door.*)

JANE. Very well. (*To her brother*) Take this cup. It's to be inhaled first and then sipped slowly. Mark me well: slowly. Impart this unto her and see that she both understands and obeys. This whole fortnight she's wont to be of a contrary disposition and disregards instruction.

(*From his chair the young man rises. He tucks the book under his arm and takes the cup.*)

SON. Should a son be tutor to his dam?

JANE. Just see that she obeys. As do thee.

SON. Aye, Jane, aye. As you will.

(*He crosses the parlour. The little girl at the cradle looks to him, her brows purled up with care. He smiles upon her. At the door he pauses and surveys his family: the girl and infant in the corner, Jane and Ann exiting down the stairs, his father drunk asleep and John shuffling idly. He turns his back upon them and enters his mother's bedchamber.*

The room is dark and smells of sickness. It is modestly furnished: a writing desk in the corner, quill and inkpot upon it, and a bottle of liquor and two goblets. Peeking from beneath its lid some sheets of paper. In a stack beside, two book chests of oak and fairly carved with featherwork and fleur-de-lys, the topmost so crammed its lid will not close. By the door, a mirror of polished steel, with linen draped over it. Candlelight. Shadows trembling on the walls.

Half hidden by curtains and coverlets, the lady of the house in her blood-spotted nightshirt reclines on her pillows. The young man hesitates before her. Framed by four turned posts and a simple tester, she is the very picture of decline.)

MARY. Approach, my dear boy, approach. Let me look on thee.

(*There is a small table at her bedside, with a stack of clean cloths upon it. The young man sets his book beside them. His mother's figure lies shrunken, her cheeks pallored, her eyes swollen and raw. The illness has bereft her of her beauty. Another chest beside the bed is turned on end to makeshift a stool, from which the girls have nursed. He sits and offers the cup.*)

MARY. It's not leeks, is it? Afore God, I'll have no more of your leeks.

SON. No, Madam. Only holy thistle in honey water. To break the fever and settle your cough.

MARY. Thank the Lord for that. (*She sits up further to receive the cup.*)

SON. Inhale it first.

MARY, *sips.* How doth my little Bess? Is she well?

SON. Aye. She's a mere whisper these two hours and more. The wet nurse came, and will again i' the morning.

MARY. And does your sister have a care of her?

SON. Aye. Easter sits with her, and the cradle ticks like clockworks.

MARY. There's comfort then. See you feed her better than you've done me, with your leeks and leeks.

SON. She's almost weaned. Time comes, we'll feed her best we can.

MARY. An you do not there'll be a reckoning. She hath lungs—a choir's worth. (*She attempts to drink again, but is overtaken by a violent cough—a frightful sound. When it subsides, her nightshirt is stained with drink and fresh gore.*)

(*Her son produces a cloth and wipes her mouth.*)

MARY. Fret not, fret not. It's the spots within have got me worried.

SON. Be still, Mother. What, should I stand by and watch you bleed?

MARY. Pah! What else is women's lot? For husband, for child … for old mother moon. A woman's tale is written in blood. (*She inhales deeply at the cup, holds in another cough.*) It's why your father comes not to see me this whole sev'n-night. He's back from the alehouse?

SON. Aye, but still at the barrel.

MARY. Perhaps it's best. His breath would only further foul the air. I miss the smell of new rushes in the house. He might have replaced the mats in the fall when I asked.

SON. Easter beat them clean this afternoon.

MARY. Aye, I heard her at 'em. She's a good lass. (*She places the cup on the table.*) Come here, lad. Let me look on thee. (*He leans forward. She puts her hands to his face.*) Oh, your poor nose. An excellent nose, very like your father's, and that ruffian half-ruined it.

SON. It's all one. And almost mended. Besides, 'twas bent in a noble cause.

MARY. I should think it was. That intruder was not a man so much as Monsieur Monopole's cudgel. Your father would have come to your aid, only he was not well.

SON. Well he should have been. To be so oft in drink when the wolves do daily lick their lips and haunch about our doors.

MARY, *strokes his cheek, then takes his hand.* You're constant then? You'll not stay?

SON. My new master awaits. My clothes and necessaries are already fetched.

MARY. I could command it.

SON. But not for long. Come the new year I'll be of age to govern myself.

MARY. Thy sisters will have much need of thee. Thy father too.

SON, *sits up straight, passes his fingers over his nose.* And where was he—

MARY, *raises her palm.* Aye, but he's not the man he used to be. Nowadays, your father's more like mine who's dead and gone, if not so bad. For he was, as you know, of a drunken, mean, and miserly disposition. His vices suited him as well-worn clothes.

SON. Aye, they were habitual.

MARY, *laughs.* Exactly so. (*She coughs a little. He wipes.*) But yet, say thou wilt stay. For now, if not forever.

SON. I cannot. I have said. Yet I will visit. Nightly, if thou wish.

MARY. Then get your mother a brandy at least.

SON. Brandy's not allowed.

MARY. Nonsense. Get the bottle, and quick, lest your sister return.

(*He goes to the writing desk, half fills a goblet and conveys it to her.*)

MARY. Good lad. (*She sips.*) O what a world … only yesterday it seems I held you mewling in my arms. Now mine's the bib needs wiping. There should have been time … (*She sips again, then lowers the cup to her lap.*) But shall we talk till the wee hours? From curfew to cock crow? I am not weary.

SON. And what shall we speak of?

MARY. Old tales, child, to make us laugh and weep. And I'll make much of thee, and tell thee how thou wast the goodliest babe that e'er mother nursed. Albeit, from time to time, a biter.

SON. You'll not say so!

MARY. I could, and worse. And yet, in truth, you were ever a goodly child. Even at your christening, where many a child is wont to wail, you smiled and cooed and wriggled fondly in your swaddling clothes. 'Tis the talk of the rushes hastens my remembrance of it. We had not so many as at a grand christening—we hadn't the coin for't—but those your father strewed across the floor were new, and they breathed a little sweetness into the church in St. Olave's. Papa wouldn't spend so much as a halfpenny on 'em, but your father said he would to have you well and properly blessed. For he was kinder then, you see.

SON. Indeed, though now he hates me.

MARY. Thy father hates thee not, dear boy.

SON. At the very sight of me he rankles, from his eyelids to his bowels.

MARY. Well, he did not then. No, that day he wore a shameless pride. 'Twas only Papa marred the occasion, who was so foul and brutish he couldn't smile upon the birth even of his own grandchild.

SON. I should have thought he would rejoice, if only for th'excuse to drink our healths.

MARY, *rueful*. He could indeed, upon occasion, drink himself merry. In's cups from time to time he found some measure of jollity. But in truth he was possessed of a sickly heart. There was little joy in him for us, nor indeed for anyone.

SON. Indeed, but why?

MARY. Experience, child, is a great teacher of heartsickness. I remember a time when I was not yet ten, when the streets did abound in protest. You could not walk two corners but club-waving prentices would menace you right into the nearest house of wares. Papa would spit in the street before them, but I held tight to Mama whenever we went out, and hid myself as best I could within her skirt-folds. Our neighbour then, Mr. Pierson, urged us to be patient. He excused the mob for they were young and fearful of unemployment, and he prayed we recall Our Lord's example and turn the other cheek. But the mobs did frequent Threadneedle Street of a Sunday expressly to curse our parishioners after worship. They took us for itinerants and vagrants, mocked us with hateful imitation of our foreign tongues, and terrorized us one and all, even children younger than myself. Papa asked, did Mr. Pierson likewise suffer their intimidation, or for that matter any other Englishmen or denizens, or was it not true that it was only aliens and refugees they threatened? Then he cursed Pierson in the street, and Pierson called him a gangrenous toe, and said he hoped the mobs would excise us and all our kind from the city, and that London would be better for't. So Father dry-beat him i' the street and kicked him home, and dared the other denizens of Silver Street to likewise urge his patience.

SON. To knock him about for some misbegotten words … this was a severe retaliation.

MARY. Nay, but Papa had seen it all before, in France. Within that city, and without, our people were despised. Were the summer too hot or winter cold, 'twas Huguenots were maledicted. If the harvest failed, 'twas our heresies infected the air and withered the crops i' the field. Each storm or thunderclap or tremor of the earth was God's displeasure at our infiltration. Then, early morning on St. Bartholomew's, the Black Queen gave command—a cannon did crack, and a bell did ring, and Paris streets ran red with slaughter. White crosses adorned their burgonets, and white linen scarfs their arms, and all their multitude wore black vengeance in their eyes. In bloody improvisation, they chained the streets and murdered all that they could find, not sparing woman, nor child, nor age, nor infirmity. Prayer could not save our people, nor repentance, nor conversion. They even killed our dogs for sport. Then came the pillaging and sacking of houses—they were as jealous of our coffers as our lives—and families and households did also suddenly divide and sunder. Husbands turned on wives, and wives on husbands, and children 'gainst their parents. Friends and neighbours made us strangers in an instant and betrayed us to the ferocity of the mob. Any they could find they dragged, alive or dead, and threw them in the river. Those that sought to prolong their wretchedness by swimming were shot at, bolt and stone, until they sank and drowned. Babes were thrown from the bridges—and mutilated corpses—and the citizens did laugh and drink and make merry while the Seine, choked with flesh and blood, could scarce swallow what the people fed her. In the frenzy they did kill even their own kind, not only by mistake, but some disposing of unwanted others: beggars and vagrants, elderly relations, unfaithful spouses. They killed with prejudice at first, and indiscriminately after. Papa was just a boy, and was preserved only by the charity of a Christian brother. Some days later he escaped from the city to the countryside, but word had spread and even there the people did rejoice in our extermination. So many had been dispossessed or murdered that it seemed the sky itself was not fit for our roofs, nor the soil for our floors, nor even the woods for our bedchambers. The vaulted heavens themselves were more accommodate than we deserved.

SON. In our own country, even, we were strangers.

MARY. Aye, we were. And after that to have the English smiths and mercers, these native sons, with their show of kindness and accommodation, invite us to their shops, laud our artifice, engage us in trade, almost clothe us in their very liveries, and indeed so wind their wares and ours as to marry us to their fortunes ... to have them then grow sudden strange, complain that their sons and daughters cannot thrive while we persevere and bring our goods to market, curse us for encroachment and usurpation, and rouse their prentices against us. When in the street or park, or in the Exchange, or e'en the church they boast to whet their knives against our children's throats and promise blood more than Paris Massacre did spill, then you see 'twas ever thus, that all along your alien's double-taxment makes you but half-welcome, and no Act or Patent will ever make it otherwise. So, you see—

SON. I see why Papa would dry-beat Pierson. But why maintain such ill will towards you? Or Father?

MARY. Aye, but after Paris ... he could not help it. His heart was a rat's nest of resentment and suspicion, even for his kin. And 'twas worse, methinks, for that he had such ill luck in getting children. When I was four, he and Mama had a son. It lived three hours, and Papa could naught but count its desperate breaths before it died. And once, when your grandmama was some dozen weeks with child, he beat her for that she'd trumped him with Mister Wood, the mercer. She lay in bed a week and then miscarried. (*She falls silent, her eyes distant, searching.*) This was about the time your father was apprenticed to Papa. (*She smiles.*) By my troth I remember't well, for when your father first came into the house, I felt my chastity soften most notably.

SON. Madam!

MARY. Nay, blush not. Art not grown enough to hear? Was't not your boldness had Master Brown a-knocking at the door complaining of his daughter's virtue? And are you still innocent enough to blush at your young mother's natural desires?

SON. But Madam—

MARY. Nay, stint thy squeamishness. I tell you plainly, your father was then a pretty piece of flesh, with strong arms and a fine leg. In the shop on Silver Street, spinning Damask gold or silver thread—I do remember well those steady hands, twisting wire between his fingertips, and his forearms. He tied his knots with such firmness and dexterity it used to make me quiver.

SON. Mother, please—

MARY. 'Twas just so when Mama fell in love with Papa too. Or so she said. They met in his master's house, where she did come round of a Saturday to help tidy the rooms for twopence. They were sweet for one another then, though after a stillbirth and half a dozen miscarriages—God bless her, she had such tremendous ill fortune in bearing, she could miscarry by a sneeze. It would perhaps have been more easy had they been altogether barren.

SON. Being his only child should have made you the more precious.

MARY. Nay, but a heart can be drawn too thin with pulling, and his had oft been through the mill. Nearly all his family killed in France, his alien coffers twice culled for every denizen's once, and a son-in-law who straight away hit the jack and bowled a son when all the stones he cast got him but one child, and that a daughter ... he had much to make him sad. And what's worse, he was a man that carried in his heart each hurt he e'er received and fixed upon it, as a cut man whose wound lies fresh a-bleeding and, instead of seeking out the surgeon, prefers to meditate upon its bloodied shape, its breadth and depth, until the hurt becomes more fouler and infects the whole anatomy. (*She lifts her hand to her brow.*) Be a good lad. A fresh cloth for your poor mother.

(*He lifts a handkerchief from the bedside table and dries her brow and cheek. Now and again he continues, whenever there is a need and his mother is silent, which is not often.*)

MARY. No. When at last your Papa died, he was all but friendless. I could no longer love him then, and between your father and him was naught but rancour. When Mama died we returned to Silver Street to help him in's affairs, but not for long. Six months of quarrelling. Then we departed into St. Giles and did not return, and Papa ... thereafter did he drink and whore, and later get a pair of bastard children by his maidservant, and defraud us to every whit he could of the dower he promised when we were betrothed, and nor the courts nor no fatherly imperative could soften his resolve against us. (*She becomes silent, frowning. She sips again at her brandy. Smiles now, and studies her son.*) And yet, 'tis no virtue to speak so ill of one's own sire. The world thus fallen, what else should man's heart be but evil from his youth?

SON. This is uncommon charity, Madam. Were he living he should not deserve it.

MARY. Nay, but as the scripture says: in sin did thy mother conceive thee. If not us all, then none deserves forgiveness. Be kind, therefore, and judge him not too ill. He was good enough when he could be, though mean when he could not.

SON. Your illness thus inclines you. Else you could not defend him.

MARY. 'Tis possible.

SON. Nay, 'tis certain. Grant him the horrors of France, grant him too the London riots, being squeezed with Frenchmen and Dutchmen and aliens of other sorts into itinerant enclaves, restricted with taxes and sundry punitions, grant him even his wife's infidelity. Yet this is circumstance, in the crucible of which are good hearts forged, hardened against evil, so that they melteth not, nay, though the fires of hell surround them. What you speak of, though it goes a little to explain, not excuses him. There was a flaw latent in the mettle of his heart, else all this circumstance would have but strengthened his love for thee.

MARY, *Smiling, fondly.* Thou art full of decency, child, but also youth. The wide world's not yet unfurled to thee.

SON. Is a man not bound by Nature to love his child?

MARY. Is it less monstrous for a child to despise his father? Or his mother?

(*A brisk knock at the door. Ann bursts in.*)

JANE, *from the parlour.* God-a-mercy, Ann, mind the draught!

(*Mary draws up her covers, but with the cup of brandy in one hand struggles and indeed spills some. Ann notes it, and notes as well the infusion of holy thistle, which is on the bedside table and hardly drunk. She takes it up. It has gone cold.*)

JANE, *outside.* And see there's no brandy.

ANN, *calls to Jane.* Fret me not. I know my business. (*Ann frowns and looks as though she would speak, but stops herself. She empties the holy thistle water into the chamber pot. Then she kisses her mother's forehead and kicks her brother's shin.*)

ANN, *again calling.* See to the kettle, Jane. (*Ann departs and closes the door, leaving her mother and brother alone once more.*)

MARY. She's a good child. Now come, wilt patiently attend? (*She reaches for her son's hand. He softens.*) Now that my span's stretched out to its limit—

SON. Nay, Mother. The doctor insists thou improvest by the hour. He says—

MARY. He says what thou wouldst hear, but he knows better. Come, there's a swelling in my bosom and I'm ripe for talking. Wilt listen? I will tell thee all, as best I can.

(Her son smiles sadly and nods. Reassured, Mary leans back into the pillows and headboard. Her eyes close briefly, then open again. She gazes upward into the canopy.)

MARY. 'Twas many years ago—our goodly Queen yet living—and your father was newly apprenticed. He had already lodged some time with us. Even then he and Papa got on but middling, but your father was familiar, bound by his apprenticeship, and, as we were strangers in London, familiarity was enough.

One afternoon I overheard him in whispered conference with Coles, Papa's other prentice, and he confessed he found me sweet and liked me well. I cannot tell you, child, the delight that tickled the very heart of me. I could not help but shuffle in to sweep the floor and most unchastely turn and banter and play the flirt-girl ... more even than I was wont to do ... and when I did excuse myself to my own chamber, ere I closed the door I heard Coles say, "Mind her father doesn't catch you gaping, Stephen. 'Tis wit to pick a lock and steal a jewel, but wisdom to leave it be." Coles might have heeded his own counsel. He got a maid with child and fled the city. But your father persevered in chase of me, careful only avoid his master's ire. And he was a fine angler, i' faith. In the workshop daily did he bait me with his eyes—his sweet grey eyes—until I hungered for the hook.

All that spring he courted me in secret, and I—a pretty thing, and witty and wild, but inexperienced, indeed in the very down of youth—well, I was sorely tempted. He would squire me through the town upon some errand, and offer his hand, and I would take it, and my belly quake to feel its roughness in my palm. We went a-maying too and tripped the maypole round, though 'twas already out of fashion and in spirit more ironical. And we played awhile with other men and maids at barley-break amid the tall grass. Later, as we walked alone, we laughed to hear them play at codpiece-kissing, with their chants resounding o'er the fields of gold of "Codpiece up and codpiece down, there were but a few in Southly town." He and I played too, but by ourselves, and more in earnest. 'Twas an education, believe me! Not that I was less worldly than any father's daughter, but there's knowing and there's knowing.

Once, when I was a young girl, indeed just a child, there was a night—Of what years was I then, ten? Not a dozen, sure! Let us say some nine or 'leven years—I asked Mama and Papa to be given a greater understanding of the privy parts and their uses. O, how they quarrelled! What should I be told? and how? and who would do the telling? That any subject that could so unhinge the domesticity ... I knew it must needs be a thing exciting, or sinful, or indeed both, and I was keen to know't.

Son. O Lord, Mother.

Mary. Papa insisted on some primer or manual, called *A Discourse on the Proper Attitudes and Uses of Courtship, here enlarged upon to chasten the pre-nuptial urges of our imperilled children, with Appendix containing (for the proper names of the parts of generation) suggested substitutes deemed safe for the protection of their maiden understandings*, or something like. But Mama urged him to bear a brain and recollect his own initiations, and, for a time, she prevailed. She said to me, "When between two young people there be mutual love and good liking, they needs must wed (though only after begging and receiving of their parents' blessing). And after the minister speak the words, and the congregation bear witness, yet the two young people must, in the privacy of their chamber, consummate the union. And this act of union, truth be told, is much like dancing. First the man entreats until you yield. Then you exchange hands, and there begins much standing and falling, and clipping and clasping, and spinning off, and much fondling besides, to say nothing of climbing."

And I asked her, was it really just like dancing, and she said, "Verily, child, and as jolly at times. Indeed, 'tis more than pleasure to draw up and shake a man's back, and dance with one's heels." But then when I asked how our parts involved, Papa grew out of temper. Said he, "What you need, child, is not such foolishness but rational understanding"—O, I remember as 'twere yesterday—he said, "Therefore, heed you this: such pleasure of your genital parts, if sought with a married man is called adultery; if with a bachelor, fornication; if with a cousin, it is called incest; if without your consent, it is called rape; if with a dog, it is called bestiality; if with a corpse, necromancy, for it seeks to raise the dead; if with yourself—the sin of Onan—it is called pollution; if with a dildo or some other object, it is called idolatry, which Our Lord's second commandment doth expressly forbid; if between two women, it is called tribadism; if between two men, then sodomy; and what you needs must know, for it encompasseth all this and more, is that such pleasure is a sin, and lawful marriage, ratified by the church and your parents' consent, the only means to avoid it."

SON. Good God!

MARY. Dull, dundering thing that I was, I understood but little what he spake. And Mama, bless her, railed at him for his brutishness. But later, after I was sent to bed, I heard them fall to't in their chamber and make such merriment, that I concluded this must be the dancing of which Mama spoke and Papa warned. Yet, if 'twere sin and they did it still, methought, it must be worth the burning. Indeed, my overhearing did engender in my loins such a fire I knew not what to do but rub it out.

SON, *bolting upright.* God-a-mercy, Mother, mind your tongue! Some things I can't unhear.

MARY. O peace! Ignorance is no virtue. In spite of Papa's hostility to't, Mama taught me well what men desired, and to defend against it. I knew well what your father wanted in those barley fields—yea and, in truth, I wanted it too, I was so fond on him—but I gave not easily in. Instead, I did entice and not-entice, and yield and yet not-yield. And your father, bless him, endured my torments like a gentleman. For though he desired to lie with me, he did not ask that I put-to before my troth-plight. (*Her eyes go vacant. For several moments she loses herself in the past.*)

(*Her son wipes her brow.*)

MARY, *gazes once more upon her son.* 'Tis foolish how your poor mother fancies her remembrances. (*She waves off his ministrations.*) But we were so careful that none at home knew aught of our secret, happy love, excepting Master Shakespeare that now is dead these six or seven years.

SON. Master Shakespeare?

MARY. Aye, dost remember him?

SON. I remember him but little.

MARY. 'Tis a great pity then, for you were great friends, and he did love you dearly. Oft times he brought you sweetmeats from Bankside, and bounced you on his knee. He would inquire about your day— what news from the shop? and what gossip from the patrons?—and would entertain you with tales in miniature from the theatre. You and he wasted many a Sunday afternoon in talk.

SON. Thom Newcome once asked me to recollect something of him. I told him how, when I was a youth of seven or eight, some school-fellows and I played truant to see the bear-baiting in Paris Garden, and by chance, Master Shakespeare intercepted me. He urged me not to go.

MARY. You never told me this! Right glad am I that he did send thee back to school.

SON. He did not send me back, Mother. He only held my hand and painted for me the picture I would see there. The bear chained and staked, and the dogs unleashed upon him, tearing flank and ear, tail and leg, the cries of pain, and flights of gore, and torn fur and spittle, the bear's frantic desperation. But all this, he told me, would be the lesser horror. For when I looked about the garden I would see my fellow Londoners, delighted by the bloody spectacle. When once I looked upon those smiles, said he, I would not quickly trust another. He did release me then to mine own governance.

MARY. And you went anyway?

SON. Aye. Without hesitation I hurried to the market, where my fellows waited. Then hastened we to Bankside for the baiting. Afterwards I wished that I had not.

MARY. Had I known this then, I would have thrashed thee black and blue o' both sides. (*Wryly.*) But that's all one. I cannot thrash thee now, my boy, can I? Lord, what years have passed since then.

SON. Methinks that Master Shakespeare was not long with us.

MARY. Not above a year or two. Nor were he and Papa ever more than civil. What friendship there was between them was due not to mutual liking, but timely remittances. Indeed, 'twas Mama did engage him to be our lodger. She took a fancy to him after she furnished him, at Mrs. Field's urging, with a refurbished tyre for his playhouse. He was a kind man and a jovial, though sometimes haunted by melancholy. His daughter and I were of an age, and he and Mama both had lost a son, and that, methinks, did work to knit their sympathies. Master Shakespeare's renown, it must be said, did also play a part. Though she would scarce have owned it, Mama conceived herself somewhat above her station and, not to be thrifty in her praise, she had an ingenuity with people and counted among her friends or clientele many men and women of note and influence, from poets and men of fame to lords and ladies of the courts. Even the ladies of the Queen's wardrobe would spend Her Majesty's own money in our shop. Yea, Mama liked Master Shakespeare well, but methinks she liked his reputation better.

When he came to stay with us he was already known by sight to many as the poet of the Globe. He was also a gentleman, arms bearing, and a man of property with a share in the playhouse and a house in Stratford-upon-Avon, where his wife—God bless her, she died but recently; Condell said so when he and Bess came to call, and kindly brought that book there for me; alas, we are but mortal—but, I say, he was a man of property in Stratford too, where his wife did supervise his holdings and rear their girls far from the plaguey London air. Under the rank of his betters there were few so well esteemed as he, and Mama flattered herself by his acquaintance. But to me and your father, child, he was much more, and likewise he seemed fond of us somewhat beyond the common bounds of friendship.

Of an evening he might read us riddles, or extemporize sundry entertainments from the idle talk of sailors dockside, or chambermaids i' the markets, or court news, or tales of monstrosities in other lands—all done in voices for our amusement. And he did teach us courtly dancing such as we had never seen. We knew only your base jigs and roundels then, and such steps as Gathering Peascods or Jenny Pluck Pears. But he showed us how the lords and ladies trod the floor. And though we lacked the music for't, yet 'twas no matter. His foot did keep the time. We learned the galliard out of Arbeau and the seemly cinquepace, and even—when Papa was not at home—the volte, in which your father did oft embrace and heft me high in's arms till I did blush, and not maidenly as from modesty or lack of wind, but rather from the tourdion that danced about my heart. We had but one poor room and few candles, and only the meagre melody of Master Shakespeare's humming to accompany our steps, but to us the homespun revelry did seem a masque, and we a pair of delicate courtiers.

There was one evening when Papa, lion drunk and smelling like a brewer's apron, discovered us in a sarabande. O how he cursed Master Shakespeare's expedition of our wantonness! Mama did entreat him not to grouch. The dinner table was furnished with some cheese and cakes and ale, she said, and our diversions were nothing more than festive hospitality. She reminded him that as a youth he loved to dance, and had a fine leg for it too. But Papa would not hear't and they quarreled. He vilified her for a bawd, apt to turn a Petticoat Wag into a Saturday Night and Sunday Morn. So she warned him to amend his temper, lest he find himself alone and dancing Cuckolds All in a Row!

O child, how the victuals flew! I laugh to think on't. A cannon-aded roast, a trebucheted pudding—'twas a wise man then who had his dancing shoes. Papa demanded was your father implicated with me. And your father, though it stung me to hear him speak it so indifferently, wisely swore it was but pastime, and that he cared for me naught but as a sister. Papa would perhaps not have believed him, but Master Shakespeare's warrant secured the peace. He vouchsafed both mine honour and your father's honesty.

SON. 'Twas a kindness.

MARY. Aye. And a wonted one. Master Shakespeare was ever pleased to do us good. Sometimes he recommended, and did once or twice attend with us, the concerts of a Sunday afternoon at the Exchange. And often he invited us to hear the plays—and not just his own. Once, before Michaelmas, in the year before the great plagues, he even took us into the privy places of the Globe to see the makings of a play, and there we made acquaintance of some of the players, including Richard Burbage himself! I assure you, there was no handsomer man upon the stage than he, with an eye to melt all womanly reserve, and a leg as would cause a nun to waver in her faith. 'Tis known he delighted many a well-born lady with an epilogue in her private box. But what most fondly I remember happened ere all this had come to pass.

SON. And what was that?

MARY. Mark you. 'Twas high summer, after Whitsuntide. A great bank of clouds that afternoon had intervened betwixt the lofty heavens and our more humbler earth, and a pitched darkness did besmear the upturned face of London-town that would not be made clean. The storm did rage all day, and into the evening, with such lightning and thunder as one would think another Noah's Flood were come. Master Shakespeare was yet new in my acquaintance, but I was so enchanted by the novelty of his inhabitance that, my parents being absent—but where were they then? My mind plays truant with me now. They could not have been at home, else I should ne'er have had courage to approach his chamber door. I wonder ... but this is off the mark. To the point: with the house thus empty, and Master Shakespeare's chamber too, I breached the threshold and committed a most brazen and unpardonable rummaging of his affairs.

SON, *smiling*. Mother!

MARY, *rueful*. 'Twas a grave impertinence, I do confess, but when pleasure and shame are even scales, which of us is not prone to mischief? Some of his things were strewn about, and some tucked within a large chest: a comb and shoehorn, some apothecary wares and perfumes, a picture of his son in miniature. There were book chests by the bed too, and those filled to overflowing with sundry volumes and pamphlets. Near the window was a writing desk, with pen and ink, and pages written o'er in's secretary hand. And though it took some labour—for in that time I read mainly from my Bible, and with some difficulty too—yet I thought I recognized the matter, for I had seen it played upon the stage not many years before, the play of Falstaff, the scene where he did read the roll for young Prince Harry's wars. Hungry for more, I took some other pages from the floor and tried to read aloud, but in doing so seduced myself withal that I did not hear't when Master Shakespeare stepped through the chamber door. And there he found me, a-sitting on the bed, encircled by his pages—

SON. Like a woodcock in a springe.

MARY. Aye, and the noose of my own making. O, how I tried to speak in my defence, but he prevented me. Said he, "Is't not strange that, coming home, I find thee rifling here and not in young Master Stephen's chamber?"

SON. Ha! He had you doubly apprehended.

MARY. Son, the disgrace of it! I've ne'er been so ashamed. Nor knew I neither which of his discoveries I feared the more—the plunder I had made of his belongings, or the disclosing of my true love's passion, for both had set my cheeks alight. But Master Shakespeare fixed upon it straight. "Come now, Mistress Mary," he said. "Add not the sin of perjury to here deny what thy cheeks do openly confess."

SON. And what did you then?

MARY. What could I do, my child, but like the storm outside let loose a torrent o'er the seared fields of my poor visage?

SON, *with sympathy.* O Mother.

MARY. Aye, but Master Shakespeare was more kinder than I could have dreamed. When I begged his forgiveness, he gave it. Without hesitation. And when I told him how I wanted nothing more than to rise again where I had fallen in his esteem, he said, "Then I propose, from this time forth, we shall each other's secretaries be. For my part, I'll keep a swan's song for you and young Master Stephen, and for your part, you will copy out the parts for my *What You Will* once I've finished it."

You must understand, I was luckier than many girls and went to a dame school. Nonetheless, I knew not then the skill of writing, nor could even make my letters. For though Christ's Hospital was nothing negligent of its poor charges, yet young women were for husbands, not for universities, and could we read a little from the

Bible and the *Book of Prayer*, and learn a grocer's list and cancel out its items, and not come home with corn when cakes were wanted, then were we literate enough for our utility. Indeed, once I began to learn the grammar of wire and wig, Papa sold my hornbook to a neighbour with a boy grown old enough for petty school. Therefore, never before had I been conscious of any defect for that I could not write. But now, how ignorant and incapable I felt that, notwithstanding Master Shakespeare required so little, I could nothing

And yet he bolstered me up. He was well ware of my ignorance, he said. Indeed, 'twas the very inspiration for my penance. For he did intend to teach me, which he hoped would be not only to his profit, but especially mine own, so that whilst I paid my debt to him, 'twas I would gain in interest! I told him how I no longer had my hornbook, as Papa had sold it for the neighbour's boy, but he said 'twas no matter, we could begin without. Besides, he would teach me the Italian hand, for 'twas the hand the ladies of the court now used—and easier to shape besides—and like enough in time to dispossess the other scripts. Some days later he gifted me a hornbook unlike any I had seen, for it did show the curling Italianate letters, which I suspect was made for me in special. O, then what a fiery purpose did this ignite in me! I burned to be made perfect in his teaching, and to well deserve his kindness. Thereafter, many an hour I spent in private study o'er his Ovid or Plautus, and I did set down all that I read therein verbatim, no matter their Latin strangeness. He bade me mind my *k*s and my joining strokes, and counselled me to hold the pen but lightly in my hand and dip but lightly in the well, and these and sundry other dictates did I patiently attend. Before long, such was my handiness, that he pronounced me able to begin my work in earnest, called me his blushing parakeet and bid me then his pages for to parrot.

We were forced to proceed most carefully, I assure you, for had Papa found it out he would have cursed it for a wasteful exercise of liberty—under his gables, superfluous industry was by and by supplied with occupation—but in truth, lad, come what may I would still have found some covert hour to labour with those pages. Indeed, 'twas most of my entertainment, for though the

wearing of wigs had set upon the worthies of London like a conta-
gion, Papa pinched his pennies tighter than a bench vise and, to tell
you plainly, refused to give e'en the smallest sum for any common
pleasure. To Mama he was more a moneylender than a husband.
Nor would he pay for your father's apparel, nor the cutting of his
hair, though he had promised to when he took him on, nor lay
out for stockings that our legs would not be cold, nor for wax so
that our candles would not reek. Only he lived in expectation of
another levy 'gainst his foreignness, made husbandry turn vice, and
cultivated the purest strain of parsimony I ever savoured of. E'en
meat at meals was discouraged, as fish was cheaper—though he
had copper enough for the tavern-keeper's ale.

The theatres were closed that summer too, because of plague,
and Master Shakespeare went forth for many months into the
countryside to tour the parishes beyond the long, contagious fingers
of our London streets. Lacking, therefore, other means for entertainment, when I had finished writing out Master Shakespeare's
parts, I practiced writing out his other plays. By summer's end,
I was grown so self-assured I wrote my first composition: a letter
to your father, professing my dear heart's faithfulness to him. Of
a Sunday we would often steal away and stroll through Moorfield
together, and in the tall grass there I delivered it to him, whereupon
such amazement did beset him that it did enflame my very heart.

He was a doting youth, already skilled in's trade, and soon to
be released from his indentures. 'Fore long he would be wanting a
wife. When he asked how did I learn to write so well when I could
not at all before, I told him, "'Tis a thing that I did teach myself
i' the quiet of my chamber, love, where I did dream of you." Then
I pressed a twig into his hand and, taking his in mine, upon a patch
of bare soil, with my hand guiding his, our two hands scratched
out *M-a-r-y B-e-l-o-t-t*.

SON, *touched*. This was, Mother, very sweet of you, and charming.
Albeit uncommonly forward.

MARY. I know it well. For your father thrust his hands into my petti-
coats so suddenly that I was forced to push him from me lest he
ravish me outright.

SON. Good Lord.

MARY. 'Twas unkind of me, though, to enflame him so and then deny him. He was like a coiled spring, poor dear! He begged me leave to express the full measure of his love, and mustered many arguments, which I discarded, such as—

SON, *raises his hand to prevent her.* I do have some knowledge of these arguments.

MARY. And some familiarity, perhaps?

SON, *looks away, bashfully.* Perhaps.

MARY. Well, in despite of his sundry urgings and my denials, I did relent anon. For to speak true, I did desire it every whit as he, only I liked to watch him earn it. But once he delivered his trothplight unto me, and I to him, he kissed me soundly and I opened up the gates—

SON. Yea, I know what follows—

MARY. —then off with our garments—

SON. Nay, but madam—

MARY. —that they not be soiled and gossip after us—

SON, *loudly.* Enough already!

MARY. *quickly, reaching for him.* Hush.

SON. For your sake I have been patient, but a child cannot listen … 'tis more than … 'tis too much, surely—

MARY. I prithee, not so loud. (*Her cough flares.*)

JANE, *from the parlour.* Is all well? (*The door partly opens. She tilts her head in.*) Is anything the matter?

(*Mary takes the handkerchief from her son and lifts it to her mouth. When her cough has settled, she hands it back. Gouts of blood have seeped through.*)

MARY. A tickle in my lungs is all, Jane. It took me by surprise.

JANE. Well. Hast need of anything? The holy thistle shan't be long.

(*Mary shakes her head. The door closes.*)

MARY, *laughs quietly.* Forgive me, child. I have forgot myself again.

SON. Indeed, and most appallingly.

MARY. Yet you must be quiet, lest your noise betray us and wake your father.

SON. Go on then, madam. I'll not a peep. But, I pray you, tell me only how you then did marry. You may omit the rest.

MARY. Ah, but we did not marry.

SON, *hesitates, in confusion.* How now, not marry?

MARY. We did not. Not yet, at least. Nor shortly neither.

SON. But then—

MARY. Just attend, my boy, and softly, as I said. We had not yet disclosed our affections to Mama and Papa, much less received their blessing, but as your father soon would be released from his indentures, we determined to conceal them a while longer. And when this came to pass and your father was released, we had a gathering at a tavern spitting distance from our corner. It was not a grand celebration, for Papa wanted it nothing and swore he would not pay for it. Indeed, 'twould have been a sorry, mean affair had Mr. Fludd (your father's mother's husband) and Master Shakespeare not each consented to a share in the dispense. Yet, for all that, 'twas grand enough for us. There was music and dancing, and some dozen or more friends and relations in attendance. Papa, despite his surliness, even bowed to entreaty and spoke a little.

"He hath been a good and diligent apprentice, and hath behaved himself well in my service," said he. "He hath not drunk much of my beer, nor often pilfered stores, nor slandered my person more than any other, nor gotten any children by my daughter that I know of, nor by any other's. And 'tis well he hasn't. Some of us may recall how young Antony Pistol, our neighbour's prentice, was whipped for getting a young maid with child, and then was married to her ere the sting had left his flesh. Y'are wise not to meddle with them, Stephen. A young man married is a young man marred." Many in our company laughed at this, and your father smiled a little and demurred o'er the contents of his cup. Mama swore 'twas true for young maids too. She asked had Master Shakespeare not written so himself. Then a hush fell upon the table, and the air was still with expectation while Master Shakespeare drank a little of his beer and temporized. At last he replied, "I know little enough of marriage, but perhaps three things. What was not marred before, no marriage will harm. Nor, what was marred already, no marriage will amend. And lastly, notwithstanding matrimony was designed to save our souls, yet if we wed before our ripeness the preservation cannot but savour bitterly."

SON. This was but slender wisdom.

MARY. 'Twas wisdom enough. For—mark you—Mama boasted then how already I was ripe enough to be a bride, and how it was a daily occurrence for some young gentleman or other to inquire after me. Said she, "When once we give our daughter leave to court, no doubt the suitors will like pigs to the trough." But Papa said, "Will they indeed? Then be assured, if they do come, they'll find no fodder. For what have I to give that I may safely part withal? Nor lands, nor properties, nor wealth in coin. No, I thank you. If they will have her, let them take her for nothing. Let herself be the dowry. 'Tis all they'll get from me. Here's more instruction for you, Stephen. Before you take a maid, be sure she be well-dowered. Plough not a field will yield no harvest."

I'll tell thee, child, to have my *ripeness* so discoursed upon, and my worth assessed, among my friends and neighbours, to say nothing of the sundry idlers, taverners, and drunks—

SON. No doubt 'twas hard.

MARY. Hard indeed, but not the hardest. O, I wished your father would speak for me then, though indeed 'twas not the time. But when he rose among the company and begged their leave speak, I could never have imagined ... He gave thanks for their good wishes, called himself most fortunate to have such good and true acquaintances, and said he wished now to impart that which his disposition did intend for him. Though he did love us all, he said, yet he longed for more than one could spy out of a chamber window. He would, therefore, go forth to seek his fortune, and his mind was bent on Spain.

SON. On Spain? No.

MARY, *nods*. One and all they did congratulate him on his adventure, clap him on the shoulder, wish him well, and … I was such a fool. The presumption of the man, methought, that he should make such plans for us and not confer with me.

SON. O Mother …

MARY. I know. Such a poor, green thing your mother was! So unpracticed and unschooled—

SON, *growing angry*. And he … but did you not see—

MARY. Not a jot, boy. I was somewhat drunk just then, which out of question undermined my wits, but in truth it would have mattered little. I was so blinded by his assurances and mine own affections that I was incompetent to apprehend that he did mean to leave me.

SON, *loudly, rising from his seat*. O Villain!

MARY. Hush, now! Hush!

SON, *paces. Nears the chamber door*. Scoundrel!

MARY, *with much urgency*. Not so loud, I say!

SON, *desists from pacing, but with menace stares at the chamber door, as though he would his gaze could pierce it, through and through, and strike the man beyond*. A faith-breaking, double-dealing scoundrel. Thy tale confirms the baseness I have witnessed in him all these years. And thou would have me reconciled with this cheat, this leasemonger?

MARY. My child, sweet boy …

(*A knocking at the door. Enter Jane, with the infusion. She hesitates, sensible to her brother's mood, then conveys the drink to the bedside table. Her brother returns to his seat. Jane studies them both, but they give her nothing. Mary smiles and pats her hand. Uncertain but satisfied that his hostility has cooled, Jane leaves them. She closes the door behind her.*)

MARY, *firmly*. I do beseech thee, adopt some quietness. We must not rouse thy sisters' curiosity, nor wake thy father. Believe me, we would not long be left to gossip were he conscious.

Son, *angry, but giving way.* Well. I will do my best to obey you, madam. 'Tis certain he's not wanted in here. But at least assure me that, once you understood his meaning, you did not merely suffer his duplicity.

Mary. Indeed not. No. On the very morrow, after my drunkenness had lifted, and I had more clearer brains to think with, at the earliest opportunity I fronted him. I asked him plainly did he really mean to turn me away.

Son. And how did the hollow man reply?

Mary. With the most pathetical hems and haws, and *you-must-understands,* the coward. O, and after that, I promise you, there was no hole he could weasel himself into where I would not ferret him out! Was I no more to him than an appurtenance, some trivial accessory? A chain, perhaps, for to wear about his neck until it grew too weighty?

Son. Now this is better. To unmuzzle your fury and let it loose upon him … this is business I can savour of.

Mary, *looking away, embarrassed.* Yea. But, to tell thee true, my fury was unmuzzled only because I did not think he would desert me in the end. (*She slumps back upon her pillows.*)

(*Her son slouches. He takes a little brandy, directly from the bottle.*)

Mary, *gently.* Do not judge your mother too unkindly. Freely, I confess. I was too credulous. 'Twas so incredible to me that I could scarcely compass it. E'en when he was three days gone, I held out faith he would return anon. And when at last I understood that he intended ne'er to return … O! Then cracked my heart in earnest. Then were my spirits as addled eggs, suspended in their own distress, and my bosom an empty shell that wanted filling.

Son. No true lover could have done't. He was a pilferer. Even for him, this was a shameful piece of work.

Mary. 'Twas as though a lock was picked, a gate swung open, and my heart laid bare for anyone to rummage.

Son. O, poor my mother. But was there no one for you to confide in? No friend, or trustworthy relation?

MARY. For some seven or ten days after his departure I did enclose my grief and guard it jealously, but when I felt I could no more, then did I seek out good Master Shakespeare, for—true to his word—of our courtship he had always been secret and close. Besides, there was none other worthy of confidence, none to lend an ear who would not censure or execute some worse consequence upon me.

All full of tears I did betake me to his chamber, and he did rise from his writing desk with a kindly smile. "How now, girl?" he said. "Thy tears could rinse thy mother's dishes for a week. What's the matter?" Then followed such a sobbing! Such an inundation as London Bridge could not withstand! But his kindness did. All mutely he rode the flood, swanlike and calmly, and enfolded me in's wings as I unfolded all my signet heart to him.

SON. You were most fortunate in his friendship. He sounds a good man.

MARY. He was my schoolmaster. He taught me a spiritual stiffness for to bear your father's abandonment, as well as the burden which my misdemeanours shortly laid upon me.

SON. What burden?

MARY. Why, thee! Thou pretty fool!

SON. Indeed?

MARY. I did not fear at first. Monthly my courses still appeared and, after all, 'tis the usual sign that one is not with child. And yet it is not always so, and was not then the case with me. Afore long there were other signs, the which I could not ignore. I fell a-vomiting for little cause, and though I disliked my meat, yet contrarily I grew a more capacious appetite than I was wont to have. For a time I told myself 'twas sorrow made me to gorge myself, but by four months I was grown so round I could no longer conceal it from others, much less myself. Indeed, I felt as though I were anatomized, a porthole cut in my belly to expose to one and all my ruinous condition. I lived in terror of its evidence and, to tell true, for fear that Papa would disinherit and expel me from his house, I often prayed for some catastrophe.

(*Her son frowns, but says nothing. She sits forward, encloses his hands in hers.*)

236

MARY. But then thou quickened. I felt thee quiver in my flesh. Thereafter I feared nothing more than that I should miscarry as Mama had so many times. Yea, though thou wast unbidden, yet I wanted nothing more than to guard thy life and shield thee from the world's censure. Alas, with every day it grew more plain. (*Mary's eyes glow in remembrance.*) My belly bragged of my condition. (*Her son smiles, lifts the brandy to his mouth again.*) And my nipples too. (*He chokes. The drink burns in his nose and throat. He puts down the bottle and fights to contain his coughs.*) Lord, most wondrous long and hard they grew. 'Twas almost miraculous. Whenever with child, I promise you, your mother's teats could serve to hang a traveller's coat upon, or point his way home after.

SON, *eking breath enough to object.* Lord-a-mercy, Mother, mind your tongue!

MARY. Peace, peace. Th'art i' the right, I do forget myself. I'll better master my discretion. However, mark this well, my son. Secrecy is a plague. Fear it. It infects not just the carrier, but all that breathe within the house.

SON. Thou needs not be secret, only more modest, if thou please. For my comfort. (*Mary nods her head, acquiesces.*) Well. Come then, if truth must out, tell me what happened when they discovered it?

MARY. One night at supper, as we were gathered all in the parlour, Papa demanded how it was that I had grown so sudden fat.

SON. As always, a master of discretion.

MARY. Aye, he was. Methought I was prepared to counterfeit, I had a thousand times rehearsed it o'er in private. Alas, I could not. Tears instead, like started quarry, bolted from the marches of my eyes.

SON. And then?

MARY. Lord, what fiery calamity there followed. Papa erupted. Called me cuckoo bird, and hobbyhorse. Denounced Mama for a breeder of harlots, said I had sucked falseness from her breast. We and all our sex were naught but beasts, he said. "Like polecats in heat you will be climbing. Write that, Shakespeare! You'll ne'er write a truer word." After that the furnishings began to fly, and his scourging fell on any who dared to counsel reason or restraint. I fled to my chamber, and Mama with me, and Master Shakespeare escaped to the tavern, fast as feet can fly, and with him the poor, helpless prentices.

Long time Papa railed, like a Catholic sermon or a Puritan lullaby, cursing the several multitudinous whoredoms of women and demanding to know who 'twas that made me. I would not say, but he was unrelenting and would have it out of me. He was so beside himself that with a chamber pot he hammered at my chamber door, and hollered he would have the name. And—bless me!—if your father, all smiles and new-returned from Spain, did not that very moment cross into the parlour. "Goode'en all," he said, "is something the matter?" (*She smiles, and sits forward, conspiratorially.*) He woke up sometime later with a bloody hurt upon his head and the smell of piss upon him.

SON, *laughs suddenly, without restraint.* It serves him right, the rogue.

MARY, *laughing too, but less, and growing serious.* Marry, there was some justice in't for him, but not for me. For when he woke and saw how I was with child, and he suspected, and Papa armed for bear, well … there was no sweet reunion. His paternity he denied outright.

SON. Surely not!

MARY. Marry he did, in terms most categorical. And, moreover, called me a beet-eating wench, said that I endeavoured to restrain my terms and stuff my belly for to ensnare him. Either that or I did lie for to lay another's crime upon his head.

(*Mother and son alike fall silent. There is shuffling in the parlour, again the sound of the cradle rocking, an occasional fit of snoring. Betwixt mother and son, however, the air is thick, coagulate with silence.*)

SON, *at last, disbelieving.* Did he deny you still? And in your extremest need?

MARY. He did deny us both, my boy, when he swore he had not fathered thee.

SON, *hopeless.* He goes from ill to worse.

MARY. Indeed. (*She frowns, studies him. His disappointment at his father's betrayals, greater than he had imagined, is legible in his eyes, advertising his despair.*) I can say, in fairness, that he tried to compensate in private. His indifference was not in earnest, he assured me, but a stratagem for to beguile my father into giving a marriage portion greater than the nothing that he promised all those months before. But, for my part, what cared I for money? I required no portion but your father's love. It would have been enough had we but solemnized what we had spoke, and left my father's house.

I remember how, one evening not long after, Master Shakespeare discovered me a-weeping in my chamber. Mine was a broken heart, sutured up with your father's *please-forgive-mes* but still not mending. Even thinking on your father's treachery was to infect a wound with too much scratching. "Then think not on't," said Master Shakespeare. "Nothing breaks the heart so much as thought." So I asked him what I should do instead, and he bade me consider my state. That I was with child and in want of a husband, and your father a tyre maker in need of a wife, and moreover that your father loved me, though he showed it very ill just then, and lastly that, unless he was mistaken, I did love your father in return.

SON. An inventory is ill comfort.

MARY. I thought so too, and thereupon I 'gan to weep all o'er again. But less for my circumstances than that I knew not why I loved your father still. He was as a stranger, landed from an alien shore. The man I knew would not have wronged me so, could not have done. I told Master Shakespeare this, that he might understand my misery the better, but all he said was that he thought he knew his Annie more when he did know her less. "To think," he said, "that a sea should grow more strange with sailing it."

SON. And what then?

MARY. Marry, first I told Master Shakespeare where to stick his wisdom. Then I confessed to Mama and Papa that 'twas Stephen put the baby in my belly, and I swore I would have not him, nor any other man, to be my lord. In sum, I did confound them all.

SON, *gazing upon her, his face proud but uncertain.* This was a noble passion, but—

MARY. But untenable. Aye.

(*A strong wind buffets the windows. Mary breathes too deeply. A cough threatens to break forth. She contemplates the brandy, but takes instead the cup of holy thistle and drinks.*)

MARY. Hear me, child. Experience is a glass, and perspective a remedy for rue. Your father bargained for me as a butcher for his meat—and Papa too—but as I had to marry, 'twas a question not of love but of market. And your father was right. We could not yet have sustained ourselves by industry alone. In time we would have a tyre shop of our own, but 'twas a horizon farther than our capacity to reach it.

SON. And what? You therefore forgave him his abandonment?

MARY. What's he that can fetch aught from the abysm of Time? No, child. As it was past cure, your father's crime was past care. Mind you, I made suffer for it. For a riot in Spain your father spent that dividend I gave him gratis out of mine own heart. Therefore, I assure you, I did not go easily along. Nay, I made great show of my determination. Nor argument, nor imploration, nor even bribe could sway me at the start, such that, ere long, the house was in such turmoil that Mama did entreat of Master Shakespeare his assistance, that he might prove the shoeing-horn to slip me into a marriage contract.

SON. It must have been quite the barter.

MARY. It was indeed. Papa complained that, as your father had violated and defiled mine honour, he was compelled by law and duty to wed me. Your father then indifferently replied that he who marries for love and no money, hath good nights but sorry days. The sum he named was so outrageous, methought 'twould end in murder, and thereafter Master Shakespeare did pigeon their proposals, for they could no longer share a room but it would come to blows.

SON. But in time they reached an accord.

MARY. Aye. In the end Master Shakespeare prevailed, and Papa promised a good dowry, with a goodlier portion to be paid on his demise. (*She laughs a little.*) He also cursed me and Mama both most thoroughly, and threatened to box your father's ears if e'er he asked for aught thereafter. Had Papa not afterwards reneged on his promise, who knows? Our threads, perhaps, had spun out very differently. We might have been a long time happy.

SON. Bethink you so?

MARY. Why should we not have been?

SON. You yourself have said.

MARY, *nods, sadly.* Perhaps I have. The more pity. For, in spite of the precedent conflicts and their consequences, there did follow a time of great happiness for us.

(*Her son frowns and drinks from the bottle.*)

MARY. Nay, doubt me not. Your father and I were newly joined. All was honeymoon between us. And, most notably, my child, you were soon to be born. (*She smiles, her eyes afire in the candlelight.*) Thy little life waxing full within me ... I still feel the bodily remembrance of it. It was wondrous. I was all joy and apprehension all at once, and patience and impatience, and hope ... and love, most especially love. Such a mingling that I'd never felt before, nor ever since, save when I was with child. I often trembled with amazement and uncertainty, and I wondered what the Fates were weaving for us. A little world was there concealed in me: my belly the vaulted sky, my womb the wide circumference of the sea, and a little sailor within did steer his bark. From whence? I wondered. And where to? And by what stars did he steer? For though thou wast invisible, yet I sensed thine every motion and did marvel at it.

Thy father marvelled too, and asked me many questions, the which I could not answer for all was new to me as well. Abed at night, when all was quiet, I did sympathize and sometimes think I heard thy little heart beating out a rhythm for you to row by. E'en now—five children later—I cannot say if it were aught but fancy. And after thou wast born, and my gossips had bathed thee, and swaddled thee, and brought thee to me, and I did hold thee to my breast ... Thou didst wail a while, at first. Then thou didst ope thine eyes. Blue they were at first, the deepest blue, whole seas within 'em—sapphire waters ringed with pearl. My heart did quake to see you look so like your father, though all insisted you took after me.

(She leans forward, once again takes his hand in hers and squeezes. Twice she strokes his cheek and then falls back, laughing.) But God-a-mercy the smarting of my privy parts! The way you yawned forth from me—it left me so dreadful swollen and sore, methought my Venus glove had stretched into an old sack.

(He cringes. She laughs harder at his squeamishness, risking a coughing fit. Then he slumps somewhat. His eyes linger on the brandy bottle in his hand. He sets it down.)

SON. And how fared my father?

MARY. Yours as every other, boy. Proud and foolish. When he and the other men returned from the tavern, he strutted like a peacock. Some two or three days after you were born, he took you from my arms, and placed you on the dining table. Whereupon he undid your wrappings and exposed you utterly, so all could witness that you were a man-child and well made. Enough to make men quail and women quiver, he boasted.

SON. Fah!

MARY. Three days old, child, and already such lungs you had. You screamed to feel the chill air upon your poor, unused flesh when all you knew was wrapping. I feared some consequence, some cold or fever, but by my faith you were more heartier than a mother could wish. And I too, then, was stronger. I do believe my lying-in did last no more than a fortnight, from birth pangs to churching. 'Twas not so with your sisters. What trials I had with them! But by then we were no longer in Silver Street, but at Wilkins' Inn.

SON. Wilkins' Inn?

MARY. Aye. 'Twas there we went when we could no longer abide Papa's temper. At first, he and your father aided one another in business, but as the one was a pinch-fart and the other had apprenticed under him … well, they quarrelled over the cost of wire, or thread, or some such thing, and we did shortly take our leave. Mama begged them to be reasonable, but no accord could there be made between 'em. When she died, God rest her, we returned to offer him what help we could, but ere long we were in St. Giles again.

SON. But who is this Wilkins?

MARY. George Wilkins.

SON. What, the playwright?

MARY. Part time. For the most part he called himself a victualler, but he fed more than men's stomachs.

SON, *astonished*. He was a bawd?

MARY. Or a pander, or a pimp—he kept a brothel. He was also a drunk and a cheat, and that on good days.

SON. 'Twas no place for a family, then.

MARY. O Lord, no. The place was so full of corruption, I wondered that God and the laws of architecture allowed it to stand. The woodworms would not touch the timbers, nor birds would not nest in its gables, nor even rats breed in its corners it was so rotten. Had it been within the city walls, every alderman within the mile would have condemned it, but we had little choice then. Having departed Papa's business, and selling so few tyres, 'twas all our purse could purchase. Indeed, it would have cost us more, had Master Shakespeare—who had some obscure acquaintance with our landlord—not bartered him down for us.

SON. But a house of sale, a whorehouse, Mother … Did not its viciousness cry out against it?

MARY, *laughs*. When anyone accused him for a brothel-keeper, he swore that he maintained an inn. "Look you, do you not keep some cheese within your house?" he would ask. "Yea, and does that make you a cheesemonger, sir?" And, in fairness, the premises were well liked. E'en more than the stews of Turnmill Lane. Bankside could offer more exotic fare—like a strange banquet, boasting dishes from divers countries, far and near, brought directly from the docks—yet for earthen entertainment and good English provender, that rascal's inn was the very place. All manner of gentlemen were welcomed, and fleshing boys. Ladies too.

SON. Not truly.

MARY. Yes, truly. All with coin were welcome. And though he was violent in his humour from time to time, and like to beat a dog or kick a strumpet with equal indifference, he was nonetheless a marvellous spokesman, and had a sure eye for what's vendible in women. To entertain his customers he would inventory his services, ex tempore. (*Impersonating*) To kiss your cod or pipe your flute, we have the girls! Or, if your taste be ravishment, we have some Sabine women will provide resistance.

SON. A foul incitement.

MARY. For a small superfluity, you can trim a maidenhood.

SON, *smiles*. Fie, this is worse and worse!

MARY. We have your tickle-tail mistress, your courtesan. Your fricatrice and tribade (for either watching or enjoining). We have your sodomite and valet too (if such be your leaning). Or indeed anything your fancy conjures.

SON, *joining in*. Wouldst play Jove? We have an Io or a Ganymede for you.

MARY. Wouldst be an undertaker? We have girls will lie still as corpses.

SON. Or a shepherd? We even have a curl-haired girl will bleat for you.

(*They fall to laughing.*)

MARY. They are expert in sundry attitudes and positions, as vertical or horizontal, inferior or superior, lateral or penitent, seated or astride. (*Laughing more and more loudly. Mary feels a cough coming and tries to calm herself.*)

SON. You, sir, my aged gentleman. Let me take your cane. You'll not need it. We have within our stores such provocatives that will give thee another leg to stand upon.

(*Footsteps approach from the parlour. They stop at the threshold. Mary hushes her son. Their smiles fade. Both look for an interruption, but ere long the footsteps move away.*)

MARY, *after a moment of hesitation, turns back*. You do remember.

SON. No. Not really. Or nothing sure.

(*Mary gazes on him with the sweet sadness of recollection.*)

SON. Perhaps a little, though. The ghost of a memory.

(*Growing uncomfortable, Mary shifts in her bed and arranges her pillows anew.*)

MARY. It was an ill house for lodging, but diverting at times. And always safe. The girls would pick a purse, but not your pocket. And though the patronage did at first solicit me as well, Wilkins gave them warning. I was not to be harried, he said, and, as he expected to be obeyed, offenders should expect to be kicked. In truth, while for others his hospitality was mostly counterfeit, to us he sometimes showed real kindness, and though the house did reek of license, yet I remember fondly of our time there. There was one evening, I recall, ere thou could walk, thou fled into the common room below. When we found thee gone, in fear we hurried down. But there thou wast, in the arms of one of Wilkins' doxies, with a stolen tyre upon thy head, holding court there like a tiny princess, the wagtails pinching thy cheeks and quite crowding thee with kisses. (*She smiles fondly and shakes her head in wonder, seeing the infant child within the man before her.*) We scolded thee roundly for fleeing, but thy tears only encouraged their affections. Thou could command them with a frown, those night-horse ladies. The minorest quivering of thy lip could conjure them on thy behalf.

SON, *smiles.* Fondness for a whorehouse? You amaze me, madam.

MARY. Verily, child. Fondness without measure. Thou'lt have someday a child, and then will understand me. 'Twas there thou took thy first steps, and there thy first meat. There Master Shakespeare gave thee thy first rattle to stint thy crying—and was a lovely rattle too, not of parchment or gourd, but of kid leather and shaped by's own hand. And there did he attend sometimes thy training, and warned thee when thou pissed a-standing not to shake with too much vigour, lest thou besmot thy shirt or, worse, the stockings of the man beside thee. 'Twas also at about that time we went to our first Frost Fair. You don't remember it, perchance?

SON. Sometimes, when you or others have spoke of it, methought I did remember.

MARY. You were but two years then, or maybe three.

Son. Was't much like winters since?

Mary. 'Twas a thing most wondrous to behold. That year the frost was so severe that cauldrons were wont to crack and garments grow stiff with ice. Doctors envied their patients' fevers, whole flocks of sheep and herds of cattle were said to have frozen in the fields, and the dockers and watermen—indeed all who made their living by the flowing of the Thames—were hard beset with poverty and lack of work. And not them only, but all who were dependent on cheap goods for sustenance, as these grew scarce with the river frozen o'er and the shipments overland forestalled with mounting snow.

Not all men grew poor, though, for there was buying and selling aplenty on the ice. There were booths for sale of fruit and food, and also beer and brandy. Shoemakers and barbers lit fires and set up stalls, and printers printed cards that sold for sixpence to mark the occasion. Oxen were roasted, and chestnuts, and brandy drunk in vast quantities. For want of coal to heat their chambers, the prentices did shoot at marks and play at football on the ice to keep themselves from freezing, though often they were past their knees in snow. And, now I do bethink me, the fripperers did a brisk and busy trade, and kept us layered o'er with cast-off clothes.

We took you through the frozen streets, down to the stairs at Paul's Wharf, and marvelled at the industry of our fellow Londoners. By chance, we there met Master Shakespeare, who had heard of puppet shows being played and thought to have a look. Together we walked all about the place—you well-bundled, and we helping you to mount the drifts of snow—but we could nowhere find these puppet players. Instead we took some beer, and then you three gentlemen—Lord, I had almost forgot!—you withdrew behind the tapster's booth for to relieve yourselves, whereon I heard such laughter coming from you that I was compelled to spy around the corner. And what found I there? What but three fools a-practising their penmanship! There was your father's name, well scripted, and yours an illegible yellow scribble, and Master Shakespeare's name truncated, reduced to *Shakes* for that his well ran dry.

O! and then—bless me, how it comes back to me!—then did I see a horse-drawn sledge! Can you imagine? I so much desired to be driven in't—a most rare extravagance in me—and your father indulged my fancy. It was exceeding kind of him. So much so that, once we mounted, I covered him in kisses with such brazenness as would make a harlot blush.

SON. And was't exciting?

MARY. I do believe his britches strained—

SON. Nay, not that, madam! The carriage, the carriage!

MARY, *laughing.* That too, that too. For I had ne'er been driven in a carriage of any kind, not e'en i' the streets. And he paid a shilling for't! Can you believe it? Master Shakespeare kept you with him while our driver took the sledge upriver to Westminster and back, and all the way, beneath a pair of heavy furs, we pecked like turtles true (*with tears coming*)—God's mercy, do you see? E'en now mine eyes do water with remembrance.

SON, *laughing kindly.* This was most wanton entertainment.

MARY. Nay, we must have our indulgences. Besides, we were but two among many, and less brazen than most. A good winter maketh women handsome and men companionable. Trust me, many a slippery thing was done on the ice, as many a mound of snow could testify. As for your father and me ... 'twas enough to nuzzle under cover while the sharp winds nipped our cheeks. And when we arrived back we found Master Shakespeare, with a little cone of roasted chestnuts, teaching you to peel and eat them.

SON. Did he not think me like to choke?

MARY. He minded thee closely. Besides, they were so hot, at first you feared to more than nibble. O do you remember, child? How you took the cone from Master Shakespeare's hand, and one by one withdrew the nuts, and dropped them in the snow to cool them for us? Thou wast so solemn and diligent in our protection, we could naught but laugh. (*He smiles and looks away, somewhat embarrassed.*) Nay, blush not so. Thou wast always a loving child. That afternoon your father and I danced outdoors with other young couples, and took turns a-carrying you as we danced, whilst Master Shakespeare applauded and encouraged from a bench beside an open fire. And later, back at the inn, your little hands seized the icicles that hung from your father's beard, and you were fascinated for to see them melt and slip from your grasp. Such was your joy and affection that you planted your face into his cheek, and after, though you were laughing still, it left your face so wet it looked for all the world that you did weep for that the day was over. Ah! 'Tis a shame that we could not return.

SON. No? With so much mirth and divertissement ... Was't too costly?

MARY. In part. And also our loss of labour. We had no prentice to carry on without us, nor no shop girls to encourage buyers, nor indeed no shop. Two rooms in Wilkins' Inn and our two pairs of hands were our entire company. But what's more, we did not go again for that my health did greatly suffer after. I discovered, too, that I was again with child and my too vigorous exertions in the cold, the doctor said, had placed both me and child alike in jeopardy.

SON. I did not know such trifling outward influence could hold such sway.

Mary. 'Tis hard to credit, I know, for you were conceived amidst a great plague, and yet not sickly, born in winter and yet not cold. But, Ann, whom I carried throughout those frigid months, did suffer chills her first year and more. So who's to say? She is a hesitant child still, often afeared, like a beaten hound who lives in expectation of a boot. More's the pity, for that she hath like thee a tender heart.

SON. Methinks I remember it a little. It was a difficult birth.

MARY. Most difficult. Perilous, in fact. And Jane and Easter's not much better. When I do bethink me of that time ... (*She hesitates, looks away from her son, towards the chamber door.*) Well, in truth, it was the beginning of all our unhappiness. If you remember little, 'tis just as well, for there is little good for to remember of. Five years and more we had not lived in Silver Street and, what with all our quarrelling, and then Mama's death, Papa had not given us, nor would not consent to give, no portion of the monies he had promised. We had you three already, and Easter on the way. We were forced, therefore, to bring a suit against him.

SON. A suit? Was the sum so great that you would drag your own father before the magistrate?

MARY. Drag him, thrust him, catapult him into court if necessary. Would not you for sixty pounds in dowry, and two-hundred more to be inherited?

SON. So much? This was a more than modest fortune!

MARY. It was on this promise that Master Shakespeare made us sure. After we were wed, though, Papa sent us only some paltry household stuff worth not even five pounds. What could your father do but bring the matter before the courts of law?

SON. Indeed, for sixty pounds ready money, with thrice that and more to inherit ... And yet, 'tis pity ... a tawdry business.

MARY. I liked it not neither, but what could we else? Papa hoarded all his capital, endeavoured to defraud us even of the law's third part for his only child, declared to's friends that he intended to leave us not one penny, and that he would rather rot in prison than give us more than he had done. O before the magistrate, of course, he vouched that, loving us as he did, he would deal with us at the time of his death as is fitting for a father to deal with his only daughter, except he had not the means, nor was like to have while he yet lived. This from the man who, not a quarter of an hour before, had denounced me on the courthouse steps, called me blood-sucking pelican, and threatened to wring my neck should I seek to further feed upon him. We only asked that he keep his promise. But, you see, there remained no natural affection in him.

SON. And did his avarice prevail? Received you nothing?

MARY. A little. But not much. A mere tithe of what the courts instructed, and less than that of what he promised.

SON. But surely, the court could not have been indifferent to your complaints, nor the witness of your friends in the matter.

MARY. Except that there was only one who witnessed, in his own person, what my father promised, and that was Master Shakespeare.

SON. Why, then you should have been saved.

MARY, *smiles sadly.* Ah ... well it had been some years, you see. In the interim what love there was between him and your father had grown rather cold. Remembering our old friendship, your father sent me to ask him what he intended to speak when called before the court. He thought it best not to accompany me, but I was then with child almost to bursting, so he sent his friend, Mr. Nicholas, along. But when we called on Master Shakespeare, he received us only at his door and would not invite us further in. Why he held himself aloof—whether his discomfort with the court proceedings or the presence of this other man—I knew not, but when I did inquire of him what he would speak, he said that some fifty pounds or thereabout were promised, but he remembered not when they were to be given. And what of the two hundred for a legacy? I asked. But he looked away and, as a child, made strange, and said that he remembered not what sum was settled on. Surely he would recall when he testified before the magistrate, I said. But 'twas plain— great though our need was, he intended to deny us.

SON. What else said he?

MARY. Nothing. Only he thanked us for our visitation, and excused himself for he was vexed with writing of a wedding masque. I pestered him, that I might infect his conscience with my urgency, but in defiance of my protestations he closed his door upon us. I told your father that I believed our Master Shakespeare's reticence would thaw. But this was a lie.

SON, *frowning.* This is not the man I remember.

MARY. Anon I was delivered of your sister, and we both fared ill. A fortnight or more I stayed abed, in the care of my gossips and midwives. But on the day the court did hear our case, though it was before my churching even, I took up Easter and went to the courthouse, all the way to the stairs of Westminster. As I arrived, the doors gaped and vomited a scourge of attorneys into the yard. I was in time to witness Master Shakespeare fleeing.

SON. And what said he to the interrogatories? Did he remember?

MARY, *as a proclamation.* He said he did know the complainant, Stephen Belott, when he was servant to the defendant, Christopher Mountjoy, and that he did well and honestly behave himself, and that the defendant's wife did solicit and entreat him to move and persuade the complainant to take the defendant's daughter to wife, and that the defendant promised to give the complainant a portion of money and goods, but what certain portion he remembered not, nor when to be paid, nor knew he of any two hundred pounds that were promised at the time of his decease. (*She is sullen.*) This was the deposition he gave, and with it he our hopes deposed as well, beyond uplifting.

(*For a time neither speaks. The wind is silent, the sounds in the next room are small and few.*)

MARY. What say you, child?

SON, *hesitating, then looking over at the book on the table.* But set he his name beneath this deposition?

MARY. Hurriedly, your father told me, but verily. Within the week he came by the house to offer up an explanation, but your father threw him out, since when his name is not spoken in the house. Not within your father's hearing.

SON. Quite right. This lapse … 'twas unforgivable.

MARY. I confess, 'twas hard.

SON, *agitated.* Nay, impossible.

MARY. Soft, soft.

SON. Hear me. If he got to the courthouse, he remembered how to walk. If not lean with starvation, he remembered how to eat. Did he not go to sleep at sundown and rise again i' the morning? Had he lost the faculty of speech? The ability to read? Make money? Make water? He forgot not his name, nor how to sign it. How, then, could he not remember not to perjure himself in a just cause on which the hopes of friends depended? (*His face twists, disbelieving.*) Your expectations hung upon his testimony. How could he forget what mattered so dearly to you he held so dear?

MARY. Tell me. Dost remember when we saw him last?

SON. Mother, answer me.

MARY. Thou shalt be answered, but tell me: dost remember?

SON. Only dimly. That age is naught but patches to me.

MARY. What dost recall?

SON, *carefully, as though through a fog.* I remember 'twas a bright day, and warm, which should have made me glad, but I was not. Father was not home, and I did feel obscurely some discomfort that we should be so secretive.

MARY. Were we secretive, boy?

SON. 'Tis my recollection. Perhaps we worried Father would discover ... Master Shakespeare called and we received him.

MARY. What else do you remember?

SON. That we did meet him on the steps, and you and he did talk. Coldly, methinks.

MARY. What else?

SON, *frowning, with thought.* That you were not only angry, but also very sad, and Master Shakespeare too, although a different sad. His face I do not remember well, but I suppose he knew it to be the end. He acted as though it were a play he had rehearsed before.

MARY. Go on.

SON. He did look upon me often, but always briefly. The length of a breath, or sigh, no more.

MARY. Thou remembrest well.

SON. I felt that something between you was amiss, something I did not understand. I wept and knew not why. And ... did not Master Shakespeare reach down to me, to dry my tears, but that you snatched me from him?

MARY. Is that all?

SON, *hesitant, at first, then rapidly unfurling.* He gave you something, did he not? Some token? Or, 'twas a paper. A note, perhaps. And then he bid you goodbye and looked quite strangely on me. I was hard by your hip. Then he departed. 'Twas the last I saw of him. Mother, what was this thing he gave you? You did not open it at first, but I remember that you examined it quite closely later. I saw you from my chamber door, though you bid me lay me down a spell.

MARY, *points to the book chest with fleur-de-lys, by the desk.* Go you now. Open the lid there. (*He does as she bids him.*) Empty it completely, child. This box was given to me by my mother ere I wed, to hold such things as were dear to me. Good. Within, on the left side, there's a little lever. Press it. It unlocks a hatch. (*He does.*) Is't open? Open it and bring me what thou findest there. (*He brings her the contents.*) Lay it all upon the bed. (*He does. She struggles to rise. He assists her.*)

SON. This is my rattle, the which you spoke of.

MARY. It is.

SON. Remembering whence it came, you kept it anyway?

MARY, *sifting through many dozen sheets of writing paper.* Where is it, now? Where is it? (*She seizes a piece of vellum. It is folded shut, but the waxen seal is broken.*) Here, take this.

SON. What is't? (*He receives it and turns it in his hand.*)

MARY. Do but open it and read.

SON, *reading aloud.* This Indenture made the twelfth day of June in the Ninth year of the Reign of our sovereign by the grace of God King James of England and Scotland defender of the Faith et cetera. Between William Shakespeare of Stratford-upon-Avon and Edward Kepysit, of Cheapside within the City of London, goldsmith. Witnesseth that the said William Shakespeare hath deposited with the said Edward Kepysit monies in the amount of ccxl^{li}. The aforesaid sum well and truly paid to be held until such time as William Belott, son of Stephen Belott, of London, tyre maker, and Mary Belott, his wife, upon reaching his majority present the aforesaid William Shakespeare's part to the aforesaid Edward Kepysit his heirs and assigns. At which time the aforesaid sum shall be paid and delivered to the aforesaid William Belott without any other charge to be set upon. In Witness whereof the parties first above named, unto these present Indentures Interchangeable have set their hands and seals the day and year first above written.

Wm Shakspere   Edward Kepysit

Mother, what is this? What does it mean?

(*A knocking at the door.*)

ANN, *from the parlour, softly.* Will, does she sleep? 'Tis almost day.

MARY, *urgently.* At your father's insistence, the magistrate summoned Master Shakespeare to be deposed a second time, but he did not go. Instead he came to the house, where he knew your father would not be, to deliver his farewells and this, your legacy.

ANN, *knocking, more loudly.* William. You've done yours and more. I'll spell you.

MARY. O, the knocking—

SON, *to Ann, through the door.* I will tarry a while longer. Get you some rest.

MARY. —such a frightful knocking at my bosom. How it batters. (*Panicked*) O, William! It will out!

ANN, *opens the door and looks in.* Art sure? Is anything the matter?

SON. I have said, Ann! Go thy ways!

(*She hurries out, but there follow other noises: a sharp scrape of wood, the sound of chair legs across the floor, and bootsteps, heavily.*)

MARY, *in a desperate whisper.* O God, not yet! The rattle! The pages! (*The materials are spread wide on the bed. She paws wildly at them, burying them under her covers.*)

BELOTT, *in the parlour, but closing in.* For the love of God, peace! Is there no respect of time, but thou'll hammer and prate while a man sleeps?

MARY. The indenture! Hurry! (*Her cough breaks through.*)

(*Will tucks the indenture into his shirtsleeve. The door bursts open. Belott stumbles just over the threshold.*)

BELOTT. What's this?

(*Mary's cough is uncontrollable. Will does his best to settle her. The handkerchief is overwhelmed, the holy thistle useless till he can check her barking. With aimless anger, Belott subjects the room to scrutiny. The blankets ruffled, the cups and brandy on the bedside table with*) *the handkerchiefs and the heavy book. By the door, the wedding chest open and its contents on the floor.*)

BELOTT. Thou disturb her rest too, I see.

(*He glares, but Will ignores him. Mary needs a fresh cloth.*)

BELOTT. Thy too much worrying hath made her throat and lungs more sere. Is this how a son ministers to's dying mother?

(*Will gazes on her, pale and shrunken in the candlelight. Her lips and chin are spotted, her hands too that could not catch the spatter. Her eyes are frightened, but not of the cough. They fix upon him. They beg his patience. With the fresh cloth he dabs her face and then her hands. Her breathing calms.*)

BELOTT. Go thy ways, then. But remember: for a fortnight yet you belong to me. Rested or not, come morning the shop will open and there's tyres in need of mending. Well. I have said. (*He lingers a moment, but soon turns and exits. He closes the door behind him.*)

(*They can hear him walk across the parlour floor and down the stairs. His footsteps fade.*)

SON, *once he is sure they will be left alone.* How is't with you, madam?

MARY. Well enough. A little hounded by disease, but that's all one.

SON. Then can you tell me? Will you? What means this? (*Removes the indenture from his sleeve, holds it out to her.*) Why would your Master Shakespeare forget the sum, and relieve your father of his promise, only then to compensate from his own purse? And to put the money not in father's name, but mine?

MARY. Canst not see? Hast thou not attended me these hours? Were this played out upon a stage, wouldst thou not foresee how it must end?

(*He is bewildered.*)

MARY. Papa threatened Master Shakespeare, and my good friend surrendered. He was a gentleman, arms bearing, but newly so and by purchase, still a glover's son, and by trade a poet and playwright. His gentry sat but doubtfully upon him, he had a reputation to uphold, therefore he could not afford accusations. Not that Papa knew, methinks, but rather guessed at it, and when he confronted him—well, I suppose that Master Shakespeare's countenance confirmed it.

SON. But what sayst thou?

MARY. Marry, that Master Shakespeare and I were ... When your father left for Spain he was so kind to me when I came to him. He took my hands whilst I did tell him all my woe, and then he held me in his arms—

SON. O God! ·

MARY. —and hushed me. "There is no wisdom below the girdle," said he. (*Dreamily*) Then he touched my brow and caressed my hair. Then were we kissing, and then abed, and ... e'en now do I remember the ruffle of the bed sheets, like two great white wings beating around me. (*She reaches for her son, but he retreats.*) In short, child, I cannot know for certain, but by the timing and thy looks ... Thine eyes you seem to have from Master Shakespeare, and the rest derived from me.

(*He does not reply. He only glances at the indenture and his own hands that strangely hold it.*)

MARY. You must understand, child, it was no deliberate enterprise. I did not plan it. But now ... looking before and after ... was't not a clever thing t'have done? You'll soon have near three hundred pounds, the which your father cannot touch.

SON. Who kissed first?

MARY. Does it matter?

SON, *firmly*. Tell me!

MARY. In truth, child, I do not recall who first advanced, but neither did retreat.

SON. And ... Father knows?

MARY. Your parentage? He has eyes. I should say he's guessed it.

(*He cannot look upon her.*)

MARY. Thou art sad.

SON. Should I not be? Bethink you. Would you desire your arm be cleft in twain? Your hand? Even so small a thing as your finger? How should I fare, then, with a heart divided? What am I now? A tyre maker's son? A playwright's bastard?

MARY. O Will—

SON. No. For now I am neither, having two fathers lost—the one by cuckoldry, the other by his dying ere that I was ware of what he was to me. (*Rising to his feet, struggling to control his temper.*) How couldst thou? 'Tis why he hates me! 'Tis why my very face appalls him! What am I now if not my father's son?

MARY. O William! Do not be so unkind to her that bore thee.

SON. 'Tis thou that hast unkinded me! And what do you ask? Forgiveness?

MARY. Yea. I would have it so, as would your father—

SON. Aye, but which one?

(*Mary begins to weep.*)

SON. You place this writ upon me, inscribe it into my very flesh, such that I can neither renege nor discharge myself of it. Did you forgive your father?

MARY, *sinking down*. I did not.

SON. I thought not.

MARY. I have tried.

SON. And failed. For you cannot command it. No, not you, nor Master Shakespeare, nor your husband, nor indeed anyone.

(*Mary now is weeping freely. Will's eyes scan the room, it and all that lay within suddenly alien to him. He glances at the chamber door and then at his mother, bedridden and miserable. He hesitates. At last, he approaches Mary. He sits once more beside her.*)

SON, *softer, with effort*. And yet I would command it of myself, if such a thing were possible. (*He takes her hand.*) O Mother, teach me to forgive thee.

MARY. Sweet, my child. Dear boy. This is not the golden age, and th'art too old for easy teachings. Look around. Lessors scheme to seize our tenements. Companies endeavour to monopolize our livelihoods. The wide city is lousy with pimps and lawyers, pickpockets and moneylenders. The people of London are full of suspicion. They view their neighbours crooked if they drink not, and eat not, and speak not just as they do. The world is hard, meagre of accommodation. The cruelty of man doth flourish everywhere. But mistake not: for all that, there is much love here for the gleaning. Master Shakespeare failed me, and thee, but above all himself. And yet, I'll swear't, he loved thee. As do I, most dearly of all my blessed children. Your father loved you once too, and may again, though now he all but drowns himself in drink. (*Her hand goes to his breast.*) O William, do not block up this your articulate heart. Let it love freely, and as it loves forgive.

SON. But wherefore tell me all of this?

MARY. Because a bosom's not a lockbox. One cannot seal it up forever 'gainst the world's misfortunes.

SON. But with him dead and you ...

MARY. I am sorry I could not conceal it till you were of age, but had I died before ... Well. I cannot now be heedless of time. There is much that I wish I had said to Papa, and to Master Shakespeare. I would not leave things so with you. The past can be a deadly anchor to contend with. If there be time, you raise it up. If not, you cut it free. Poor Master Shakespeare. How he must have suffered when he bid another son adieu!

SON. And what of this? (*He indicates the rattle, pages, and indenture.*)

MARY. They are yours. In a few weeks, when you come of age, you may collect the promised sum. Guard it jealously till then. Your father will see it as his due.

SON. And what should I then?

(*He looks upon his mother. Like unused wells, his eyes begin to fill.*)

MARY. Thy next apprenticeship need not be long. Thou hast already your father's instruction and mine. When th'art released, thou mayst do whate'er thy heart desires.

SON. And the girls?

MARY. Should you return they'll be no better off, nor no worse if you do not. They're witty enough, and trained in useful skills already.

There'll be no shortage of stout craftsmen wanting them for wives. Now, wilt take my hand? Say thou canst forgive me?

SON. Madam, I do not know. 'Tis much. But I will try—

MARY. O William!

SON. And, come what may, I will love thee ever. (*He kisses her forehead.*)

(*Fresh tears flood her cheeks. Then she coughs briefly, but with violence. He wipes some blood from her lips and encourages her to lie down.*)

SON. Now to sleep. Thou hast much need of it. I'll return tomorrow evening, and every evening after, for as long as thou hast need.

MARY. Nay, my child. I would wake awhile longer, if thou will sit with me.

SON. Aye, madam. I will.

MARY, *lies back, closes her eyes.* Read something to me. From Master Shakespeare's book, there.

SON. If you wish it, though I should think you know it by heart.

MARY. Some of it, my dear heart, but I would like to hear you read it.

SON, *takes the book and opens it.* Where do I begin?

MARY. Begin at the beginning, and just carry on. Perchance 'twill give me dreams.

SON. I doubt it not. (*Reads.*)

A tempestuous noise of Thunder and Lightning heard: Enter a Ship-master and a Boatswain.

MASTER. Boatswain.

BOATS. Here Master: What cheer?

MAST. Good: Speak to th' Mariners: fall to't, yarely, or we run ourselves aground, bestir, bestir.

Out from the bedchamber and into the parlour. There's one girl knits, and two asleep. And the infant and the prentice too—she in her cradle and he in his chair. Down the dark stairs, through the scullery to the shop-front where the drunken master sips his wine and sags upon the countertop. Into the cold night air of Long Lane, which opens into Smithfield, its small expanse deserted. The snowfall has thinned, the moon begun to show its face more clearly through the clouds. The pinched streets are empty, and the gleaming, mantled earth lies stainless, all untrodden and unblemished in the early morning. Newgate and Christ's Church, Cheapside and St. Paul's. The city is quiet. It is waiting. The very shadows seem aquiver in the moon-glow. The inns and tenements, companies and hospitals, and even the yew-filled cemeteries, where congregate Christians in their dormitories lie, do seem to hold their breaths for morning bells and cock-crows.

Onward, down Old Change and Lambert Hill to Castle Hill and George's Yard, where the heavy Thames glows silverly in the moonlight. The river squeezes eastward, her waters breaking as they shoot the bridge and rush into the Pool. Her tidal waters press, her progress quickens. She pulses against her confines, surging under Greenwich, passing Gravesend first and then the muffled, snow-bound countryside, her every wave and surge a laboured breath that seems as it will last forever, till … release. The pressing of th'embankments lessens, the current slows, and the swollen waters of her estuary breach, at last, into the sea.

The storm now is abated, now the river's breath is eased. The channel now is fit for transit, and from forth the cold, forbidding waters where the Thames and North Sea meet, may many ships be seen. No doubt some trim their sails for Amsterdam, and others make for Calais; still others take the channel west and then lean south for warmer climes and Iberian shores. But some, perhaps—with a clear sky, and a full moon, whose glowing ring they hope betokens not another storm, but only that this evening's one is past—the wind propels, propels them o'er the wide Atlantic waters to the Americas, and to certain sea-side settlements, where hardy, pioneering men and women set out to make a world less strange.

PART SIX

The Cloven Pine

II

Snowstorms in March left Cecelia ambivalent. At the cusp of spring there is often a stirring of relief: the worst is past, the warm weather is coming, the days are longer and the reassuring hand of the sun settles on your shoulders more and more. To Cecelia, though, this was at best a mixed blessing. Term would soon be over, soon there would be time for many things, indeed anything; and yet she always felt unsettled, as though unmoored by the pull of aims and expectations. Without fail, a creeping irresolution spread over her, a crossbreed of sibling anxieties, equal parts yearning and fear. The sentiment filled her, but didn't fill her. Like a substitute or stop-gap, it framed the void inside her while she worried what to fill it with. Most often she tried out things she thought she wanted—books she could read, trips she might take, old friends she hoped to reconnect with—only to discover that she didn't want these after all, these nothings she confused for somethings, in that deeply dissatisfying bait and switch people use on themselves. Following the promise of spring, the return of the snow was like a kiss from a dubious boyfriend. Nature was having second thoughts, and Cecelia was getting cold feet too.

To be fair, it had been a mild winter, but it had also been miserable. It rained the first two weeks of January, and when finally they got a little snow, it didn't last long. February then was warm and mostly dry, except for a couple of days of rain, which rid the city of what little snow there was, leaving everything grey or brown or dead. It was worse between Kingston and Quebec City, if you happened to live there. Three storms in six days. Freezing rain and freezing drizzle, and ice pellets, and fog, and inches of ice, the hardest nature knows how to produce. It swallowed everything. Maple trees buckled. Roofs sagged and then fell in. Eaves bowed and collapsed. Farms shut down. Herds grew sick and could not be saved. In the cities, transit was crippled and even ambulances couldn't get through. Thousands of soldiers were deployed. It wasn't enough. Traffic accidents, ice chutes, carbon monoxide fumes from propane generators. Thirty-five people died. A million lost power. No one could remember seeing anything like it. Not that that meant anything. Some things you can learn from the past, some things you can't. This is what a flood looks like in winter.

Noah had flown to Halifax just before it hit. As soon as he heard what was happening, he called Cate and Felix. In Toronto, the real weather was passing them by, but he said he would keep in touch in case that changed. Then he called Cecelia and asked if she would maybe check in on them from time to time. After his dramatic near-exit, he had stayed for the holidays. The whole thing had been overblown. He and Cate made up, after a fashion, and were civil again before he left. Still, Cecelia found it unsettling. In ten or twelve weeks she hadn't seen him, and heard from him infrequently. His birthday was coming.

Although it was not yet evening, the sky was dark with snow. The backyard and her mother's garden were dressed all in white, likewise the trees, fringed as though with lace. Across the city, the parks and squares and streets were disappearing under this same delicate and uniform whiteness. It was like a work of art, indifferent to utility. A feeling of wonder encroached upon her, and she almost gave in to it, except she knew that cars would be skidding out there, and the elderly. People would get careless and the hospitals would be busy. The shelters would be full up too, and they were short-staffed even at the best of times. People forget how everything beautiful has a cost, and even when you're not paying it, somebody somewhere is. This was thinking a bit too finely about it, but Cecelia was no stranger to thinking herself out of a good time.

Janet was gazing out the kitchen window. A cup of mulled wine warmed her fingers. "It's like a wedding out there," she said.

"And just as inconvenient," Cecelia added.

Susan Lines was at the sink, cleaning soil from her fingers. "I don't see how it affects you. I thought I'd be able to get the burlap in and get to cutting back the perennials. So much for that."

Cecelia, who had been leaning against the countertop, joined her friend at the window. A hot cup was nested in her hands too. "It's more like the idea of a wedding. Before the audience comes to wreck it."

"Killjoy," Janet said.

The cold glass began to fog from the nearness of their faces and their cups. Behind them, Susan stopped the water and dried her hands. Cecelia and Janet then followed her through the kitchen door.

Over the course of a few weeks, the main floor had become more like a greenhouse than a dwelling. Dozens of plants had come up from the basement (which somehow still seemed full). Cecelia knew most by sight and many by name. There were cut-and-come-agains: aster and cosmos, pansy and Sweet William. Several species of larkspur, which she could never keep straight until they flowered. Damascene nigella, called love-in-a-mist or devil in the bush. Yarrow and corn-flower. And forget-me-not, which her mother always preferred to dig up in the fall to keep it from taking over. Many others she could not identify, but they were everywhere: atop the buffet and on the piano bench and end tables, in bunches behind the couch, perched on the mantel and arching over the television, even hanging from brackets on the walls or merely shoved in corners, taking up whatever space was not otherwise occupied by the furnishings of year-round living. Some were destined for re-potting on the back porch; some for transplanting in the gardens once the spring made up its mind to begin in earnest. Once the last frost had come and gone, they would be ready to bloom.

Cecelia and Janet sat down at either end of the couch, knees side-ways. They cradled their cups and looked out the living room window. The streetlights were on already, and they shimmered and glowed like snow globes. For several minutes the room was silent but for the sound of Susan shuffling between pots.

"I'm sorry, what?" Cecelia asked.

"I didn't say anything," Janet replied.

"Oh."

"Something on your mind?"

Cecelia slumped forward and sipped the spiced wine. "They're getting this down east too, only worse. They'll be digging out for days if they're lucky. If unlucky, it'll turn to freezing rain. Either way, he's really in for it."

"Are you two still … ?"

"I sent him some articles. And an introduction for a monograph bibliography. I guess he hasn't finished with them." Janet's face, Cecelia could see, was impassive. "That's not what you meant."

"It is not."

Susan took up the shears. Her pruning snip-snipped over and between their chit-chat. Cecelia frowned.

"Trover's been asking too. I keep having to put him off. I told him I can't give it all my time. I've got three classes and papers to write. I also told him Noah had to go take care of his grandparents, but we've been stalled for weeks now, and he's getting impatient. I take it he's not used to waiting."

Susan's voice cut between them: "It sounds like he's not the only one."

Janet quietly smirked and drank some wine. Cecelia swirled hers pointlessly.

"He wants me to get a move on."

"He may have the right idea," Janet said.

A pair of headlights swept along the road and Oliver's truck appeared. It turned and climbed the slick driveway with little difficulty, disappearing from view as it neared the house. They heard a door slam shut, and then the truck reversed down to the road and rolled away. Rose was coming in. Each time they visited, she appeared more plump and ripe. Cecelia lifted the mug, warm and boozy, to her lips to counter the strange, unspecified anxiety that began to fold and fondle her insides. She imagined Oliver walking through the door with his strong arm and large hand around her sister's round-bellied readiness.

Noah's hands were thin and long, more deft than strong. They were a reader's hands, a writer's, but nimble like a musician's or a puppeteer's. They were insistent at times, at times tenacious, but at times solicitous and even, on occasion, unsure. In respect that they were gentle hands they were good hands, but in respect that they were soft hands they were not. When he curled his hand around her hip, she sometimes felt the meetness of a well-made handle, but also the obedience of one when he used it to steer her on a crowded street. They both had laughed when she said thank you but she could pilot her own ship, and when she threatened that if he tried it again he would lose that hand; but for all her levity she had been quite serious, and he seemed not to apprehend his impropriety, or not to care, and carried on. His hands pleased her when they rubbed her back or shoulders, or massaged them gently, or pressed her feet or (once) painted her toenails; and they pleased her likewise when they rested on her thigh, affectionately; but when they squeezed, she found his hands possessive, and she disliked it when they dug into her knees, which she had told him tickled—but which he seemed to think meant that it was fine to tickle only once, or maybe twice, or just once more in jest or feigned forgetfulness—and it always made her feel defensive, though she tried to be good natured. His hands brushing her hair from her eyes so he could see into them she liked, and also when they traced her lip to remove a crumb or daub of sauce, unless he looked perturbed, or licked his finger first as her mother and father had done when she was a child, and pressed too firmly, in which case she liked it not at all, nor neither when his fingers smelled of garlic or raw onion, or the secreted evidence of her arousal (although the scent of his she did enjoy when it was fresh, though not when it was stale). For the skill with which his fingers pleasured, dexterously, she was grateful; but that often he used them to merely push her buttons, as though she was a touch-tone whose pleasure he could dial up at will, she resented, especially when it seemed that he was dialing it in long-distance although, to be fair, sometimes he got the number right. She liked his hands to begin, entreatingly, beneath her breasts, but this he often forgot and he got out ahead of her; and even when he (thinking better or suddenly remembering) thought to double back and make it up to her, each stroke or press or pinch said hurry up, or are you ready yet, as though his pleasure was beholden to hers and hers to his, which was true enough, but she didn't like to think of it that way. And yet if he rested his hand upon her cheek to kiss her—especially while they made love and she, in turn, hooked her fingers a round his runner's thighs, taut as bowstrings between her thighs—his tension and his gentleness and sometimes not-so-gentleness could shoot a trembling right through her and she would cry out in the dark of her apartment. And then there was how his hand half-covered his mouth and chin when he was thinking hard, as it did when she first met him in the stacks at Robarts, and she could see by that hand how hard he was thinking and how supremely important she was to him for as long as his hand remained there. It was also those same hands that had tried to interfere, not trusting her, when she first handled the indenture.

These thoughts occurred to her not sequentially, but in binaries of emotion—on and off; in and out; yes, now or no, later. They were the knotted threads of experiences that even afterthought could hardly untangle, and in the moments between Oliver driving off and Rose coming through the door, Cecelia felt them cinching tighter. It was so tedious the way it was always hands-on, hands-off with Noah. She could not remember exactly when was the last time he called. How could his hands do all of this to her and yet somehow be incapable of picking up a phone?

Rose was stamping her boots on the mat and then removing them. Then she began to remove her coat, which Cecelia could observe as her sister's belly peeked into the living room while the rest of her remained out of sight in the foyer. In fact, Rose was now more spherical than her arms could compass, so large she had become a stranger to her navel, which stood out like an uncharted island, resistant to discovery. Her breasts, too, had become swollen and protuberant, so much so that, at the pool, when she floated on her back, she formed an archipelago: like her very own Antilles. When Rose at last came into full view, however, Cecelia could only marvel. For what her sister really most resembled was a tropical flower, dew-covered and radiant, perched atop a round bulb.

Rose greeted Janet and Cecelia, and then her mother, who crossed the room to embrace her. Susan held her daughter at arm's length, appraisingly, and ran her fingers over the soft, cold, snowy wetness of Rose's hair.

"I still can't believe how red it's grown," she said, "and how long and thick it is. C., look at how thick it is. When was the last time you had it cut?"

Rose looked away. "I don't remember. Probably not since the summer."

"Well, it's the baby that does it, so don't get used to it." Susan ran her fingers through it. "Once you're a mother it will start falling out in clumps. It's disgusting."

"I guess I'll need a trap for the shower drain," Rose said.

"Such a shame, though. It's so beautiful. Oh well, that's motherhood for you."

"I never understood why people say you'll be a mother once the baby comes," Janet said. "I mean, if Rose will only be a mother after she delivers, what the hell has she been for the last nine months?"

"Maybe it's to keep you from getting ahead of yourself," Cecelia said.

"Cecelia!" her mother snapped.

Cecelia met her stare with confusion, and Rose quickly intervened. "It's OK. I certainly don't feel like a mother yet."

"Soon enough," Susan said.

Rose twisted free of her mother's fondling and lowered herself into an armchair. Her abdomen cantilevered out over her waistband. "Mostly I feel like a Christmas oven."

"My sister said she didn't feel like a mother for months after she delivered," Janet said, "and for the first week she actually felt nothing at all, like she was so drained she was kind of dead inside. Of course, now she's so fond it's appalling. She can't leave my nephew alone for even five minutes. If she were my mother, I'd take out a restraining order."

Susan surveyed the seated women. "This conversation has turned irritating." She retreated to her plants and pruning.

Cecelia rolled her eyes and waved off Janet's searching expression. Not only was an apology unnecessary, but one would hardly make a difference. Her mother was in a mood.

"It's too bad Oliver didn't come in," Janet said. "I haven't seen him in forever."

"He was disappointed too. He wanted to ask C. about that thing she's doing," Rose said.

"Oh, really?" Cecelia asked.

"He asked me to find out, but I told him I wouldn't be able to explain it so he'd have to wait until the next time he sees you. What I want to know is, how's Noah?"

"He's fine," Cecelia said. She looked out the window.

"He's been gone a long time now."

"Yes, he has."

"It's been a party of one for, like, ten weeks," Janet said.

Unsure of her meaning, Cecelia and Rose stared at Janet. She thumbed the zipper on her jeans as though playing a bass guitar. They laughed, all three, but Cecelia looked over her shoulder at her mother. Rose did too.

"Maybe you should write him something," Janet said, trying to speak below the whisper of Susan's shears. "Something a little ... you know..."

Susan interrupted. "Don't bother being sly about it, Janet. I know what you're talking about and I don't like it. It's not proper."

Janet ignored her. She leaned towards Cecelia. "Or phone him. For a little you-and-he time."

"What would your mother say if I told her?" Susan said.

Janet's laughter this time was voluminous and unrestrained, rolling over any impropriety.

Cecelia frowned. "In his grandparents' house? I don't think I could do that." The location was the least of her reluctance.

"He's been gone for weeks," Janet said. "If you don't show him you're still interested he might get interested in something else."

Cecelia stole a glance at her sister. Rose was contemplating her belly and rubbing it in slow circles. Cecelia asked her, "Have you ever known a long distance relationship that worked?"

"Without being married?" Rose shook her head.

"Janet?" Cecelia asked.

"Unless you want to be disappointed, you should probably ask me something else."

Cecelia conceded that, in fact, she had no idea what was going on between them.

"You should go see him," Susan said, butting in.

"And look desperate? Not likely."

"Do you want to see him?" Rose asked.

"Just find an excuse," Janet said. "What about that thing in Halifax?"

Rose turned to her. "What thing is that?"

"Noah has a friend he said could help them with that thing they're doing," Janet explained.

"Noah was going to talk to him," Cecelia said.

"And has he?" Janet asked.

"I don't think so. He hasn't said so."

"So ..."

"I don't remember his name. Anyway it's his friend, and he would want to do it," Cecelia said. Her stomach turned a little as she said it, though, and although she didn't say so, she admitted to herself that she really didn't know what Noah wanted, except that when he finally left town after New Year's, he didn't seem like a man who wanted following.

"Why should it just be about what he wants?" Susan interrupted. She was at the buffet, pinching a dwarf shrub. "Really, Cecelia, stop being so timid."

"Yeah. Go see his friend. Then, go to his grandparents' and surprise him," Janet said. She sipped her wine. "And after that you should fuck him."

"Janet!" Susan shrieked.

Cecelia, unlike her mother, tried to conceal her irritation. She got a fortunate distraction when, at that moment, her sister let out a sharp gasp.

"Sonofabitch!" Rose cried. Cecelia and Janet jumped to the edge of the chesterfield, and Susan raced into the living room, but it was not what they thought. "This thing's got a foot like a sledgehammer. Like it's trying to break down a door." She groaned and rubbed her belly. "You're not chained in you know! You can come out any time!"

"Just a few more weeks," Susan said.

"God, I hope not. If it gets any bigger it'll feel like it's coming out sideways."

"It'll do that anyway," her mother said.

"For a while they talked about sewing my cervix shut," Rose informed them.

"Is it really that big?" Janet asked. "What does your doctor think, will it need inducing?"

271

Cecelia relaxed and leaned back casually on the sofa. "If it knows where it's headed it will," she said.

Susan slammed the shears on the dining room table. She fled into the kitchen, and Rose's eyes followed her. Cecelia had meant it to cut her mother, but only gently, and only in jest. Bewildered, she turned to Rose. In the kitchen their mother was making a racket with some glasses.

"She's just anxious about the delivery," Rose said. "After us, she delivered a stillborn baby girl in her eighth month."

Janet's eyes grew wide. "Those things I said about my sister ..."

"It's not your fault," Rose reassured her. "Nobody talks about it. Not even our parents."

"I didn't know," Cecelia whispered. She looked back to where her mother had escaped. "She never told me."

"She thought at eight months she was safe. Then one day the baby didn't move as much. The next day it didn't move at all. She didn't want me to find out like she did." Rose shuddered visibly. "I hardly slept for a week after she told me."

In the kitchen, the assault on the glassware had stopped. The women sat in silence. Janet and Cecelia nursed their drinks. Rose, pressed back into the armchair, continued to hold her abdomen. Again, she grimaced and quietly groaned.

"Like a sledgehammer," Janet repeated. "That must be a comfort, at least. To have it knocking things around in there."

Rose remained as still as scales.

"I should go see him, shouldn't I," Cecelia said, surprising herself with a feeling of decisiveness. Then she got up from the sofa and went to her purse, from which she pulled her notebook and a pen. She wondered would Cate even be home. Or maybe she would find a babysitter on the other end of the line. Or maybe have to leave a message if neither Cate nor Felix were at home. Notebook in hand, she entered the kitchen from the front hall, just as her mother was leaving by the side through the swinging door. She watched her mother's straight back and proud shoulders march out into the dining room and the door swing shut behind her.

She punched Cate's number into the telephone, which was Noah's number too. Another reflex of frustration shot through her as the ringing—three, four, kick the door—continued unanswered. She pulled the phone from her ear to disconnect, but then Cate's voice answered crossly amidst a terrible racket. Cecelia could almost see the chaos at the other end of the line.

"Clean those up now. I could have broken my neck. I'm not your maid—I'm sorry, yes? Oh, hi. Sorry about that. Felix has been on a tear tonight—Now, mister!—I think he misses Noah. He calls every few days, but it's not the same as him being here. You must miss him too. I know I do when Felix gets like this—No! Like I told you: on the shelves where they won't be underfoot—Sure, you mean Andrew. I'll get the number. Noah called for it a couple of weeks ago, actually. He forgot his address book. Yeah, Felix has been a great nuisance since he left, I can tell you—That's what I said, mister. You heard me!—That sounds nice. I'm sure he wouldn't mind a change of company. His grandmother too. I bet she's going loopy—Yes, we're talking about your father. Yes, it's her—Sorry. Felix says hello and wants to know when you're going to come and visit—She can't, sweetie. She's going away for a bit. Maybe after she gets back—You're not driving, are you? That's good. It's a long, lonely drive on your own. Alright, here it is: Andrew Coyle, Public Archives, Halifax." She fired off the numbers. "Do you have the address in Mission Point? OK. You know, I was thinking of you the other day. That guy from the university called for Noah. He was so weird. He would go on about something for a couple of minutes and then just wait, like I was supposed to fill in the blanks. Oh, and Felix says to give Noah—Sorry!—give Dad a hug for him, and Great-Gran and Gramps too—There, happy? Yes, as long as you stay in the backyard. And put on your snow pants too. No buts!—Sorry, what was that? Oh, just tell him we're fine. Yes. Alright, take care. Bye."

It was over quickly, and a little hard to follow. A stenographer would have had a time of it. Cate sounded exhausted. Between Noah's aloofness, Janet's fussing and her mother in the next room, and Trover's occasional prodding, Cecelia felt it too. He never said he'd talked to his friend—he was just handling it all for her. She closed the notebook and forced herself to straighten and take a full breath.

She exited the kitchen and found her mother showing Janet the sweet pea she had spent months training up a trellis. With dexterity,

Susan was deadheading and entwining unruly shoots, fanwise, in and out of the trellis-weave. She had meant for it to move outdoors eventually, but thought she might instead continue raising it inside, it had behaved so well.

"It's settled," Cecelia announced.

Janet looked up from the climbing plant. "Awesome. So I should be getting home?"

"It's up to you. Stay if you want, but I need to get back to my place. I've got to book a flight and let my professors know I'll be absent. I've got to call Noah's friend too."

"I don't understand. What's happening?" Susan said.

"I'm taking a short trip to Halifax, and then I'm going to surprise Noah with a visit. It's his birthday next weekend. He's turning thirty."

"What about your sister? What if she goes into labour?"

"She's not due for a couple of weeks."

"It's OK, Mom," Rose said.

"It's unacceptable is what it is."

Cecelia stared her mother down. "You said I should go see him. That's what you said."

"Yes, but not now. Not when your sister needs you."

"I'll give you the numbers. You can reach me if anything happens."

"Mom, it's fine," Rose said. She hefted herself out of the chair and planted herself beside her sister.

"Rachel Rose, you stay out of this," Susan commanded.

"What's she going to do, poke around the delivery room? We don't need any more bowlers in the alley."

Susan was silent, waiting, but Cecelia's anger was running wild on the inside. She had no intention of cutting it back. "I'm not changing my mind," she said.

"You're not going and that's final."

"C., don't you dare let her tell you," Rose said. "If you do, I'll never forgive you."

"I don't need your help," Cecelia shot back. In the seesaw of her emotions, resentment was easier to leverage than gratitude, and only after snapping did she see that Rose was hurt. Cecelia retargeted her mother. "Mom, I'm going. And that's final."

Janet light-footed her way towards the front door. She smiled as she navigated the crossfire of angry eyes, but only her mouth was smiling. "I'll be in the vestibule."

Cecelia joined her. Quickly she pulled on her boots and coat and collected her gloves. Looking back she could see, even from the door, that her mother's hands were shaking. Their entire relationship was right there in those hands: a thumb for pressing, a finger for pointing, another for cursing, a third for expectation, and don't forget the fourth for good form and not forgetting. Rose joined Cecelia at the door as she was leaving and entwined her in her arms. Her belly made hugging difficult. Cecelia tried to push up the gratitude she thought she felt beneath her anger. Then she bolted out the door. As her feet imprinted on the freshly fallen snow, Janet followed uneasily at her side, but Cecelia wasn't paying attention. It persisted in her ears, no matter how much ground she put between them: the sound of her mother's snipping and the unending tsk tsk of her shears.

The snow had been falling heavily for hours, blotting the dark vaulting of the sky with a faint, dense whiteness. Conditions were dangerous. Noah wore a pinny with reflective crosses, and the road, despite the salting, was so slick that at times he was forced to shuffle. He shuffled, too, to protect his foot, whose sole had grown inflamed with overuse from these long midnight runs. Incapable of steadiness on the wintry roads, the muscles in his feet, legs and hips, were increasingly exhausted. Sometimes the effort was enough to clear his mind, but tonight it had come to nothing and he despaired that sleep was now more distant than when he'd lain restless in bed an hour before. Worse, the run had only further irritated his plantar fascia. By morning his ankle would be almost frozen. He was running himself down.

A plow approached from behind and it caught him by surprise. He crossed the road and gave it the widest berth he could without climbing over the guardrail. The driver too, for hours having navigated deserted lanes, must have been surprised, seeing a runner at that hour and in that weather. Despite Noah's raised hand and apologetic smile, the driver looked at him as though he must be mad. The plow threw up waves of snow on either side and, as it roared past, Noah climbed the wake back over to the fresh road.

He stood still for several minutes. The visible landscape was soft, like rolled muslin or bolts of fustian, but underneath all that it was hard as a tooth, biting his heel with every step. You could break your shins against it, and Noah knew that was exactly what he was doing. He tried not to think about it, which was difficult, and even tried not to think at all, which was more difficult still. He tried listening as his breathing slowed.

High up the roadside there was a small waterfall, one of the myriad along the Trail. It was fed by the pumping heart of a mountain spring, but the freezing temperatures had all but locked it up and it hung there, congealed into long, thick ropes of ice and gently weeping. Noah imagined his bearded face looked much the same, seized up and frosted white anywhere his breath pushed through his whiskers. He gazed a long time and tried to see it clearly, but it was so dark out and the snow was falling so thickly that, even standing still, his sight was almost useless. All he could see clearly was that he was tired of losing sleep in a bed that no longer belonged to him, and tired of caring about what he knew he couldn't help.

Cold and silent, the snow lighted on his face like a ghostly presence, and although it was his skin the snow fell on, he felt it touch those inward and hidden places he seldom spoke of to himself and to others never. He felt an unaccustomed need for prayer—or maybe poetry—or something else extraordinary. He was unsure what it meant exactly, but it was not the time for too curious consideration. The snow was already filling in around his shoes. There might be days of this ahead, or worse.

His grandparents' house was not far off and he navigated by the cleared road and the line of votive lights atop the telephone poles. By the time he arrived he was favouring one side, like a ship with too much sail, over-canvassed and heeling. Rather than fumble through the freezer for an ice pack at this hour, Noah trudged into the snow towards the water. He was warm from the run, but knew that as the minutes passed his tissues would grow cold and constrict and limit the inflammation in his foot. The tide was in and laying a beating on the shore. Before him, spray after spray of salt water was thrown into the air as the water struck the stones and sea stacks, causing it like aspergils to sprinkle sweet forgiveness on its own transgressions. Something welled inside him too, rising to his throat before he breathed it down. He ran his hands all over his face, washing it clean with the ice and snow from his beard. A quarter of an hour at least he stood there before he started to shiver. It was getting to him. He needed to take care not to catch a chill.

The flower beds around the house were buried under mounds of snow, and the eaves, under the weight of ice, were bent out of shape, undoing all the reparations he had made in the fall. The pavers leading to the back door were slick underfoot. He would have to get out and shovel them before his grandfather woke, and fetch wood from the shed while he was at it. There was little time for sleep, despite his need.

The screen door swung open easily and the storm door too. Noah had oiled them, and the others too, when he'd arrived. He wiped his feet and passed through the vestibule, but stopped in the kitchen door to jam the ball of his injured foot against the frame. Then he drove his heel into the floor. Gripping the trim with his fingers, he straightened the rest of his body, from his calf up through his hips and spine, and forced his toes towards his shin in acute dorsiflexion and, conversely, an extension in the plantar fascia. It hurt badly at first, like someone had driven the fangs of a garden rake under his heel, and he could feel all the little micro-tears in the connective tissues of his foot, thousands of tiny pockets of distress from countless footfalls exploding the length of his sole. But gradually, with deep breaths and with rhythmic contraction and release, the tissues a little loosened, and the pain lessened, and he felt a little better, although he might yet need that ice pack. Only then did he remove his shoes and step, toe first then cautiously heel, through the kitchen door. Without a squeak it closed behind him and he grimaced in envy—his own hinges wanted oiling.

Two night lights cut the darkness enough for Noah to find his way. There were others in outlets all over the ground floor to prevent his grandfather getting disoriented should he wake in the night (though Noah and his grandmother were now such alert sleepers that there was little need to worry). He took a glass from the cupboard and filled it from the tap. The initial draught of water was so cold it made his teeth ache right into his jaw with one of those dull, throbbing discomforts you can't rub better but have to suffer through until it dissipates. He should have properly insulated the walls years ago, but there was never the money. Leaning back against the counter at the sink, he waited with his eyes squeezed shut. As he did, a sharp whispering, barely audible, wound its way into the kitchen. He opened his eyes and listened.

Something in his grandparent's bedroom. He crept into the hall. Their door was open and feebly lit. Trying to measure his concern, he stepped closer and cocked his head. Their voices were low, but agitated—"I can't, Love . . ." "Please try, for me . . ." "No no, I can't."—then some muffled confusion and, after, quiet sobbing. Noah quickly turned away, embarrassed to have overheard. He limped up the stairs and willed his stupid feet to hush, as every rotten, creaking footstep sold him out.

Once in his room he divested himself hurriedly. The chill was creeping into him. He threw off his running gear and swapped it for a hoodie and sweats. Then he went to the dresser. It was covered in papers and correspondence, some of it messages from people who had called while he was out, some of which he had even answered. It had been accumulating for weeks. Those from Cate he had answered, mostly. One, from Felix, he had answered immediately and learned how Felix had scored six goals in floor hockey and helped a boy he said he liked score his first, and how excited the boy had been because he was always terrible at sports.

Noah pulled out a pair of socks, glancing as he did at all the other messages on little slips of paper he had allowed to pile up. Three or four were from Raymond, whom he had seen twice already since returning. One was from Amelia Phee, who had invited him to her and John's house for his birthday with the promise that everyone would be there: Ben McPhail and Charlotte, Nadine and Louis Clarke, Pete Farry, Jim Mahon and Annie Leblanc, maybe Adrien Gaudet. Henry Rambeau maybe too. Odds were Maggy would turn up as well. Her name, Margaret Horne, written in full in the careful hand of Noah's grandmother, appeared on another two slips he wished would slip his mind.

Two large bubble-lined envelopes from Cecelia were on the dresser too, largely ignored. They had been cut open, their contents skimmed and stuffed back in. The one contained a few dozen pages of updated descriptions, which he could hardly proofread without the originals handy, as well as an introduction to the bibliography, which she had titled with striking dullness, A Descriptive Catalogue of the Ledgers, Letters, Bills of Sale and Other Miscellaneous Items in the Lately Discovered Archive of the Belott Firm of Boston and Halifax. The other envelope contained articles of several lengths and bents: for *Notes and Queries*, a thumbnail sketch that she could later spin for the *Star* or maybe the *Chronicle Herald*, called "'How Possibly Preserved': A New Shakespeare Discovery;" for some Renaissance quarterly or other there was a paper titled, "The Discovered Country: The Belott Family in the New World;" and, for the popular press, one called "'Twixt a miser and his wealth': The Belotts and Shakespeare's Banker." Even without reading it that last one struck him as melodramatic: a suggestion of scandal, hints of betrayal. Her Shakespeare was a question whose answer she glimpsed in a shadow cast at her own feet. He hoped she would get someone who actually knew something, and not just him, to look it over once Trover let them off the hook.

Noah frowned. There were also, sitting atop the envelopes, two short messages from his employer, whose impatience was evident enough, even mediated through the courtesies of Clement Rowse and his grandmother's note taking. These messages had been easy to ignore. He was running twice a day, and watching the old man so his grandmother could go to bridge nights, and cleaning and shovelling, and making small repairs that, unlike those on McCaul Street, were not beyond his skill. He could not ignore those messages forever, though. He was slowing down Cecelia's work and there were bills that needed paying. He decided he would call soon. As soon as he figured out what to say.

A noise from downstairs. Unlike the one before. A voice, low. The heavy thud of a door. Afraid what he might find, Noah didn't want to go, but he went anyway, down the stairs and around the landing. The bathroom light leaned out into the hallway, and the door was swung all the way in. As Noah approached he found his grandfather, dressed in trousers and an undershirt. His head was down and in his hand was a key chain with many keys. He was going through them quickly, one after another, trying to insert and turn them in the lowered zipper tab of his trousers. He was shaking his head angrily and muttering.

"Gramps, what's wrong?" Noah asked.

The old man reached into the mouth of his fly and Noah watched, horrified, as with a sharp tug his grandfather fished out his old-man penis and slapped it on the vanity. He pointed at it. "This is dead!" More than describing, it was an accusation.

Noah looked at it: lank, bloodless, doughy. He didn't know what to say. It was hard to gather what was happening. His grandfather shook the keys in irritation and turned his sad eyes to him, while Noah struggled to communicate something useful or kind or, in fact, anything at all. "Oh," he said at last, as offhanded as he could. "Well, don't worry. It happens to the best of us from time to time."

A painful silence followed, but then the old man burst into laughter and threw his arms around Noah. He was still terrifyingly strong. Noah hugged back, dazed, but also tried to avoid the length of exposed geriatric flesh between them. He couldn't quite. His progenitor's genitals pressed against him. The old man released Noah from his hold.

"You're a ... you're a good egg," the old man said. "You remind me of someone."

Noah said nothing, only patted his grandfather's shoulder and sort of smiled. The old man stood there a moment, silent and increasingly uncertain. He frowned and left the room, but Noah lingered. He couldn't help but examine himself in the mirror. The ears, the lips, the bearded cheeks. The eyes. His eyes and not his eyes—behind them where he was and wasn't. He felt disjointed, disarticulate. His grandmother had received a second offer on the house, but still she wouldn't sell. Noah stepped out into the empty hallway. He listened, but all was silent. Reaching back, he cut the light, and as he made his way to bed, he thought about Felix and Cate in Toronto, and about Cecelia too, and about being here and not being there, and about being there and not being here, and how, wherever he was, how much he missed.

Andrew Coyle's woolly smile greeted Cecelia at the door of the Public Archives. His beard seemed to begin somewhere below his neckline. She shook her feet to prevent more water soaking through her boots. The weather was grisly. The streets and sidewalks were slushed over and a fine mist was falling. She had walked much farther than she meant to, and it left her wet and dishevelled from cuff to collar.

She offered Coyle her hand. His fingers were large and spongy. His belly was likewise. He gave the impression of a man unused to exercise, but his eyes were brisk.

"You didn't take a taxi?"

"I rented a car, but then I mixed up the address. I'm parked a few blocks away."

Coyle ambled towards his office with sloth-like economy. Perhaps he was capable of urgency, but Cecelia suspected it would take some doing.

"It always turns ugly after a dump," he said. "Freezing rain sometimes. Slush and road salt. Mostly it gets worse before it gets better."

The office was ill lit and full of boxes. A clammy shiver rolled up Cecelia's spine, and her eyes cast vainly about for a coatrack. She settled for the back of a chair. The hem of her coat settled on the floor. "Thanks very much for this. I hope it hasn't been too much trouble."

"Yet man is born unto trouble—as the sparks fly upward," Coyle intoned.

Cecelia sensed she ought to laugh, but she couldn't quite grasp his intention. Not wishing to be impolite she smiled, she hoped not condescendingly. She wished he would get on with it. He wrapped his thumbs and fingers around a steaming cup of tea. Then he sat in his chair and invited her to sit in hers. He asked her to excuse the mess. He was taking a job at the National Archives and hadn't finished packing up his things. He was moving to Ottawa the following week and was still negotiating to store his things with his parents.

Cecelia looked around. The office was indeed cluttered. It was not, however, disorganized. The boxes were stacked neatly along one wall. An antique chest of drawers—something like an apothecary cabinet— was wrapped in plastic to keep the drawers secure. A half dozen or so framed prints leaned safely in the corner. It was, she had heard, what the rooms of people who committed suicide often looked like: everything orderly, everything in place, everything in a state of readiness for whatever unforeseen thing was coming next. Even Coyle's stationery was carefully arranged on his desk. A pen and two newly sharpened pencils were all aligned on one side and, on the other, a stapler and a square tin of paperclips. Between these margins lay a thin folder with *Lamarck* written neatly in large, block capitals.

As her eyes looked down on the folder's thinness, Cecelia felt a slight impatience creep over her, and something else. A sensation she couldn't quite pinpoint or name. It seemed to come and go, dangling on the edge of her perception, acting on her at a distance. Maybe it was the cold air coming in from the ventilation ducts overhead. Or the odd smell that she began to catch. Or maybe even the huge fish mounted incongruously on the wall behind the desk, which Cecelia had somehow only just noticed. The sheen of its belly and the blood-red slash of its flank stood out from the wood platter to which it was mounted. Cecelia had never seen taxidermy before, except in a classroom or museum. Coyle followed her eyes.

"Oh, the fish!" he said.

"Is that a salmon?" she asked.

"Trout, actually. Steelhead. Pulled her out of the Bras d'Or one winter. Noah was there and caught nothing but shit luck, if you'll pardon my French. Not that he'd mind me saying. He can't fish worth a damn and he's the first to admit it. You'd swear there was a conspiracy down there, all of them with the understanding that no matter what he fishes with they ain't gonna take it. I never knew a feller for such poor fishing."

The trout's mouth gaped, and its one eye stared stupidly at her. Cecelia wondered if fish experienced astonishment.

"She fought hard, that one. I bet I never catch another like her: six point two and twenty-three inches. That was a good day." Coyle's admiration was evident, but his smile was not altogether happy. Thus ending his memorial, he turned forward again in his seat. "The steelhead's an anadromous species, sea-run," he said. "Noah's a bit like that sometimes."

Cecelia decided she didn't care what he meant. The file lay there waiting. Coyle spun it around for her.

"Here. I'm sorry there isn't more."

"I'm sorry for the short notice." Cecelia hesitated. "I was surprised Noah hadn't called you already. He gave me the impression he meant to." She hoped her voice did not sound defensive. That olfactory infestation in the air was nagging at her again.

"He probably did mean to, but then he probably didn't want to be a bother. Or, more likely, he hasn't had a spare moment. My great-grandfather was the same way when I was a boy. It was mostly just confusing for me then, but I never forgot how it hurt my mother to watch it happen."

Cecelia nodded her head. She began to flip through the pages and hoped. Coyle began to explain.

"I could have gone further, but a week and a half isn't enough time to be comprehensive. And I didn't really know how wide a net to cast. A lot of the families around here are prolific. They branch out all over the place. I mean, technically speaking, it goes on forever. It's hard to know where to cut off. But the main branch was pretty simple, actually. Not too many children and not too far to follow. And Belott's an uncommon enough name."

Cecelia looked over the photocopies. Mostly they were census and parish ledgers, the shorthands and conventions of which were unfamiliar to her and difficult to understand. Much of it was nearly illegible. Where it was not, the spelling was often improvisational. She frowned.

"I know," Coyle said. "They're hard to get your head around. My eyes get so buggy looking at the microfilms sometimes I get narcoleptic. Nothing a smoke wouldn't fix, but still, enough to make you feel dopey. There's a summary at the back where I've distilled it. The line goes more or less directly down to him." Cecelia flipped to the last page and saw a neatly drawn family tree. "They're in the 1891 and 1901, and luckily they don't leave Halifax until after the war, so I found Margerie Belott marrying John Avy in the parish records. They turn up again in Sydney, baptizing their children two years later. And then—this is the pearl—Modeste Avy is baptized in Sydney—in 1927, I think it says, you can check the photocopies—then it's just a hop, skip and a slide to Noah."

Cecelia's eyes, like the lineage on the page, narrowed.

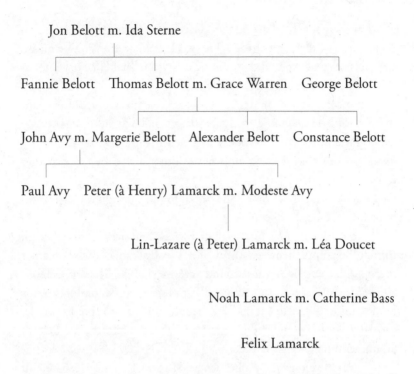

Jon Belott m. Ida Sterne

Fannie Belott   Thomas Belott m. Grace Warren   George Belott

John Avy m. Margerie Belott   Alexander Belott   Constance Belott

Paul Avy   Peter (à Henry) Lamarck m. Modeste Avy

Lin-Lazare (à Peter) Lamarck m. Léa Doucet

Noah Lamarck m. Catherine Bass

Felix Lamarck

"I stopped once I saw the Avys were the link. I mean, I could still branch out if you want, but I figured this was all you needed."

"I'm sorry. What is this?" Cecelia read it three times more and still could not believe it.

"Did I misunderstand? Aren't you helping him with his family tree?"

"No, he's helping me, damn it." Cecelia's voice was starting to break on her.

"With his family tree? I don't get it." Coyle's head listed to one side.

"I'm researching a family of London Huguenots who rented a room to Shakespeare," she said.

"What, and it turns out Noah's related?" Coyle said it glibly. Then he saw that she was serious. "What, really? Well, I'll be jiggered. That's a strange one."

"Do you think?"

"Mind you, I've seen stranger," he added, helpfully.

"Really?" Cecelia felt like she was being mocked.

"Actually, no. That is pretty surprising. I mean, go back a bit and everybody around here is related. It's a shallow pool. But still …" Coyle scratched at his beard. "And it all boils down to the Belotts? You'd think Noah would've mentioned it."

"No shit!" Cecelia looked again at Coyle's handwriting. It was hardly credible, but there was no mistaking it. It cut cleanly across the page. She tried to swallow down her vexation, but it roiled and curdled within her. Noah's great-grandmother was a Belott. Nearly nine months she had known him—and for six he had known what she was looking for—and still he had said nothing. Now here she was, on the barb of a question set all the more firmly for the tug he had on her affections: what else had he been keeping from her? The whole thing was fishy. Rotten. Noxious. It befouled the air itself and lingered, like that indistinct, acrid odour she had been trying to ignore since she arrived. It was all too much for her. "Jesus, Andrew, what is that smell?"

"Oh, I'm sorry," he said, nervously. "Is it bothering you? It's the tea. I know, it's kind of off-smelling, isn't it? The wife makes me take it. She's one of those naturopathics. A bit harsh. The tea, I mean, not the wife—most of the time." He swirled the cup and the odour increased. "I don't like it either, but she says it's good for me."

Cecelia leaned back, exasperated. She looked away and her eyes settled inadvertently on the steelhead.

"She's a beauty, isn't she?" Coyle said quickly. "A miracle of evolution, Noah called it. Millions of years of adaptation. Almost all of them get eaten up, but this one makes it and grows to six point two and twenty-three." Coyle frowned. Cecelia still wasn't saying anything. "I guess I could have thrown her back—Noah wanted me to."

A few minutes later they said their goodbyes and Cecelia thanked him for his help. It was his pleasure, he said, and asked her to say hello to Noah for him. As she stepped outside the Archives, the air was still cold and thick with precipitation. She looked up at the sky and a large bead of water snaked its way down her temple and deep into her ear. She tried to shake it out, and then pry it with her finger, but it was lodged inside.

In frustration, she formed two fists and pressed her shoulders down hard. She persuaded herself that she was working on a second wind. First, though, she needed an umbrella.

At first, Noah had thought it was just the thunder. He was hurrying down the stairs, through the kitchen and into the vestibule. Knock, knock, knock! Someone had been out there hammering awhile. He turned the knob and jerked. Cecelia stood on the other side of the screen, wet and getting wetter. In the wind her umbrella was proving useless. Her hair was pressed to her cheeks in mats and strands.

"What's wrong with your face?" she snapped.

"My face?"

"Jesus, does everyone around here have a beard?"

Noah had never seen her so determined, or irritated. "How did you get here?"

"I rented a car. I guess you didn't hear that either."

"No, I mean how did you get *here*."

"I asked at a convenience store in town. The scruffy guy inside gave me directions. He was very nice. Nicer than some." Cecelia waited while Noah stood there dumbly. "Can I come in, or what?"

Noah threw open the screen door and stepped aside to let her into the vestibule. He took her umbrella and placed it open in the corner to dry. "Sorry. The sound doesn't carry well back here."

"I tried the front door. I assume that was your grandfather I saw. He took a look at me through the window, then he went away."

"Only strangers ever use the front. Friends always come around back. It's where the kitchen is."

"Noah!" It was his grandmother calling from inside. "Noah, is someone here?"

"It's a friend. From Toronto."

Noah stepped from the vestibule into the kitchen, but Cecelia refused to move from the threshold.

"Why the hell didn't you say anything about your great-grand-mother?" she said.

"What?"

"Why didn't you tell me she was a Belott?"

Noah spun around. "What? Who's a Belott?"

286

"Fuck, Noah!"

Entering just then from the parlour, Noah's grandmother stopped sharply. "Do all your Toronto friends use the fuck word when you invite them in?"

Noah turned to her in surprise. "Gran, was your mother a Belott?"

"Yes," she replied.

"Modeste Lamarck, née Avy, daughter of Margerie Avy, née Belott," Cecelia listed. She had repeated it over to herself, four hours and more, all the way from Halifax.

Noah felt suddenly unsettled. His grandmother too, it seemed. She looked at Noah, who looked at her. Then both looked at Cecelia in the doorway. It was a whole lot of gawking.

"It's a Huguenot name, you know," his grandmother said finally.

"We know it's a Huguenot name," Noah said. "Why didn't you ever tell me?"

"I don't think you ever asked. How was I supposed to know it was important?"

Cecelia rolled her eyes. Noah was incredulous. His grandmother turned and went to the cupboards. "Now, should I go ahead and make us some tea or do we want to wind ourselves up a bit more?" Not waiting for an answer, she put on the kettle. "And Noah, the poor dear's sopping. Take her coat and get her a towel before she says anything else to shame her mother."

ᠸ

The storm continued. The wind made the windows shiver in their frames, and the rain, like the impatient tapping of ten thousand fingers, trembled on the brink of an outburst. In the parlour, Noah's grandfather was in his rocking chair, frowning. He did not acknowledge their arrival. He sat with his back to the mantelpiece, staring at the faded Botticellis. Noah and Cecelia sat at either end of the small loveseat, and Noah's grandmother sat in the armchair facing them.

Noah was shaking his head at Cecelia. "But I don't understand. How exactly did you work this out?"

"Andrew traced the Belotts from Halifax."

287

"So Andrew says I'm related to these friends of William Shakespeare," Noah's grandmother said. "And you think maybe even to Shakespeare himself, in a back door sort of way?" She shook her head. "My Lord, what a world. You know, I imagine that's where I got my way with words."

Noah looked at his grandmother, then back to Cecelia. "And where does that leave us?"

"I have absolutely no idea," Cecelia answered. "If I wrote a book about this, no one would believe it."

Cecelia sipped her tea. Noah likewise. It was all he could think to do.

"You don't have anything that might be connected?" she asked. "No heirlooms?"

"I think I would know if I did."

"Sure you would. Like you knew the whole time you were researching your own family."

Noah thought about it. Only one thing came to mind. "Gran, how old is your wedding chest?" His grandmother did not answer immediately. "Gran?"

"Oh, I don't know. Old, but probably not very. Maybe a hundred years. But it's just full of toys and things. There's nothing in there I didn't put in myself."

"Can we look at it?" Cecelia asked.

"I don't even know where it is."

"It's up in the crawl space," Noah said. "I helped you put it there."

"Did you? Well. Sometimes, I swear, my mind's going too. You know I used to be a girl as could find a fish in a graveyard."

Noah got up and left the room. "I'll bring it down," he called, the groans of his feet on the stairs mingling with the low rumble of thunder. The women said nothing for several minutes, until their mutual observation grew uncomfortable.

"Noah's told me a lot about you," Cecelia said.

"How long have you known each other?" his grandmother asked.

"Since last summer. We met in the library."

"Are you a student, then? You look a little old for that."

Noah returned quickly and Cecelia saw that the chest, though large, was not unwieldy, his arms easily long enough for his fingers to grasp the bottom. He set it down and she kneeled beside it. The wood was dark with age and the sides carved with feathers and fleurs-de-lys. He knelt beside her. Cecelia lifted the lid.

"See, it's full of toys," Noah's grandmother said.

Ignoring her, Cecelia said, "I think it's old, though. Much older than a hundred years." She removed a heavy plastic apple, bright red with a face painted on it, and with a weight and bell inside. It rocked when she set it down, and it rang as it rocked. She then pulled out two small stuffed bears with eyes and noses and other bits missing, then a large wooden boat and some small plastic animals.

"There used to be twenty or so, all in pairs," Noah's grandmother said. Then she addressed Noah. "You kept misplacing them and, Lord, you got cross when you did. Three years old, rummaging everywhere with your serious face on. We thought it was funny at the time. You were already such a fusspot."

Cecelia then pulled out a hairbrush, small and blue, with baby-soft bristles, and shaped like a whale.

"That was my father's," Noah said, happy to set aside the animals. "He called it Blub-blub."

"He once tried to pick it up from the bottom shelf of a bookcase," his grandmother said. "Stuck his head right under to reach it, and then couldn't figure how to get himself out. Just kept lifting his head up against the shelf, over and over, and screaming his lungs right out." She grew quiet and thoughtful. "He got out on his own eventually. Face red and furious. Took him a while though. Probably we should have helped him out." She worked her fingers around in her curls. "Lord, he was stubborn."

There was more in the chest. A wooden train set; some toy soldiers; a small, flat cardboard box; three hockey pucks; and a child's skates. Noah took up the skates and turned them over in his hand. The leather was stiff and cracked, the blades dull and pitted with rust. "We both used these," he said. "Gran, could I have them?"

Cecelia removed some more toys, a couple of children's hardbacks, and an envelope box. Once the chest was empty she tilted it up on its edge and studied it, inside and out. "Noah, this chest is too shallow. Look, it's smaller on the inside." Noah leaned closer. His grandmother rose and came to stand over them. "They had a thing for secret compartments and oubliettes. If it's as old as it looks …" Cecelia's fingers slid carefully along the inside. "Down here, in the front. You'd never see it unless you were looking." She pressed and the bottom popped up slightly.

Noah's grandmother gasped. "Well, Lord dyin'."

Cecelia used her fingernails to lift the lid. It resisted at first, as though reticent, unaccustomed to exposure. It soon gave in, though, and swung more willingly the more it opened up. Underneath, Cecelia found a wooden paddle with an alphabet and numbers on one side, and the Lord's Prayer on the other. "It's a hornbook," she said, handing it to Noah. "It's like a schoolboy's slate." On the floor of the compartment lay a stack of paper, an inch thick or almost, contained within a larger sheet, double the size and folded over as a wrapper. Noah reached in to help, but she elbowed him away. "Stop it." She withdrew the stack and set it on the floor. The wrapper was higher quality than the leaves it enfolded. She opened it. The pages were yellow with age but otherwise intact.

"Well?" Noah asked.

"Don't rush me," she said sternly.

"You know, I had it from my mother that it wasn't always a wedding chest," Noah's grandmother confessed. "Noah, quit leaning in so much. Let an old woman see."

The writing was faded, but not much. The pages numbered in the dozens at least. Cecelia frowned as she scanned them. Then she frowned some more. "Shakespeare wrote in secretary hand and this is cursive. And it's a little hard to read because of the bleed-through. But it's definitely the plays. Some of them anyway." Then she settled back on her haunches, turning the pages loosely in her grasp. "I have no idea what this is."

Noah's grandmother looked inside and closed the hidden compartment. "If there's nothing else inside, can I tidy away the box?"

Hastily, Cecelia began to replace the contents of the chest, and Noah began to hand her the items. "Relax, Gran, no need to get a sweat on." Then he picked up the envelope box and paused to examine it. "What's in this?"

His grandmother did not answer, but her eyes skipped to her husband, who was still in his seat, frowning but otherwise impassive. He had stopped rocking. Cecelia noticed and looked up from the pages. Noah opened the box. Inside he found a number of folded letters, maybe twenty or twenty-five. He withdrew them and opened a few. He wasn't saying anything. Leaning over, Cecelia saw the salutations and endearments. Each one Noah opened was signed either *Laz* or *Léa*. His hands were trembling.

"Oh my God," she said. "Noah, it's your parents."

"I've—I've never seen these."

After that, he lost track of time, and lost track too, as he held the pages, of Cecelia and his grandparents, and even of his own bodily awareness. Yet he could hardly concentrate. It was as though he were prying open a tomb and stepping into the darkness. During those first, fearful moments his eyes were useless. They jumped around the page, taking in only the occasional phrase or expression, each no more than a shadow. His parents were incoherent to him in the fragments his distraction lighted on, and yet the more he settled, the more he gleaned.

The letters were full of the overstated protestations and endearments common to the young, the kind scoffed at by those who don't remember what it felt like, or who do and are still embarrassed by their former selves—their intensity of feeling and the depths of their foolishness—those who have grown afraid of feeling, or who have forgotten that emotions cannot be made safe, or that in order to really live we have to gamble with our hearts. The dead alone are safe, and the safe already dead. Laz and Léa lived when they were young, as this boxful of their hyperbole testified. But for many years, Noah had crafted an idea of who his father was, or might have been. Having so long worried it round and smooth, like a soft stone under his thumb, he was not prepared for the hard and faceted shape of the real thing. A little sadly, he found that his father's voice seemed quite alien. He thought he could hear his mother's, though. Dark and sweet and gentle. He heard it less as a reality than as a faint and distant memory, foggy and perhaps invented, but nonetheless comforting in a primal, instinctive sort of way. He wondered if there were some quality of it that he did indeed remember, some timbre or inflection, perhaps only by association, the way by crossing a trumpet with a French horn in your mind you could imagine the mellow, brassy sound of a flugelhorn, even had you never heard one. It was somewhere so deep in his consciousness that he was never likely to reach it again. It had retreated and receded and shrunk during the course of his life, so that now it was nothing more than a line trolled so far behind that he could no longer tell if anything was hooked at all, or if the tug was just his imagination. It did tug, though, all the same. Her letters spoke of school dances and kitchen parties, alliances made and unmade, her sisters, her father. Most of all she spoke of how much she liked Laz, and how good she felt when he was with her. Noah glanced at the bottom of one of her letters. She called him Puffin.

A sharp crack in the sky, and his grandmother's hand went instinctively to her breast. It was followed by a long metallic rattle of thunder so loud it knocked around inside Noah's chest and made him realize how his heart was pounding. "My God," he said. "They were so young." He smiled a little.

Cecelia leaned close and put her arm around him. "Are you excited?"

"If I was more excited my pants would be getting shorter."

Then Noah looked up at his grandmother's pale face. She averted her eyes and he understood. "You knew about these. You put them here."

He shrugged Cecelia away and shuffled quickly through to the bottom of the pile to the final letter. It was his father's. He read it carefully. Then he read it again. His face stiffened, and his hands and forearms grew tense. For several moments he said nothing. Then, in anger and confusion, he thrust the letter towards his grandmother. "What does this mean?"

Cecelia shifted back to her hip and slightly away from their confrontation. She saw the rocking chair was now empty. "Noah, where's your grandfather?"

Noah looked around. Then he leapt to his feet. The old man was gone.

They rushed into their boots and ran outside. It was coming down harder than when Cecelia first arrived. With rain crisscrossed like a wire screen in a confessional, the storm was leaning hard on the byland now, and the downpour, through the nearby forests, penetrated to the understory. The sky above them was dark and tainted with an eerie greenness. Upland, the island's taut ropes of muscle, the Appalachian hills, were all but obscured. Their distant silhouette was visible only in the fleeting whips of lightning that flickered in and out of existence, obedient to the violent whip-snapping of the atmosphere. It was a gale of wind out there, and there was no sign of the old man. The women started down the drive towards the road, but Noah was looking to the shore and, in the distance, to the wave tips slashing whitely on the long hefts of blackwater. It was a long road, and if his grandfather had taken it they would find him without difficulty. The greater danger was by the sea, and Noah just knew the old man had scampered down. Calling them back, he ran to the rock ledge and picked his way towards the shore.

The old man was there, evading the water's wagging tongue, which was throwing up brash ice and clinkers. He was struggling, with fretful sidling, to climb out onto a small outcrop that rose dangerously above the swells. Noah's grandmother scurried down to the shore and closed in on her husband. Reaching him, she shouted, "Peter, you get your arse back here right now!" When he ignored her, she grabbed hold of his arm, causing him to cry out.

Impetuous in his struggle, he struck her with his arm so hard she would have fallen had Noah not been there to catch her. With Cecelia's help, she staggered to safety. "I'm fine," the old woman said. "Just get him down from there."

Noah's grandfather, with an eye like a stinking eel, was staring into a wind as growly as he. What had gotten into him, Noah could hardly imagine. Who knew what the old man had knocking about in that skull of his.

As within a machine, when two great unbalanced forces contend and the housing is not strong enough, the old man stood there shaking. "Hush now, hush now." He put a finger to his lips. "Shhhhhhhhhh."

Noah feared that if this went on any longer his grandfather might slip and pitch himself right into the water. If that happened, Noah wasn't sure that he could fetch him out. Careless in his haste, he himself slipped, scraping both of his hands and banging up his knee. Below them, little puffs of water swirled up from the surface and winged into the air. In the storm's nimble sleight of hand, they seemed like water spirits, evaporating almost before they were seen, but here and there, fleetingly, they gave to the vagaries and shifting violence of the wind a substance and a shape. Noah shouted and pulled on his grandfather's arm. "Please, Gramps, you have to come in!"

But the old man resisted, holding out against him and peering into the storm like there was something out there. "They'll be talking," the old man was shouting. "Talk, talk, talking."

It can be hard to believe, with the brunt of a storm upon you, that—notwithstanding how the North Atlantic's weather can be erratic and capricious, disposed to sudden shifts of temper and flabbergasting violence—there are nonetheless mornings in that corner of the world when the sea all up and down the coast is smooth, and it shines in the sun like a mirror you could shave in, and above it are open skies, and wide and blue, and underneath the surface schools of quicksilvery capelin, and the bob and dart of eiders, thick-billed murres, and terns, and hardly a breeze to disturb its shimmering veneer. But this calm—however beautiful—is brief as peace, and momentary as a dream. Danger lurks in the darkness underneath, with its swift jaws ever unfolding. Sometimes, the fin of a minke whale, its white belly flashing, will cut sharply across your bow; and sometimes, a colossal mass, the leviathan of the North Atlantic, the humpback whale, with its fearsome tail, will erupt without warning into the air, scattering a retinue of gulls, and crash so hard by that you'll lose your nerve and fill your pants. Sometimes it's less dramatic: a silent undertow will catch you by the heel and reel you out to sea. But sometimes—just as tapping lightly on the bottom of a glass will cause a tremor in a drink's meniscus—some black current or unseen reverberation, from deeper down or farther away than we can really fathom, will trouble the waters. Then follow on the surface gentle ripples, hardly perceptible at first, but with every oscillation growing, until, like an insurrection feeding on its own disturbance, the winds come a-howling and the waves threaten to spill over and escape the compass of the shores.

Were the rain to fall all day and night for weeks, and the sea swell with it and rise to the steeples, and the world, all unprepared, be given up to perdition—what remedy then except to overturn our churches and bail like crazy in their inverted frames and pray they keep afloat? Sometimes, the calm is just the storm we don't see coming.

Behold therefore the cold rain, like splinters of ice, bite into Noah's flesh, and his grandfather's flesh. The old man confused, and perhaps demented. His eyes narrow, searching. He wrenches his arm free and points. "There, there!" he cries.

A heavy wave, spitting white vengeance like a charging bear, sprints towards them on their rocky knob. There's no time to escape. Their eyes grow wide. A stroke of lightning overhead, such as would cleave a man in two, falls like the fearful downbeat of some dreadful choir-master, and the air howls like a host of choristers, and the sky shakes with the pronouncement of a terrible organ blast. Behind them, Cecelia screams and the old woman too, and Noah, exposed and helpless on the outcrop, in desperation pulls his grandfather hard into his arms.

The water exploded around them. Noah felt the thunder kick his ribs and echo in his inward parts. His grandfather seemed to feel it too. Both men shuddered. Around their ankles, the water threshed and threatened to wash them away, but by some miracle they remained rooted.

Oblivious to his good fortune, the old man scanned the ocean, but there was nothing out there. Then his legs began to unstring and he fell to his knees. Noah, fearful that he would topple in, kneeled down and held him close. A spirit of brokenness had overtaken the old man. His shoulders dropped and a look of desolation appeared. His eyes were large and brown. Bovine, they seemed to Noah, glassy and oddly beautiful. The rain continued to give them all a scouring, but it was letting up a little. It slid down their faces, like meltwater when an ice dam starts to go and, with the shards unlocked, the water starts anew. When the old man spoke, his voice was gentle and resigned. Noah almost didn't hear him.

"He's gone." Then the old man turned to Noah and stroked his head. "Laz, my poor boy."

Noah felt his chest tighten. His heart lurched. "Gramps …"

With a wave of his hand, the old man cut him off. "I know. Got it wrong again."

Noah and his grandfather sat rigid, like bookends on a rocky shelf. The old man mouthed arng-arng, chomping his teeth. Then he slumped still further and gestured with his nose towards the water. He spoke without looking, and when he spoke he seemed possessed by some hideous bloodguiltiness, and his voice was full of piteous contrition. "Gulp! The water got him good."

Above them a deep groan resounded from between the pursed lips of a pair of clouds. With drones and whistles, the entire sky went on reverberating like some heavenly instrument, but more gently now. Still, it was foolishness to linger. Noah looked back over his shoulder. He saw Cecelia, her expression feared-over, struggling to hold his grandmother back. He shook his grandfather gently and spoke in his ear. "What do you think? Can we go in now?"

The storm had done its office and, though the rain continued, the thunder was becoming less frequent and quieter. The old man wiped his face and nudged Noah with his elbow. "Bit of a wash. Feels clean." His body was shivering so hard Noah could feel it, but the old man smiled and laughed a little. "C'mon, old son," he said.

It was a good job of work to get the old man off the rocks. With the immediate danger gone and his adrenaline spent, Noah's legs were hardly able to support even his own weight. Stumbling, he retreated with his grandfather towards higher ground. Cecelia, he realized, had raced to the house and back. She had her umbrella and was holding the edge with one hand to keep it from inverting as she held it over them. It was pointless, though. Before they had gone more than a few steps it popped inside-out and then was blown right out of her hands.

Cecelia watched the umbrella go somersaulting across the lawn. "Sonofabitch."

The old man watched it too. "It's veering," he said to her.

"It sure is," she agreed.

"No, no," the old man corrected, tapping his skull. "In here."

Noah's grandmother was a few steps ahead of them. "All right, fetch a heave onto him."

As they struggled to deliver him back to the house, Noah began to give instructions: he would need a towel and a change of clothes for the old man (they could all do likewise after they got him dried off and into bed), then he would need an extra duvet for warmth, and one of them could get the water boiling and maybe set a can of soup on the stove. Noah's grandmother interrupted.

"Relax, will you? He's had a bit of a cobbing, is all. He's had worse. Just let's get his arse to an anchor and then we'll sort him."

Noah, frowning, hooked his hand under his grandfather's belt to steady him. As they stumbled their way back, the old man looked up, apparently bewildered.

"Jesus, Noah, where'd the roof go?"

Though she dismissed Noah's instructions, his grandmother followed them as though his anxieties had been her own. She got the old man dry and into bed, and covered him up, and gave him hot tea. She also turned the heat up. At first they wondered would they need to take him to the hospital. It might still be several long, tight hours of watching before they knew. As the evening passed he was still shivering in his bed, and they worried he would catch more than a cold. The strain of watching wore on them, particularly Noah's grandmother, whose face was drawn close and whose complexion was pale almost to ghostliness. She seemed haunted, and Noah became aware—not for the first time, but now with the suddenness and clarity of a revelation—how something elemental was seeping out of her and had been doing, really, for a long time, the full extent of which he only now was allowing himself to see. It was worse than he had thought. She too was fading. The rain had ruined her hair. In some places it had gone lank, and in others it curled waywardly. She kept running her fingers into it. Several times, when he thought she would not see, Noah glanced at her in worry. She seemed so small and frail. How strange that she should seem so when his grandfather's rounded pine knot of a fist was as strong and tough as it had ever been.

The hours passed. As midnight came, it became clear from the old man's deep, even breathing that he was in no immediate danger. He had a journeyman's stone chin. Noah's grandmother, confident in her grandson's vigilance, rose and left the bedside. She returned briefly and handed Noah the box of letters. Then she went to join Cecelia in the parlour and plunked herself into a chair. Cecelia asked how he was doing.

"Which one?" the old woman asked. "Oh, Peter will be fine. His brain doesn't give his feet much work these days, but he's strong as an ox. And Noah … well, he's stupid as a bag of hammers sometimes, but he'll be fine too. He'll be in there reading those friggin' letters." Her eyes grew distant and she sighed. "Up and down he looks like his father. It frights me awful sometimes."

"Could I make you some more tea?" Cecelia asked. The old woman thanked her, but no. Long minutes passed. Cecelia had no idea how many. As she sat there, something began to trouble her increasingly. "Mrs. Lamarck, how did Noah's mother die?"

The old woman did not answer immediately and, when she did, she did not look at Cecelia at all. She spoke dreamily, the way you might if you thought an invisible witness were nearby, sitting there in the room, or lurking by the door, or even hovering in the air. "Léa was never right after Laz died. She took to moping around the house, and taking long walks by herself, and not eating much. Mostly she ignored Noah, though she was so unhinged I don't think she could help it. It went on like that till winter the next year. Then one night, Noah came and woke us—not that that was unusual; he wasn't yet three and already running around like he owned the place, making himself toast in the middle of the night, and pulling his games out and having a grand time; it got so bad we had to unplug not just the toaster but the oven too in case he got ambitious; Lord, the first time he realized the toaster wasn't working you should have seen the tantrum 'cause he couldn't figure out why it wouldn't work, and we wouldn't tell him 'cause then he'd just plug it in himself—anyway he woke us, crying just awful, and dragged us up to their room and she was gone. I guess he got scared when she wasn't where she was supposed to be. I says to him, "Not so funny when the shoe's on the other foot, now is it?" But then I couldn't find her either and I got scared too. Peter and I put Noah back to bed and locked him in and went looking outside.

There'd been a bit of snow, but it was clear by then, and there was plenty of moonlight. The tracks weren't hard to follow. There's woods nearby have been logged more than once, and in it there's a clearing where she and Laz used to play when they were young. It wasn't fifteen minutes from the house so we found her quick. It was a large clearing then, as I remember, and there was birch and beech and sugar maple, and some spruce, and white pine. The snow was shining and she was right there in the middle, laying back and looking up at the sky. There was a circle of snow around her, and little shoots of wintergreen poking up like little fingers. She was still in her nightclothes and making snow angels like it was nothing. I liked Léa. She was a good girl, but foolish. The next time she wandered off we didn't find out till morning. By rights, she should have been with her own parents, but they'd left town by then. And those Doucets don't know but to hold a grudge. The doctor figured she'd been dead a couple of hours by the time we found her. I think about her sometimes, in the winter. I think about her damned snow angels. It really was awful beautiful."

"He doesn't talk about her like he does his father," Cecelia said, cautiously.

The old woman shook her head and frowned. "No, he doesn't."

"Maybe it's something subconscious?"

"Likely as not," the old woman said. "Men are like that. Unconscious all the hours they sleep. Subconscious all the rest." She looked in the direction of the bedroom. Then she looked at Cecelia. "But then, maybe it's not the same for them as us. No matter how old she is, when a girl loses her mother she just keeps on losing her. My mother lived every day till she was eighty-four, but when she went it was like someone cut a birth cord I never knew was still attached. Is your mother still living?"

Cecelia said she was.

"Then you've got that to look forward to."

Cecelia wanted to say something, but she didn't know what. She felt like apologizing. "I'm sorry for the way I spoke when I arrived. I didn't know you were there."

"Dear, that's no apology. You just wish you hadn't been caught."

When Noah came into the parlour, he was carrying the box in one hand and in the other he held a single page. Cecelia could guess which one. He sat down and handed it to her. "It's his note," he said. She was about to read it, but Noah's grandmother began to speak.

Softly, at first, the old woman's voice crackled with evident discomfort. Then she seemed to give in. She slouched back in the chair, reciting from memory:

I had a dream last night that I've had many times before and it's always the same. It's a stormy day and the wind is bad, and I'm the captain of a schooner making for home. I'm following the shore, but even near the headlands the sea is deadly and the crew is terrified. I tell them to be careful and hold on tight, but they cry out. My first mate's gone overboard and I see him struggling in the water. The ship is right over to her hatches and the waves are getting in. I was always told that in a storm like that no man would ever ask to turn back, not even for his own brother. No captain would even try. You'd just get wrecked and everyone would drown. So I know I should cut my losses, but those flailing arms are flesh and bone, not thrum yarn. He's crying for help, and there's something so pitiful in his voice that I can't stop myself. I turn back every time, even though I know I shouldn't. Even though I know it means everyone on board will die, I just can't bring myself to leave him behind. I should have told you this before. Not now that you know everything already, and there's nothing left to be done about any of it. I want you to know I tried harder than I ever thought I could to keep it locked up. It was like my body was divided into two camps, each making war on the other, laying waste to my insides. And just when I thought I might finally be able to kill my feelings for him, they would rise again in my chest and choke me in my throat and I would have to swallow them back down again. I used to think I could hide it, but now I know I'll be found out no matter where beneath the sky I hide. And then what am I to my parents? Or to Noah? Or especially to you? I would sooner have cut this from my living body than hurt you if I could have, and I've split my heart in trying. I just can't keep pretending to be all you deserve. And I can never be anything but what I am, which I can never be at all. I love you so much and always have, but I can't go on hurting myself and you as I have and always will. I imagine the worst is when you're underwater and you know that you'll die if you breathe and you'll die if you don't, and it's got to be one or the other. After that, I imagine the drowning itself is easy. Forgive me.

She was weeping as she finished. Noah observed her and Cecelia dazedly observed them both. The old woman was not really looking at anything or anyone. How many years away from it was she, and there it was still rustling inside her.

"We found it after your mother died. I read it every day, for a long time. Then I put it away. Even now, he dies all over again when I talk about him. Reading it so much … it's like one of those Sunday school songs when you're young. I guess I wore it in. Once Felix was too old for you to come looking for toys, I thought … safely stowed."

Then Noah's grandmother explained it all. How Laz and Léa were always peas in a pod, even when they were little, and there was this other boy who used to shy around with them too. The three of them were always together when they were in school, shoulder to shoulder, like yearling lambs, and they were great friends after. Zephyr was his name. His parents were from away, she thought. She never really knew them, although maybe Peter taught some of their other children. Zeph came by one day not long after. He wanted to deliver his condolences again and asked to see Léa. Had they any letters from Laz, he asked. He was half-wrecked himself and Léa got angry, so he left. That was the last they saw of him. He left town soon after, she remembered. At the time, they had their reputations to think of. Peter taught at the school and she was on the church board. They had friends who wouldn't have understood. Noah had to understand, she said, back then parents would not cut their children's hair or nails or let them see themselves in a mirror before their first birthday because they believed it would keep their kids from being mentally defective. They'd figured it out years before, but they never spoke of it except in hints that neither had courage enough to pick up, and then, after Laz died, there was an empty space left between them where their son had been that neither wanted to venture into. She sometimes wondered if they had let him down or done something wrong to make him that way. It didn't seem like such a big deal now, but it was different then. They were just so relieved when he and Léa got married.

"Why didn't you tell me?" Noah asked.

"You were young and it was complicated."

"I haven't been young in years."

"I didn't know how. I kept hoping you would let it go, and your grandfather would forget about it."

"I'm pretty sure he remembers. I think that's what he was going on about outside."

"For the love of old cock robin Christ. Of all the things for him to remember." The old woman reached hurriedly down into her dress and pulled a folded tissue from her brassiere. "Soon he won't remember that either. Or much of anything else. Damn him." She dabbed rapidly under her eyes, but it was a losing battle. "Well, no sense going into one now about it. What's done is done." She blew her nose, and seemed to intend a kind of finality, but the tears continued unabated.

"Gran ..." Noah's face was tense, his voice hesitant. "Do you think he loved Mom too? Like he did Zephyr?"

Modeste Lamarck's eyes grew wide. She seemed taken off guard. "Oh my, yes. He loved her. There was never any doubt about that. But he couldn't only love her, you see? Even though I guess he tried. I don't think we ever thought bad of anyone for it, except for him. A man shouldn't be ashamed to love." She paused in reflection. "And he gave us you. That's something."

The room seemed darker, the shadows not exactly growing, but asserting themselves in their corners and crevices. Noah was still for some time. Then he addressed his grandmother carefully. "You really need to get help with Gramps. There were three of us tonight and we still couldn't stop him."

The old woman leaned forward and, assisting herself with her hands, she got to her feet. "I told you. There's no money for help."

"Then you need to sell the house and find a home for you both."

"There's no point. A few years ago we started needing money, so we borrowed against the house. I saw an advertisement about it, on the television. Now the bank owns about as much as it wants and there's no credit left."

"If you needed money—"

"The roof was leaking—"

"But I could've repaired that—"

302

"And then there was the windows on the north side—"

"I could've helped."

"Noah, quit trying to fix everything. You can't always be here. And you shouldn't be. Besides, it isn't worth as much as you'd think. We only own a sliver where the house sits. I always assumed we had it down to the water, but it turns out the rest is Crown land." The old woman walked over to the mantel and fiddled with the photographs. She looked like an aging priest before an altar, hallowing objects of worship in an empty chapel. In the glow of the faux–candle sconces, her hair seemed impossibly silver, burnished and brightly shining over her stooped shoulders. She turned to face Noah. "I should've been more careful, but I never thought your grandfather would hang on like this." She raised her finger vaguely in the direction of one of the prints. Her mouth twisted to one side and she shook her head. "The other day he asked me if I painted that."

Noah looked over at Cecelia, who was silent and uncomfortable, but she smiled at him a little and took his hand.

"Oh, don't worry. I know how to make do. Now I'm going to go in and see to your grandfather. I'll sleep if I can. Cecelia, dear, eat or drink something if you like. You're welcome to whatever you can find."

"We'll think of something before I leave," Noah said, firmly. "We'll start with that money you've been setting aside for Felix."

Noah's grandmother approached him and placed her open palm on the crown of his head. She ran her fingers through his hair. "Don't be so hard on yourself. You're less good than you mean, but better than you think." Then she kissed him on the forehead and left.

Cecelia had set the letter down beside her, and as Noah picked it up Cecelia saw that the Shakespeare pages were still on the floor beside the wedding chest, weighed down by the hornbook. They couldn't leave them there; they should remove them to a safer place. However, that could wait. "Are you disappointed?" she asked.

"I don't know." He was handling the letter without opening it. "It's not what I expected."

"Me neither." Cecelia still had his other hand and when she squeezed it she thought he squeezed a little in return. She looked at her watch. "It's tomorrow," she said. "Happy birthday."

Noah smiled. A moment later he was crying. She had no idea what to do.

It would occur to Cecelia when she thought back on this night, and on the one that was to follow, that the more we hate something within ourselves the more we see it manifested everywhere around us: in a kindness someone else performed that we did not; in a joke bearing no reference to ourselves that nonetheless strikes our conscience; in the suspicion and contempt in which we're certain others hold us, but which we've altogether invented. Our anger at others too is often just a despising of something in our own nature we're ashamed of, some weakness or jealousy or vileness they bring out in us. This is true with strangers and acquaintances, she thought, and even friends, but always more so with family and loved ones because it's they who know us best. Some indiscretion from our adolescence they were witness to; some hidden insecurity they know too well; some terrible longing we confessed in an unguarded moment that we would never permit ourselves with others less intimate. Loved ones, more than others, are capable of bringing out in us a kind of autoimmune response. They turn us into cannibals eating our own flesh, or suicidists turning our knives into our own hearts. In return, we treat parents and siblings, lovers and spouses, in ways more careless, more hurtful than we ever would a stranger, our negligence proportional to our closeness, for nothing has power to hurt us more than what we love. All things considered, not to love at all would be the safest course. But was it even possible, she wondered, to live a human life not loving, forever hiding out, not ever really being seen? She wondered too if a heart, once it had been broken, could be more supple, more articulate, indeed of much more use, than one that was altogether whole. She thought this might be a kind of wisdom; and if this were the extent of someone's wisdom, it was not insubstantial. Perhaps it could do.

She and Noah would talk this over, but not until a long time after. For that evening, if they could abide it was enough. Cecelia leaned into him, and their breathing—his long and deep, and hers shorter and more frequent—phased in and out of time. She lost track of how long they stayed that way. As she waited for sleep to come, her gaze lingered on the mythical figures in the prints on the far wall, and especially on the bemused eyes of Botticelli's naked goddess, luminous even in faded reproduction, watching silently over them. She waited patiently for Noah to give her a sign.

And William the Bard begat William of Mary that was the wife of Stephen. And William begat Samuel, about the time they departed into Boston. And after they were settled in Boston, Samuel begat John, and John begat William, and William begat Matthew, and Matthew begat John, and John begat George, and George begat John, that was beset by creditors. And John begat Augustus, and Augustus begat Henry, about the time they were carried away to Halifax. And after they were brought to Halifax, Henry begat Leo, and Leo begat Jon, and Jon begat Thomas, that departed from Halifax and came into the shores of Cape Breton. And Thomas begat Margerie, and Margerie married John Avy and bore him a daughter Modeste, and Modeste married Peter (à Henry) Lamarck and bore him a son that was called Lin-Lazare. And Lin-Lazare was espoused of Léa (née Doucet), and she bore him a son Noah, who was called Plugger. And Noah took to wife Catherine Bass, that of her body bore him a son Felix that she carried away to Toronto, whereto Noah followed and there took up with her in her house for a time. And the house they lived in was crooked, and crooked too their domesticity, and there was strife between them and a great schism.

Now, it came to pass that Noah departed from Toronto and returned once more to the land wherein his father was born, in Cape Breton, in the land of Nova Scotia, for to shed the weight of his burdens. And before his eyes the sky was dark, and the land beneath dark too, and dark shadows abiding in his heart. And Noah said unto himself, I will run, that my body may breathe more deeply the breath of life, and that this darkness in my heart may be lifted, and my troubled spirit be assuaged.

So Noah ran and, as he ran, from out of the ground around him sprung up plants and herbs of every sort that is pleasing to the sight, as cattail and dandelion, pearly everlasting too, and coltsfoot, which some call son-before-the-father for that it blossoms almost ere it be sown.

And beasts of the earth appeared around him, and also fowls of the air and creeping things abundantly. But Noah was heavily burdened, and his spirits troubled, and he took no note of these, nor cared for anything that was not putting his one foot in front of the other.

Then the ground beneath his feet grew steep and he began to labour. There was sweat upon his brow, and the road was long and steep, and he laboured exceedingly. His gait, however, was even and his heart was strong, and into his mouth he breathed the breath of life, and his spirit began to be assuaged. Then he did rejoice in his living body, and the darkness began to be lifted. And beneath his feet was the dry land, and above him the wide firmament, and gathered all around him the broad waters.

And it came to pass that his father's father, Peter à Henry, appeared unto him in a cloud in the midst of the sky. Peter stirred not, however, nor spoke not to Noah, but lay on one side with his eyes still and open, as one that is dead. And Noah saw that his hair was white, and his eyes white, and his sides were small and bereft of strength. His raiment was poor and torn, and it exposed his nakedness. And from his loins there hung a branch, large as a fallen trunk, but all withered, and this branch brought forth neither leaves, nor flowers, nor fruit of any kind. And Noah hid his face in his hands for he was afraid to look upon his grandfather's nakedness, sore afflicted with age and frailty.

Now behold, how the clouds above grew many, and a mist went up, and soon the wide ring of the horizon was obscured. And a strong wind rose up and the withered branch that hung from his grandfather's loins lost its hold and fell from his body into the sea. And along with it no blood but three drops did fall, for it was wasted and no longer quick.

And where the trunk fell into the waters the sea grew incensed and the waters were lifted up. And where the clouds were multiplied the sky bore down and the rain increased exceedingly. And betwixt the sea and sky could no line be drawn, nor no horizon be seen, but everywhere there was nothing but storm both high and low.

And where the blood dropped, there the waters grew violent and the sea boiled, and three creatures sprung up with white wings, three angels of vengeance, and they were as the seas incensed. And the angels were called Catherine that was his wife, and Felix that was his son, and Cecelia that was his friend. And their eyes did fix upon Noah, and from their eyes they wept the very blood whereof they had sprung, and they rose up out of the water's fury.

And in the face of the storm, Noah beheld in the distance a ship beset by the water's white teeth, and at the helm was a captain, and at the gunwale a boatswain. And the captain was Lin-Lazare that was Noah's father, and the boatswain too was Lin-Lazare, and when Noah saw that the ship was beset and like to be broken he was sore afraid.

Then it came to pass that the waters rose up, and the boatswain knew for whose sake the storm was upon them, and he let go the gunwale and cast himself forth into the sea, that the captain should not perish. But the captain could not leave him behind. He unblocked, therefore, the tiller and brought the vessel hard about, and the vessel pitched over to her very hatches. And though the hatches were stout, yet they could not hold, and they soon gave way, and soon were choking down the sea. And behold the waters were tempestuous and not to be allayed, and the ship was overcome and foundered utterly, and the sea smacked its lips and swallowed.

And Noah saw the vessel founder, and it repented him that Lin-Lazare was drowned and that Lin-Lazare was also drowned, but he was on the headland and could do nothing to deliver them. And all their days were twenty-three years and then they died, swallowed by the sea, and their bodies ripped open, and down they went to their watery tombs. And neither were the waters abated, nor the hunger of the storm allayed, and it ceased not from its raging.

And Noah in his sadness stumbled, and he fell down upon his knees. And his knees were bruised and his heart was grieved, and he sent up a cry of anguish. Noah's angels of vengeance then rose up from the waters and spoke unto him, saying, "When our hurts were raw and we sought relief, you did nothing. And when we made known the suffering in our hearts you did nothing. And you did nothing neither as our hearts grew cold and desolate of remedy. Wherefore have you forsaken us and why your oaths forsworn?"

And their countenances fell, and Noah spoke not for he was sore ashamed, and his face was as a whited sepulchre. And they spoke unto him again, saying, "Take you the sum of all our grievances, after their kinds and number, and repent." And Noah took the sum of his trespasses against them, after their kinds and number, as many as he could remember.

Against Catherine his wife, Noah was guilty of the following offences and trespasses and transgressions: He kissed her on the mouth without asking when their years numbered eleven, and when they were fourteen he kissed her again, with her permission and often, and took joy in that her father disapproved. And behind the woodshed, when their years numbered fifteen, he kissed not only her lips but her other parts too, and he did this as often as she would let him. But he heeded not her counsel, nor her fear that they surely would be seen, and his desire grew reckless and thereafter they were seen of her sister, who told her father and betrayed them.

Furthermore, he opposed her father's religious teaching, from the age of seven and upward, for that he thought it mean and unlearned, nor did he conceal his disdain, nor cared he not for what her father thought. And he did not honour her father, and with subtlety encouraged the increasing rift between them, and likewise the rift between her and her sisters, though he knew himself the import of a father's love and a family, and the hole it leaves when it is lost. But he wanted her all to himself.

And after they were come of age and married, he made poor provision for the home. He failed to lay up sufficient store whilst they were married. And he several times in secret lent from their savings to deliver a friend out of his distress, and several times he did not recover the sum.

And he increasingly uncovered himself before her, and not only displayed himself in all his nakedness, but preened and flaunted when he knew that Catherine in those days was shy and reserved, and did not like it. And it pleased him that she was uncomfortable. And it pleased him to tease her by frequent exposing of his private parts, and swinging them both up and down and side to side, and also windmilling them around and around. And he rejoiced in the slapping sounds his parts made against his thighs, and the unease it caused her.

And many times he exposed himself expressly because he knew she did not like it. And impatiently, by means of these continual assaults upon her eyes with his nakedness, he sought to undermine the walls of her reserve and diffidence, and make her more congruent with what he had imagined a wife would be.

And he enjoined her to lie carnally with him more than she desired. And he often showed off how he could skill to pleasure her. He learned of diverse techniques, such as *coitus reservatus*, which he practiced to delay the onset of his climax for her pleasure, and sundry positions through which he often dragged her, willy-nilly and without warning, that he might surprise her with his learning and earn her gratitude and admiration. And he sometimes made her climax ere she wanted to because it boasted of his skill.

And once he knew her carnally in the night ere she was fully awake, without asking first if she consented. And that night also he was guilty of nocturnal omission for he did shun, for his own ease and pleasure, the condom that he should have worn, the consequences of which she bore the burden of more than he.

And after when their son was born, and she returned to school, he would not understand why she pursued not a degree and was satisfied with her license and diploma only. And he did not believe that she was really satisfied. And he did not seek to understand what she desired and why. Instead, his idea of Catherine he made into a graven image, and he bowed himself down to it, and desired that Catherine should bow herself down to it also.

Then he laboured in his trade, and in the home, but all in vain, for he knew Catherine not as she was, but only through the strange impressions he created out of his desires. And when he saw that she valued not his labours, neither in his trade nor in the home, he would not understand the reason, and thereafter he grew angry.

And he ceased to heed her counsel, or confide the cares of his bosom. And he no longer took pleasure himself when they lay together, nor allowed her to pleasure him, but practiced coitus reservatus to defy her and resist her. And in this wise he continued for many months until he no longer knew how to take pleasure, or allow her to pleasure him, and grew so angry that he could hardly remember when he knew how to do otherwise. And he lost all patience, and grew sore with his grandparents, and with his infant son also, and with Catherine, who by then no longer desired to lie with him either.

And he struck the walls of the house in anger. And he forswore many oaths he made to Catherine in her youth. He removed his wedding ring and placed it on the dresser, and told her she could put it back upon his finger when she was ready once again to be his wife.

And through his anger and negligence he caused her to lie carnally with another man, and therefore he put Catherine aside for fornication. But afterwards, when he was come to Toronto, he boasted to himself that he did so out of charity only, when in his secret heart he still longed for Catherine, and he told her not.

Then once again he made poor provision for the home, and laid up not sufficient store, and guarded not against the loss of employment. And thereafter, when he lost his employment, he unwisely sold his service to a man who kept him under heel, a man with means to cause his wife and child to be uprooted and cast out, a man who would, without mercy, subject them to poverty and destroy them utterly. And Noah confided this not in Catherine, and he abandoned her rather than unclasp his bosom unto her and all its secrets.

Against Felix his son, Noah was guilty of the following offences and trespasses and transgressions: He was for a long time absent. And he was often ignorant of his son's condition, such as was he well or ill, or unhappy or vexed. Or was he confused. Or was he frightened. And Noah kept his son from visiting at his grandparents, not for the child's sake as he pretended but for his own, because he wanted not to explain the dwindling of their condition, nor the approaching grief he was not ready to endure.

And when asked why he and Catherine could no longer be together, he told his son that he did not know. And when asked if this meant that they were no longer a family, he could nothing say to relieve the sadness and confusion in his son's eyes, but like a hypocrite assuaged his son with commonplaces that he himself disdained.

And the sum of all was this: However Noah was justified in putting Catherine aside, it did sore repent him in his heart to do it. And he could not say this to his son without saying all. And so his son, by soft inheritance, was learning Noah's habit of concealment, and how to closet up his hurts. And it was this that made Felix always seem to be fine, and Noah therefore unable, even when he asked, to learn from him what things he had need of, and it made his son, like a lockbox, to remain impervious.

And Felix too would run himself into the ground. And it was Noah himself who was guilty of departing, and it was he who rent his son's heart and his own. And some holes cannot be mended. And history is only ever repeated.

For Noah was the author of confusion, now as then. For he lodged with Catherine his wife and Felix their son, when before he said that he could not. And he used Cecelia as a concubine, and he invited her into the house. And in the house, which was built neither straight, nor tight, in which he suffered them to grow cold for that he had not means for better accommodation, he was uncareful. He flirted with Cecelia in the sight of Catherine, and with Catherine in the sight of Cecelia, and with both when Felix was near at hand, and he so tangled all of their threads that he no longer knew how to free them. And Felix, who was always near at hand, did not know what his family was, nor how he should belong.

And against Cecelia his friend, Noah was guilty of the following offences and trespasses and transgressions: He did not take her seriously when she confided her apprehensions at school, and he teased her for her insecurity, and found cause to laugh at her dismay. And he condescended to her in her research, for he asserted himself too strongly, in his methods and his views, and forgot that the archive and the researching thereof were hers to oversee.

Too often, by means of his insistence, he merely interfered. He would not credit that her practices were well-ordered, yet insisted that she credit his own, and he diminished her spirits thereby. And he disdained her theories regarding the indenture, and did not keep this to himself, but expressed his disagreement carelessly, not considering her feelings.

And he was guilty too of lies of omission, for he confided not in her neither that he had sold his service to a man who kept him under heel, who had means to cause his wife and child to be uprooted and cast out, who would subject them to poverty and destroy them utterly. And he told her not what the man demanded of him, how he was to oversee her, and steer her, and that he communicated her progress without her knowledge or permission.

And he deprived himself of her counsel, and he deprived her of his confidence. And thereafter he quarrelled with her, who knew nothing of his tribulations nor his compromises, and he abandoned her rather than confess how he had sinned against her. And he did not return her calls, and did not read her communications, for he was ashamed and incapable of explanation.

And he did lie carnally with her before his affection for her was grown ripe, and he continued to lie with her when in his heart he could not put his wife aside. And he never let her entirely into his heart, because the spaces there were already supplied. Nor did he learn how she and his wife differed from each other in the desires of their flesh.

And sometimes was he guilty of taking pleasure without giving it, and using her as a concubine when she deserved to be more to him than this. And several times he lay with her while in his heart he wished she were Catherine, and twice while he imagined her sister, and once while he imagined her and her sister both. And though he did not know where some of these thoughts came from, and some of them he resisted, yet had she known she would have grown exceeding wroth and smitten him with blows most furious and fell, and he would have deserved them.

Of the trespasses and transgressions of Noah, after their kinds, from the age of seven and upward, were these and countless more he could remember.

And Noah saw how he had wasted the substance of his heart through lack of understanding, and how he had destroyed his own soul. And then he humbled himself before his angels and he prayed. For mercy, he prayed, and for understanding. And he prayed for someone to come to him to be his helper and assister, for his thoughts were evil from his youth and he was desolate of remedy.

And he prayed to be delivered of his bloodguiltiness, and to be forgiven for his trespasses and unrighteousness, and for his negligence and sins. And he prayed that not every one of his sins be taken into account, because his spirit was broken and his heart contrite.

And he prayed for a clean heart, and for unity and peace within himself, and wisdom enough to repair the breaches he had made in his own house. And he prayed for food for the hungry too, and direction for the lost, courage for the feeble-hearted, and above all love and understanding for all that dwell upon the earth, both now and world without end, for we all of us have sinned and come up short. This supplication Noah made before his angels, but unto him and to his supplication they had not respect, for sin lay ever at his doorstep, and in wrath they turned away.

And the angels on their white wings rose up, and where they rose the waters followed. And the white fingers of the waters rose and tore at the headland and all the high hills, and they seized upon Noah and cast him into the sea. And Noah trembled exceedingly for that he knew he was like to be drowned.

But he was not drowned, albeit a long time he was carried upon the waters. And Noah saw that carried upon the waters too, like a piece of driftwood, was the withered branch that had fallen from loins of his father's father. And around it white seafoam grew in great abundance, and the currents carried Noah nearer.

And it came to pass that a strange and antique music passed over the waters. And the music grew and, as it grew, the water's fury was allayed, and the clouds were restrained, and the skies grew calm. In the sky was set a rainbow, and the wide ring of the horizon was no longer obscured.

Then a ring of monsters, half men and half fish, with tails and chiseled torsos gleaming, arose from the waters and encircled the seafoam. And the monsters pressed together the seafoam within their circle, and the withered branch sank beneath the waters within the circle. And behold the seafoam parted, and a cockle shell appeared and was lifted up, and Lin-Lazare that was dead came forth, and he was carried upon the shell.

And the monsters all did clasp and kiss their brethren on either side, and embrace one another, and rejoice that this was Lin-Lazare come again from his deathbed. And the body of Lin-Lazare was all uncovered, and his back was broad, and his buttocks as an apple cleft in two. And the nakedness of his body was young and beautiful, and it gleamed with seawater and sunlight, as though anointed with oil, and his eyes gleamed as white pearls in the sunlight, and he went naked and rejoiced in the midst of his brethren.

Then appeared at his side an angel of modesty, Noah's father's mother, dressed as an old woman. And her hair was silver in the sunlight, and her raiment was done up high upon her neck, and also low about her heel, and it covered all her body round about. And when she beheld her son Lin-Lazare and saw that he was not ashamed, her countenance fell, and she grew afraid because he was naked and did not hide himself.

Then a shroud appeared in her fingers, and the shroud was pale and white as mountain snow, and large as a sailcloth when it is unfurled. And she approached her son in haste, and she threw the shroud upon his shoulders. And she would have bound him hand and foot in the shroud and bound his face also, but Lin-Lazare disdained the frippery she wrapped around him, and he cast it off. For he was as one that is awoken from a deep slumber by a strangling sheet. And the body of Lin-Lazare glistened with seawater and sunlight, and his mother wept with shame, and she departed and went with her face backwards, and she refused to look upon her son's nakedness. And Noah's heart was filled with sadness at the sight thereof.

Then in the distance there appeared two winged figures, shining angels of desire, and their wings were black, and their arms and legs were altogether entwined. And albeit Noah could see that they were male and female, yet he knew not which wings belonged to which, neither did he know which arms and legs, for that they were entwined as serpents that become entwined.

And the angels approached, and lo, Noah beheld that one of the angels was his mother Léa that was dead and gone. And her hair was long and golden, and her cheeks shone like sport-red Gravensteins. And on her garments she bore snowy-blossomed wintergreen, whose leaves drop not in winter, nor fade, and on her shoulder she wore a harebell. And she inclined unto Noah, and her eyes were tender, and she smiled as one who knew him, although he was altogether changed and resembled not the child that once he was, and Noah's heart grew warm and was lifted up. But of the other angel Noah knew not his name, nor his features neither, only that he was beautiful.

And gliding low above the waters, the angels approached Lin-Lazare, and the circle of monsters parted to admit them, and Lin-Lazare inclined unto them and opened his arms to embrace them. And the angels embraced him on both sides, and he was entwined by them as a caduceus is entwined, and the circle closed around them.

And Léa leaned upon Lin-Lazare's right shoulder and he inclined his head unto her. And on his left the other angel leaned, and Lin-Lazare embraced him with his arm and drew him close, although he kept his face backwards to him and inclined still unto Léa.

Then into Lin-Lazare's ear the other angel whispered, and he touched the hollow of his thigh. And his whispers entered into Lin-Lazare's ear as a serpent to its hole, and Lin-Lazare's flesh grew hard as a staff, and it was lifted up. And in Lin-Lazare's ear was the angel's breathing, and his chest pulsed with his own breathing, and his hard flesh pulsed as though it were breathing too. And Noah looked on at what the angel did, and his own breath quickened, and the monsters in their ring ceased not their rejoicing.

And Lin-Lazare inclined unto this other angel, whom Léa envied and fought with to uncoil his limbs from Lin-Lazare's, but the angel was not removed. Then unto Lin-Lazare, whom she loved, she gave a multitude of flowers that she took from her bosom. And some were showy lady's slippers that bear the pink-hearted blazon, and some were tansies, whose yellow buttons clear the bowels of worms, and some were short-lived, painted trilliums. And the flowers multiplied abundantly and filled the air around them. Unto the other angel she gave flowers also, but they were ragweed, that causes wheezing, and bittersweet which is poison, and water hemlock also.

And Lin-Lazare embraced her and drew her close, but he kept his face backwards to her. And when Léa saw that he inclined still unto the angel, and cleaved not unto her only but also unto him, she grew sore distressed and broke from Lin-Lazare's embrace. And lo, Lin-Lazare reached out his hand to catch her, for that he knew she loved him dearly, and he was fond as much on her, but Léa, seeing how he doted upon his other angel, was not capable of understanding, nor of consolation, and when she broke free of him she broke the monstrous circle that encompassed them also.

Then Léa approached Noah, and she inclined unto him, and him she garlanded in many flowers, such as beach pea and bindweed, and yellow-eyed forget-me-not, and woundwort. Then she kissed him and placed her hand upon his forehead. And she wept bitterly, and Noah wept also, and so they parted ways.

And though that Léa was now departed, and Lin-Lazare was sore distressed, the angel at his side ceased not his whispering. And the angel's whispering provoked Lin-Lazare most bitterly, and he shrugged mightily and cast the angel from off his shoulders and sent him forth from him with anger. Then stood Lin-Lazare alone atop the cockle shell, amidst the broken ring.

And Lin-Lazare groaned in his spirit, and he wept most bitterly. And his hands covered his face, and his chest and shoulders glistened with seawater, and his frustrated flesh did pulse and run with issue.

And Noah saw his father's sorrow and felt it in his heart, and it lamented him. And Noah beat the waters under him, and breasted towards his father and the ring. And where the ring had frayed, Noah took in his right hand one monster and in his left another, and he pulled it back together. And behold, Lin-Lazare saw Noah and inclined unto him, and smiled as one who knew him, and Noah's heart was lifted up.

And Noah climbed atop the cockle shell, and his father's arms encompassed him about. And his father's flesh ran abundantly with issue, and Noah knelt before him to receive his blessing. Then Lin-Lazare anointed him upon his forehead, and Noah felt how his breath quickened, and saw how his own flesh grew hard and was lifted up. And the body of Noah's father stood naked before him, and it was beautiful, and the monsters that encircled them kissed their brethren and rejoiced greatly at the sight thereof.

But lo, in the heavens the clouds now reappeared and multiplied, and the seas grew rough and threatened. A great mist went up, and the wide ring of the horizon became obscured, and the waters rose suddenly up against them. The monsters broke away and melted back into the sea, and Lin-Lazare fell backwards from his cockle shell and disappeared again beneath the waves. And Noah strived to keep his head above the waves, but he could not. The waters raged and rose up around him, and they rose within him also, and in his flesh he felt the pounding of the surf, and everywhere the storm. And his loins pulsed, and all the members of his body were squeezed and much pained. And the waters pressed in upon him, and bore down hard upon him, and the sea's white fingers dragged him under and began to rip him open.

PART SEVEN

Deeper Than Did Ever
Plummet Sound

12

A shower. To put things in perspective. Cecelia needed both. Her arms and thighs, the coping of her small breasts, the gentle round of her belly. She soaped in little rounds all over and down the slender architecture of her body. She might have found it relaxing, but she had the water hot enough to hurt and it kept the bathroom steaming like a canner. It was hard to breathe, hard even to stay conscious. A few more minutes of this would start the wallpaper stripping. Swooning was an option and she was keeping it open.

With her hands she braced herself against the wall beneath the shower head and let the water wash the suds from her hair. It ran down hotly over her eyes and lips and dribbled from her chin. Her mother had called early that morning. Rose was in labour. When Ray arrived to pick them up for the party, she said she would join them later. She wanted to wait around a while, in case there was any news. She watched the pool of water swirl around her toes and down the drain.

After dressing she went downstairs to the parlour. A pair of cheap accordion folders lay out of the way on an end table. Noah had gone out first thing to get them. In the one he put Andrew's research and the letters, in the other the mysterious manuscript. This second one she took and from it carefully removed the manuscript pages again. She had been studying them all day.

A hundred and twenty loose leaves a little larger than folio. The edges brittle, but not badly chipped, nor as worn as they should have been. Not terribly discoloured either. One would think they hadn't been handled—or looked at—in four hundred years. The writing bled through a little, front and back, but not enough to obscure the text. Six plays, written in a consistent and legible hand. Lines very close together. They could have been drafts, except for the care and regularity of the cursive. They were almost like presentation copies, only those were usually ornamented in some way, and the pages before her were not. Nor was there a dedication. Nor any signature. And the ink changed from time to time, brown at first, then elsewhere greyish and even slightly yellow. Maybe it was written over a string of weeks, or months. It was the return business of somebody's favourite scribe, maybe. Or maybe a performance copy, like the Douai Manuscript. *Twelfth Night* and *Troilus*, *Measure for Measure*, *All's Well* and *Othello*. She studied the pages with the intense vagueness of utter confusion. Nothing made sense: "The Historie of King Lear. Enter Kent, Gloster and Bastard." Whole chunks of Lear's address to his daughters missing, a single *nothing* from Cordelia. Just three *never*s as Lear cradles her cold body in his arms. No dramatis personæ. A continuous text without acts or scenes. "Nor live so long," the last word given to the Duke. Something about it was familiar, but what?

Noah's grandmother came in from the kitchen. "Tea, dear?"

Rapt as she was, Cecelia did not answer at first. When she did, it was with a shake of her head and a poorly articulated "No, thank you." The old woman approached and looked over her shoulder.

"Feelin' a bit down, are you?"

"Not exactly. I was expecting something exciting. Or revealing at least. But this …"

Noah's grandmother shrugged. "You were hoping for a scandal. I read the tabloids. I know what sells."

"I guess that was wishful thinking."

"I'd say. But you never know."

The old woman left her to it, but there was little point. Cecelia had read it through already, but repeated examination only deepened her confusion. She flopped back and sagged into the chesterfield. She had no idea what it was or what to do with it. A scholar should have found them, not her. She didn't know enough about Shakespeare, or indentures, or history, or manuscripts, or handwriting, or archives, or anything. She didn't know enough about boys either. She had no idea what Noah wanted, only it was obvious that she couldn't simply hand the pages over to Trover. Not now. They were Noah's inheritance.

It was early evening in Ontario. Trover might be at home. She ought to let him know at least. Cecelia slipped the pages back into their folder and ran them up to the bedroom. Then she went to the telephone, which sat on a small table in the hallway, and removed a small notepad from her back pocket. She placed a call, as she had been told, to the number she had been given, collect. At the other end, Clement Rowse's gentle voice asked her to hold. A few moments later Trover was on the line, undertaking to meet them in Mission Point the next day. Enthusiasm, of the ancient kind, possessed him—the antic disposition, a kind of frenzy. Cecelia found it frankly unsettling. She couldn't understand the rush. They didn't even know what they had, and certainly the pages weren't going anywhere. She tried to reassure him that there wasn't any urgency, but he was maddeningly insistent.

"Don't be silly. I claim the privilege of urgency. If I fly out in the morning I can be there before noon."

"But it's not that simple. I can't just give them to you. They're Noah's. As in, they're really his. I haven't any right to hand them over."

"Yes, isn't that something," he said. "Just a staggering improbability. Not to worry, though. He and I have an understanding."

He said it so matter-of-factly that it took Cecelia a moment to recalibrate. "What do you mean by *understanding*?"

Trover then explained it all—how Noah had agreed from the outset to be his invisible hand, so she would not feel interfered with. There was something casual in Trover's excitement, something negligent, an almost childlike oblivion, as though he could not or would not conceive of what this revelation might be costing her. It was nothing, he assured her.

Cecelia took it nicely, as a reflex—"I see," was all she said—said with her nice-girl's accommodating niceness. As though it were indeed nothing and she were not perturbed at all, nor rattled, not even a little. As though every word he spoke were not the ripping out of a stitch in her habit of forbearance. Her mother would have been proud, the way she took it so well, not giving anything away.

Contrariwise, by the time she hung up she was well on her way to a decision: she was done letting other people fucking decide.

"And that was it. I woke up," Noah said.

Noah and Ray had gone to the front hall for a breather. They and the others hadn't all been in the same place for a long time, and they were making quick work of the cases. John and Amelia's boys were at her cousin's, and anyone else with kids had sitters, so no one was counting. Noah related how he woke up with a piss-boner on and a violent need to take a leak. After that, he said, he didn't want to go back to sleep. He wasn't sure he wanted to that night either.

Ray shook his head. "I don't blame you, fella. That's a weird dream. And gross."

"Yeah, well you were one of the mermen, so fuck you."

"I bet I was dead sexy."

"Sure. Why not."

Noah leaned against the wall, from the alcohol in part, but mainly from fatigue. He took a swig of beer and looked down the hall. The others were either in the kitchen or the living room. Jim and Annie couldn't make it—her mother wasn't well and they were staying close to home in Dartmouth—and Andrew and his wife, the new one, from London, hadn't been able to, what with all their packing for the move. And no one was sure what was going on with Adrien and Henry. But most of them had come, just as Amelia said they would. Ben and Charlotte, Louis and Nadine and Pete. Maggy had come too, which was good of her. She was even staying sober—relatively—which he hoped would make a difference. The girls were on the couch tending their bottles, except for Maggy, who was with the boys around the kitchen table. The music wasn't so loud yet that he couldn't hear them.

Noah righted himself and gave Ray a straight-up listen-fella kind of look. "Just keep it under your hat, though, will you? I really don't want to talk about it."

Ray raised his hands in mock injury. After all these years, how could Noah doubt him?

In the kitchen, Ben and Louis were standing on either side of the sink, dishing dirt on Henry, which is the chance you take not showing up.

"When did you see him last?" Louis asked.

"A couple years at least," Ben said. "He was still in Moncton."

"How many kids is it now?"

"Five, far as I know."

Louis whistled loud. "That's a handful."

"Handful," Maggy muttered, laughing.

"You're telling me," Ben said. "Char was one and done. I can't even bring it up without her getting cross with me."

"Jesus. I don't know how his wife can take it."

Maggy laughed again.

"What?" Louis asked.

"Oh, she can take it," she said.

"Oh grow up, Maggy," John said, joining in.

Louis looked at them, still noticeably confused. Maggy just laughed again, more loudly.

"Henry's got a big one, is all," Ben explained.

"He does?"

Pete, overhearing, confirmed it. "Seriously. Like, ten inches."

Louis sneered and leaned back on his heels. He wasn't going to let them rag him. "Yeah, right. Maybe if he measures from his rectum."

"No really," Pete said. "Why do you think we called him Moose?"

"I thought that was because of his nose."

"It was also because of his nose."

"And the way he used it," Maggy said. "Like he was stripping bark off a tree."

Ben winced. "Thanks for that, Mags."

"If Annie were here she'd tell you," Pete added. "They used to go together in high school."

Maggy agreed. "Remember how she used to get those nose bleeds?"

Even Pete seemed uncomfortable with that image, and Maggy burst into laughter.

Through the kitchen door, they could see into the living room. Amelia was sitting forward on the edge of a cushioned chair. Charlotte and Nadine were huddled on the sofa. Several half-drunk bottles lay

before them on the coffee table, and Amelia was gesturing emphatic-
ally. Her hands were spread a foot wide or more, giving the others an
estimation of length.

Pete frowned. "Hey, John. What's your wife measuring out there?"

John hesitated. He saw how Amelia's hands then moved closer
together—much, much closer. "There's no way they heard us from
in there."

Louis shook his head. "Not a chance."

"Right. They're probably talking about the scarf she's knitting."

"You hope that's it," Maggy said.

John gazed worriedly at his wife. Maggy only laughed harder.

ʊ

In the living room, they were indeed talking about the scarf, for the
most part.

"My grandmother taught me when I was a girl," Amelia said. "I've
been meaning to do something about it, but it's been two weeks and
that's all I've got." It was an unimpressive length for two weeks of
knitting.

"Switch to crocheting. It goes faster," Nadine said. "I can do a scarf
this long in an evening."

She held her hands wider than Amelia's, shoulder-width. Then she
winked and bent her head in the direction of the kitchen. Through the
doorway they could see their husbands wearing troubled expressions.

Charlotte adjusted her hands to match and raised her voice almost
to a holler. "Really? That long?"

The men hurriedly looked away, feigning ignorance, and Amelia,
Charlotte, and Nadine all fell to laughing. They settled back into their
cushioned seats, but Nadine first grabbed her bottle and raised it in
victory. "That oughta keep 'em off balance."

ʊ

It was much later when Cecelia finally arrived. By then the little kitchen
party had turned into a soiree. The stereo was blaring and you could

324

hear *Road Apples* in every room, which was how she more or less snuck in. Though no one seemed to notice her, from the front door she had good sightlines into the adjoining rooms. A couple of girls were dancing in the living room, and someone was in front of a TV with the hockey on. Everyone else was mixing it up in the kitchen. They were all at least a little intoxicated.

Despite the time she'd given herself to simmer down—a good two hours plus the fifteen-minute drive—she was still in no mood for having a time, so it only made it worse when she barged in to find Maggy more or less throwing herself at Noah. If she'd come in sooner, she would have seen the way Noah kept trying to fend her off without being impolite about it, but some device of Fortune wouldn't have it so. No, she arrived in time to see Noah let his guard down just a little, just long enough for Maggy to curve in close and land a little love bite on his neck. You can imagine what it looked like. "Jesus, Maggy, get off!" Noah said. Good thing he did too. It may have saved his life. Just. Then he noticed Cecelia by the door. "C.! I was starting to worry where you were."

"You were right to worry," she replied.

Noah hurried to introduce his friends. "Everybody, this is Cecelia."

Maggy leaned back against the counter. "So you're the reason I haven't got a date tonight."

"Easy there," Ray said quickly. Then he announced to the room: "Noah tells me Cecelia here's got a lot of schooling, so everybody play nice and try not to hold it against her."

"Hang on now," Ben cautioned. "What's a lot? How much are we talking?"

With so many people to account to suddenly, Cecelia was a little daunted. "I'm working towards a doctoral degree."

"Oh good!" Pete said. "When one of us passes out you'll know what to do."

"No, a PhD. In literature."

"Well isn't that big fiddle," Maggy chirped.

Cecelia hardly knew what to say. She felt they must be joking.

"So you must read, like, all the time," Pete said.

Ben asked, "What do you have to do to get a PhD in reading?"

"Well … I'm studying Shakespeare—"

"Sweet Jesus! Shakespeare?" Ray made a show of exasperation, and even let his hands go up in protest. "Shakespeare's got to be the worst writer in history. No matter what I tried I couldn't understand a word of it."

"Is he serious?" Cecelia asked.

"Hardly ever," Ben reassured her.

Cecelia was at a loss. She turned to Noah, but he wasn't any help. "Don't look at me. I'm not crazy about Shakespeare either."

"You … wait, what?"

Noah hurried to the fridge. "Let me get you a beer. It'll soften the blow."

"Better get her two," Maggy said. Then to Cecelia she added, "Two-fist it for an hour or so, love. You'll be less boring in no time."

Everyone went on a bit, taking it in turns to give Cecelia a rough-housing sort of welcome, until Ray rescued her with an accommodating change of subject.

"Don't let 'em cramp you, it's just their way. Besides, everybody gets their turn. For example—Hey, listen up everyone! Plugger just found out his dad was gay. Discuss."

Noah nearly dropped his beer. Pete choked on his. Ray smiled at Cecelia, like he was throwing her a lifeline. After that everyone got quiet and there was a momentary atmosphere of dis-ease, with a right lot of feet shuffling, and people fidgeting with bottles and not making eye contact. In the midst of this community of discomfort, John with several big, deliberate steps sidled himself away from Noah. The others watched him. "You know," he said, "just in case it's contagious."

It broke the silence. And although Noah wasn't laughing, the others' tongues loosened up again:

"What are you saying? Noah must be gay 'cause his dad was?"

"My father's Irish. That makes me half-Irish."

"Jesus, Noah, how did you find that out?"

"More like, how did you not know?"

"Idiot. Do you think they wear a sign, or have it stamped on their foreheads?"

"Or shop at Gay-mart?"

"That's deep, man."

"Yeah, balls deep."

"It's 1998. Who cares?" Ben interrupted. "As long as you don't picture them doing it."

"Methinks I see your father," John said.

Ray clapped his hands to his face as if to ward off the offending visions. "Oh, my mind's eye!"

Noah headed for the back door.

"Come on, Plugger," Ben said, "lighten up. We're just having a go."

"I just have to take a leak." Except for Maggy and Cecelia, who watched Noah exit, everyone else went on laughing.

"You guys ever take the quiz?" John asked.

"The what?"

"The quiz: would you rather have sex with the best-looking man in the world or the worst-looking woman?"

"Somebody asked me that in high school," Ben said. "I didn't like it."

"But seriously, right? Which would you choose? If you had to. No opting out."

"Fuck off," Ben said.

"No, no. Really. But don't decide until I tell you what they look like."

"Listen, I don't care what they look like—"

"You know, they say statistically one in eight men is gay," Cecelia said. Like a schoolmarm grabbing an errant child by the collar, she had pulled them up short. "And one in three has had a same sex encounter." With her finger raised, she began counting heads.

"Oh, I like her," Amelia said, laughing. "She can stay."

The boys studied each other with suspicion. They looked a little nervous. Then Pete spoke up. "I had a same sex encounter once."

Once again the room grew quiet and for a time they all remained studiously aloof. It seemed no one, after this bout of candour, knew what to say.

"I was in Montreal, and this transvestite came up to me and asked if I had any change," Pete explained. "I told him I thought he had enough already."

♎

Noah unzipped his pants and began to unwind his bladder. The laughter inside was loud, not easy to ignore. It took him a minute. He aimed into the cedar shrubs and tried to concentrate on the rustle of the leaves. It worked well enough, until Maggy banged open the door behind him. It caught him off guard and, reflexively, he cut his stream. He had to fight to get it going again.

"You fuck with that thing?" she asked. "It's like someone startled a turtle."

"It's cold out. And I don't see anything worth the erection."

She came up to him. "You've been in town for weeks and you can't even return my calls."

"Maggy—"

"'Cause you're with that sweetheart now?"

Noah shook it out and stowed his gear.

"You know, your new girl's a bit of a sook," Maggy continued. "She riles easy." Maggy snuggled in closer to him. "I brought you a beer." She held the bottle out to him. It was already open.

"No thanks."

"Come on, just a kiss of booze."

"Maggy, listen. It was alright for a while, but it was what it was. I thought you knew that. I'm sorry if you feel different."

Maggy put her bottle to her mouth and took a long drink. She shivered as she did. "Fine. But next time you want to wet a line, you can do it somewhere else."

"Maggy, it's not me that's been angling all night." Noah turned and went back in, with Maggy following, to the warmth of the kitchen, where Ray was holding forth, as was his tending.

"Let me spell it out for you: do you know why we wait twelve hours at the hospital for stitches, or to get a bone set? Why the government keeps cutting services? Why they're terrified of the deficit? Why companies are downsizing? They lay off the young and buy out the old because everyone in the middle wants lower taxes and higher yields on their investments, so they can buy the next stereo or television, or get a cell phone, or tart up their kitchens. They want to Debbie-fucking-Travis the bathrooms

328

in their shitty little bungalows or shove a useless dormer into their roofs just so their neighbours can eat their fists. I swear to God, the other day I heard my boss on the phone offering an unpaid internship to a girl who's worked on contract for us for five years. He said maybe they could find a little in the budget to offer her a per diem. Can you fucking believe that? I'm telling you, they're all like trust fund babies, burning through their inheritance. Only it's the public trust, and the inheritance is everyone's. Fuck them. Bunch of ungrateful, shiftless parasites."

"Try reading the newspaper once in a while," Noah said. "There are millions dying in Africa."

"Yeah, well, I gotta clear the mote from my own eye before I can get to work on theirs."

"That's not what that story means, you idiot."

"Cecelia, dear," Maggy said, interrupting, "how long have you known Noah anyway?"

"We met last summer," Cecelia answered.

"So, before last August then?"

"That's right. He helped me with some books and got me out of some fines."

"Sounds like Noah," Maggy said. "He's a good man in a tight place."

For all that the words sounded innocent enough, she put such a slant onto it that you could hardly miss what she was getting at.

"Anybody know the score?" Pete asked, changing the subject.

Nobody answered, but with Ray's harangue blessedly derailed, they'd gotten busy on other things, indeed anything: a pee break, a beer hunt, current gossip, uncurrent gossip, whatever it was coming out of the oven. Pete wandered into the living room to check for himself. By the other door, Cecelia exited the kitchen too. She was keeping silent, but as she left she heaved a look at Noah that said enough. When he joined her in the front hall, he could see how angry she was. The music was blaring, but they could still be seen from the kitchen, so he gestured to her to follow. They went into a nearby room, John and Amelia's, as it happened, and Noah flipped the light on. Behind him, Cecelia slammed the door. There was no point being casual.

"I'm sorry about Maggy. We used to see each other."

"Used to?"

He sat down on the edge of the bed and took a haul on his beer. "I know. She's a piece of work."

"You're the one I'm furious with." She stood there before him, seething.

"Listen, I've told her over and over, but she won't—"

"Just shut it. I called Owen about the pages. He's coming out. He says you have an arrangement."

Noah faltered. "C.—"

"Don't call me that. I hate it."

"But everyone—"

"I hate it. Every time." Her fists were squeezed tight and she was trembling. "God, Noah, I defended you. I told him the pages were yours and I wasn't going to just hand them over. And then I find out—the whole time!"

The drive of the music from the living room was insinuating itself into the bedchamber, but it was nothing to the earful Noah was getting. He slumped forward. "I'm sorry."

"You're sorry?"

"I know, I shouldn't have, but he didn't give me a choice. And now—"

"But you didn't tell me." She began pacing the short length of the room and tugging on her hair. For several lengths she didn't even look at him. "I worked for months on this," she said, finally, "and for what? To find out I'm a footnote?"

"I don't understand. Why would you—"

"I have no idea what I'm doing! It was dumb luck. Get it? I'm the latest in a long line of accidents somebody else is going to write about."

"You're sulking because you got into this by accident?" Noah stood up quickly. "Everything's just an accident! You being here. Me being here. Us meeting in the library. Owen-fucking-Trover! Everything."

"But I want it to mean something!"

"Like what?" Her mouth clamped and skewed into a frown, but she said nothing. Noah grew insistent. "Well?" When she didn't answer, he tried to go to the door, but she barred his way.

"How do you not get how unfair this is?" she demanded.

Although she didn't spell it out, Noah understood what she meant by *this*, and *this* was stupid. No stupider, of course, than any number of things he had said or thought, especially when, like Cecelia, he had laid down time and energy, and gambled his self-worth, vainly, on something beyond his actual control. By now, though, he was too angry to think of this. Instead, he opened his stupid mouth.

"I may—possibly—be distantly related to the son of somebody who knew Shakespeare. Only an idiot would think that means something."

"Fuck you, Noah."

Flinging open the door, she fled from the chamber, down the hall, and into the kitchen. Amelia was laying out a plate of food. The others had moved to the living room. Cecelia yanked her shoes on and, in her haste and anger, stood there doubled over, clawing ineptly at the laces. Noah had followed and was trying to prevent her departure.

Then Maggy stumbled back in from the living room. "What was that, five minutes? That's fast, even for you, Plugger." Then to Cecelia, she said, "What happened, love, did he stick it in your ear?"

Cecelia had got her laces done at last, and her hand was on the doorknob, but she stopped. "Keep baiting me. See what happens."

"Hey, now," Amelia intervened.

"I thought we were playing nice," Ray said from the doorway. He and John had just wandered in.

"Don't look at me," Maggy said. "She's just being soft."

"You know what," Cecelia shot back, "you can go stuff your box."

Maggy's eyes lingered on Cecelia a moment, then she looked Noah over, with purpose, like she was taking it all in. "You know, love," she said, "maybe I'll do that."

It all happened so fast that, even with the benefit of sober reflection, it would be hard to catalogue everything that went down in the brouhaha that followed. A rough account would show that Cecelia landed the first punch, and a fair few after that, and Maggy nearly held her own, and John got an elbow in the mouth trying to break it up, and there was a fair amount of scratching and hair pulling too. Then they really got into it. And when it was over, there was more blood than you'd think, and already a whole lot of swelling, and one of Maggy's teeth was missing.

Later, Noah was sitting on the porch in the cold and Ray came out to join him. Ray offered him a beer. "I think I've had enough," Noah said, though he took the bottle.

"Solidarity," Ray insisted. "I shouldn't drink alone."

They sat there awhile. The altercation had briefly put a halt to the festivities, and although the music inside was still loud, and there was laughter in the kitchen, it never really got going again. Not like before. Still, nobody wanted to go home yet. They were all adults after all. Besides, who knew when they would all be in one place again. Outside, the night was serene. A sliver of moon was going down, and stars beyond number shone through the gauzy overcast.

"She's gone, I guess?" Ray asked.

"She went back to the house. How's Maggy?"

"Not bad, considering. That girl of yours can handle herself. The way she reached down for that punch. I mean, Maggy oughta know better than to go into a fist fight slapping, but still. And then when she jerseyed her! You know, I always thought a girl fight would be kinda sexy, but that was just awful-looking. The way she was just filling her in there at the end, with those haymakers. I never saw anything like that before. Not that she didn't have it coming. Maggy was right awful tonight."

Noah scowled. "Was she always like this? Trouting for attention all the time?"

"Yeah, only you've got a good heart for forgetting." They sat thoughtfully for several moments before Ray continued. "Hard to blame her, though. Every guy she's ever been with left her." He raised his bottle. "Well, here's to the first day of spring. Here's to new beginnings."

"That's tomorrow," Noah corrected.

"The stars say otherwise. This year, March 20. The birth of Ovid. Walter Raleigh paroled. Einstein's theory of relativity." Ray winked. "I looked all that up. I wonder what it means when someone's born on the cusp?"

"I don't think it means anything," Noah answered.

"No, you wouldn't. Well, happy birthday, Plugger." Ray drank a mouthful. He also nudged Noah with his arm to encourage him.

Noah shook his head. "I think I should get home. What about you?"

"I think I'll drink this beer, go find a couch, and distend. You want a lift? That's a long walk."

"You're in no shape to drive."

"You're not wrong there. Let's call you a taxi."

"You mean *the* taxi? Nah. I'll cut along the coast. I could use the air."

Noah rose from the porch. From the street it was a five-minute walk to the water, then half an hour by the shore to his grandparents' house. He started towards the side of the house. His foot was stiff, but it would loosen up.

"You'll have to hop a couple of fences," Ray called to him. "There's assholes and heiresses put them up since you went away. I had a run-in last fall."

"I'll mind my way. Say goodbye for me, will you?"

"Yeah. Hurry home, you gimp."

"I'm ambling."

"Any slower and you'd be loitering."

Noah turned and smiled at his friend. Then he raised his hand, and Ray his bottle, in farewell.

13

It was after nine when Cecelia came down to breakfast. Noah and his grandfather were sitting there, the old man in his nightshirt and Noah in his day-old clothes. Their cups and empty bowls lay before them. The first thing they noticed on her was the shiner. Then the scratches and other marks she'd acquired in the ruckus the night before.

"Wow," the old man said.

"She gave worse than she got," Noah informed him.

The old man raised his fist into the air and shook it in commendation. "Beware!"

There was a pot of warm porridge on the stove. It had been keeping warm an hour or so and was stuck to the bottom now. A wooden spoon was planted in it like a flagpole. It was past the point of appetizing. There was a pot of tea beside it, and on the counter an empty bowl.

"It'll take some chewing," Noah said.

"I'll just have some tea."

"I was talking about the tea."

Cecelia sighed and took a cup from the dish rack. She half-filled it and added almost as much milk. Her hand ached to do it. As she sat down at the table, she rubbed some sleep from her eye and winced.

"You OK?" Noah asked her.

"Yes."

"Are you sure?"

"Do me a favour. Don't ask me again."

Noah's grandmother entered from the next room. "Oh, good you're—sweet humpbacked Jesus! You met Margaret, I take it."

"I ... encountered her." Cecelia painfully articulated her punching hand.

The old woman only nodded. "Time to dress, Peter. Company's coming."

She heaved her husband from his chair and they marched off to the bedroom. That left Noah and Cecelia at the table, not speaking and, with every silent sip of unpalatable tea, stringing each other along.

"How was the couch?" Cecelia eventually asked.

"It was fine."

"You could have come up."

"I know."

"My mother called before you got in. Rose had the baby. Ten pounds, eight."

"A bag of potatoes."

"She named her Lily."

Noah smiled. "It's lovely."

"It's my middle name."

"Is it?"

"Yeah. She named her after me. Go figure." Cecelia looked down into her cup. Then she asked, "Noah, how long have we known each other?"

"Since last June. End of June, I think."

"What's that, two hundred ... eighty days or so?"

"I guess," Noah said. "Or forty weeks."

"Or nine moons."

"Seven floods."

Cecelia laughed. "At least two ultrasounds."

"One stroke of luck."

"Just the one?"

Her eye twinkled, and they both were smiling, but sadly. As the silence grew up again between them, their minds wandered, seizing on things extraneous and irrelevant to the matter at hand: the warmth of the stove, the clicking of the electric coils, the dull hum of the refrigerator, the orange countertops, vile and impossible to get used to no matter how many times you saw them, the sound of the wind against the windows—anything to distract themselves. Each knew what needed saying, but neither wanted to trouble the waters. And, anyway, they each knew it, and knew the other knew, way down in their stomachs where all matters of emotional importance are finally settled, that however pleasing it was to pretend, none of this was what they really wanted. It was just a surrogate for what they'd each been hoping for.

"Did you talk to Felix?"

"While you were sleeping. He called to wish me a happy birthday. He was sorry you missed him."

Cecelia smiled. "You know, you have a great kid."

Noah nodded. "And you throw a hell of a punch. Maggy never did find that tooth."

Cecelia reached into her pocket and dropped an incisor on the table. Noah would have commented, but the slamming of two car doors outside cut him off. He frowned.

"What are you going to tell Owen?" Cecelia asked.

"That, I don't know." Noah put down his cup and pushed back his chair. "I guess I'll see what he says."

ਧ

By and by the knock came on the front door, and Noah went and let in Owen Trover and his assistant, inviting them into the parlour, where Cecelia was waiting. "You're early," he remarked.

"It doesn't take long to charter a small aircraft if you know who to call. And what was I doing on a Saturday morning anyway?" Trover directed his gaze at Cecelia and noted the change in her appearance. "Ms. Lines, I didn't take you for a brawler."

"Neither did the other girl," Cecelia countered coolly. "Now she does."

"I bet."

As Noah took their coats and folded them neatly over the back of the couch, Trover crossed the room, passing the television and rocking chair, and stood at the mantelpiece. As he did, Noah's grandmother entered from the hall. His grandfather leaned in the door and looked upon the visitors with suspicion.

"This is my grandmother, Modeste," Noah said, "and my grand-father, Peter."

"Mr. and Mrs. Lamarck. Nice to meet you. I'm Owen Trover." With a nod Trover indicated his assistant. "This is Clement Rowse. He keeps me in line."

Trover's attempt at humour elicited only silence from the Lamarcks. Cecelia merely shifted in place. Clement proposed that they all sit down, which he and Trover did on chairs and Noah and Cecelia on the couch. Noah's grandmother, however, remained by her husband in the doorway, arms crossed and steady as a fencepost. Next to her, on the end table, lay an accordion folder which caught Trover's eye. He hinged forward in his seat, elongating towards the folder, as though compelled by a pointing instinct.

"So, where's my baby?" he asked. "Is that it in the folder?"

"Owen, it's like I said," Cecelia cautioned. "The pages are Noah's."

"I've hardly had a chance to think about it," Noah said.

"What is there to think about? We had an arrangement. Anything you found was mine."

Noah frowned and weighed his words. "Our arrangement was for the archive you bought. Anything it led to, you were always going to have to pay for."

Leaning back again into his seat, Trover passed a critical eye over the furnishings and inhabitants of the little cottage. He smiled and crossed his legs and let his hands fall patiently on his lap. His posture conveyed no discomfort, only an attitude of relaxed readiness.

"Noah, that's a fair point. How much do you want for them?"

"But they aren't mine either," Noah said, evading. "They belong to my grandmother. And they're a family heirloom, most likely."

"So they have sentimental value?" Trover glanced up at Noah's grandmother. "Even though you don't know what they are, and you only just found them. Noah, are you improvising your caveats?"

"What's wrong with this blowhard?" the old woman said. "Coming into our house, and talking like that."

Trover ignored her. He was calculating. "For an orphan copy ... Cecelia tells me it's not in a recognizable hand. Two thousand."

"It's a manuscript," Noah countered.

"It's insulting," Cecelia said, making it clear to Trover where she was throwing in her lot.

When Trover said nothing immediately, Noah added, "It looks old enough to be contemporary. It's worth more than that no matter whose hand it's in."

Trover took his time. Then: "You want five?"

"Owen!" Cecelia snapped. "Don't do it, Noah. Don't let him push you. What if it turns out it has authority, even a little? Think what it'll be worth then."

"Ms. Lines," Trover said, "I really don't think—"

Cecelia cut him off. "If it's worth real money, you couldn't afford it. You told me yourself. So why would he sell it to you anyway?"

"Ms. Lines, do you know how a mortgage works? How it really works? Do you, Noah? Do they?"

His remarks were so casual, so oblique, that at first only Clement, with a wavering of his usual aloofness, reacted. "Owen," he began, but a slashing, sidelong glance from Trover silenced him.

"You wouldn't know this, I imagine, but there's good money to be made in mortgages. Normally, you would buy a portfolio, hundreds of mortgages or more, you would buy it for cents on the dollar, and make your money foreclosing and reselling. Now, that kind of thing is much easier to pull off in the States, but as it happens I had some leverage with a friend at the bank. I said to him, I'm not interested in starting a collection agency, and I don't need a portfolio. I just need one."

Apart from Trover and his assistant, only Noah grasped the implication. The others stood there, only sensing the threat and waiting. It was Cecelia who finally gave in. "I don't understand."

"He bought their mortgage," Noah said. He fought against the urge to fold over in his seat.

"That's illegal," Cecelia said. "It has to be." She looked over her shoulder at Noah's grandparents.

"No more than insurance fraud, Ms. Lines." Trover was looking straight at Noah.

"Fraud? Noah ..."

Noah could only answer dumbly. "Owen, this is their home. They've been here their whole lives."

"It was theirs. Then it was the bank's. Now it's mine. That's what a mortgage means."

"He's lying," Noah's grandmother broke in. "It's a loan we don't have to pay back. Not as long as we live here. That's what they said."

"They say a lot of things, Mrs. Lamarck."

"But why?" Cecelia asked.

"Because, like you said, why would he sell it to me anyway?" Trover's tone was flat and factual. "All right, how's this? I'll give you fifteen right now, without even knowing what you've got there. If you take it somewhere else, you may get nothing."

"Or you may get more," Cecelia said to Noah. "Maybe thousands more. Or hundreds of thousands." She was staring hard at Trover, but speaking still to Noah. "Then you wouldn't need his money. And he'd never get his hands on it."

"Stop helping, Ms. Lines," Trover barked. "If I have to I'll squeeze hard and fast, instead of slow and gentle. I don't know exactly how long it will take to foreclose, but I promise you it's less than the years it'll take you to get those pages authenticated and auctioned off. I doubt these people have another house I don't know about. I doubt they even have a lawyer." He studied Noah and his grandparents.

"But you can't do that!" Cecelia cried.

She had leapt to her feet, finally unable to restrain herself, and Trover rose to meet her. The confines of the parlour emphasized his height and he loomed over her.

"I can," he said. "And I will if I have to. Things will get awfully tight around here."

Trover seemed as though he might go further, but Noah's grandmother had started to laugh. She strode in from the doorway and wagged a disdainful finger at him. "You go on, you soft-headed sook," she said. "I lived through the depression. I lived when money was tight enough to pinch a ghost."

"We'll have some conditions," Noah suddenly said.

His interjection was strangely quiet, but it nonetheless brought everyone—Trover, Cecelia, and his grandmother—to a stop. He had not risen from his seat. He had hardly stirred. He had simply cast his eyes about the room and taken it all in: the photographs on the mantel, the cracked plaster, the dinged-up piano, the worn chairs and couch and all the room's faded beggary, Cecelia toe to toe with Trover in his defence, and his grandmother standing there, in the house Trover threatened to wrest from her, with more firmness than the stone foundation it stood upon. "There will have to be some conditions," he said again.

Trover stepped back and calmed himself. "Look, I've handled this badly."

"Oh, don't even try it," the old woman said.

"No, please, let's start over. What would you like? Just name it."

"First, you clear the mortgage," Noah said. "That's bullshit and you know it."

"Agreed."

"And Cecelia gets exclusive access."

Cecelia tried to object. "Noah—"

"Exclusive, for as long as she wants."

"I don't like indefinites," Trover said.

"Well, we all get disappointed sometimes." Noah rose from the couch and stood with Cecelia and his grandmother. "Now, hypothetically, what are an auction house's fees?"

Trover frowned at Noah's question, as though perhaps he would not answer, but from behind him the answer came nonetheless: "Twenty-five percent on the first two hundred thousand." It was Clement Rowse, the only one of them still sitting down. For the second time, Trover looked in annoyance at his assistant, but Rowse was firm. "Twenty percent from there to three million. Owen, just play ball."

"In that case, you pay for an appraisal," Noah said quickly. "We get the equivalent of the house fees. You get to skip the auction."

Trover stood pondering the offer and, seemingly despite his efforts, his mouth drew almost into a smile. "I knew I liked you, Noah. But I'm not agreeing to anything until I see those pages."

He pointed at the end table, where they all expected to see the folder. It was, however, no longer there. Then they realized that Noah's grandfather was no longer in the doorway. Nor was he in the hallway or the kitchen. Only when they looked out back did they discover: there he was, nearly at the shore, with the folder in his hands. "Goddamn it!" Noah said. "Why are we always doing this?"

Quick as he could, Noah seized his shoes, and his grandmother and Cecelia likewise hurried, but Trover was quicker. He shoved right by them and sprinted out the door. Across the meadow he ran, all the way to the coast, screaming the whole time for the old man to stop and give him back the folder, and as Noah (not far behind) closed in he saw what had occasioned Trover's screams. Although the tide was in and the water swayed gently a mere eight or nine feet below, the rocky outcropping the old man stood upon might as well have been the summit of a cliff: he had the folder open and with an unaccountable leisure he was tossing the pages out over the water a few at a time. Worse, as they came sliding out the pages did not drop at once into the sea. Instead, the wind's phantom fingers snatched at them, flung them into the air, turned them over, somersaulting, every updraft teasing them out over the water and farther out from shore. Trover was hysterical. "Stop! Stop! Stop!" he cried. A more fitting torture for him could hardly have been designed, and he scrambled out onto the promontory as though it were his children being murdered, pitched a few at a time from off the brim and into an abyss.

Noah was yelling too, "Gramps, wait! We're sorting it out!" But the old man either didn't hear or wouldn't. He only scattered a few more pages as Trover, his arms extended in outright helplessness, begged him.

"Sir, please."

Perhaps the desperation caught his ear. Perhaps it was the way Trover half-collapsed in supplication. Perhaps, instead, he saw his grandson's careful approach and the urgent arrival of Cecelia with his wife. Or perhaps it was all of these that stayed the old man's hand. Whatever the cause, he hesitated, his hair wild from the chase, and his shirt blown open. In spite of it all he stood there, unmoving, like a monument or effigy. Noah could only wonder did he even understand just then what he was about. Trover risked a small forward step, and then another. At the third Noah's grandfather smiled. Then he overturned the folder.

Trover lunged for the pages, but as he did he lost his footing, and the old man, without hesitation, took him by the hip and helped him right off his feet and into the drink. As she watched the pages go, Cecelia lost her legs too and collapsed to her knees, but the old man, like it was nothing, just tossed the empty folder over his shoulder and strolled back towards the lawn. He patted Noah on the shoulder, frowned a moment, then to Cecelia he smiled and pronounced a single word: "Hoodwinked."

Noah's grandmother threw her arms up in exasperation. "Peter, I swear to Christ your brain is like a bingo cage sometimes."

The old man approached and threw his arms around her. "You're it, Avy," he said. "You're the one."

Cecelia was still on the ground, cold and wet from the sodden meadow. A limpid, clean despair was soaking in too. "Oh God, Noah, those were your letters."

Noah was watching Trover as he flailed in the water. "Yeah. I thought so."

Though no one had paid him any mind, Clement Rowse had followed them out. Approaching, he offered his apologies. "If I'd realized, I would have said something when your grandfather snuck out. Owen is usually on top of everything. I guess he didn't see that coming."

Cecelia shook her head in disgust. "How can you stand working for that clown?"

Clement did not answer immediately. "One time, he told me that his father was a gambler. He sold everything except Owen's books. And then he sold those."

Cecelia shoved her hands in her pocket. "So what?"

They observed Trover, out of his depth and floundering at the water's edge. He had a cut on his forehead and something was wrong with one arm. He was in no immediate danger, though. The sea was rather calm and the waves beat softly against the rocks.

"I suppose it's hard to trust people after that." Clement himself seemed doubtful.

Noah was still watching Trover. "I suppose we should fish him out."

"He's a strong swimmer," Clement said. "And he'll be fine if he lets the pages go. You know, I'm curious to see if he can do that."

Most of them were already heading out to sea. A few, still caught up in the wind, circled in the air above, only to plunge moments later, one by one, like diving birds into the water. Trover was steadying himself against the rocks with his bad arm, and reaching with the good one. A small circle of sheets drifted near enough to tempt him, but it was hopeless—even they were already out of reach.

14

"Hair of the dog," Ray was explaining. "Nothing like it."

"That was two days ago," Noah reminded him. "I don't think this counts."

"I know, right? I've never had a two-day hangover before. It's like I'm being punished twice for being foolish once. How is that fair?" In disgust, Ray shook his head. Gently, though.

It was Sunday, late afternoon, and they were sitting on a pair of stumps at the firepit out back of the house. The weather was fine, better than seasonal. Even so, they shivered a little now and then, and when the wind cut in from the water it ran right through their sweaters. A fire had seemed in order. A small stack of wood lay between them, and a case of beer.

"Jesus, I drank so much I think I gave myself a concussion. Is crapulence a word? 'Cause if it isn't, it should be."

"That's your third beer," Noah pointed out. "After your second I think you gave up the right to complain."

Between them, they had half-emptied the twelve and now they were taking it easy. Evening was still a ways off, but a crescent moon was out already. Like them, it was getting an early start.

"That girl of yours was able, I'll give her that," Ray said. "Too bad she didn't stick around."

"She has classes. And papers to write." The complications waiting for Noah when he returned he was trying not to think about. Still, he shook his head in amazement. "You know, he would have ruined us all. And for what?"

Ray shrugged. "Small things make mean men proud. That's why we'll be the first generation in modern history to be worse off than our parents."

Noah sat there with his friend, on the back lawn behind his grandparent's house, gazing into the fire, ruminating between snaps of his beer. He thought about the mill on the outskirts of Mission Point, unused for decades, and, a little back from the main street, the decrepit old building that used to be the town hall. Both were in terrible disrepair, but some local preservationists had got the council to protect them. They were ugly and ill-made. Not worth saving. People were running around raising money to restore them anyway, even though you could have built them new and better at half the cost. Then he thought about the city, where they were converting churches and heritage buildings into condos at a premium. The first stirrings of a boom.

As clearly as he could see the sky above them, and the field around them, and the dying flames at their feet, he could see how it would all unfold. In the decades to come there would be endless development, and towers going up all over, but smaller spaces and more expensive, where you couldn't fit a family, much less afford to raise one. And if you tried you'd only find there was nowhere safe and pleasant to take them for fresh air on a Saturday or Sunday afternoon. Homelessness and poverty. And whole neighbourhoods turning to ghettos, and the inhabitants blamed. And in the city's bedroom towns, pavement and sprawl would muscle in on farmland and moraine alike. People would go on electing apologists and ignoramuses and bigots. And they would demand a subway they couldn't pay for, forgetting the other unpaid-for subway that still wasn't finished. Unpaid billions would be kicked down the road, and no one would want to talk about what that would really cost.

Right there before him, where the ocean stretched out from the shore, there used to be a fishery. At one time—or so the story went—the waters were so thick with cod that Cabot's sailors complained of obstruction. The fish could be caught just by lowering a basket. Now there was a moratorium, already six years old. At the other end of the country, the Pacific salmon runs were touch and go now too. In twenty years they'd all be worrying about the capelin. Ray was right. It was coming. There was a time, Noah felt sure, when these things could have been prevented, or at least mitigated, but he had no idea when that might have been. Up and down the coast, ghost-gear and other manmade debris accumulated with every tide, while beyond the shore the waves kept turning over, like the pages of a book that never ends.

"Maybe once the oil runs out. Or the ice caps melt and hundreds of millions of us are underwater," Ray said. "We're under the impression that we still have choices. Once that illusion's gone, then we'll see what we're made of."

"Maybe we'll feel different when we're forty," Noah suggested.

"Maybe. Maybe then our hangovers will last three days."

Noah nodded. "While the earth remains. Seedtime and harvest." It was a strange time for doxologies.

The fire had been reduced to a smoulder. Just a couple of blackened birch logs barely going. Noah took up a piece of cherrywood and stirred the embers, then he tossed it in and nudged it into place with his foot. It was well seasoned. Fresh flames were devouring it in no time.

Ray stretched his legs out and his arms overhead. "So. Do you think you'll move back?"

"I doubt it. Felix would have to change schools and leave his friends. And there's nothing for Cate here anyway."

Ray picked a little at the label on his bottle. "You're still in love with her, aren't you?"

The question was rhetorical. Noah just gazed into the fire. The bark was beginning to curl.

"Plugger, you really know how to complicate your life. Most guys hate their exes and have fathers who aren't gay."

Noah frowned, but not altogether unhappily. Ray was the only person Noah knew who would have said it that way. It felt like home.

"Well, don't be too hard on yourself," Ray said. "After the party I phoned my ex."

"Oh? Which one?"

Ray raised his bottle. "The one that hurts the most."

Noah raised his in reply. He understood as well as anyone. Sometimes it's a train you can't get off. He wondered what Cate was doing, and Felix. Then he thought of Ray's brother. "I don't think you ever told me. Did Joe end up marrying his girl?"

"Yeah."

"She'd be due anytime now, wouldn't she?"

"She would have been," Ray said. "She miscarried a month after."

For several minutes they sat there nursing their bottles in silence. It said all they needed it to. That was something about being on the coast, Noah thought, with the wind and the sky and the rout of the waves. You feel like you can hear just everything.

"You know," he said, finally, "when I was walking home the other night I got to looking at the stars. You can hardly see them in the city, but even with the moon out the sky was just full of them. And I started wondering about God, really wondering, like I haven't in—I mean, not since we were kids. And I wondered, assuming there is a God, did He make any other worlds? And, if He did, did He make them like this one? Does He look down on them too, and are there people there like us? And then I wondered if they have the same trouble with their parents and their children. And with their mates. Or is it really just us He's punishing?"

"Methinks you were raised in the church too."

"I was indeed," Noah said. "They told us God was merciful."

Draining the last of his beer, Noah lifted his eyes and looked, and Ray looked up with him. The moon was just hanging there, hanging with its crooked, shit-eating grin, like a dog's shit-eating grin. Ray tossed his empty bottle back into the case. Then he grabbed another and deftly twisted the cap off with his sleeve. The wind across the field was tranquil—just a whisper really—but the chill of the evening nonetheless was creeping in. Hunched forward for warmth, Ray stared into the flames and went on staring, turning the bottle cap end over end in his fingers. Noah's gaze, however, remained upturned, his eyes following the trail of sweet-smelling smoke, following as it rose in a delicate thread and spun away into an empty sky until, at last, it disappeared.

Finis

Sources

Most of my research for this book centred on part five. Sources of historical and technical information that I consulted (some a little, some a lot) include:

GENERAL INFORMATION: *London Weather*, by J.H. Brazell; *Birth, Marriage & Death: Ritual, Religion, and the Life-Cycle in Tudor and Stuart England*, by David Cressy; *Elizabeth's London*, by Liza Picard; *Shakespeare's England*, by R.E. Pritchard (ed.); *The A to Z of Elizabethan London*, by Adrian Prockter and Robert Taylor.

SHAKESPEARE WITH THE MOUNTJOYS: *The Women in Shakespeare's Life*, by Ivor John Carnegie Brown; *Shakespeare, the Later Years*, by Russell A. Fraser; *Shakespeare: A Life*, by Park Honan; *The Shakespeare Documents*, by B. Roland Lewis; *Shakespeare the Man*, by A.L. Rowse; *William Shakespeare: Records and Images*, by S. Schoenbaum; *William Shakespeare: a Documentary Life*, by S. Schoenbaum; *Shakespeare's Lives*, by S. Schoenbaum; *Shakespeare in the Public Records*, by David Thomas; "New Shakespeare Discoveries: Shakespeare as a Man Among Men," by Charles William Wallace (*Harper's Monthly Magazine*, Vol. CXX, No. DCCXVIII, March 1910); "Shakespeare and His London Associates As Revealed in Recently Discovered Documents," by Charles William Wallace (*University Studies*, Vol. X, No. 4, October 1910); *Shakespeare For All Time*, by Stanley Wells.

TECHNICAL MATTERS: *Elizabethan Handwriting: 1500-1650: A Manual*, by Giles E. Dawson and Laetitia Kennedy-Skipton; "A Seventh

Signature for Shakespeare," by Giles E. Dawson (*Shakespeare Quarterly*, Vol. 43, No. 1); *Shakespeare at Work*, by John Jones; *Trade and Banking in Early Modern England*, by Eric Kerridge; *A Shakespearean Grammar*, by E.A. Abbott; *Shakespeare's Words*, by David Crystal and Ben Crystal; *Shakespeare's Grammar*, by Jonathan Hope.

ADDITIONALLY, AND OF PARTICULAR USE: John Stowe's *A Survey of London*, for its style and its descriptions of that city during the reign of Elizabeth I; Morris Palmer Tilley's *A Dictionary of the Proverbs in England in the Sixteenth and Seventeenth Centuries*, for its extensive compilation of early modern sayings and witticisms; for its depiction of the Saint Bartholomew's Day Massacre, Christopher Marlowe's *The Massacre at Paris*; and Charles Nicholl's *The Lodger*, for Shakespeare's time with the Mountjoys on Silver Street (and especially for its ingenious reading of Christopher Mountjoy's bafflingly worded last will and testament). Fortuitously, Nicholl's book was published not long after I began drafting part five (the first I drafted). As well as filling in some holes in my research, and providing me with additional local, historical details, it gave me the confidence that my framework was sound, and that within it I could give Mary Mountjoy a voice of her own.

FINALLY: Father Anselm Chiasson's *Chéticamp: History and Acadian Traditions*, a wonderfully rich study of the town in which my paternal grandfather Éli-Charles was born, and where some of my distant relations still reside. Many of my grandfather's experiences there, and many of Father Chiasson's accounts of life among the Chéticantins, have passed into me and, through me, into this book.

Acknowledgments

My sincere thanks to the librarians and staff at the Fisher Library, particularly P.J. Carefoote and the late Richard Landon, who allowed me to consult their copy of Shakespeare's First Folio ("The Rosebud"), as well as a number of early modern indentures.

For their instruction, thanks to Michael Bristol, Gayle Ebbesen, and the late Fred Flahiff. For their support and friendship, thanks to Andrew Brock, Elissa Defalco, the late Christopher Holmes, Matt Huculak, and Liisa Stephenson. Thanks also to my friends Joel Deshaye, Harold Hoefle, Anna Lepine, and the late Larry Weller, each of whom was kind enough to offer early feedback and encouragement.

Thank you to Blossom Thom and Elise Moser for their careful editing, which improved the text in a variety of ways and prevented not a few blunders. And thanks to Kenneth Radu, whose unwavering faith, generosity, and most excellent good sense were invaluable to me down the home stretch.

Finally, I would like to thank my families, in particular my in-laws Peter and the late Gail Chellew, my parents Dave and Wendy, and above all my wife Megan—my best friend—to whom I am indebted beyond words, beyond measure.

I started writing *Full Fadom Five* a number of years ago and, regretfully, some of those mentioned here have since passed away. Their kindness and friendship and love I carry with me always.

About the Author

David C.C. Bourgeois was born in Kitchener-Waterloo, Ontario, and grew up in Port Perry, for which he played hockey, achieving some notable victories, but suffering many more defeats, in towns up and down Ontario's Highway 401. He holds degrees from the University of Toronto and McGill University, and his work has been published or shortlisted for awards in several Canadian literary magazines. He now lives with his wife and their two adoptive alley cats in Montreal, where he writes fiction and drama and teaches English Literature at John Abbott College. *Full Fadom Five* is his first novel.

Also from Baraka Books